ALL PARTS TOGETHER

a novel by

Tom Mach

It is Love that holds all parts together!

...the trilogy continues from the author of SISSY!

Hill Song Press

Lawrence, Kansas

ALL PARTS TOGETHER

—Book 2 of the Jessica Radford Trilogy—

Copyright © 2006 by Tom Mach

All rights reserved

With the exception of historical figures, all characters in this novel are fictitious, and any resemblance to living persons, present or past, is coincidental.

Published by:

Hill Song Press
P. O. Box 486
Lawrence, KS 66044
www.HillSongPress.com

Library of Congress Control Number: 2005910120

Publisher's Cataloging-in-Publication

Mach, Tom.
  All parts together: a novel / by Tom Mach.
  p. cm. – (The Jessica Radford Trilogy; bk. 2)
  LCCN 2005910120
  ISBN 0-9745159-4-9

  1. Kansas--History--Civil War, 1861-1865--Fiction.
2. United States--History--Civil War, 1861-1865--Fiction. 3. Women pioneers--Fiction. 4. Historical fiction.   I. Title.

PS3613.A224A44 2006   813'.6
                                 QBI05-600199

PRINTED IN THE UNITED STATES OF AMERICA BY
CENTRAL PLAINS BOOK MFG., WINFIELD, KS

Acknowledgements

I am indebted to a large number of individuals for their insight and helpful comments. People with a passion for the Civil War, such as Michael Koessick, Kevin Frye, Lamarr Eddings, and Bob Taubman have freely donated their time to give me advice on specific matters in my book. I am also grateful to the National Park Service for their extensive knowledge on battle sites and to the people at the Lawrence Public Library and the Kansas State Historical Society for their insight into Kansas history. I owe a debt of gratitude to Thomas Goodrich for his keen insight into the Lincoln assassination, to Bob Spear for editing, and Angela Farley for creating my cover design. I am indebted to my son Mark, an author in his own right, my sister Florence Helmetag, and Jessica Vanness for proofreading these materials. In addition, I appreciate the wonderful support I received from writers in the Kansas Authors Club as well as writers in critique groups. Above all, I especially thank my wife Virginia. Without her encouragement, I could not have written this book.

Foreword

On August 21, 1863 William Quantrill and 447 marauders burned down virtually the entire town of Lawrence, Kansas and killed as many as two hundred unarmed men and boys.

☐ The following day, some citizens of Lawrence hanged an innocent man because he was a stranger in town.

☐ The next day, people went to church to pray.

☐ And three weeks later, farmhouses, outbuildings, houses, and farms in far western counties of Missouri were burned in retaliation.

Savagery during the days of the Civil War existed on both sides of the conflict.

...and so did compassion

All Parts Together is the second book in the trilogy of Jessica Radford, a 19th century fictional character who is sensitive to the pain of slavery, experiences the horrors of the Civil War, and eventually becomes an advocate for the emancipation of women. If you have not read *Sissy!*, the first book of this trilogy, I have provided a summary of that book in the "What's Happened Before..." section of this novel.

Four "battle" scenes are alluded to in *All Parts Together,* although I use the term "battle" loosely. The Baxter Springs incident was a massacre rather than a battle in that innocent, unarmed band players, as well as soldiers, had immediately surrendered when confronted by the enemy but were killed in cold blood. The other three battles included in this novel are: Chickamauga, Chattanooga, and Franklin. Where historical facts were available, I integrated these into my novel, even though I also included fictionalized scenes where historical characters interacted with characters in my novel. Maps of battles cited in this book are shown after the Foreword, while highlights of these battles are presented at the end of this book.

Each of the major characters in this novel plays an important part, and taken as "all parts together," they form a cohesive look at that incredible era of 1863-1865, as experienced through the emotional sinews and expressive souls of these people. Historical characters include Abraham Lincoln, Jim Lane, Walt Whitman, and various officers—such as Ewing, Plumb, Grant, Rosecrans, Garfield, Pond, and Bragg, as well as other minor characters. Fictional characters, such as Jessica, Otto, Matt, Tinker, and Nellie, can be considered archetypes of people who may have existed back then. I subscribe to the position that best-selling author E.L. Doctorow takes, in that *all* characters—historical and otherwise—are, in a sense, "real."

If I have missed something in my research for historical accuracy, I offer you my sincere apologies. Please note that when there was no known historical record of an event, I fictionalized details of the scene, but otherwise, I wrote these events as close as I could to historical truth. There are areas, such as dialogue, that even nonfiction writers fictionalize because no one recorded the exact words of all their many conversations. And speaking of dialogue, I had to slightly modernize it so that today's reader could understand what people said or may have said, without having to wade through the verbose naivety and pious sentimentality of their language during those times.

All Parts Together can be viewed, in a sense, as a history book that is strongly entwined with the emotions of that era. It is also a novel that allows you to enjoy the journey through the eyes, hearts, and minds of the characters.

And maybe the experience of that bygone era will help you appreciate the current times in which we live.

Figure 1: Location of the Battles of Chattanooga & Chickamauga*

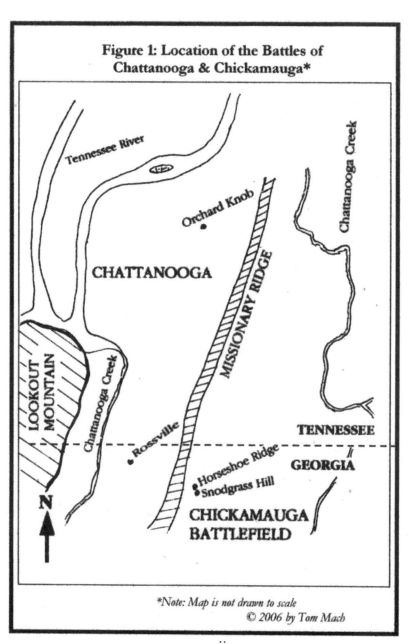

Figure 2: Some of the Locations Mentioned
For Tennessee, Georgia, & Alabama*

● Nashville

● Franklin

● Murfreesboro
(Stones River)

Crab Orchard ●

Tennessee

Chattanooga ●

Chickamauga
Rossville ● Dalton ●
● Union Point

N

Birmingham
●

Atlanta ●
● Leeburn

Pine Mountain ●

Alabama

Georgia

*Note: Map is not drawn to scale   Leeburn is a fictitious town
© 2006 by Tom Mach

Highlights from *Sissy!*
The first book of the Jessica Radford Trilogy
(This summary shows events preceding All Parts Together.)

In *Sissy!* Jessica Radford is a spirited nineteen-year-old who, in June of 1862, returns home to her parents and to Nellie, an adopted slave girl who had been rescued at the bank of the Missouri River by an Underground Railroad conductor named Otto Heller. Jessica's parents are murdered by border ruffians and Nellie, who had always claimed to have seen Sissy, her guardian angel, is kidnapped. While three of the murderers are executed, one is still loose and Jessica swears revenge.

Matt Lightfoot, a part-Cherokee minister, is fond of Jessica, but she questions whether their friendship will blossom into a serious relationship. One obstacle she sees is that while she is passionate about the right of slaves to be free, Matt believes in slavery and, in fact, once owned a male slave named Tinker. Jessica admires men like Otto Heller—a widower with two young daughters, Mitzi and Emma—who had helped more than thirty slaves escape. It is Otto, now married to a self-willed mulatto woman named Penelope, who supports Jessica's decision to disguise herself as a man to fight in the war rather than be a field nurse like her devoted friend, Mary Delaney.

Initially, Jessica helps the Union cause by bringing needed medical supplies to Perryville, Kentucky, the site of a major battle. Wanting to become more involved, however, Jessica later disguises herself as a Yankee soldier to go on a skirmishing mission some twenty-five miles south of Murfreesboro, Tennessee.

A Southerner named Roger Toby later discovers Nellie in the company of her kidnapper, and taking pity on her, purchases her so he can take her to the safety of his home in Chattanooga, where he lives with his wife Sara. While masquerading as a male soldier, Jessica finds Roger, now a wounded Confederate lieutenant, and mistakes him as Nellie's kidnapper. About to kill him in revenge, Jessica is stopped by Sissy, who makes a stunning appearance on the battlefield and tells Jessica that Roger had actually rescued Nellie from her kidnapper. Unsure as to whether or not she was delusional at the time, Jessica struggles later with Sissy's insistence on forgiveness. During the Quantrill raid of Lawrence, Kansas, Jessica kills Nellie's kidnapper, but in an act of self-defense rather than in retribution. Penelope, who has also witnessed the town's destruction by Quantrill's marauders, saves men fleeing their attackers by hiding them in a secret cellar. She also saves her husband Otto by hiding him under her hoop dress as she makes her way to safety through the burning town. The scene closes with the marauders leaving Lawrence, Kansas, in flames.

— Fictional Characters in *All Parts Together* —

Jessica Radford

A young, spirited and independent woman writer who feels a strong need to help former slaves find freedom. In 1863, she disguised herself as a male soldier so she could fight in the war, only to be discharged after her identity is revealed. Having experienced the brutal Quantrill raid of Lawrence, she is now faced with the hellish aftermath of that raid.

Mary Delaney

A close friend of Jessica, she goes about her tasks in a quiet, unassuming way as a nurse who comforts the wounded and dying.

Matt Lightfoot

A Methodist preacher who had a Cherokee father and a mother of Irish descent, he pursues Jessica as the woman he wants to marry.

Penelope Heller

A mulatto and Jessica's aunt, she is strong-willed like her niece Jessica and had formerly owned a store in Lawrence until it was destroyed in the Quantrill raid. Having divorced George Radford years earlier, she is now married to Otto Heller.

Otto Heller

A widower married to Penelope, he had been a conductor with the Underground Railroad. An abolitionist publisher, he has two children from his former marriage—Mitzi, nine, and Emma, six.

Tinker

A former slave of Matt Lightfoot, he deserted the Union in 1863, but through Otto's influence with Senator James Lane, he manages to join another regiment.

Nellie

A slave girl who, as an 11-year-old in 1857, had been rescued at the bank of the Missouri River by Otto Heller. She enjoyed her subsequent adoption by the Radford family, but in 1862, she is kidnapped the same night that Jessica's parents are murdered by border ruffians.

Roger Toby

A Tennessee man who was in the banking business before enlisting to fight with the Confederates. He secured Nellie's freedom by purchasing her from her kidnapper.

Sara Toby

A South Carolina woman and Roger's wife, she had always considered herself a decent, church-going woman. Her ambition for the stage as an actress is thwarted by the events of the war.

Devin Alcott

A free black man born in Canada, enlisting with the Union to fight for emancipation, his goal in life is to someday become an accomplished musician.

Sissy

Although not an actual character in the novel, Sissy is Nellie's young, black guardian angel, whom most everyone else believes is a figment of Nellie's imagination.

"Great is Life, real and mystical, wherever and whoever;
Great is Death—sure as Life holds all parts together,
Death holds all parts together.
Has Life much purport?—
Ah, Death has the greatest purport."

—Walt Whitman, *Leaves of Grass*

1863

Prologue

President Abraham Lincoln, his bony hand shaking as he put the War Department telegram back on his desk, collapsed in his chair. The information had now been confirmed. An estimated 150 men had been killed in a cruel raid on Lawrence, Kansas by border ruffians headed by some jackal named William Quantrill. The president leaned forward and pressed his hand against his forehead, wondering how much more tragic news he would have to bear before this war was finally over.

Almost four years ago, he had been in Kansas Territory, stumping for his election, knowing that people there had been suffering from the divisive slavery issue. He realized it was ironic that while he had been in Atchison preparing for his campaign speech, news reached him of John Brown's execution. Lincoln told a reporter that Brown had shown great courage and rare unselfishness. In the same breath, he went on to say that even though he thought slavery evil, it "cannot excuse violence, bloodshed, and treason." But Lincoln could not shake off the feeling that most people with abolitionist leanings had vehemently disagreed with him on that point.

Hatred, he realized, existed on both sides of the slavery issue. It was especially contentious along the Kansas-Missouri border. Even his abolitionist friend, Senator James Lane from Kansas, would probably rejoice at seeing proslavery factions eliminated from the face of the earth.

The muscles in his hands tensed as he read the telegram again. *My Lord! When will all this savagery cease?*

"Mr. President, are you ill?"

Lincoln lifted his head and looked up at his young male secretary.

John Nicolay, his eyes not hiding his fright, stared back at the President. "Mr. President?" he repeated, lowering his eyes to the letters he held in his hand.

With the tip of his forefinger, Lincoln smoothed the creases

3

of the telegram on his desk. "I'll be fine. I'm just fatigued, that's all. Is that my mail?"

"Yes, Mr. President." He took a step forward to hand the envelopes to Lincoln, and then took a respectful step back.

Lincoln took a cursory look at the return addresses. "These are probably prominent folk inviting me to give speeches." He pushed the envelopes aside and rubbed his hands together, as if they were cold. "But, alas, I cannot afford an absence from my duties here."

Nicolay eyed the telegram on the President's desk. "I understand Senator Lane was unharmed in the raid."

"Yes, and I am greatly relieved to learn that, John." Lincoln rubbed his hands together to relieve the stiffness in his fingers. He would be forever grateful to Lane who, as Captain and Commanding Officer of the Frontier Guards, had stationed his men at the Executive Mansion to protect the President after the Fort Sumter attack. But Lane made him uncomfortable as well...his rashness, impetuosity, those rumors about him stealing goods from Missouri towns....

"May I get you some tea, Mr. President?"

Lincoln studied the gray Saturday morning sky through the window to his right. Mary wanted to go to New York to do some marketing, but it was really to escape from all of this. To get away from the memory of their eleven-year-old son, Willie, who had died from typhoid last year...to get away from this horrible war, this senseless brutality.

But those innocent folks in Lawrence, they could not get away. What was it like for them to have gone through such an ordeal, to have seen their husbands and sons butchered? It must have been horrific for them to have witnessed....

"Mr. President?"

Lincoln returned his gaze to his secretary. "I want to be left alone for awhile."

After John left, closing the door behind him, Lincoln rose from his chair and walked toward the large window. A column of Union soldiers marched in formation down Pennsylvania Avenue. A woman, possibly a teacher, sat on the lawn talking to a group of children. A black man passed by and tipped his

4

hat to the woman.

In the South, that man would not have been allowed to even look at a white woman, Lincoln thought. Negroes were regarded as chattel, often having no more worth than a horse. But this war proved the rebels wrong. Negroes in the First Kansas Colored Infantry in Kansas showed the Union that this land was their land, too.

Would his Proclamation truly free negroes, he wondered? What would happen to them when this conflict was finally over?

The grayness of the morning convinced him that there was no answer.

Chapter 1

August 22
Lawrence, Kansas

This was indeed Hell, she thought, as a buzzard beat its wings and disappeared into a drab sky.

Twenty-year-old Jessica Radford cussed under her breath. She was not afraid of those proslavery, hate-peddling murderers who did this. If she could, she'd make them pay for their butchery yesterday. Shivering in the warmth of the morning sun, she stumbled along with a negro named Tinker down what used to be a busy thoroughfare with shops lined on both sides. Now Massachusetts Street was a shadowy graveyard of debris. Smoke filtered through the ruins, and the acrid smell of burning flesh still hung stubbornly in the air. There were five charred bodies piled in a heap in the rear of what used to be a livery stable. A dead man lay on the street, his mouth open in a frozen cry. One woman holding a blackened skull in her hands and crying over it, sat along the ashes of a building. Duncan & Allison Dry Goods Store, Ward Meats, Danvers Ice Cream Parlor, Brechtelbrauer's Saloon…nothing but rubble now.

Jessica recalled how poor Mr. Speer, the once proud owner of the abolitionist newspaper, the *Kansas Weekly Tribune*, sorted through wreckage back on Winthrop Street, groping for the remains of his son Robert. Speer had discovered the dead body of his other son, John Jr., in the cellar of another newspaper office yesterday afternoon. "I never," he said, "wanted to outlive my sons. Never!"

John Speer, she thought, was one writer she always admired. He was a Kansas voice against the evils of slavery, but now his press was silenced. And there was no voice.

A half-hour into her walk, Jessica saw a crowd gathering in the distance, near the entrance to South Park. Perhaps, she thought, they were assembling for a funeral. There would surely be many funerals taking place in Lawrence, just one day after the slaughter. To Jessica's right, a woman shooed a crow from a blackened corpse that two boys dragged out of a burned-out building. A white dog chased chickens in a lot fronting the shell of a brick farmhouse. Jessica wondered if it was the same dog Tinker insisted had saved his life yesterday by barking him awake when he had fallen unconscious near a burning building.

But Tinker claimed it was Nellie's medallion he wore that saved him yesterday by stopping a bullet. While she adored her negro sister, whom her family had adopted, she wished Nellie would have stopped claiming the medallion had angelic powers. Of course, Nellie was now living somewhere with some Confederate folks, but Tinker now carried Nellie's superstition with him. All because the inscription on the back of the medallion said: *"For God has given His angels charge concerning thee, to keep thee in all thy ways."*

Angels, she thought, certainly did not protect this town yesterday morning. So why would they even bother to protect him?

Tinker walked a respectful distance behind Jessica. "Why the Lawd do this!" he moaned. "Why?"

Jessica turned to face him. "The Lord didn't do this, Tinker. Bill Quantrill and his horde of murderers did it. Just like those other devils who kidnapped Nellie." Her old feelings of hate and revenge returned. While she still carried a Colt .31 in her dress pocket, she wondered if she would ever have any need to use it.

Tinker dug his hands in his pockets. "I sho wish Mastah Lightfoot still like me after what I done yesterday."

"Mr. Lightfoot is not your master any more." Besides, she thought, you should never have been a slave to begin with. All men—and, by God, all women—were created equal.

"I know, Miz Jessica. I forget sometimes."

"Besides, what did you do that was wrong, Tinker?"

"I feel bad 'bout draggin' dat dead rebel—the one they call Larkin Skaggs—to the river yesterday. Dogs ate him. Feel bad like the time I kill another no good man in the woods."

Jessica remembered the letter Tinker had written her when he thought he shot the rebel who had killed her parents. *Miz*

7

Jessica, I feel bad. I shoot rebel and not save him from dying. He call me names so I leave him in woods. He cry for help, but I don' come back.

"Tinker, are you feeling compassion for a man who helped murder the people in our town?"

"I don' know what I feel, Miz Jessica."

Jessica clenched her jaw. How could God expect anyone to feel compassion for these animals? For a moment, that absurd vision of hers, the one she had months ago in Tennessee, returned. Sissy—Nellie's guardian angel—asked Jessica to forgive, to show kindness. To the enemy? Ridiculous. People ought to show kindness to slaves. Set them free and let them live as our equals. Someday, she would write a book about that.

"You were right to feel outrage, Tinker. Why yesterday, some of these rebels heard an infant cry, and they ran into a cornfield, shooting a man dead—with the man's infant still in his arms. These pigs don't deserve compassion."

"Except dat the Good Book say dat we should—"

"I don't care what the Good Book says." She stopped, spun around, and glared at him. "Tinker, this is foolish. Walk next to me. I don't have any dreaded disease that you have to walk behind me the whole time."

"I jest don' feel comfortable walkin' next to a nice, respectable, white lady. But I'll come up, if yah say so, Miz Jessica."

"I do say so, Tinker." She waited until Tinker came alongside before resuming her pace. "I'm delighted that you're no longer afraid of being seen in public and being reported as a deserter. Now you can—"

Jessica stopped in mid-sentence when a commotion arose from a crowd that had gathered in South Park. The throng had formed a circle about a tall oak, a rope hanging from one of its limbs. They were chanting "Guilty! Guilty!" and clapping.

Immediately, Jessica and Tinker rushed over, but Tinker stopped at the edge of the crowd while Jessica pushed and shoved her way to the front. Skipp Forester, the burly town blacksmith, was restraining a feisty bearded man, while another struggled to put a noose around the man's neck.

"You're gonna hafta answer to God now, Jake Callew," Skipp shouted, "if that's who ya are."

Jessica's mouth dropped open....*Could this be happening?* A wave of dizziness swept through her. Maybe she was imagining all of this. The lack of sleep, a lingering odor of burning flesh, and the ghastly sight of the charred remnants of storefronts, were perhaps making her feel delusional again. Just like she felt two months ago on a Tennessee battlefield, when, disguised as a male soldier, she thought she had seen an angel.

But this was no delusion, Jessica assured herself. This was real. The people of Lawrence were about to hang a man. A bystander told her that Jake Callew, the condemned man, was a stranger who had ridden into town earlier this morning.

"Make him pay!" one person yelled. "Murderer!" screamed another.

"No!" Jessica shouted. She turned to find a minister standing near the fated man, his Bible in hand.

"You had better make your peace with God," the minister said to the prisoner, "for you don't stand much chance with this crowd."

"You need not trouble yourself about my soul," Jake Callew said.

Jessica grasped the minister's arm. "Make them stop, Reverend."

The minister returned a sad stare and released himself from her grip. "It's out of my hands, ma'am."

Skipp jabbed a stubby finger at her. "Jessica, this ain't none of your concern!" he snapped. "This is a man's business. Ya ought to be takin' care of the widows and orphans. We just had ourselves a trial and although the judge rendered that the evidence didn't prove his guilt, we know Jake here is guilty of being one of the Quantrill raiders. Justice must rightly be done."

"Justice?" Jessica exploded. "You call this justice? You get the folks here all stirred up, hold a hasty trial, and then condemn him? I suppose you felt it was justice when you were about to whip Tinker for wanting to serve in the Union."

Skipp glowered at her, but his expression changed to a smile when he caught sight of Tinker among the people in the crowd. "Hey, boy," Skipp shouted. "Do ya always show up to cause us white folks trouble?"

Tinker, she thought, had every right last year to demand that he be entitled to enlist in the war. Skipp said it did not concern her. Well, this hanging *did* concern her. In desperation, she pulled out her revolver from a dress pocket. Her hand twitching, she waved the gun in Skipp's general direction. She swore she'd never use it.

"Let him go!" she demanded.

"You're a fool, woman!" Skipp snapped. "Of all people, ya ought to be grateful we got one of these here dogs who murdered our folk. Jest like ya ought to be grateful we hung the men who done kill your pa and ma last year."

Skipp's sharp words sliced open a memory vein in her mind. *No, I swore I'd never think about that again.*

She glanced at Jake Callew and pointed her pistol at Skipp. "All this killing has got to stop."

"Please, Jessica," the minister added, "put that down. This is no way to settle things."

Someone from behind her grabbed her arm and twisted it, causing the gun to drop to the hard, sun-parched ground.

Jessica spun around and recognized the woman who restrained her. She was a neighbor who had lost her husband in the raid. The face of the young widow was red with fury. "My husband's soul cries for justice. These men must pay for what they did!"

Her words resonated a familiar chord to Jessica. Last year, four border ruffians had kidnapped Nellie, a former slave girl, and had murdered Jessica's parents. All four had since paid with their lives for what they did.

Skipp tightened the noose about Jake Callew's neck. "Any last words, you swine?"

"I'm innocent," Jake said, his eyes surveying the crowd before focusing on Jessica.

She shuddered. Yes, innocent indeed, she thought. Perhaps just as innocent as a wounded, defenseless man she had almost

10

killed on a Tennessee battlefield.

The thump of a falling weight was followed by a cheer from the onlookers. The body swayed like a pendulum.

Jessica ran back to the graveyard of burned-out buildings.

*****

That afternoon

Although he had served here in the past as a guest preacher, Reverend Matt Lightfoot hardly recognized the interior of a Methodist church on Vermont Street. Most of the wooden seats were removed and the floor was covered with draped bodies. Occasionally, a relative or friend would pull back one of these sheets to identify a body. But some bodies were so blackened from the fire, they resembled negroes.

Jessica Radford was now but a dreary form wandering in the stark grayness of the church, surveying the bodies. She looked up at Matt for a moment, the skin of her face as tight as a drum, except for a mean anger etched into her young forehead. It was the same expression Matt had seen when she had attended the funeral of her murdered parents last year. Like then, the light had disappeared from her eyes.

Jessica pointed to a corpse dressed in a sooty nightshirt. "This one does not have a tag," she said with icicle coldness.

Matt was about to answer when a voice shrieked in the distance. "God, no!"

Two men restrained a hysterical woman dressed in a cape and a filthy wool hoop slip, her arms thrashing about. "God, no!" she repeated, twisting her body as if she wanted to escape from their grasp. "Why did the Lord take him away? Why?"

A dirge of other sobs reverberated throughout the old church. Heart-piercing weeping fingered its way through the shadowy room—a wailing mostly from women walking dizzily around the random maze of bodies, hoping to identify a husband, relative, or friend among the deceased.

Another scream echoed from somewhere near the tall cross on the wall at the front of the church. The mournful

11

shriek tore its sharp claws into Matt's nerves. The words from *Matthew 5:1* came to mind: "Blessed are they who mourn, for they shall be comforted." But a question nagged Reverend Lightfoot's soul—*when* will they be comforted?…how *long* must they wait?

"Matt," Jessica said in a shivering monotone, "help me move this one outdoors."

He pondered the ghost in her voice as he lifted the torso of the corpse and she raised its lifeless legs. He could not believe it was just yesterday evening when, as the City Band played those nostalgic strains of "Battle Hymn of the Republic," he reclined next to her near the bank of the Kaw River. After the band had finished that piece, Matt asked why she was crying. "Just sad, that's all," she explained, dabbing her eyes with his handkerchief. "I don't want to go back to my empty house tonight." *It was a good thing she stayed with me through the early morning hours*, Matt thought. *Who knows what would have happened to her if she had been home by herself when Quantrill's marauders arrived?*

Once outside the church, he felt the hot sting of the August sun. The smell of decaying flesh unfolded like a blanket, and Matt reared back from the odor and forced himself to breathe through his mouth.

Jessica took the lead with her end of the corpse that she helped carry. With each step, she pulverized the hard ground with the heel of her boot. Then she stopped. "Next to that one," she ordered Matt, with a nod of her head toward the end of a long row of dead bodies.

Matt lowered the corpse to the lawn and stared at her. Her unsmiling face avoided his and she put a kerchief to her mouth. "The stench is going to be unbearable in this heat."

"I know that. No coffins, too. Men tryin' to find lumber to build them. I'm thinkin' maybe we'll have to put these bodies here in a mass grave. Can't leave them out here and treat 'em like excrement!"

She turned away. "Seeing all these dead people makes me want to vomit."

He touched her shoulder. "Refrain from doin' this, Jessica.

This is not a proper task for a lady."

She moved over to one side, forcing his hand to drop. "I don't care," she said. "I have never shirked from doing a man's work. You know that, Matt."

"Yup, I do. But you ought to be with your Aunt Penelope, comfortin' the widows and assistin' with their needs."

She looked back at him for a long moment, and Matt wondered if she had heard him. "I am not capable of giving others comfort," she finally said. "That is the reason I could never be a nurse like my friend Mary helping the wounded in this horrible war. Ask me to drive a team, charge the enemy on a battlefield, or even rescue negroes from slave states, and I would gladly do it."

"I know you would."

"I wish I were like other women," she said, her mouth twitching. "Docile, humble, obedient, and helpless. I wish I had all those qualities you would expect in a lady."

"Shucks, Jessica, it don't matter to me. I—"

"Matt," she interrupted, pressing against him, "I don't belong here. Take me away from this horrible place."

Matt pondered a moment, wondering whether this would be the best time to tell her what had been on his mind and what he knew she had to hear.

Chapter 2

Chattanooga, Tennessee

From her kitchen window, Sara Toby stared at the vertical cliffs of Lookout Mountain, shrouding the high, wide plateau with fog. Her husband Roger used to tell her it was the fist of God, daring any intruder to climb its steep slopes. And this town, at the foot of that mountain with the Tennessee River running through it—before it became Chattanooga—was once the home of Indian settlers. Roger explained it was the place that the Cherokee Indians used as a boat landing before they were forced away, dripping their sorrows along a "trail of tears" toward Oklahoma Territory.

Sweet Jesus! I am going to miss this town—which I'm forced to flee because of those Yankee fools.

She would no longer see any of this—that grand mountain, this river, the railroad, a bustling town that became the gateway to the South—and this very house she and Roger owned. Soon it would be only a memory. She dried her eyes with the sleeve of her dress and sat down to finish her letter to Roger…

> *Darling, I wish you were here today to console me. The Chattanooga Rebel newspaper claims General Bragg is in control of the city, but it is difficult for me to accept this on faith. Our town was shelled yesterday by light artillery fire, and while I was in church with Nellie praying, I heard the awful crash of shells, and I ran out of the church with the others. I learned the bombardment managed to sink two steamers which were docked at the landing, and even the 32-pounder we had in the fort was silenced by a Union shell. It put the fear of God in all of us.*
>
> *I don't take much stock in Bragg maintaining a secure position on Lookout Mountain. If*

14

the Yankees are able to get as far as the Tennes-
see River and bombard the town, like they did
yesterday, I fear that Chattanooga must soon
surrender. I met with some of the ladies from the
Daughters of the Confederacy, and they reas-
sured me that I am wrong, that Bragg will call
in reinforcements and the Yankees will be
pushed back. While I admire their optimism, I do
not believe they are realistic. I've read articles
about General Bragg being in severe disagree-
ment with his own officers and how some main-
tain he has lost the confidence of his men.

How often she stared at that framed daguerreotype of Roger on the wall of the kitchen. He looked so handsome, the way his chestnut hair and thin mustache framed his handsome face. He had this picture taken three years ago in South Carolina, where he first met her. Back then, he was twenty-two, while she was thirteen years his senior and already an aspiring actress in a local theater group. Nonetheless, it made no difference in their plans to marry. They were both eager for the possibilities of a new future—she, as a stage actress and he, as a bank president. Unfortunately, they were both deaf to the rumblings of a conflict that would disrupt everything... .

I am annoyed that you must be out there fighting
with the Army of Tennessee while I have to be here
alone with Nellie, trying to forage for food and won-
dering what to do when those Yankees take over our
beloved town. I am seriously considering moving to At-
lanta, where my aunt now lives alone ever since her
husband who served with the 8th Georgia Infantry was
killed at Gettysburg. As you know, Jane Millicent is a
wonderful, caring woman, although I don't know if
her neighbors would take too kindly to treating Nellie
as a free woman.
The trains now carry military personnel and sup-
plies, so I wonder if they would accommodate fleeing

citizens. If not, I would somehow procure another horse and take Nellie with me on that arduous journey. Do not be concerned for our safety, darling. If I do decide to leave, I will seek the assistance of others, as we have many friends here in town. Needless to say, I will not wait for those awful Yankees to overtake our beloved town, and I refuse to endure whatever cruelty they might impart upon me and Nellie. Yet it is you, my dear, which most concerns me. Night and day I think about you, hoping and praying that you are still alive.

However, I am thankful that you managed to escape from the clutches of that Union camp near Shelbyville, when you were wounded. I was curious about something you mentioned in your letter about a Union corporal who helped you escape. You mentioned the corporal was a lady, which would be impossible since only men are allowed to fight in battle. How could this be? Perhaps you will provide me with details of your escape when this horrible war is over.

As far as Nellie is concerned, our neighbors have accepted my notion of caring for her as our own daughter, even though she was once a slave girl. Maybe people are becoming more tolerant because of their greater concern for survival. Nellie, thankfully, no longer has illusions of being visited by some angel named "Sissy." Maybe I have succeeded in convincing her that, at seventeen, she is a young lady and not a small child. She does have a wonderful voice and loves to sing in church. If I could afford it, I would hire someone to train her to play music.

I wish you Godspeed, Roger. I look forward to the day we can resume our life together.

With all my love,

Sara

*****

16

Early that evening
near Leavenworth, Kansas

At one point during his long trek from the Grand River in Missouri with seven other riders, including Senator Lane and General Thomas, Otto Heller rediscovered the letter he had been carrying in his trouser pocket. Because of the confusion of the early morning raid of Lawrence yesterday, he had forgotten he had it on his person. He would share it with his wife Penelope when he returned to Lawrence, and he would offer her a sincere apology for his quick departure.

Penelope, I regret following Lane and his men in that futile attempt to hunt down those evildoers while leaving you alone in that town of sorrows. I felt I had no choice at the time, but I pray that you and the children were able to endure the agony of my absence.

He jammed the envelope back into his pocket. *I have enough damn things to worry about.*

After spilling water from his canteen into the palm of his hand, he slapped its coolness against his eyes and yawned. He could have slept in the grassy fields of Paola last night if it had not been for that sharp pain in his back. Felt like an arrow lodged in his spine. And all of this for what? For a fruitless search for Quantrill and his horde who burned Lawrence to the ground and killed its unarmed citizens.

Earlier, at the bank of the Grand River, where William Quantrill and his men were last seen, Senator Lane brought his horse to a halt and dismounted. Lane ground the heel of his boot into the dirt as General Thomas Ewing took his time getting off his horse. Lane tossed his hat to the ground and stomped over to Ewing.

"General," he thundered, "you are the most incompetent commander I have ever seen."

"How dare you address me in that manner, sir!"

"I have every right. When I return to Washington, I will see to it that you are relieved of your command. You were

17

charged with protecting the Kansas-Missouri border. How could you fail to prevent over four hundred men under Quantrill to pass through and devastate Lawrence? Were your men asleep at the border outposts?"

"Senator, with all due respect, by the time word reached me that—"

"And look how long it took your troops to get here," Lane shouted, his eyes betraying a dark anger, his black hair in disarray. "You told me it was ten hours before you even knew about the Lawrence attack. And even then, it took you all day to get to this point, with Quantrill long since gone."

"Events delayed us. We had to wait five hours before we could be ferried across the Kansas River and some of our horses collapsed from the searing heat of the day."

"I don't want to hear any more excuses, General. I've had to flee my house, have my poor wife subjected to being terrorized, see our home destroyed, and our citizens killed. All because of your incompetence, sir."

Lane's heated exchange with the general seemed to go on indefinitely, but at some point the argument ceased, and the party took a westward retreat back to Kansas. Ewing's officers rode in silence behind both the general and the senator while Heller took up the rear. Once the party crossed into Leavenworth, Lane and Heller took a fork in the road that led to the military compound while the rest of the party continued on.

Otto sighed with relief at the sight of civilization—a large, four-story brick structure, just up ahead.

"That's the Planters House," Lane remarked. "Have you stayed there before?"

"No, but I recall reading a column by Horace Greeley once about that establishment. He called the Planters a wonder of elegance and comfort."

Lane smiled. "You are quite a literary man. I've heard about some of your fine accomplishments from John Speer."

Otto dismounted at the hitching post. "I've great admiration for Mr. Speer, Senator. His fearless written attacks on pro-slavery factions were remarkable. His *Kansas Weekly Tribune* will be deeply missed."

Lane nodded as he tied up his horse. "John will find a way to put his paper out again."

"But first," Otto said, walking with him toward the registration desk, "he'll need to bury his two sons who were killed by those madmen."

Lane's face darkened. "I could have overtaken those monsters, if they would have left me in charge. Good Lord, I could have overtaken them!"

Otto grunted as if he agreed with him, but he didn't. When Lane's makeshift army met up with Major Preston Plumb's men, Lane insisted on being in command. Lane lost the argument, but continued to find fault with the way the pursuit was being conducted. Perhaps, Otto thought, Lane felt humiliated when he appeared in his nightshirt and a pair of ill-fitting trousers after the raiders left Lawrence, insisting that all men and boys give chase to Quantrill and his men. About forty people who volunteered grabbed whatever weapon they could find, whether it be shotgun, a knife, squirrel rifle, or an old musket. And they took whatever animal was available, be it dray horse or mule. Otto followed the ragtag group on a mare which refused to go faster than a trot. At least the Ninth Kansas later loaned him a steed to ride, but what use was that now? Quantrill was gone.

Otto was about to bid goodnight to the senator after he signed in at the registration desk. But Lane took hold of his sleeve. "Just a moment," he said, his slender face ashen, his eyes weary, his eyelids drooping as if they too required rest. His countenance was that of a beaten man, not at all like the raging senator some papers portrayed him as. "Mr. Heller, would you have dinner with me before retiring?"

Otto agreed and went to the center of the hotel restaurant, but Lane insisted that they take a seat in the corner of the room. "You never know," Lane said, in a weak attempt at humor, "when a bushwhacker might recognize me and use me as a target."

Otto winced as he shifted his weight on the wooden chair. "I can understand that, Senator. My back has been in considerable pain ever since proslavery ruffians pummeled me one evening after I left my publishing house. I suspect our long ride today

19

only served to irritate it."

Lane's eyes conveyed his sympathy at Otto's plight. "It is unfortunate you had to sell your publishing firm last year. Do you plan to get back into the business some day?"

Otto thought a moment. Now that Penelope's general store in Lawrence was gone, her dream had also disappeared. "Nothing would please me more, senator. But for now, I am just looking for some way to survive all of this."

A server came by to take their orders. Lane ordered the stew along with a glass of ale. Otto nodded to the woman and said he'd have the same. After she left, he focused on the senator. "You were fortunate to have escaped the devastation. How is your wife holding up?"

Lane's face was drawn and tired. "Mary is holding up quite well under the circumstances. Quantrill paid her a personal visit to destroy me and, instead, destroyed our home. I assure you, however, that snake will not escape. I plan on returning soon to Lawrence, but first I need to meet with Ewing tomorrow and firm up that order he promised to issue."

"What order?"

Lane's dark eyes darted across the room before he leaned forward as if beginning a confidence. "A government order that will prevent Missourians from harboring bushwhackers like Quantrill and his ilk. They are nothing but snakes and devils."

Otto gazed absently at the roaring flames in the fireplace nearby and returned a questioning gaze back at Lane. "I don't understand. How would a government order prevent that?"

Lane leaned back in his chair. He opened his mouth slightly as if he were going to answer, but then he pursed his lips, studying his friend. He smiled politely to the server who poured his ale.

"A toast," he said, raising his glass while Otto did the same. "To the triumph of the Union in this Rebellion."

Otto winced at the large painting above the fireplace. It showed Union soldiers raiding an Indian village. One Indian standing outside his tent, held his hand up in an apparent greeting while a soldier on horseback fired at him. Otto turned away from it in disgust and stared at the senator, wondering why Lane never answered his question.

The senator frowned. "What is the matter? You look concerned."

"I'm curious—what about that government order you referred to a minute ago?"

Lane smiled slightly. "I wish I could be more specific, but I cannot. This is strictly a military matter."

The words "military matter" struck a resonant chord with Otto. "That reminds me, senator. I wanted to thank you for your favor concerning Tinker."

Lane's eyes narrowed. "Tinker?"

"That former slave I had informed you about, the one who had deserted the First Kansas and made it to Lawrence. He admitted he had made a terrible mistake and wanted to return to the war without recrimination. You were going to use your influence to see if he could avoid a charge of desertion. Remember?"

A hint of recognition crossed the senator's face. "Oh, yes. There is a possibility of a need for him in one of our regiments. I have learned that negroes make excellent soldiers. Have Tinker report to Lieutenant Colonel Clark with the Ninth Kansas Cavalry next week."

"With all due respect, senator, the town has been devastated and Tinker will have no way to get here."

Lane shrugged. "No cause for concern. I'll arrange it." His eyes appeared to sparkle with a sudden thought. "Clark's regiment will require additional recruits for an upcoming engagement I know he has planned." Lane explored his jacket pocket for something, and returned his attention to Otto. "Do you have anything to write on? I would like to make a note to remind myself."

Otto stuck his hand in his trouser pocket and pulled out an envelope. He had forgotten until now that it was there. He removed the contents and handed Lane the envelope.

Lane scribbled some notes on it and glanced at the letter Otto held in his hand. "That appears to be an official government document of some sort, am I correct?"

"Yes, very observant of you. It's an order from the Federal government to enroll for military service. I received it last week and had intended to tell my wife, but with the recent devastation of our town, I did not have an opportunity to relate this to her."

Lane rubbed his chin, no ready answer apparent in his eyes.

"Look, Senator, as much as I would like to serve my country, it's impractical at the moment." He felt his blood boiling, but took a deep breath. "You know as well as I do that my home has been destroyed, my wife is out there in the ashes of Lawrence trying to survive, and I have two young children to tend to. It's impossible, damn it!"

The senator leaned forward. "Relax. You won't have to serve. The Enrollment Act allows you to find a substitute for the price of $300."

"Indeed, I realize that, but I have no intention of paying my way out of service to my country. I am not afraid to fight for the Union."

"I was merely exploring options concerning your dilemma."

Otto relaxed a degree. "Any advice you can give me?"

The senator asked to examine the letter and stroked his chin in thought as he read it. Otto was about to say something to break the silence, but Lane shushed him. "There can be more than one way for you to serve the Union. Hmmm, I think I have an idea."

"What is it?"

"It might be a perfect fit, considering your past experience as a publisher. As I told you before, newspapermen like John Speer hold you in high esteem."

"But what does that have to do—?"

Lane shushed him again. Otto leaned forward, curious, both of his elbows on the table, his chin resting in his fists.

With the slightest twinkle in his otherwise tired eyes, Lane looked up at him. "Mr. Heller, how would you like to move to Washington, D.C.?"

Chapter 3

Lawrence, Kansas

Into a large cloth bag, Penelope placed a bar of soap, some rags, and scraps of food she had managed to find in the rubble. "All my worldly possessions," Penelope muttered, gritting her teeth. The sun had already set, and she could not help but recall reading somewhere that darkness was a great equalizer. After all, she was a 31-year-old mulatto with charcoal black hair and dark copper skin that made some people assume she was a negro and probably a former slave. But she had always been a free woman, having been born in Canada where slavery was not tolerated.

Fortunately, the people of Lawrence accepted her as she was—the owner of a now-destroyed general store and an educated lady. Perhaps they silently questioned why her children were not colored, but it was no one else's affair. While her two girls were Otto's by a previous marriage, Penelope never thought of them as stepchildren.

Penelope hoisted the bag on her back and took her two young daughters to the edge of the Kansas River to bathe. Six-year-old Emma, her wet cheeks caked with dirt, looked as if she were going to cry again when they arrived at the river.

Penelope stooped and held her gently by the shoulders. "What's wrong?"

"I miss not having Papa here. He should be home now."

"I've told you before that he will return soon."

Nine-year-old Mitzi peered into the darkness, her fingers on a button of her dress. "Are we alone, Momma?"

"Yes, now off with those things and into the water." Penelope was thankful that at least it was a warm autumn evening and the river temperature was tolerable.

Emma handed Penelope her clothes and entertained herself by splashing her feet at the river's edge. But Mitzi, removing her petticoat with deliberate slowness, glowered at her mother. "I hate you. I hate this town. No food, no home, people dying, and everyone crying and afraid."

Penelope just shook her head. *You're so much like Jessica—demanding to leave when the situation becomes unpleasant.*

Just today, Penelope happened to meet Matt Lightfoot, who told her that Jessica begged him to take her far from this wretched town. He hadn't yet informed Jessica that he planned to return to his regiment on Tuesday. A detachment from the First Kansas Infantry would be passing through and take him back to Lexington, where he would be mustered back into the Kansas Eighth. "She'll be furious," he had said, "that I'd be leaving without her." Penelope had to agree. Jessica would probably insist on going with him.

"Mother! I will *not* stay here another day," Mitzi declared, her arms folded defiantly across her bare chest, her pantalets encircling her feet.

"I'm not terribly fond of the situation either," Penelope said. "But we must make the best of it. Now, pick up your clothes and hand them to me."

Mitzi did as she was told, but she turned her attention to the sluggish river. "Mama," she said, after a long pause, her voice softly straining, "aren't you the least bit worried about Papa?"

"No need to worry. I know your father, and he will take good care of himself, believe me."

Penelope was about to add that it was all in God's hands, but then how would she explain to the girls that this horrific murder last Friday was in God's hands too? This morning, Father Favre Sebastian had a short Sunday Mass for some three dozen people, mostly women, at St. John's Church on Kentucky Street, one of the few buildings that had been spared. Fourteen parishioners had lost their lives in the raid, and Penelope tried her best to console two of the widows. All about her, just before the service began, women with disheveled hair, gaunt faces, and dressed in filthy clothes were hugging each other, and there was so much crying Emma started crying as well, telling Penelope she did not like this place. Penelope endured the Mass and was relieved that in place of a homily,

24

Father Sebastian read a few lines from Scripture.

But she despised the words he read from *1 Peter 4*: "Do not be surprised, beloved, that a trial by fire is occurring in your midst. It is a test for you, but it should not catch you off guard. Rejoice instead, in the measure that you share Christ's sufferings. When His glory is revealed, you will rejoice exultantly." A couple of parishioners walked out after hearing that. And if it were not for the sake of her children, Penelope would have walked out as well. Why indeed did these good people of Lawrence have to suffer while those evildoers plundered, murdered, and escaped? Why rejoice?

As the girls waded hand-in-hand into the river, Penelope looked about in all directions to be reassured of privacy. Grabbing the bar of soap, she followed them in, not concerned that her dress would be soaked.

Emma's face wrinkled in pain as she stood chest deep in the water. "I miss Papa. I miss him so much."

An impatient frown crossed Mitzi's forehead as she glared at her young sister. "Stop it! You keep talking about Papa all the time. We all miss him."

Emma began to cry. "I'm afraid, Momma. Will those evil people come back and kill us?"

"Of course not, darling," Penelope said, applying soap on Emma's dirt-streaked back. "I won't let anyone hurt you."

Crickets chirped, a yellow moon rippled across the river's surface, and in the distance the glow of campfires punctured the awful desolation of the night. The survivors out there were probably thinking the same thing. Would they come back and finish their task?

Penelope was about to scrub Mitzi, but she insisted on doing it herself. "I'm nine years old already," she said. "Don't treat me like a child!"

Little Miss Independence, Penelope thought. *Just like Jessica.*

"Momma," Mitzi said, handing the soap bar back to her, "do we have to go back in that dark cellar tonight? Must we?"

"Yes, we must." That hidden underground cellar on Vermont Street may have saved their lives. It certainly saved the

25

lives of a dozen men and boys fleeing from the marauders Friday morning. But she wondered if she would have courage now to do what she did back then...

Three horsemen rode down Vermont Street and reined their horses in front of her. "Men keep disappearing here," one of the men growled, looking down at her with black, contemptuous eyes. "Yeah," said another. "Where're they hidin'?"

"I'm not going to tell you," Penelope said. Who did they think she was, she thought, a fool?

The first man drew his horse nearer to her and pulled out his pistol, aiming it at her face. "Tell me, lady, or I'll shoot you!"

No man, Penelope thought, should ever dare tell her to do the wrong thing. She lived her life believing that. And she'd die—if she had to.

She glared back at him. "You may shoot me if you will, but you won't ever find out where the men are."

The explosion of the gun never came, thank the Lord! What would Emma and Mitzi have done without a mother?

The children emerged from the river and Penelope dried them with the rags she had in her bag. "You girls are shinier than a pair of new pennies. Now let's get dressed and make our way back."

As she was about to hand Mitzi and Emma their clothes, gunshots permeated the night air. In the distance she heard screams...."They're coming back. Run for your lives!" More gunshots.

Penelope's heart skipped a beat as the tumult increased. Were those footsteps she heard?

She grabbed a rock.

Chapter 4

While angry guns from the white men blazed behind her, Jessica ran with the others, many of whom began scattering into the open field. The people running with her were all negroes, and they shrieked as they fled through an open field of a Southern plantation. "Sweet Jesus, save me!" a negro woman closest to her shouted. "Doan let 'em kill me!"

Jessica turned towards her. "Why are we running?"

The woman's face was beaded with perspiration and her large eyes beamed back a look of dismay. "Doan yah know why? We try t' escape 'n now deys tryin' to kill us. Dat's why."

As gunshots punctuated the air. Jessica spun around to see a line of armed white men still chasing after them on foot. About a dozen screaming negroes scurried between the endless rows of cotton plants.

The woman who had been running with Jessica waved her arms in desperation. "Yah wanna get yerself killed, woman?" she said. "Keep movin'."

"Why would anyone want to kill me?"

"Cause yah is a black slave like the rest of us, 'n our massah got no use fer slaves dat done run away. Now, git goin', woman."

"But I'm not a slave and I'm not black."

"Are yah crazy? Take a good look at yerself."

Jessica looked at her hands. Black. Her mind spun as if it were caught in a whirlwind. *I'm a negro. A negro slave. How could this be?* Her mouth dropped open as she stared at her black companion

"Yah plumb crazy," the negro woman said. She took off in another direction, but had not gone more than a few yards when she was shot in the back.

Jessica gasped. "Oh, dear God!"

Her scream was still on her lips when she awoke. The morning sun, peeping past a small cloud mocked her. Jessica looked at her arms. White. Of course, what did she expect?

27

Maybe Matt was right. She *was* obsessed with the slavery issue. It even dominated her dreams..

Jessica pushed herself up. By now, she was getting used to sleeping in the open, using the grassy field as her mattress, and thankful that at least it hadn't rained. Although some of the townspeople now slept in tents donated by nearby towns, Jessica refused. She recalled how she had to sleep outside when her parents were en route from Missouri to Kansas in a canvas covered wagon. *I'd lay beneath the wagon with Ma pressing against me, already fast asleep. But I'd just look up at the stars and try to count them all, wondering what it'd be like to be way up there in the sky, looking down here.*

She felt lonely when she thought about it. It reminded her too much of that tragic line from Shakespeare:

"But I alone must sit and pine,
Seasoning the earth with showers of silver brine,
Mingling my talk with tears, my grief with groans."

Tears and grief. That's all she had been witnessing. "And I'm sick of it!" she snapped. A pesky breeze blew her blond hair across her face as she pumped the handle of the well with an anger that filtered through the sinews of her arms. "Why am I even bothering with this?" she muttered as she washed her face. "I might as well be out in the pasture with farm animals."

People from as far away as Kansas City rode into town yesterday, eager to help in any way they could. Food and medicine arrived, as well as blankets and clothing. She now had a hand cart, some undergarments, an ill-fitting dress, blankets, towels, food, and water.

Nonetheless, if it were not for the scorched writing tablet and the pencils she managed to find while searching through the ruins, she felt she would have gone mad. At least she had been able to write down her thoughts about the devastation and perhaps use them in the future in one of her stories or poems. She had started a novel seven months ago, not that she had gotten far along on it, but it was gone in the flames, as well

28

as everything she kept at home. But while all her books were destroyed by fire, she was pleased she had memorized lines from poets such as William Wordsworth (*"We will grieve not, rather find strength in what remains behind."*) or Henry Longfellow (*"And the night shall be filled with music...and as silently steal away."*)

When two total strangers—a Leavenworth couple eager to assist Lawrence townspeople after the devastation—appeared, Jessica waved off their offer of food. She needed conversation more than a slice of bread.

"Sit on the grass for a spell and talk to me," Jessica insisted, opening her arms toward them. "Loaf and invite your soul," she added, reflecting on the opening lines of Whitman's *Leaves of Grass.*

"I am sorry," the Leavenworth woman said, taking a cautious step back, "but we have other people to tend to."

Jessica scowled back at her. The couple did not understand her, just like the others....

"What do you want out of life?" Mama once asked Jessica as they toiled in the garden patch.

Jessica examined the weeds in her soiled hands. "To be understood, Mama. People just don't know who I am."

"Bein' understood don't matter as much as understanding, child. More important that you understand."

The couple waved goodbye and began walking away.

"If you will not talk to me," Jessica shouted back at them, "let me at least recite the poems I have memorized. Do either of you have a favorite poet?"

The man accompanying the Leavenworth woman turned around. "We really must be on our way."

"Please," Jessica pleaded, chasing after them, "let me go back with you to Leavenworth. I have no money, but I can work as a—" She stopped short of asking for work as a servant-girl. "—as a farmhand. I can chop wood, drive a team, shoe horses, plow a field, or anything of the sort. Believe me, I can earn my keep."

The woman's brow was lined with exasperation. "I'm sorry."

Jessica glared at her. *Ma'am, does your compassion have limits?*

This was likely the way Tinker felt, begging for a job from strangers after Matt reluctantly gave him his freedom. People were probably repulsed by the color of his skin, just like they were repelled by her torn clothes and unkempt hair.

"I have some worth, you know, I'm a writer," she said, panting, as the couple hurried to leave. "I need to read something, anything. Can you at least do that much? Will you let me have a book?"

The couple looked at each other as if wondering whether she had lost her mind. Finally, the man returned and handed her a copy of the *Leavenworth Daily Conservative.*

When they were finally out of earshot, Jessica screamed back at them, "And a good day to you, too!" After tossing the paper to the ground, she picked it up and scanned the pages. This damn newspaper was the only thing she had read since last Thursday. The dozen stories written about the raid were interesting, as was the criticism of General Ewing's lack of adequate defense of the Kansas-Missouri border. It laid the blame on the do-nothing policy of Ewing, who, with five thousand soldiers under his command, allowed some four hundred guerrillas to get to Lawrence and destroy the town and murder its citizens.

She approached other Good Samaritans as well, but all anyone was willing to do was to provide her with material necessities, not transportation and a paid position, no matter how meager the wages.

Grabbing the handles of the handcart containing her scant belongings, she pulled the cart behind her, all the while wondering where her friends were. After the raid, everyone had scattered, many to Mount Oread—where they apparently felt safe on higher ground, others to partially-burned buildings, and still others, like herself, on the grassy plain.

Two days ago, late Sunday evening, she had seen Penelope and her children racing down Massachusetts Street. "Qunatrill has returned!" Penelope screamed, almost running into Jessica. "We are doomed!" But Jessica assured her aunt it was only a false alarm. Apparently, someone had fired several shots at some animal, and some of the townspeople thought they were being raided again.

But that was the last time Jessica had seen Penelope and the children. *Where were they?* The question lingered on her mind as she searched for wood to use for coffins, brought in water from wells, erected temporary shelters, repaired whatever dwellings were capable of repair, cleared the rubble—and before sunset, wrote down her anger. At night she returned to the river, calling out for Penelope and children. *Did they leave the area?* Jessica wandered the streets, peered into the Methodist church, searched the ravine, walked through cornfields. *Were they harmed? Oh, Lord, no! Where were Penelope and the children?*

Maybe Otto should not have left them in search of Quantrill. But how could he not do what he felt was right?

Jessica picked up a twig and tried to bend it with both hands. *Otto, you're an obstinate fool, but I admire you for it.* She grunted as she bent it a bit more. He had once told her that bending a twig was akin to breaking the resistance of society....the more controversial the issue, the thicker the twig and the harder it was to break. Just like the hardships he surely must have undertaken in bringing slaves to freedom. *What a fine, unselfish man you are! Penelope was certainly fortunate to have married you.*

The twig snapped and Jessica tossed the pieces aside as she took up the cart containing her belongings and pulled it behind her. A wheel stuck in a rut along her path, and Jessica cussed as she pulled the cart free.

"Let me give you a hand with that," a familiar voice called out to her.

She spun around. "Matt! I thought you had already left."

Matt's smile shone through the Cherokee features of his rugged face. He had let his black hair grow long, and it was tied in the back. The tense lines in his forehead, so evident last Saturday when he helped her carry the bodies out of the church, were less prominent.

"I'm delighted you haven't left this miserable town. I need to talk to someone to keep my sanity."

Matt grabbed her cart but avoided her eyes. "No, I'm not stayin'. The men from the First Kansas are waitin' for me by the ferry. Told them I couldn't leave without sayin' farewell "

"What!" Jessica exclaimed.

"I'm sorry," he said, pulling the cart as she walked alongside. "I feel badly for you that I must leave so soon."

"You're *sorry?*" she said, her voice rising. "Why didn't you tell me you had reenlisted?"

"Shucks," he said, waving an apologetic hand, "I planned to tell you after spendin' Thursday evenin' with you at the river."

Jessica stopped, staring hard at him, her eyes narrowing into thin slits. "Perhaps because you did not want to spoil your chance of having your way with me, is that it?"

A muscle in Matt's jaw ticked. "Now see here, I'm sorry for havin' taken liberties with you. But what you said just now was uncalled for."

"I apologize, but I am still furious with you."

"We've got a crisis loomin'. The Union needs more men to help the cause. I had to reenlist, and I'm not goin' to excuse myself for it."

"Aren't you the least concerned about getting killed?"

Matt took a deep breath and his face softened. "Yup, I sure am, but I'll have someone watchin' over me." He taunted her with the medallion around his neck. "Tinker gave me this. Said it carries with it the protection of an angel. Told me it kept him from gettin' killed in the Lawrence massacre."

Jessica frowned. "Mr. Lightfoot, you don't believe that nonsense about angels, do you?"

"Don't know why I shouldn't. The Bible is filled with stories about angels who got involved with folks. In *Genesis*, an angel appeared to Abraham—in *Judges*, to Gideon—in *Luke*, to Zachariah—in *Revelations*, to John. Need I go on?"

"No—and I really don't need or want a Bible lesson from you. Look, Matt, I think it is grossly unfair for you to go away like this and leave me here in this wretched town."

"I had hoped that you might reconsider joinin' our unit as a nursin' assistant. You would be able to see your friend Miss Delaney again as well."

Jessica shut her eyes. Mary Delaney! The name conjured up mixed feelings. There were indeed some warm moments Jessica had shared with her. They had gone to the same school, played together, and once, when they were both nine, took a riverboat ride with the Radfords on the Missouri River. But now there was that horrible time, just this year when, stationed in Murfreesboro, Jessica witnessed Matt alone with Mary in the grass near the creek and overheard her whispering to him.

Jessica flinched when Matt attempted to pat her tearful cheek with his handkerchief. "Jessica, what's wrong?"

She moved his hand away. "How fortunate it is, Reverend Lightfoot, or should I now refer to you as Lieutenant Lightfoot, that you will be seeing Mary again. I suppose the two of you will now resume—" The rest of what she intended to say caught in her throat.

Matt's eyes, hurt and questioning, flashed back at her. "Good Lord, Jessica. We've had this discussion before. I agreed it was all over between Mary and me—and how I truly felt about you."

"I believe you," Jessica said, relaxing. She remembered how he proposed marriage to her after the City Band had finished playing their first performance the night before the raid….He had held her in his arms as he asked a question that demanded only one answer: "How could it be wrong for me to want you?"

Jessica dug her heel into the ground. "It's not fair, Matt. You'll be gone fighting the rebels while I'm here sinking in all this misery, in this horrible town where people have been stripped of everything, including their own dignity."

Matt, his hard features softened by his caring and gentle brown eyes, held her by her shoulders as he brought his face close to hers. "I've already talked to Otto. I reckon he's searchin' for you to tell you all about it. He's thinkin' of takin' you along with Penelope and the children to Washington, D.C."

Jessica's shoulders slumped. "Our nation's capital? That's incredible. Whatever for?"

"You need to talk with him about that. I'm only relatin' that fact to you now so you won't have to worry about your survival. I know how much you want to leave this town, and I believe Mr. Heller has the solution to your problem."

"But—"

He kissed her while the word was still on her lips. "I'll miss you, and I'll always consider you my beautiful, special lady. Besides, I feel this will give you time to think about us and our life together."

Our life together? Jessica hoped that in time she would feel the same about Matt as she had when she first met him at her high school graduation picnic in Lawrence. Her father had introduced her to Matt, a lanky, dark-haired man who disarmed her with his friendly smile. Pa said that Matt was single and aimed to become pastor of his own congregation someday. While she was extremely fond of Matt at first, she began having doubts when he later defended his belief in slavery because the Bible supported it.

"Jessica?" Matt said, searching her face with tenderness. "You haven't heard a word I've said, have you?"

"Oh, indeed I have. You informed me that the Hellers want me to accompany them to Washington, D.C.."

"But I have also told you that you mean more to me than anything in this world."

Although his face seemed to beg for a response from her, she said nothing.

"Jessica, I only want to know one thing."

"What's that?"

He struggled for the words. "Do you love me?" His piercing eyes were demanding as he held her close.

She bit her lip and looked away, grasping for an answer that might please him. Maybe in time she could love him. An ancient

34

Roman poet, she instantly recalled, wrote that absence makes the heart grow fonder. But Shakespeare had a better vision: *"Love's not Time's fool."*

"I have tender feelings for you, Matt," she said, bringing her face close for his kiss. *I wish it were true. Maybe some day it will be.*

Chapter 5

Jessica found the monotonous dull thump of hooves and the creaking of wheels of the stagecoach hypnotic. Sitting between Emma and Mitzi, she scribbled on her writing tablet:

> *...and so Mr. Heller enters a new world of wonder, becoming an assistant to Mr. Defrees, the Superintendent of the National Printing Office in Washington. No military service awaits him either. Senator Lane convinced Mr. Heller he would be entitled to a deferment. Men with back problems do not good foot soldiers make, so sayeth the senator.*

As Jessica continued with her script, Emma squirmed closer to her. "What is it you're writing, Miss Radford?"

"Just some things I want to remember. If I don't write them down, I will forget." She smiled back at the little girl and resumed writing...

> *All the world's but a stage. Yet I am not a poor player on it. Alas my dear Shakespeare, my hope rests in the newness of it all. Mr. Heller now has his salary advance...Penelope will clerk at the Printing Office...and me, pray tell...Tis pitiful that on the one hand, I will be domesticated as a nanny for the Heller children. But on the other hand, I am blessed by my greater distance from that wretched town. I will be in our nation's capital, where I will be able to write as well as be near to Mr. Heller, a dear man about whom I care a great deal.*

Jessica struck out the reference to Mr. Heller. Those were sinful feelings to have about a married man. She wished she wouldn't have had that dream about him last night. She still felt guilty about it.

Emma leaned her head against Jessica's side. "I am so happy you will be with us."

"I am as well. Are you looking forward to your new home?"

Emma looked up at her and nodded, a huge grin encircling her face. "That's where Mr. Lincoln lives, isn't it? Are we going to live with him?"

Mitzi turned a sour face toward her young sister. "Don't you know anything? Mr. Lincoln lives in the Executive Mansion. He doesn't live with ordinary people like us."

Emma looked hurt, but Jessica rubbed her shoulder to soothe her. "Everyone needs to live in her own place." As soon as Jessica said this, she thought of the irony that she'd be living with the Hellers and not in her own home. But maybe some day.

Otto, outside the coach and seated next to the stage driver, gave a muffled order. The stagecoach began to slow as the sprawling town of Leavenworth came into view.

Penelope, seated directly ahead, turned around. "Jessica, we are going to stop in town while Otto visits with one of his old friends. I would be delighted if you would accompany me and my daughters in shopping for some decent clothing before we leave later for the railroad depot."

"I have no money, so I hope they will allow me to purchase a few things on credit."

Penelope smiled. "Don't be concerned about that. I am certain in due time you will be able to repay me. I hope you will come with us."

"Yes, please," Mitzi said, her eyes sparkling with enthusiasm. "You must come shopping with us."

"And," Emma added, "you don't want to wear those smelly clothes anyway."

Jessica laughed, putting an arm around each of them. "You make a good point. Yes, of course, I will join you."

*****

Fort Leavenworth bustled with activity, with one group of men lined up in formation just outside the entrance. A captain called off names from his roster to another group. Inside the headquarters, two officers engaged in serious consultation as they walked quickly down a hall. A major barked at a first lieutenant near the doorway to an office. Otto spotted a medium built man with a salt-and-pepper beard fixing himself a cup of tea in the main dining area. It was Second Lieutenant James Pond of the Third Wisconsin Cavalry, and his guarded look turned into a grin.

"Otto! You are fortunate to have found me today. I'm due to leave for Fort Scott this afternoon. The adjutant in my regiment informed me that Senator Lane had paid a visit to our quartermaster a few days ago. The senator told him you had been chasing after Quantrill but failed to capture any of his men."

"Unfortunately, that is the situation."

"Well, please, have a chair. Let me know what has been happening since that godforsaken raid of Lawrence. It must have been quite a shock to you and your dear wife."

"Yes, it was." Otto took a seat across the table. "By now, you've probably received all of the information about it, but the experience in having gone through it was horrible."

The lieutenant leaned forward in his chair. "How did you manage to avoid being slaughtered?"

Otto wasn't about to describe how he escaped by hiding under Penelope's hoop skirt, crawling on his knees like a dog, while she took small steps from her shop on Massachusetts Street to their secret underground cellar across from the Johnson House on Vermont Street. "It would require a rather involved explanation." Otto pressed the fingers of his hands together, almost as if he were initiating a prayer. "I need to tell you the purpose of my visit."

Pond maintained his smile, but he glanced about as if expecting to hear a dark secret.

"Lieutenant, I'm inquiring about a negro soldier who goes by the name of Tinker."

Pond cocked his head in thought. "That name sounds familiar for some reason."

"He was to have arrived here yesterday to meet with Lieutenant Colonel Clark with the Ninth Kansas Cavalry, per Senator Lane's suggestion."

"Oh, yes, now I remember. A tall, strapping negro in his thirties, I would guess. I was conferring with Adjutant Sanders when this man arrived, claiming he was directed by Senator Lane to meet with Clark. While I helped Tinker find his way to the lieutenant colonel's office, I gave him some information about the Third Wisconsin Cavalry. I had rather hoped he might be mustered into our regiment instead of the Ninth."

"Why is that?"

"I fear that his recruits might be required to implement General Orders Number Eleven."

Otto raised a questioning eyebrow. "I beg your pardon?"

The lieutenant's face quivered into a nervous twitch. "Orders Number Eleven. They were issued to prevent border residents from supporting Quantrill and his gang—although I suspect retaliation for the Lawrence raid was a hidden motive for the action. General Thomas Ewing ordered all inhabitants of certain Western Missouri counties that are not within a mile of Union military posts to leave their homes. They have been given until the ninth of September to do this or else we would take military action."

"What!" Otto rose from his chair, his head spinning. Innocent people thrown out of their homes and deprived of livelihood? No wonder Lane had been evasive at dinner when Otto asked him about a mysterious "government order" he slipped out during the conversation.

Damn that Lane and his personal favors.

September 9
La Fayette, Georgia

"Maybe Bragg wants t' give Chattanooga t' the Yankees, as a goin' away present," one of the officers sneered when he learned about Bragg's decision to evacuate Chattanooga. After

39

he shared the news with Lieutenant Roger Toby, Roger stormed out of the man's tent, picking up a rock and hurling it toward a tree. *General Braxton Bragg is an idiot and doesn't deserve to be the Confederate commanding officer.*

And though he had first heard the news three days ago, Roger still felt his muscles tighten and a vein throb in his neck whenever General Bragg's name was mentioned. "I don't rightly care if even his own generals have no respect for him," Roger told a colleague. "It don't make me feel any better about the situation." *And I don't know why Jefferson Davis continues to support him after losing Kentucky to the Federals and not making any real progress in Tennessee.*

Roger curled and uncurled his fist as he thought of Bragg while waiting for Lieutenant Colonel Watt Floyd to wind up his talk to his men. "We will be returning to Chattanooga," Floyd concluded, "and as I say, the plan is to surprise them from the south where we expect to garner strength from Confederate reserves."

Roger visualized himself running up to the lieutenant colonel and saying, "So we're here to correct Bragg's mistake, is that it?" Instead, he bit his lip as he thought about how the Confederates had abandoned their key position on Lookout Mountain and by now, the Federals had probably overtaken the Crutchfield House—Bragg's former headquarters.

Roger took a deep breath and exhaled slowly. If only he had the opportunity to see Sara again. It was all the more unbearable because home was a mere two hours away. But was she there? Her last letter to him said that she would likely be leaving for Atlanta and staying with Jane Millicent, her only surviving aunt.

He lit the oil lamp in his tent and began writing. But after only a few words, he crumpled the letter with his hands and tossed it to the ground. There would be no point in writing to her, not knowing where she was. *This was one damn, poorly executed war!* Perhaps the sacrifice would be worth it if he could help achieve a major Southern victory. But the Confederates had already suffered significant defeats at both Vicksburg and Gettysburg. He did not think he could suffer through yet another loss for the South.

Calhoun, Georgia

"Does your aunt know we're coming?" seventeen-year-old Nellie asked Sara Toby after they boarded an Atlanta-bound W&A Railroad car.

"No," Sara answered, looking about for an empty seat in a car crowded with uniformed soldiers. "But I am sure that will not be a problem."

Just then, a lieutenant and a private got up and offered their seat to them. "Why, thank you, gentlemen," Sara said. "Are you both traveling to Atlanta?"

The private tipped his cap. "No, ma'am. Richmond. We have the privilege of defending the fortifications there."

Sara eased herself next to Nellie, who was seated by the window.

"Those Yankees would be fools," the lieutenant said, "if they think they can ever penetrate Georgia. I wish General Lee would detach himself from his engagements in the east and give Chattanooga back to us."

The private laughed. "Then we'd have something to Bragg about."

His dry humor dissolved, replaced by the monotonous clickity-click-clack, clickity-click-clack rhythm of the rails. For Sara, the mind-numbing sound of train wheels moving relentlessly over miles of tracks changed into an ominous "Yankees-acomin', Yankees-acomin.'"

Oh Sweet Jesus! Her worry over Roger's fate, gripped her like an eagle's talons. She tried not to think about the possibility of losing him. Instead, she reflected on how fortunate she was that she was able to get passage with so many military personnel traveling. The grasslands, hills, and farms flew by, while the grayish smoke from the locomotive two cars ahead attempted to obliterate it all. It reminded her of a scene she had once played as a woman riding the rails in a desperate search for her husband. But this was no play, and she was in a desperate search for survival from those horrible Yankees.

Nellie's eyes seemed to express the pain of the bitter war. "Missus Toby, I gonna miss our home in Tennessee. I surely will."

"I know, Nellie. I will too."

"Excuse me, ma'am," the lieutenant said as Nellie glanced in his general direction, "but I wondered if you and your servant girl are comfortable travelin' alone like this, unescorted by a gentleman, I mean."

Nellie beamed a smile back at him. "But I'm not her servant girl."

"Hush, Nellie," Sara said, jabbing her elbow against her. "I must warn you not to talk to strangers."

The private's face broke out in surprise. "That colored girl is not your slave?"

Sara stared back at him. "I never said she wasn't. Now please leave us be."

She took a deep breath, wishing she would have explained to Nellie before they left to keep quiet in front of gentlemen strangers. Nellie's openness was risky.

Chapter 6

"I don't care what you think, boy," Sergeant Lawson of the Ninth Kansas Volunteer Cavalry told Private Tinker, "your duty is to obey orders. Understand?"

"Yessuh," Tinker replied, gripping his Sharps rifle as if he were strangling it. "I understand, suh." He looked at the road behind him. He counted two farm wagons, four dray horses, a shay, and several people on foot—clutching each other for support, some carrying sacks over their shoulders. An elderly man, seemingly confused by all that was going on, had walked back toward a burning field and was now being escorted back to his wagon by two soldiers.

Tinker cussed silently as he followed Sergeant Lawson and Captain Coleman up a stone path leading to a brick farmhouse. *This was not why I reenlisted,* he thought. *Not to order folks out of their homes and destroy their crops.* He wanted to fight the enemy, not people whose only crime was living in the wrong county.

Earlier, Captain Coleman had mentioned that six men in Jackson County were executed by Union troops near Lone Jack, Missouri. Coleman claimed they were Quantrill supporters, but Tinker wondered if they were only simple farmers and neighbors like the people living in this building. And even if they *were* Quantrill supporters, they did not deserve to be killed.

A gray-haired man in his fifties, wearing overalls and a rumpled shirt met them outside. There was a certain rawness to his smile. "What kin I do for you folks?"

Captain Coleman was all business as he looked down on his ledger before staring down the farmer. "Mr. Jackson? Charles Jackson?"

"That's me," he said, his voice crackling with fear. "What do you want?"

"You had been directed by General Orders Number Eleven, issued by the District of the Border, to vacate the premises. Why have you not done so?"

A woman appeared as the captain was still speaking, her brown hair in disarray and a boy about five clinging to the hem of her dress. "What is the matter, Charles? Who are these soldiers?"

"It's all right, Rebecca," Mr. Jackson said. "Go back in the house. Jimmy ain't had his breakfast yet."

Lawson brought his rigid military face closer to Mr. Jackson. "Can you offer any proof of loyalty to the Union?"

"I've never been disloyal to the Union."

"If you've harbored rebels here, you have."

"Now why would I do that? I don't take any sides to this war. I'm a farmer."

Lawson fixed him with an angry stare. "Any proof of your loyalty, Mr. Jackson?"

"No, sir."

The sergeant shoved his way past Mr. Jackson and pushed open the door. "We have no time to waste. Private, see that they take only their essentials. Clear them out of here, fast."

"Yessuh." Tinker almost stumbled over little Jimmy and followed the impatient sergeant into the Jackson's modest kitchen, consisting of a wood burning stove, unpainted wooden table, large cut logs that served as chairs and a brick fireplace containing smoldering embers. A young slave woman about Nellie's age and dressed in a plain black dress and white apron, sat on a stool in the corner of the room, her eyes wide with fright. Jimmy tried amusing her by hopping like a rabbit, but the slave woman's gaze remained frozen.

The sergeant went through the other rooms and returned to Tinker. "You have ten minutes to get them out of here, Private. Have them take what they can carry and confiscate the rest."

Rebecca Jackson plunged at Lawson, digging her fingers into his arm. "No, please don't!"

He pulled away from her as if she had a dreaded disease and shifted his attention to Tinker. "Do your duty, Private. Let them have a few basic things, but take whatever valuables they've got and bring them out to our supply wagon. We can't have any folks around these parts who are providin' aid and comfort to bushwhackers."

Tinker waited until the sergeant left before facing Mr. Jackson, who stood leaning against the table with both arms, his face flush with despair. He avoided looking at Mrs. Jackson, who was tugging at his sleeve in desperation. "I'm sorry," he said, "but I hafta do mah duty. I got mah orders. Don' like 'em any more 'n you."

The negro slave ran over to Mrs. Jackson and they wept in each other's arms. Jimmy clung to his mother's leg as if it were a log that would keep him from drowning. "Please don't cry, Mama."

Tinker felt like burying himself in a deep hole. He wished the lieutenant colonel would have told him what to expect before being sworn in. He took scant comfort in Major Plumb's promise that this would only be a temporary assignment and that he would be transferred to Fort Blair at the earliest opportunity.

Mr. Jackson vanished but soon returned with two empty flour bags. "C'mon, Rebecca. We have to take what we can and leave. You heard what the man said." He motioned to the young negro slave. "You too, Sally. Get our valuables."

Sally darted past Tinker, but when he entered the adjoining room, he saw her stooping near a small end table and snatching a shiny walnut box from under it. Sally stood up with the box in her hands, but when she saw Tinker staring at her, she dropped the box, spilling its contents, and stood as still as a headstone in a cemetery. A collection of hair jewelry, cameos, broaches, and earrings were strewn across the wooden floor. There was also a folded letter.

Sally reached for the letter, but Tinker got to it first. "No, please," she begged, looking at him with both wariness and terror. "This belong to my mistress. Let me give it to her. You can keep everything else."

Tinker was about to return it when Mr. Jackson, in the kitchen and moving about, called for Sally to help pack up.

45

"Go on, girl," Tinker said, lowering his voice. "I'll give everythin' back to yah later. Go on now. Your master needs you."

"But my mistress be in a heap of trouble if you—"

"I promise."

Tinker stuffed his side pockets with the jewelry before getting up. The folded letter bothered him, and, with curiosity eating at him after Sally's concern about it, he picked it up and read it:

Mrs. Jackson,

> *On behalf of Bill, George, and me, I wanted to thank you and your husband for your hospitality in serving us a fine meal and treating us with such kindness.*

> *Respectfully,*

> *William H. Gregg*

Tinker was tempted to leave the paper behind because of its insignificance but at the last minute stuck it in his back pocket. He didn't know why. It was just a feeling that came over him, something he had to do. *Why did Sally make such a fuss about this innocent note?*

He emptied the contents of his side pockets in a kerchief and handed it to Mrs. Jackson. "If you take 'em in the box, I think dey gonna steal 'em. Best if you hide deez in your pocket." Sergeant Lawson showed up at that moment. "What are you giving her, Private? Hope they aren't valuables. We keep those as contraband, soldier."

"Just worthless items, dat's all, suh," Tinker said, trying to sound casual even though his nerves racked his body.

Lawson stared at him for a moment, as if trying to assess the honesty of Tinker's statement. Then the sergeant made a long sweep of his arm. "Everybody leave now. See those Redlegs out there? They're gettin' ready to torch this house and the barn."

46

Tinker followed him out of the house, as did Mrs. Jackson. "We'll show these damn rebels," the sergeant murmured. "We can't allow them to leave behind any sustenance for bushwhackers like Bill Gregg and those other Quantrill pigs."

"Dear Lord!" Mrs. Jackson shouted, chasing after him. "Oh no! It's all we've worked for. Please, don't do this."

But Tinker froze. Blood drained from his face. Bill Gregg, a bushwhacker? What was that note he read? ...*Respectfully, William C. Gregg.* The Jacksons had welcomed bushwhackers in their home. Weren't six men in Jackson County—who might have been ordinary farmers—recently executed by Union troops near Lone Jack, Missouri?

Tinker pulled the condemning note from his back pocket and was about to tear it up when he heard a voice growl at him. "What you got there, Private?" Captain Coleman asked.

Chapter 7

It was as if Pigeon Mountain in the distance was mocking General George H. Thomas, taunting him with its secret places that gave the rebels an advantage. In the evening, General Thomas could only make out its silhouette in the dimming twilight, yet daylight would reveal its many caves and limestone rock formations which could easily hide sharpshooters. If Bragg was in full-scale retreat from Chattanooga, as other generals seemed to believe, Thomas would send his men after those cowards. But what if that self-righteous rebel commander was expecting reinforcements and planning a flank attack once Thomas crossed the mountain?

General Thomas returned to his tent and peered over Brigadier General James Negley's shoulder at a map sprawled on the table. Thomas reflected for a moment on that imposing fracture in the mountain that served as a dangerously narrow pass. "Jim," he said, "you made the right move. I'm convinced, based on what we've learned from our scouts, that both divisions—your XIV Army Corps and Baird's division—would have been decimated by Bragg's men had you moved any further down Dug Gap Road."

"Correct, sir. We were already getting strong resistance near McLemore's Cove." He offered Thomas some hardtack. "Bragg's forces may be more concentrated on the other side of the mountain than originally thought."

Thomas frowned as he scrutinized the map. "Where is the XIV Army Corps now?"

"Davis' Cross Roads, sir. We're awaiting the arrival of Baird's division. They had been coming under a heavy barrage of fire. It would be suicidal for us to try to get through at this point."

"I wish Old Rosie was in agreement with that," Thomas answered, using the nickname some officers privately used in referring to Major General William Rosecrans. "I've already had a conversation with him, and he's understandably being pressured by Lincoln to have the Army of the Cumberland crush Bragg without delay."

Lincoln, General Thomas thought, *was a good man, but he has to be more aware of the limitations of battle. If I could crush Bragg today, I most certainly would.*

Negley rubbed the palms of his hands together to brush off the crumbs of the hardtack. "But, we also have to believe what our scouts have already learned about there being a large concentration of rebels further down the Dug Gap road."

Thomas nodded. He was thinking about his supply line. How long could he hold out here in Northern Georgia, where Bragg undoubtedly had greater access to replenishing his provisions?

Negley got up and paced the ground. "May I speak candidly, sir?"

"Of course."

"I believe that Rosecrans needs to have faith in your decision to hold up any further advance at this time. You have never been wrong in making major decisions."

Thomas felt embarrassed by the compliment, but he knew Negley was probably right. After winning two brevets in the Mexican War, he went on later to win his first victory against the rebels at Mill Springs. He was praised for introducing, along with Rosecrans, the use of combined forces by adding the massive firepower of repeating Spencer carbines at Hoover's Gap and Nashville.

"That's it, then," Thomas replied. "We're going to hold our position until we get further intelligence on Bragg's position and troop strength. I have a couple of men right now who are attempting to crack Bragg's signal code." He ran his fingers through the short, tough hairs of his beard and shot a tired look back. "It is a shame that Old Rosie didn't follow my advice."

"What advice is that, sir?"

"To consolidate our Union forces in Chattanooga rather than leave our stronghold in order to catch Bragg down south." He turned a sad face to General Negley. "Old Rosie's decision may well cost us our next battle."

Union Camp west of Union Pt., Georgia

When she heard the news about the massacre in Lawrence, Kansas, Mary Delaney felt nauseous. She dropped to the ground, gasping, her mind envisioning her friend Jessica Radford witnessing the horror. *What has it been like for her to experience innocent men being killed?*

Or worse—Mary put her hand to her mouth at the thought—was Jessica herself harmed?

A second image emerged in Mary's mind....Jessica, fearless Jessica, being approached by one of those evil men. Instead of hearing the helpless shrieks of a terrified woman, the man receives a mouthful of cursing from her, a kick in his shins, and perhaps even a bullet in his chest.

Mary smiled. She ought not to be worried about her friend. After all, Jessica probably had more courage than many men. Didn't she demonstrate this by having disguised herself as a man earlier this year so she could fight in the war?

You are one tough lady. You should have been a man.

Walking through a meadow, letting the sun warm her face, Mary thought she heard sounds and stopped. Her heart skipped a beat when she recognized them—the soft, sweet strains of "Home Sweet Home" as played on a saxhorn brass instrument. She had heard someone in the band play this same piece before and had always wanted to meet him.

The music drifted from behind a small ridge about a hundred yards away, so she put her horse into a slow trot and headed for it. The sad melody made her want to cry every time she heard it....

'Mid pleasures and palaces though I may roam,
Be it ever so humble, there's no place like home;
A charm from the sky seems to hallow us there,
Which, seek though the world, is ne'er with me elsewhere.

Mary had heard this same song when it was played by

50

opposing armies just prior to the battle at Shelbyville in Tennessee. It was a colored soldier, a private, who had played that music on a saxhorn, but it was the way he played it, improvising and changing the harmony ever so slightly that it became a delight to the ear. When he began playing it, the song was taken up by the others in the band. Then Confederate musicians, only a mile or two away, also started playing it as well. Both sides loved the melody.

Mary approached a negro soldier leaning with his back against a red maple, a musical instrument in his hands.

"Private!" Mary called to him. She dismounted and headed for the figure.

"Yes, ma'am?" He placed the saxhorn on the grass and smiled back at her. It was a handsome, intelligent face, and his eyes burned with a zest for life

"You play beautifully. What is your name, sir?"

"Private Devin Alcott, ma'am."

"My name is Mary Delaney, a nurse with the Kansas Eighth."

"I am pleased to make your acquaintance, Miss Delaney."

"How did you learn to play that way? A slave isn't given much opportunity to—"

Devin's eyes hardened into a cold stare. "Why must everyone who sees a black man assume that he's a slave?"

"I'm sorry. How insensitive of me to assume that you had been one."

He tried to smile. "Don't apologize. I understand. Many people make that assumption. My cousin Charlotte has the same problem. Her mother was a freed slave and her father a white Northerner, but Charlotte has to constantly tell people she's never been a slave. My situation is a bit different because both my parents are citizens of Québec. My father was a military attaché to King George IV and my mother taught music when we lived in London prior to moving to Canada."

Mary cocked her head in curiosity. "But why would you be fighting for the Union if you're from Canada?"

"I'm not really fighting for the Union, ma'am. I'm fighting for freedom, not mine, but theirs. I have heard dreadful stories

51

of brutality from slaves who have escaped to Canada by way of Lake Ontario. I've seen their whip marks and I've listened to their incredible tales of torture and humiliation. I suppose I just wanted to do my part in helping them get a taste of freedom."

"What are you going to do when this war is finally over?"

He picked up his saxhorn and smiled. "Music is my life, Miss Delaney. Music is my life."

Chapter 8

The carriage stayed within the perimeter of the forts as it circled the nation's capital. "I understand that the Union built 68 forts around the city," Otto told Jessica who shared the front seat. "In fact, President Lincoln even converted a portion of the Treasury Building into a bunker. So, you see, it wasn't unusual for me to find a section in the U.S. Printing Office that had once housed soldiers."

"Are you telling me that this city is a virtual fortress?"

"Yes, and it is by necessity, my dear Jessica. Washington is a key target for the rebels."

A large white stone structure came into view to her right. It looked as if someone had sheared off the top of an obelisk.

"The Washington Monument," Otto said, pointing at it. "Lack of funds and politics got in the way of its completion."

"Maybe someday Congress will erect a monument to you and the Underground Railroad." And perhaps beyond honoring the abolishment of slavery, she thought, the government will someday recognize that women were not "slaves" either.

Otto flushed and turned away for a brief moment. "Freeing slaves from their masters is something more people should have done. I don't take any special credit for that."

Jessica shook her head. "Ralph Waldo Emerson once wrote that 'we must get rid of slavery or we must get rid of freedom.' He was correct. I daresay slavery should have never existed."

"Jessica, there have been slaves even before Jesus Christ walked this earth."

"I know, and that is the kind of rationale Mr. Lightfoot had once given me for owning Tinker."

"I thought you might have forgiven him for that by now."

"I thought I had as well."

She pressed her lips together. There was no sense in talking about this subject any longer. "Mr. Heller, are you delighted to be back in the publishing business?"

"In a way. It's not book publishing, an enterprise of which I am fully acquainted, but it does involve knowledge of press work, typesetting, proofing and that sort of thing. I think the Superintendent is glad I could be there to assist him. There is a tremendous amount of work to be done at the U.S. Printing Office. We're even rapidly running out of space."

Jessica looked down at her green dress, the same one she bought when the Hellers had stopped in Leavenworth on their way here. It was wonderful to be employed again, not having to beg. She looked up at him with a twinkle in her eyes. "With your busy schedule, Mr. Heller, I suppose my services as a domestic and nanny are quite needed."

"Indeed they are," Otto said, nodding. "Especially with Penelope working as well. Ten hours a day for each of us, and sometimes we work different shifts. It doesn't provide Penelope or me the opportunity to see the children after school. You are a good friend."

"That is very kind of you, Mr. Heller," Jessica said, grazing his fingers.

"I wonder," he said, pulling his hand away and sweeping it across, "if you'd care to see more of the Capitol grounds with me?"

"Of course," she said, hoping she had not appeared too forward with him. "I'm glad Penelope suggested taking the children for a walk while you and I ride the carriage as we tour the city."

"I am glad to do it. Penelope depends on you. So do I."

Jessica regarded him carefully. There was no expression of anger anywhere, just the countenance of a man twenty-four years her senior who had a certain firmness in his chin and a resolute, steadfast gaze that could not easily be read. She had welcomed the opportunity to be alone with him, but now that she was, she wondered how she could tell him she enjoyed his company without causing him discomfort.

54

"Mr. Heller, how does Penelope like her new line of work?"

"I don't think she relished the idea at first about being a clerk at the Printing Office. But she is becoming accustomed to it. Quite a departure from being a store owner in Lawrence. Had border ruffians not burned it down, I suspect she would still be running it." He went on to discuss the particulars of his job and how fortunate they were able to find schooling for their children.

Otto had the carriage stop briefly at the Capitol grounds and he pointed to the white edifice that dominated the landscape. "Some of these structures are in a state of incompletion right now. Just like that truncated obelisk you saw earlier—the Washington Monument—the Capitol is also incomplete. The dome still has to be done and the wings of the Capitol are also unfinished."

"Maybe," Jessica said with cautious amusement, "the buildings aren't sure which side will win the war."

Otto frowned at the comment, and Jessica bit her lower lip. Had she somehow displeased him? Perhaps he was uncomfortable being alone with a single woman. If so, that was unfortunate. Some elements of society were always ready to find fault with even the most innocent of encounters.

Otto asked the coachman to take them to the Executive Mansion on Pennsylvania Avenue. "There is someone I think you ought to see, Miss Radford."

Jessica's heart fluttered with anticipation. "The President?"

Otto laughed for the first time. "No, of course not. I think even Senator Lane would have a difficult time these days getting an appointment with Mr. Lincoln. No, it's someone else." He looked at her with a big grin bursting on his face. "You don't like surprises, do you?"

He said nothing further until he approached the south lawn of the Executive Mansion. "Did you know that the British burned this fine building to the ground in 1814?"

"If you are trying to impress me with your knowledge of history, Mr. Heller, you are succeeding."

A captain on duty at the entrance stopped the coach. Otto reached from underneath his seat and removed a book, but he exited from the carriage too quickly for Jessica to see the title of the volume.

"Might I offer you my assistance?" he asked, extending his hand to her before she stepped out of the coach. She waved off his support. "Mr. Heller, you ought to know I don't require any help just because I am a lady. But I would be flattered if I could take your arm as we stroll."

He smiled politely. "I assume you want to be a lady only when the opportunity presents itself."

Jessica stopped herself from voicing an objection. She noticed he was holding his book in his other hand as he led her down a worn trail which was headed toward a long, canvas building of some sort.

"I must ask you a question, Miss Radford."

"What is that?"

Otto halted for a moment to allow two officers to cross the path in front of them. A sparrow fluttered over her young in the nest of an elm tree.

"Who in your estimation," he said, "would you believe is the greatest poet alive today?"

Jessica wondered what impelled him to come up with such a question. But for her, it was an easy one to answer. "Why, Walt Whitman, of course."

"Well then," he said, handing her the book he was carrying, "I've bought the appropriate gift for you. A copy of Whitman's *Leaves of Grass.*"

"Why, Mr. Heller. How thoughtful!" She was about to kiss him on the cheek, but he hurried her on toward the building. Groans emanated from within. Two soldiers were bringing in a wounded man on a stretcher. A legless man sat in a wheelchair near the entrance.

"This," Otto explained, "is the Reynolds Barracks Hospital. Let us go in, shall we?"

"Whatever for? You know I don't have a great fondness for such a sight. Not after what I have experienced following that horrible raid."

56

"Please, Miss Radford," Otto said, with a hint of annoyance in his voice. "Just follow me."

The pungent mixture of opiates, astringents, blood, and alcohol overpowered her, and she turned away for a moment to catch her breath. She noticed three ladies standing by a sign that read "Sanitary Commission" while two other women walked between rows of the sick and wounded, delivering items on metal trays. With not a single empty cot in sight, there were people here and there, sitting or standing near the wounded or sick. Memories flooded back to Jessica to a time after she had delivered medicines to the wounded on a Kentucky battlefield. It seemed so long ago....

In Danville, Kentucky, she had just stepped outside of the door of the Presbyterian Church— now a makeshift hospital—after hearing the screams of the wounded. Even with the large doors closed behind her she could hear their cries for help. This church was a monument of misery, with men dying and with surgeons acting more like butchers in treating the wounded.

"Miss Radford," Otto said, interrupting her thoughts, "there's a gentleman here I'd like you to meet."

She looked up to see a man whose face was framed by discordant gray and charcoal hair emanating from his head in all directions—mustache, beard, and crown. He had the wizened face of a professor with a protuberant nose, but it was his soft eyes that conveyed an empathy that overrode his countenance. Dressed in a faded blue shirt and torn overalls, he could have passed as a farmer, but Jessica intuitively felt he was far more complex than that.

"This is Jessica Radford," Otto said. "She is the one I told you about when I met you last week at the Army Paymaster's Office. I am thrilled you promised that you would be here this afternoon to meet her."

A smile crept on the stranger's face as he stared at Jessica. "It is indeed a pleasure to meet you, Miss Radford. Mr. Heller tells me you enjoy my work."

57

Jessica raised a questioning eyebrow. "I don't understand."

"I apologize. Where are my manners? My name is Mr. Whitman, Walt Whitman."

Jessica swallowed hard, disbelieving. "That's not likely. How could you possibly—?"

He laughed lightly. "No need to be surprised. I've taken up residence in this town." He ran his fingers over his beard. "I see you have my book. May I autograph it for you?"

Jessica handed it to him. "I would be thrilled, of course, but I don't understand. What are you doing here at the hospital?"

Whitman's smile widened. "While this war continues, I've been visiting the sick and wounded. The doctors tell me that I provide patients with a medicine that their drugs and medicines cannot supply. I hope they are correct about that. I try to give them hope and comfort—and, if possible, good cheer."

"Mr. Whitman," Otto added, giving his full attention to the poet, "correct me if I err in saying this, but I've read that your visitations to hospitals all over the city began after your brother George, with the 51st New York Volunteers, was wounded at Fredericksburg late last year. I understand it was not a serious wound, but after you visited and cared for him, your outlook on the war changed. Is that correct?"

"You know me better than I know myself," Whitman quipped. "My first disheartening experience occurred at the Lacy House, a makeshift hospital where I saw nothing but a heap of feet, legs, arms, and human fragments—bloody, disease-ridden, swelled and sickening. It was then that I resolved to make as many visits as possible to these men who were not only wounded, but sick at heart and lonely. I wanted them to know that they have not been forgotten."

"Mr. Whitman," Jessica said, "I hope to write as well as you some day."

Whitman's eyes lit up. "Oh? You are a writer, are you?"

"I hope to be. Someone once told me that words are but pictures from a pen, and I have so many pictures floating in my consciousness, I would like to get them down into words."

58

Whitman sat down on the edge of a cot. "Then I shall write something appropriate for you." He took his time scribbling on the leaf of the book, then handed the volume to Jessica. "Do you aspire to be a poet?"

"I don't know. I enjoy poetry, but I don't always understand it."

"Understanding poetry, like everything else, is important. But poetry is unique in that it holds a special meaning for each person. That is why I write it." He glanced at a man being carried in with a stretcher. "Now if you will excuse me, there are more men whose pain I need to share."

Chapter 9

Early morning
September 19
La Fayette, Georgia

General Braxton Bragg, commanding the Army of Tennessee, stared at the pre-dawn darkness through the slit of his tent. His body still ached from tossing and turning during the night, and his mind whirled as if he were drunk. Another damn sleepless night! How the hell was he going to sharpen his mind for a fresh attack on the Federals?

He pumped water from an outdoor well and washed his face, muttering his displeasure at his officers. Earlier, at least a dozen of them had expressed their unhappiness with his command. Lieutenant General Leonidas Polk went so far as to request Jefferson Davis for a suitable replacement for Bragg. Such insolence! Didn't they realize that what the South needed was a cautious leader who would use economy of force and strike only when the advantage was clearly on his side?

Bragg splashed more water on his tired, sleep-deprived eyes. Polk did not deserve his command; he should return to being a minister and trust those men who had intensive military training. *On the other hand, I am entitled to my position, being fifth in my West Point Class and going on to achieve a brilliant combat record in the Seminole and Mexican Wars.*

Nonetheless, Polk had command of his right wing and he would have to live with that situation. *But Polk had better follow my orders to the letter.*

While the sun took its time pushing up above the horizon, there was enough light for him to make out the thick forest and the craggy mountain ridge in the distance. The forest was so dense, it would be impossible to shoot at an enemy soldier who was further than one hundred feet away without first striking another tree. This also made cannon use impossible. Clear battle lines could not be drawn, and Bragg worried as to how his field officers would be able to give their troops commands.

Bragg dropped himself into a chair and struggled to get his boots on. *Somewhere out there*, he thought, *was McLemore's Cove, where, eight days earlier, we almost trapped Union General Thomas at McLemore's Cove—pigeonholed between Missionary Ridge and Pigeon Mountain. A division from Polk's Corps was to have attacked Thomas and his trapped division but he hesitated, waiting for a division from Hill's Corps to advance—which failed to occur.* "Five hours," Bragg muttered under his breath. "It took five hours for my orders to reach Hill, and by then, it was too late." Polk missed a second opportunity six days ago when Union General Wood was isolated at Lee and Gordon's Mill. After Bragg had ordered Polk to attack Wood's division, Polk marched in the wrong direction. Bragg stomped the heel of his boot against the parched ground. "Incompetence!"

This would not happen again on *his* watch. His plans were clear. He would order an attack on the Union's north flank this morning. And he would push back that Yankee devil, General Crittenden, and force him into McLemore's Cove where Crittenden and his men would be cornered like pigs in a sty. Then he would have some of his divisions cross Chickamauga Creek and cut off Rosecrans from making a retreat back to Chattanooga. *By God! My superior manpower, along with Longstreet's fresh reserves and Nathan Forrest's excellent cavalry, would make this a decisive victory.*

The sun finally burst through, and its brilliant rays illuminated the anticipated killing field.

******

Mid-day
Union 3rd Brigade
near Chickamauga Creek

When he passed through Crawfish Spring earlier, Lieutenant Matt Lightfoot had caught a glimpse of Mary Delaney at the Gordon Lee mansion that now served as a field hospital.

She was outdoors, dressing a man's wounds, and oblivious of the soldiers hurrying double-time toward the woods. He wished he could have veered away from his line just to pay his respects and wish her well, but it was out of the question.

*Oh, Mary, so long ago, it now seems, when you…*His thoughts were broken up by the cadence of the forced march. *…you comforted me when I was prepared to give up on myself.* Hut-hut-hut. Death was hovering out there in the grip of those woods. Hut-hut-hut. *Oh, Mary!* Hut-hut-hut. *How I miss your kindness.* Hut-hut-hut. A wagon containing two wounded had just drawn to a halt in front of the hospital and a soldier, probably a nurse, hastened toward it. Hut-hut-hut. The hospital and Mary were now far behind him. Hut-hut-hut. *Oh, Lord, let me see her again.* Hut-hut-hut.

Colonel Hans Heg, a tough Norwegian, led the brigade, and his orders were to stay together at first and spread out to form a line of battle upon his command. The Army of Tennessee was out there in the thick of the woods like ghouls thirsting for blood. Union scouts had reported earlier that the rebels were getting more reserves, and enemy ranks were swollen with fighting men.

This afternoon, Matt feared, was likely to be a bloody one.

A half hour later, Matt mentally sorted out the flags of the four Union regiments amassing at a small clearing—men from the Eighth Kansas, Fifteenth Wisconsin, Twenty-fifth Illinois, and the Thirty-fifth Illinois. Colonel Heg, mounted on a black stallion, waved his sword at the men and ordered them to form a battle line. "Left flank forward and charge," he shouted as he raced ahead of them. The men followed, screaming their rage at the enemy, flag bearers waving the flags of their regiments, drum and fife players urging the soldiers on with "Battle Cry of Freedom."

*****

Private Devin Alcott was in the rear with the Fifteenth Wisconsin, fingering the notes to the music on his rosewood fife. He was out of position with the Eighth Kansas, now marching with another regiment in the brigade because of the confusion. From his position, he could see the rebels, hundreds of them, swarming out of the woods like demons, shooting at the vanguard of Union troops. The Federals made short retreats, but came back time and again to recover lost ground.

Devin told himself that if he were a sane man, he would be frightened to death right now. But he refused to give himself the luxury of thinking about it. If he had to die, let him do it rallying the men to fight. He sang the words in his head as he sounded his fife above the noise of shouting men, of screams of agony, of murderous projectiles whistling through the air, splitting tree limbs—

> *"Yes, we'll rally round the flag, boys*
> *Rally once again,*
> *Shouting the Battle Cry of Freedom!*
> *We will rally from the hillside*
> *We'll gather from the plains,*
> *Shouting the Battle Cry of Freedom!"*

He turned to the negro next to him, who held a carbine and waved it about wildly. "Nice rifle there," Devin told the man, whose eyes were wide with fright. "What's that carved on the stock?"

"Freedom," the man said, his voice straining. "Reminds me that's what ah fight for."

"You have a name?"

"Salem."

"Well, Salem, I—"

Devin spotted a rebel taking dead aim, and he threw himself on Salem, knocking the wind out of him. A Minié ball whizzed past Devin's ear as he lay on top of his companion. A Union shell exploded back at the rebel. "It's safe now," he told Salem.

"You a hero jest like mah brother Ishmael. Some day ah'm gonna die like him fightin' for freedom"

"No, Salem, you should be fighting to live, not to die."

*****

63

The battle exploded with the fury of hellfire. The haze of gunsmoke formed putrid gray clouds hovering over the field, and Matt couldn't see the rest of the enemy. But they were there, perhaps hidden in the woods and behind dead logs.

Colonel Heg, hurrying back and forth across the line, ordered the Twenty-fifth Illinois to rush forward. Matt, from the corner of his eyes, could see that more Confederate troops were pouring through toward the left flank, bringing with them a hail of bullets, spherical case shot, and canister.

Just last week, when he leaned against a tree and began carving a small replica of a totem pole from a locust branch, Matt wondered if he'd see any action. Someone with a harmonica had already played the same song four times, a fly teased him about the face, and the hot sun broiled him like a fish in a fry pan. At least combat would not be boring.

"Stay in place," a man next to Matt shouted. Matt, jarred from his thoughts, saw the man was Colonel Martin, hatless, his hair waving in the breeze, lying prone next to him, reloading. "Colonel Heg is a moving target," Matt told him, just as a bullet whistled by his ear.

"The man has no fear," Martin replied as he aimed his carbine and pulled off a shot. "Thinks he's made of iron."

"Fall back!" Heg yelled. "Fall back and regroup!"

The brigade retreated some fifty yards back toward a bluff, took up a new line of battle, and advanced to a small clearing. The rebels came rushing out from behind the trees, and as more rebels crashed to the earth, more returned in overwhelming numbers. "Where the hell are they coming from?" Martin cussed.

The bullets came in a torrent toward the brigade, and Colonel Heg crumpled from a bullet while he remained on his horse. Face forward, toward the horn of his saddle, he continued to ride on, rallying the men. "Take them out," he shouted, still slumped in his saddle. "Hit them hard, boys!" He slouched to one side, his stallion now pacing slowly before it, too, was shot and fell to the ground. Two soldiers rushed in to pull the colonel from the front lines.

Colonel Martin rode to the front and assumed Heg's command. "You heard him," he cried. "Hit them hard!"

Bullets chopped the bark off trees. One of the men in Martin's brigade turned to his left and fired, only to be shot in the back. Three more men scurried up a small ridge and each fell in succession from enemy fire emanating from the dense forest. An officer on horseback charged forward, shouting "Rush on, boys" but his command ended in a short but shrill scream as one rebel bullet smashed into his cheek and another tore into the belly of his steed.

Martin called for a hasty retreat, and Matt ordered his men to fall back. Matt looked behind only to see more rebels emerge from the forest.

"Where the blazes are they all comin' from?" he asked a sergeant riding alongside.

"Don't know, sir. Maybe God's raising them from the dead."

*****

Union General William Rosecrans left the farm house that served as his headquarters and joined his Chief-of-Staff, General James Garfield, who had been peering through field glasses at a clearing the enlisted men made. He handed the glasses to Rosecrans, who observed his men cutting trees and building breastworks in preparation for tomorrow's battle.

Rosecrans read Garfield's face, and it betrayed disappointment.

"We still held LaFayette Road," Rosecrans argued. "Bragg's units gained nothing. General Thomas had to retreat, of course, but he's now on higher ground at Kelly's farm."

"I don't share your optimism, sir. Our scouts tell us that Longstreet is on his way with his infantry brigades. And we've already seen some fierce fighting today. I think the rebels are well prepared for fighting in this horrible terrain. It is not like Kentucky, where we had better coordination between divisions and brigades."

"I think you should be counting our successes instead of guessing our defeats. Thomas is in good position for tomorrow,

Beatty's brigade successfully repulsed the enemy, and Stanley's brigade forced the enemy into the woods."

Garfield simply nodded, and Rosecrans felt his Chief-of-Staff remained unconvinced. "See here," Rosecrans added, "we've outsmarted Bragg before, and we can do it again."

Garfield held his hands to his hips and his eyes seemed to be looking far out into the distance. "Yes, sir, we can do it again—provided...." His voice trailed off as if he were considering the possibilities.

Rosecrans frowned. "Provided? Provided what?"

"Sir," he replied, turning his head slowly toward his commanding officer, "I feel we've been fortunate in past engagements in being able to capitalize on Bragg's mistakes. And I am quite sure Bragg is now looking for a similar opportunity. I hope we don't give him one."

*****

Crawford Spring, Georgia

Stephen Himoe, a surgeon with the 15th Wisconsin Volunteer Infantry collapsed over one of the bodies in the wagon. "Oh, no! It cannot be," he whispered when Mary Delaney ran to his side.

Two men rushed to Mary's aid as she attempted to drag the surgeon away from the wagon. They finally managed to get him to sit on the stairs that led to an improvised Federal field hospital that used to be someone's spacious home.

"You have been working too hard," Mary told him, sitting next to him, her arm holding him as he wept. "You need to take a rest."

Himoe, a 31-year-old Norwegian, lifted up his tear-stained face, not bothering to look at her. "We will need to transport him to a regimental hospital up north." His head swayed in a painfully slow movement. "I can't believe that is *Oberst* Heg."

"Who?" Mary asked, straining to understand him.

"Colonel Heg," he answered, his eyes closing into narrow crescent moons that spilled out sadness. He pointed toward a wounded man that a soldier was taking toward a Sibley tent.

"Colonel Heg," he repeated. "He's been shot in the abdomen." Himoe buried his face in his arms.

"You and the colonel were very close, I assume."

He raised his head. "*Ja,* he was married to my *søster*. He was also my *venn*, my very good *venn*. We even shared the same tent together. Now he is gone."

Mary knew just enough of Norwegian to realize that Heg was Himoe's brother-in-law as well as a good friend. "You're mistaken," she said. "Colonel Heg's not gone. Surgeons will treat his wounds. He will recover."

Hunoe clenched his fists and a raw anger crossed his face. "*Ne,* you don't understand. I've never seen a man recover from a bullet wound to the abdomen."

"Then we must pray," Mary said, closing her eyes. She listened to the gurgling of fresh spring water flowing over the rocks in its path. This area, she thought, felt pain even before this battle. Matt Lightfoot had told her that Crawford Spring was once home to a tribe of Cherokee Indians, who were later forced to leave their lands to start on their trail of tears.

The path to this hospital was also a trail of tears, she thought. Often a deadly one.

Chapter 10

The thorns grabbed at his legs like vicious insects, and Lieutenant Roger Toby cussed as he pulled his trousers free and moved on. Slashes from the thorns felt like knife cuts, and if he didn't have to push on like this, he would be stopping at a stream to wash off the blood. *But no! Advance through the dense underbrush, through irritating thickets and stubborn dogwood growth—isn't that your order, colonel?*

It was not possible for him to run with his carbine and full pack without tripping, and his pace slowed until he came to a clearing that Major Davis had warned would be the crossing of the Chattanooga and La Fayette roads, where the enemy was heavily fortified.

Roger felt like only a small part of the huge machinery of Johnson's Brigade—a cog, a wheel, or a screw helping to hold it all together—as he ran, stumbled, and ran again. No room for thought, no time for flashing his mind toward home, he ran—an unthinking, unfeeling part of the Johnson Brigade Machine. He crossed a fence fronting a road along with a line of men from Tennessee regiments. Some of the men screamed their "Hurrahs" and "Kill Them Yankees" while others, like Roger, let the volleys from their guns do the shouting for them.

Lieutenant Colonel Ready fell backwards as he rushed the enemy in an open field, and Roger called out for a couple of enlisted men to pull him off the field. More blue fell than gray, however, and Roger felt more confident of victory today than he did yesterday, when rebel losses were heavy.

The roar of musketry grew louder, musket balls came nearer, shells bursting all about. The sky was pinkish-grey. Roger choked from the thick acrid smoke, but he pushed on. A farmhouse came into view, a white building in the middle of hell. "Take those men in there, lieutenant," a captain bellowed above the crashing sound of grapeshot and bullets splitting the barks of trees. "There are bound to be Yankees there."

Roger veered to his right, as did several of his men, and threw himself into a garden as a gun blast tore through an open window. Others from the Twenty-fifth, Twenty-third, and Forty-fourth Tennessee scurried to the outbuilding and barn. But Roger concentrated on the house, sending some men to the other side of the building. Fire. Load. Fire. Load. Roger was determined to be part of the Johnson Brigade Machine, shooting until he ran out of ammunition, trading fire with the enemy, not retreating. Roger tightened his grip on the weapon. He had a job to do, and he'd do it.

Finally, someone inside waved a white flag of surrender. "Cease fire!" Roger yelled. The order was passed around. The guns were silenced.

Union soldiers, with their hands held above their heads, filed out of the house. As Roger Toby and other officers trained their weapons on them, other Confederate soldiers confiscated the Union rifles as well as the swords of some of the officers. Anxious to move on, Lieutenant Toby left the details of rounding up the prisoners and the wounded to his men before rejoining his unit.

Making it as far as a line of Union breastworks consisting of logs and rocks, Roger spotted a Union soldier racing toward the woods.

"Halt!" Roger shouted, raising his pistol at the figure.

The boy, who could not have been more than sixteen, stopped and turned, his musket in hand, as Roger raced toward him. His cap off and his brown hair as wild as his eyes, he dropped his weapon and raised his hands. "Don't shoot," the boy said, his face contorted as if he were about to cry.

"Come toward me slow and easy," Roger said, training his gun at him.

"Yes sir," the boy said as he approached with his hands raised. His forehead dripped with sweat. "Don't shoot."

Roger turned away for a brief moment when he thought he heard someone call his name. But when he returned his attention to his captive, the boy had dropped his arm and had slid his hand under his frock coat.

Roger fired three shots into the boy.

It was only after he opened the boy's frock coat that he saw that the lad's hand had gripped a kerchief from his pocket. Apparently, he just wanted to mop his brow with it.

Roger went numb. A white haze of shock flushed through him while two distinct voices in his head fought for his attention:

—*I've killed an innocent boy.*

—*No, you've killed the enemy.*

—*But he was unarmed.*

—*You're part of the Johnson Brigade Machine.*

—*And my duty is to do what?*

—*Your duty is to kill the enemy, lieutenant.*

*****

Didn't General Wood believe in following orders to the letter?

Major General Rosecrans slammed his fist against the table. He didn't regret criticizing Wood earlier for his tardiness in relieving a brigade under heavy fire. "You have disobeyed my specific orders," Rosecrans remembered shouting in front of Wood's officers, "and, by God, I will not tolerate it."

He had hoped to see a turning point in favor of the Union this morning, but there was none. His entire body was fraught with raw, aching nerves. Rosecrans found himself having to constantly shift the positions of General Thomas' men, based on the intelligence he received from his couriers, with Garfield translating Rosecrans' orders into concise, written language.

By 10:30, with Garfield having left to take care of other important matters, a courier from General Thomas came to Rosecrans with an urgent request for reinforcements and to say that a reserve brigade from General Brannan was available. But then Captain Kellogg, an aide-de-camp for General Thomas, came to Rosecrans' headquarters to indicate that Brannan was not where he should be and that General Reynolds' right flank was exposed. Rosecrans thought quickly. "I wish I had time to consult with Thomas," he muttered. "He is the only general I could trust in such matters." But Thomas was in the field directing his men against a deadly assault. This time, Rosecrans would have to rely solely on his own judgment.

He drew a crude map on paper. Based on what he had just heard, Reynolds' forces were just east of La Fayette Road and north of Brotherton Road. Between Reynolds' right flank and Wood's left, however, was presumably, a sizeable gap. And just where were Branham's troops? Kellogg said he was not able to observe Brannan's division because of the heavy foliage and trees in that area. If Brannan was not there to protect Reynolds, Confederate General Longstreet would march toward Reynold's right flank, get through that gap and head on north to recapture Chattanooga.

The thought nagged Rosecrans that perhaps Kellogg was mistaken about his observations. No matter, Rosecrans thought. Pressed for time and already straining from the tension of this battle, he knew he would have to make a decision very soon. He turned to his aide-de-camp, Major Frank Bond. "Major," Rosecrans snapped, "I want you to stop whatever you're doing and write an order. Tell General Wood he's to leave his position immediately and close up ranks with Reynolds."

"Excuse me, sir, but—"

"But what?" he said, his irritation growing. "What is it, major?"

"Shouldn't that order be directed to Crittenden, the corps commander?"

"No, major. Wood. Division commander Wood. Understand?"

"Yes sir."

This is one order that Wood had better obey, Rosecrans thought.

*****

Lieutenant Colonel Starling delivered Rosecrans' order to Wood, but he had reservations. "General Garfield," Starling said, with obvious hesitation, "informs me that there is no enemy in Reynolds' right flank and does not need support."

Wood looked at the written order and glanced at Starling. "Then why is Rosecrans saying something differently?"

"I don't know, sir." Starling turned on his heel and left.

To General Wood it made no sense whatsoever to move his division from behind Brannan to meet with Reynolds. Would not that leave a large gap between Davis and Brannan? Did not Rosecrans realize that?

Wood thought about returning to Rosecrans for an explanation. But the angry remonstration Rosecrans had exhibited earlier ("You have disobeyed my specific orders, and, by God, I will not tolerate it.") still reverberated in his mind. As it was now, the Union held firm on La Fayette Road, from a mile north of Lee and Gordon's Mill to McFarland's Gap Road. That road would lead them north to Chattanooga, where they could then win the race to recapturing that town before the rebels got to it. Wood was not about to receive yet another dressing down for disobeying orders. There was no alternative. He would have to follow those orders to the letter.

Yet, he wondered whether Rosecrans had lost his mind.

*****

Lieutenant Roger Toby took deep breaths, heaving from exhaustion as he pressed his aching back against an oak. His legs throbbed with pain, but the bizarre laughter of a fellow officer forced him to get up and make his way toward the man, who was punching a finger toward the sky and happily shouting "Hurrah!"

"There is nothing to cheer about," Roger said.

"But there is. Have you not heard the news?"

Roger frowned. "What news?"

"Longstreet's corps found a breech in the Federal line."

Toby's eyes widened. "A breech? How is that possible?"

The man's grin was as wide as his face. "A Yankee error. A gap opened up between two brigades of Wood's. We may soon be going through that line like water through a sieve."

72

Toby blinked in amazement. "Thank God! The South can turn this battle around."

"We will surely do that," the man said before quickly disappearing into the trees.

Lieutenant Toby pushed on, but he now felt a lightness with each step. The South had a chance to win this one! Caught in the confusing maze of underbrush and trees, he found himself detached from his regiment. *But, aha! Look there. A stallion in the clearing, all saddled up, a stranded Yankee horse.* Relieved from not having to walk any further, he rode on and spotted General Bushrod Johnson himself, yards ahead, screaming his charge as if possessed by the devil himself: "Close up ranks, boys! Charge! Destroy 'em!"

Roger took up the cheer and the others behind did as well, charging after Union soldiers whom he suspected, based on a map he had seen, that were with Brannan's division. Now some fifty yards behind Johnson, he found himself on Dyer road, near the Brotherton house. He heard a rumor that Longstreet had befriended Private Tom Brotherton the night before, encouraging Tom to tell him all about the hidden trails in the woods and how Longstreet's men might maneuver through the stubborn barriers of the forest.

Perhaps that foreknowledge of the terrain had paid off for Longstreet's brigade commanders, Roger thought. The way General Johnson rode through this area, taking a zigzagged approach in the woods, it was no wonder that the Federals were stunned when Confederates captured their battery. He ordered his officers to bring up two of their own batteries.

Skirmishers with the Seventeenth Tennessee ran toward Roger. One of them, his face aglow with excitement, made it to the head of the group. "Lieutenant, I think we found their line. We found it!"

"What are yaw talking about, soldier?"

"The enemy's telegraph wire, running along this road, sir."

"Good work," Roger said, his pulse quickening at the idea they might have found the wire that would take them to the enemy's communication center. He swept his hand in a large circle. "Now cut those lines and trace 'em to the source. Destroy their communications."

"I have one question, sir."

"What is it, corporal?"

"Must we take prisoners if we surprise the enemy?"

Roger thought a moment. He had heard rumors of Yankees occasionally killing unarmed Confederates in lieu of taking them as prisoners. It was certainly a more efficient way of dealing with the enemy. The Johnson Brigade Machine. He was part of it.

"Sir?" the corporal asked again.

"Use yaw own discretion, soldier."

*****

Ordered to support John Beatty's brigade, Matt Lightfoot took his position near a clump of dead trees. From where he was, on the north slope of Snodgrass Hill, he saw a trail of Union foot soldiers and horsemen heading further north. Were those men in retreat or was a new battle raging further up on La Fayette Road? He allowed himself only a few seconds to hold that thought as the men in Beatty's brigade returned the heavy fire from General James Longstreet's divisions.

Matt guessed that the large stocky man waving his saber and spitting out orders was General Thomas himself. Thomas raced from one end of the hill to the other, rallying the men to fight on. Through a dark curtain of smoke, Matt saw a Union soldier spin full circle, having been hit by a hail of conical balls before crashing to the ground.

After getting five direct hits on rebels charging up the hill, Matt stopped counting. This was such a different battle from what he had experienced at Perryville. There, strategy plans were laid out and executed by brigade and division commanders. But here, it seemed as if the enlisted men determined the course of battle, the way they moved back and forth, forward and back, without any specific orders.

After an endless time, the air became heavy with a gray, putrid layer of gunsmoke. Bodies, both blue and gray, were strewn across the field like grotesque statues. A few, lying prone, waved an occasional arm—for help or for showing support for their side—and some had their mouths wide open, but their screams were drowned out by the gunfire, grapeshot, and demonic yells that thundered above all of it.

It seemed to Matt as if the entire battle was focused on Snodgrass Hill. How long had he been here? Hours? It seemed as if half of the men who were with him earlier were gone, perhaps dead. He overhead another officer telling his men to retreat, so Matt decided he would do the same and ran with them.

He was surprised to suddenly find himself rolling down the hill.

It was when he saw blood leaking through his uniform that he realized that he had been shot.

Chapter 11

Mary Delaney knew from the increasing sound of musketry and exploding canister that the battle might soon be coming to her front door. But she could not leave the wounded and dying, and she told Dr. Himoe how she felt about abandoning them.

"*Ne*, it is too dangerous for you to stay," he replied. "We've received a telegraph minutes ago informing us that Rosecrans has already left the field for Chattanooga. I have a couple of drivers ready to take you north to Rossville. You go with them."

"But I cannot leave the wounded here for the rebels."

"I am sure the enemy will treat them in their own hospital."

"And be held captive in their awful prisons? Please let me stay and help you."

Himoe's eyes burned with an immovable anger. "*Ne*, you must go. *De overtrer meg ikke*. You cannot disobey me. That is an order."

"Well then, it looks like I will have to disobey an order."

"*Tosk!* You are a fool, woman. An absolute fool!" He turned on his heel and left for the stairs leading to the second floor.

The blood drained from her face and her hands shook as if she had plunged them into ice water. After taking a couple of steps forward to apologize for her stubbornness, she stopped. She had always obeyed orders and never felt it was a woman's place to exert her independence. But did he not understand that this involved human lives? If her departure from this place meant the loss of one more soldier, she would not be able to live with herself.

She hastened to assist an officer lying on his side, his leg crudely amputated above the knee. His face was drenched in sweat. He was pale, and as he looked at Mary, he began choking with grief. "I wish," he croaked, hardly able to get the words out, "I wish the Union had not been crushed so badly. "

Tears came to his eyes. "My leg is gone, and it's gone for nothing."

"It's not for nothing," Mary whispered, but she did not believe it herself. She was getting used to the agony of the butchery about her, and it bothered her. By now, she had seen wounds inflicted on virtually every part of the body. Wounds from shells, bullets, bayonets, and sabers.

If gun explosions didn't remove a soldier from action, it was disease, and she had seen it all, too. Pyemia, or what she called blood poisoning, was fatal, as was tetanus, malaria, and small pox. There was not much a surgeon could do with that, and it was that helplessness—watching these men die needlessly—that was the cruelest part of her role as a nurse.

She did not envy the surgeon, who had to also assume the role of God in deciding which ones would live and which would die. Now Dr. Himoe asked her to leave the scene. Abandon her patients. Let someone else worry over these suffering heroes.

"Miss Delaney?" It was Dr. Himoe calling her from upstairs. "Hurry. I need your assistance."

Mary went up the stairs to see him, thankful that she could be of assistance to him. Himoe was bending over a small table lined with anesthetics and medicines. As he sprinkled a few drops of something onto a cloth, she could instantly tell it was chloroform. She was surprised he had any left after all these operations.

"Mary," he said, turning to her with the cloth in his hand, "I really dislike having to do this." He put the cloth over her nose. She recoiled for a second, but the blackness swept in immediately and she swooned.

*****

A brilliant white moon cast a stark eeriness over this godforsaken slaughter corner of Georgia. Maybe this was what hell was like, Matt thought. Viniard Field was now behind him as he staggered his way north. His chest had stopped bleeding, but the pain from a musket ball lodged therein continued to make its painful presence known. Each step resulted in a

77

burning stab. His only hope was that someone traveling on La Fayette Road would come to his aid.

He fell next to a soldier bleeding profusely and holding a large crucifix in his hand. *A dead priest?* Matt took hold of the crucifix and the words he recalled from *Psalm 116* mocked him: "The cords of death encompassed me; the snares of the nether world seized upon me; I fell into distress and sorrow."

"No!" Matt moaned as he dropped the crucifix. He picked himself up. "No," he moaned again. "Not here, not in this hell-hole cemetery."

He stumbled on. Other soldiers retreated in disgrace. Union soldiers, barely able to walk themselves, kicked up the dust, cussed that their cause was gone, and swore at God for letting this happen to them. Matt had already come across several wounded. One man with a bloodied face, his hand stretched out for Matt to help him, but what could Matt do about it? Another man lying on his back, his intestines visible, begged Matt to shoot him and let him go to his Maker.

Some Union troops on horseback rode by and Matt screamed at them to stop and help take him north to Rossville. But they didn't stop; they did not even turn their attention his way. Matt was just another weed, among other human weeds strung across the road.

Occasionally, the sound of gunfire would cause retreating men traveling on La Fayette Road to scurry off into the woods but then return back to the road. Crickets chirped their incessant taunts at Matt. An owl hooted, then flew to another nest, to continue jeering him there. A coyote poked its curious face from between the cedars. Matt barely had the strength to scare off the animal and brush away the maggots that attacked his wound.

Even the white, round ball of a moon seemed to mock him. It was safe, hanging up there in the sky, away from all this torment below. Why, he thought, did he bother to return to the battlefield? Jessica told him it was stupid, and he now saw she was right. Jessica! How he wished he could be with her tonight! She had written to him about living in Washington, D.C. with the Hellers. He wished he were there now. He would gaze upon her beauty, and she would give him strength by silently reminding him how she once defied danger by shooting a threatening rattlesnake or by kicking a town bully in the groin. Yet, despite her unladylike courage, she was all woman. Her kisses were sweet, her embrace so tender. If only she would have agreed to marry him. Did she still hold it against him that he was alone with Mary Delaney that one night in Murfreesboro so many months ago?

He groaned as he continued to crawl on the road, not even bothering to dodge a horse that had just missed striking his head with its powerful hooves. Everyone was leaving this death scene except the dead. Death. Perhaps its sweetness would be something to yearn for.

He got up, determined to walk until he dropped from exhaustion. Putting a hand to his neck, he felt the chain holding the medallion Tinker had given him. Jessica was right; it did not have any angelic powers. If there was an angel, if there was a merciful God, why did he have to go on like this, half-dead and half alive?

A military wagon approached, and Matt challenged it to run over him and end his misery. He stood in the center of the road, waiting for the inevitable.

"Stop!" a man's voice called out. Matt saw two men jerk on the reins as the horse drawing the wagon slowed to a stop only a few feet away. "Get out of the way," one of the men ordered. "Do you want to get killed?"

"Yup, I might as well be," Matt said, tripping over his own feet and spilling to the ground. "Might as well be."

"Matt?" a woman's voice called out from within the wagon. "Is that you?"

Matt knew he had to be imagining things. It sounded just like Mary Delaney. "Mary?" he responded.

The woman poked her head from behind the canvas. "Lord's sake. Stop immediately! I know this man."

After the drivers stopped the wagon, they struggled to lift Matt and drag him into the wagon where three wounded men were lying on the straw-covered floorboards. Mary helped lay him down next to the other three, but he forced himself up to a sitting position. "Oh dear God! Mary, it *is* you," he said, gasping for each word.

She tore open his shirt and winced at the sight. "I'm so sorry, Matt. We are going to a Tennessee hospital. There are surgeons there for you."

"I saw you back there at the Gordon Lee mansion yesterday."

"I wish I were still there. Doctor Himoe had to chloroform me to leave that hospital."

"What? I don't understand."

"Never mind. You are safe now."

*****

Lieutenant Toby kicked his steed into a gallop. *Didn't anyone care that the Union was in retreat? Where was Bragg? Where was Longstreet? The Yankees are heading up north, and no one cares.*

He charged east down Dover Road, shooting at the retreating soldiers. Some shot back. Others ran for cover. Stopping near the Brotherton cabin, he reloaded with the last of his ammunition. The fighting on Horseshoe Ridge near the Snodgrass house had stopped. It was too dark to see the enemy, but he could still make out the retreating cowards in this moonlight.

He turned right and headed south on LaFayette Road. There were wounded soldiers along the side of the trail, but it did not pay to shoot them. With the last of his ammunition, he wanted to be sure that every bullet in his carbine counted. Perhaps if he could find other rebels to join him, he would be able to make a decent charge at those spineless Federals.

There was something up ahead. He veered off on the side of the road, dismounted, and hid behind a tree. It was a wagon slowly making its way up the road and the moonlight illuminated the lettering on its side. "U.S.A." It was a Union wagon driven by two men. Possibly the wagon contained soldiers—not wounded men, but fighting soldiers—hidden in the wagon trying to make their escape.

If that was the case, he'd kill every damn one of them.

80

Chapter 12

Roger Toby mounted his horse and trotted toward the wagon rolling up the road. He shot his weapon in the air as he pulled up alongside the two wagon drivers. "Halt! If yaw care to see another sunrise, yaw will stop."

The wagon came to a standstill, and both drivers held their hands in the air. "This is a Union ambulance," one of them said, his voice quaking. "We are not fighting men."

"Perhaps not," Roger said, "but I'm a lieutenant with the Seventeenth Tennessee and I'm taking yaw as my prisoners."

A lady in a plain black dress stepped down from the wagon. She took a cautious step closer. "You look familiar to me, lieutenant. Have we met before?"

"That is impossible," he sneered. "I would never want to meet a disgusting Yankee woman."

She studied him, her eyes searching his face. "I cannot re-call how, but we *have* met."

"I don't know what yaw'r talking about, woman." He shifted his attention to the others. "Now look here. I aim to take yawl as my prisoners. Too many of yaw kind have al-ready deserted Chickamauga like snivelin' rats."

"How dare you!" she said, attempting to slap him, but he grabbed her arm.

"If yaw weren't a lady," he said, letting go of her, "yaw would surely be dead right now."

"I don't rightly care about myself," she answered, "but these wounded will die if we don't take care of them soon. Let us be on our way, sir."

A wounded Yankee lieutenant grunted in pain as he pulled himself up, grabbing the side of the wagon for sup-port. "You heard what Miss Delany said, lieutenant. Leave us be."

"Out of the wagon, mister," Roger demanded.

"No!" Miss Delaney screamed. "He's been wounded as well. Can't you see?"

Roger flipped his attention to one of the drivers who was about to reach for a rifle below his seat. "Drop it!" Roger snarled. "I want yaw out here, now." He turned to Matt, leaning against the wall of the wagon. "Mister—Out here where I can see yaw."

The drivers jumped down, their hands in surrender, while the Yankee lieutenant struggled, with the lady's help, to get out of the wagon. Holding his chest, the lieutenant gasped as he took his place next to the drivers and then slumped to the ground.

The wind shifted and Roger felt like gagging as the odor of blood intermingled with feces assailed his nostrils. He reached in his saddlebag for something while keeping his rifle trained on the three men. He pulled out short pieces of rope and tossed them to the ground at the feet of his prisoners. "The Yankee soldier who once owned this horse came equipped," he laughed. "Lady," he said, looking up at Miss Delaney, "I want yaw to come down from there and tie these men."

She resisted but Roger took aim at one of the drivers, threatening to kill him if she refused to obey. "I have no choice but to do your bidding," she said, pulling back the hands of one of the drivers and tying them with a rope.

"Go ahead," Roger ordered, "do the same with the next one."

After she tied the second driver, Roger ordered the Yankee lieutenant to stand up so he could be restrained as well.

"You beast!" Miss Delaney exclaimed. "Have you no mercy?"

Roger shot a look of disbelief at her. *Woman, there's no mercy on a battlefield.* While maintaining vigilance on the lady and the two drivers, he stooped down before the wounded lieutenant. "What's yaw name?"

The Yankee, his eyes half closed, mumbled something incoherent.

Roger gave him a fierce look. "Speak up, man."

"For the love of God," the lady shouted. "Leave him be."

"Quiet, ma'am if yaw know what's best." He looked at the chain about the man's neck. "What the hell is this?" He removed the chain and stared at the medallion. There was a curious dent in it, as if it had been hit by a bullet. He stood up and tried to see the writing in the moonlight. Even with the indentation, he could still make out the lettering. His eyes widened and his heart pounded in disbelief as he read the inscription on the half-dollar sized bronze object: Nellie Radford. It seemed so long ago…

"Do yah like it?" Nellie had asked him.

Roger fingered the coin-shaped bronze medallion hanging from his neck. "I like it, especially since your name's inscribed on the back of it. I wear it all the time."

"Where did yaw get this?" Roger asked him. "Who are yaw?"

"The man's name is Lieutenant Matt Lightfoot," Mary said. "He's with the Eighth Kansas, but he's wounded and I need to—"

"Silence, ma'am." He turned his attention back to Matt. "I say, where did yaw get this medal?"

Matt took a deep breath, his eyes focused on Roger's. "Belongs to Nellie. Jessica had it."

Roger's mouth dropped open. Nellie? Jessica? Oh sweet Jesus!

My dearest Sara, as I write this, I know this will be hard for you to understand. A Union corporal almost killed me as I lay dying on the battlefield. It was a woman's voice, and she tore off Nellie's medallion I wore about my neck. First she told me she was going to finish me off, then, after a brilliant flash of lightning, she took mercy on me…told me she didn't know I was taking good care of Nellie. I heard someone say the corporal was a lady masquerading as a man, and that her name was Jessica.

83

Roger let go of his grip on his rifle. "Nellie's the girl I bought from that scoundrel. I paid six hundred dollars for her."

Mary straightened up, her eyes like daggers. "You bought Nellie as your slave girl? How dare you!"

"It isn't like that at all, ma'am. Permit me to explain."

"You can do that on the way to a Union hospital," Mary said.

"I'm so very sorry for treating yaw roughly, ma'am."

"The name is Miss Delaney," she corrected. "I must insist that you let that man live," she added, pointing toward Matt, slumped on the ground. "He's a close friend of Jessica's."

"My deepest apologies to yaw, Miss Delaney, and to all the others here." He dropped on his knees to the ground in front of Matt. "Especially yaw, lieutenant." This was indeed a miracle. Somehow, he thought, they were all connected to Nellie, the slave girl who believed she had a guardian angel named Sissy.

Stop acting like a child yourself, Roger. You are a lieutenant in the Army of Tennessee.

"I may face a military hanging for this, Miss Delaney, but I will help lead him and these others toward a Federal hospital."

*****

October 3
Washington D.C.

After preparing dinner and waiting for the Hellers to return from the printing office, Jessica leaned back in Penelope's cushioned Boston rocker. It was not fair that she had no place to call her own. How could life be so unjust? The Hellers were able to afford modest furniture, while she owned nothing except the clothes she wore. This colorful moquette carpeting, she thought, could have been her own. So too, that chestnut lamp stand, or the pictures on the wall, or this badly chipped and scratched rosewood piano—which she hoped to learn to play. Not fair. She worked hard and yet had nothing tangible to show for her efforts.

84

Well, all these things would have to wait—like her need to have the world respect her as a serious writer. Perhaps one day she would be like one of the Brontë sisters, or even like Walt Whitman for that matter. *Oh, Otto, thank you for having introduced me to a most marvelous poet.*

She picked up a box of Emma's toys and looked inside. A rag doll, a ball, a cord of string, a wooden pull toy, a rope for skipping, a piece of chalk and a slate. Emma's little world in one small box. Jessica thought of her own little world in a box, but it was a box of bad memories…the murder of her parents by border ruffians sixteen months ago, the kidnapping of Nellie—who had lived with her since she was a young girl, and the horror of seeing men killed on the battlefield as well as men and boys being slaughtered in Lawrence, where no battlefield existed. Those memories went into her mental box, where she sealed and buried them into her subconscious, to be forgotten.

Jessica returned Emma's box of toys to the floor. One thing she could not hide in her memory box was the political scene all around her. Just two weeks ago, Otto had introduced her to Salmon Chase, the Secretary of the Treasury, describing him as a man alienated from white society. It was easy for Jessica to see why. In his earlier law practice, Mr. Chase had defended runaway slaves and felt that negroes had the right to vote, to be educated, and to testify against white people.

But it was Mr. Chase's newly married daughter, Kate Chase Sprague, whom Jessica found fascinating, yet tiresome. Fascinating, because she was even more headstrong and free-spirited than Jessica herself. Tiresome, because she constantly boasted about her father's political ambitions. "He truly should have been nominated on the Republican ticket for President, not that boorish Abraham Lincoln." She went on to describe her father's political common sense and his judgments in military matters that even Lincoln acknowledged.

Kate was the one to know, Jessica admitted, if ever one needed a political favor. So Jessica tolerated her, wondering if there would ever be a time when such a favor would be needed.

"Miss Radford," Emma squealed, bringing Jessica out of her thoughts. Emma's wide smile lit up the room. "Are you going to read something from *Merry's* magazine like you promised?"

Jessica noticed the other imploring face, that of Mitzi. "Yes, I will." She picked up an issue of the publication from beneath her chair and thumbed through the pages. "Would you two like to know what this article says about happy girls?"

"Yes, yes," they said at once.

"Well, then. Here's what it says. 'Happy girls—who can not love them? What cheeks like the rose, bright eyes and elastic step! How carefully they go to work! Our word for it, such girls will make excellent wives. Blessed indeed will men be who secure such prizes.'" Jessica shook her head. *What utter nonsense! Since when are women to be considered prizes? Poppycock!*

Emma raised her hand. "Miss Radford? I liked the story you wrote for us better. The one about the slave who ran away from his master and became President. Did that happen?"

Mitzi elbowed her sister. "Don't be foolish. She made that up. Former slaves could never become President, could they?"

Jessica thought about it for a moment. "I don't know. Perhaps someday, a long ways off. I hope to help negroes obtain the same opportunities we now enjoy once they become free."

Emma interrupted again. "Like Tinker? Could Tinker ever become President?"

"I don't know," she said, closing the magazine. Tinker! She wondered what had become of him since he returned to fight in this war.

Chapter 13

Tinker played his harmonica and danced when he learned he would be transferred out of the Ninth Kansas Cavalry. "Oh Lawd, I'm glad I be out o'dere," he muttered, dropping to the ground in happy exhaustion. "But please, Lawd, help dose poor folk." There was nothing much he could do about those people forced out of their Western Missouri homes by Order Number Eleven.

At night, the images frozen in his memory came to life in his dreams—farmers and their wives begging him not to take away their things and destroy their farms. *But what could I do? I try t' give 'em back their valuables when no soljer be lookin'.*

And a voice in his mind whispered to him: *but you did good, Tinker...that note...'member. the note?...don't forget the note, that nice thank-yuh note some Quantrill man gave to the Jacksons....could've got that farmer killed.*

Tinker laughed to himself. *Stupid sergeant never found out 'bout it.*

But the ugly visions returned the next night. Horrible dreams about folks having to watch their crops, livestock, and homes being destroyed. Their eyes glowed with pain as they turned toward him. "No!" Tinker said, waking from the nightmare, his face awash in tears. He stumbled out of his tent, shaking his fist at the darkness where the devil had to be. "Goddamn you," he shouted. "Goddamn you for makin' me do it." After he vomited, coughing and choking, he staggered back to his tent. But the dreams never returned.

Things had to be different now that he was with the Second Kansas Colored and assigned to Fort Blair at Baxter Springs. They just had to be better. He was all smiles as he stood in line for his pay. The sergeant gave the white private ahead of him twelve dollars for a month's pay. "Next," the sergeant snapped. "Name and rank."

87

"Tinker, suh. Private Tinker."

He pressed his hands together. *I shore could use the twelve dollars. Been needin' to save me nuff to buy me a watch.*

However, when the paymaster counted out seven dollars and handed it to him, Tinker was stunned. "But, suh, this not all."

"That is your payment for the month, private."

"But the other man, he's a private 'n he—"

"Next," the paymaster said, turning his attention to the next man in line.

Tinker wiped his brow. *Best not to complain. Wouldn't do me no good. Maybe get me in trouble.*

But Tinker was also disappointed with Fort Blair. The fort was small, consisting of a sixteen-foot-square wooden block-house in the center and a few log cabins surrounded by log-and-stone embankments no more than four feet high and a hundred feet long. It didn't provide enough room to house the 150 negro troops that should have been quartered inside. But Lieutenant James Pond was making plans to enlarge the fort. In fact, this morning he sent out a number of troops to forage for supplies.

The only things that kept Tinker company these days was his harmonica and the six-inch brass telescope which Matt, before leaving for the Eighth Kansas, had given him. "It'll help you find the enemy," Matt had told him, "before he finds you." Tinker slipped the telescope back in his knapsack. *There's no enemy around,* Tinker thought, *and hadn't been for some time.* He was anxious for action, and the idea of passing each day with camp chores, eating, and sleeping was not what he expected.

But it gave him plenty of time to wonder whatever happened to Charlotte, Private Devin Alcott's cousin, whom he had met in Nashville almost a year ago. Her skin was the color of light cocoa and her brown eyes were a bit sad. Yet she smiled almost all the time....

"There's somethin' special 'bout yuh 'n me,"
he said as he pressed his hands over her breasts.

"Been only three weeks now, Miz Charlotte, but I feel like I knows yuh all my life."

She kissed him and her eyes looked as melancholy as ever. "You're special to me too, Tinker. I wish this war were over, so we could see each other all the time. But I can't be following your regiment all across the country. I've got to go up north. My father's taken ill, and I've got to be with him."

"I understand. I sho do."

"I will miss you, Tinker. Very much."

"Write to me, Miz Charlotte. Let me know how yuh doin'."

"I promise."

But Tinker never heard from her again. No letters, nothing. Devin swore he had no idea why she didn't write, but he did hear from his parents that Charlotte's father had recovered from his illness.

"Who needs yuh anyways?" Tinker muttered as he thought about her empty promise to write.

I'm not gonna think 'bout dat no more. Charlotte is gone 'n I never gonna see her again.

His shirt off, Tinker rinsed his chest and arms with water from the spring. Matt Lightfoot once told him that the Cherokee Indians believed that this natural mineral spring had healing properties. Whether or not it did, Tinker thought it might relieve the soreness of his body, having worked earlier in helping to extend the embankment. He was glad that Matt had given him Jessica's new address in Washington, D.C. and planned to write her to thank her for wanting to do something about ending slavery. But he missed all his friends, not only Matt and Jessica, but Devin and Salem as well. He appreciated Otto's efforts in helping him return to the military without facing a charge of desertion. Now that he was back in the war, he hoped he would make up for that. It was freedom he was fighting for, and he hoped he would never forget that.

The sun was almost directly overhead, and it would be time to eat and reflect on matters. He was greatly relieved that he wouldn't have to follow orders from the Ninth Kansas Volunteer Cavalry anymore. It still bothered him the way he had to force people living in the western counties of Missouri to vacate their homes and farms. Order Number Eleven made no sense to him. He could appreciate the righteous anger against Quantrill, but to deprive innocent people of their homes and livelihood was intolerable. It was another kind of slavery, as far as he was concerned.

The dinner bell rang, and Tinker dressed and headed toward the cooking camp some twenty yards away. He was glad that Lieutenant Pond was the commanding officer of the camp. Mr. Heller said he knew the lieutenant well and that he was a brave, dependable man.

But Tinker worried about Fatty, a mail courier who was still recovering from his wounds in the camp. Despite what others in his infantry believed, Tinker thought the threat that Fatty related to Lieutenant Cook a few days ago should have been taken seriously. Fatty had been shot and captured by Quantrill's men two weeks earlier. Because of his former friendship with one of Quantrill's men, however, he was released. But he warned the men at the fort to know that Quantrill had been running short of supplies and fully intended to raid the Union garrison at Baxter Springs.

Out of nowhere, the pounding of hooves and screams of horsemen shattered the noontime peace. As the raiders moved quickly between the Union soldiers and the fort itself, Tinker felt he was reliving the Lawrence raid. The marauders, some dressed in Yankee uniforms, whooped and yelled, firing their revolvers indiscriminately at the troops, some of whom ran for the tall grass and others, for the fort. Tinker zigzagged his way to the fort, bullet pings missing him by inches, his forage cap shot and soaring into the air like a bird. His negro comrades on both sides were getting slaughtered, but Tinker knew he wouldn't make it if he stopped to help them.

Lieutenant Pond, racing from his tent, hollered at the men nearby to help him man a 12-pound howitzer inside the fort.

No one obeyed the order, and Pond raced toward the weapon, the only artillery piece there. He struggled with loading it and soon an ear-shattering explosion pierced the air like an unexpected lightning strike. Some of the rebels retreated in haphazard fashion. Then came a second boom from the howitzer and more of them withdrew into the woods.

Those retreating rebels must have stolen those Yankee uniforms, Tinker figured as he dashed toward a rifle stand within the fort and grabbed a weapon and cartridge case. He took a position behind an embankment and fired, hoping he would see Quantrill himself in his sights, but the leader was nowhere to be found.

While these men were still firing, Tinker snaked his way out of the fort to spot the enemy. Three dead Union soldiers lay in the grass, but Tinker didn't allow himself time to check if they were wounded or dead. A third firing from the howitzer caused an even greater crash, and about a dozen rebels raced for their horses, while the other guerillas had already ridden off without waiting for them. With the back of one of the retreating Confederates in his gun sight, Tinker took careful aim. "I'm gonna get one o' you rats," he cussed, "if I'm gonna hafta die doin' it."

His weapon failed to fire, but not wanting to lose sight of the men running for their steeds, Tinker charged after them. He swore as he tripped over another dead Union soldier and picked himself up. "I'm gonna get you murderin' skunks!" Tinker screamed at the retreating rebels. He fell once into the tall grass to hide when two of the men turned in his direction. Then he picked himself up and continued on. The two men mounted a white-spotted brown mustang and rode off together, the hooves kicking up dust behind them.

"Hell!" Tinker exclaimed, pounding the stock of his carbine against the ground. "Damn it!" He turned back, expecting to head back to the fort when he spotted a roan colored mount wandering behind a row of locust trees. It was already saddled, and Tinker guessed it must have belonged to one of the retreating rebels.

"Thank yah, Lawd," Tinker said, grinning as he glanced up at the sky. He mounted the horse and took off, hoping to find the fleeing attackers.

Tinker headed north on Military Road, but when he saw a rider emerge from the woods in the distance to his right, he brought the horse to a slow pace and stopped. After dismounting, he crawled on his belly. With adrenaline pumping in his veins, he pressed against a thick oak tree, and with his telescope, he spotted a sizeable group of rebels in the forest.

Damn lots o' dem probably hidden in the woods, Tinker thought. *They were pokin' out from the trees. Bet maybe there was hundreds of 'em back in there. What were they doin'? Were they goin' to attack the fort again?*

He heard the faint sound of a beating drum and strains from "Battle Hymn of the Republic" being played from somewhere. Confused, Tinker spanned his telescope across the meadow, but it was up further north, on Military Road, past Willow Creek that he saw the source of the music. A column of eight Yankee baggage wagons, two buggies, two ambulances, and—based on the glint from the sun on shiny metal—what appeared to be a wagonload of brass band players. The musicians had quit playing while a cavalry escort shouted something back to the column. A stocky Union officer headed the group.

Tinker, his mouth open in disbelief, stared through the lens of his telescope. Could that be Blunt? Lieutenant Pond made reference to General James Blunt coming to Fort Blair today with the Fourteenth Kansas, did he not? But what was the general doing here, sitting smartly on his horse watching the opposing side, his saber ceremoniously held high while the band played a grand march? Didn't the general know he was facing the enemy? Did he not see the rest of them hiding behind trees? But maybe he thought the rebels were Union men since some of them wore Yankee clothes and one of them even carried a Yankee flag.

Two Union officers moved forward toward the large contingent of men, but then they stopped and raced back to Blunt. "They're rebels," they shouted. "Quantrill's men!"

Blunt didn't appear to be fazed by the news, but instead rode forward with a small cavalry escort, ahead of the wagons, buggies, and ambulances, while firing his weapon. Suddenly, Quantrill's men raced like wildcats out from the dark of the woods while Blunt's cavalry left the line in full retreat.

The guerillas caught up with their fellow soldiers in the clearing, many of them jeering, whooping, guns blazing. Blunt, still charging, looked back and must have realized that—except for his adjutant riding with him—he was alone in his pursuit. He and his adjutant retreated, each in a different direction. His adjutant rode toward the creek, but the horse tumbled as it was shot. The adjutant flew toward the creek, and one of the guerilla's charged by and fired.

Other guerillas pursued the general, who was racing toward his wagon train. Tinker stared in disbelief as he saw Blunt lift a woman from the buggy and put her astride on a horse and the both of them rode off, with four from Quantrill's group chasing after them.

Tinker remained hidden behind the tree and watched as five Union soldiers raised their hands in surrender after they dismounted. "Yer gonna be treated like prisoners of war," one of the rebels shouted. "Just lay face up on the grass, all of you. That's right, line up next to each other. Line up and keep your mouths shut. Understand?"

As Tinker turned away for a moment he heard a series of gunshots. He shifted his gaze back to those captors, who were firing at the unarmed soldiers. One of them danced on the back of their victims. Tinker guessed the murderer might have been Quantrill himself because of the man's large brim black hat and slender build.

"Oh Lawd, help me," Tinker muttered, running into the open field. A shot narrowly missed him and he fell, pretending to be dead. These rebels would probably return to the fort, Tinker figured, so the best he could hope for would be to leave this killing zone. Run…faster…fall into the tall grass…up again, run, fall into the tall grass. A musket ball hit his belt buckle, but he was convinced he was hit. No bleeding. *Thank yah, Lawd.* He got up again…falling into the grass…rising…falling…faking death. He stopped when he got to the edge of a ravine. He looked about and saw that Blunt's adjutant, who had fallen from his horse earlier, was only twenty yards away and dead from a shot to the head.

Tinker cursed inwardly and debated with himself about shooting one of these murdering scoundrels. It would be worth it, just to make one of them pay for this and for Lawrence.

Tinker, die smart; don't die stupid.

Tinker couldn't agree with that. It wasn't stupid to give up your own life in order to end the life of a bad man.

Promise me, Tinker. Promise me to die smart, and don't die stupid.

His slave father did not realize how wrong is was to make that promise. Tinker could not just let these good men die and do nothing about it.

A volley of shots pierced the air. Obscene whoops blared from the guerillas. Hooves beat the tortured ground. A wagon driver screamed in desperation: "rush on, faster, faster!"

While Tinker lay prone, still as death, he raised his head high enough to see the Union's wagonload of musicians racing toward him, the driver deliriously whipping his horses. About twenty guerillas gave chase, but within seconds, the front wheel of the wagon dropped off, spilling its occupants to the ground. The musicians, all wearing impressive uniforms, staggered near their broken wagon, like drunken men. But one of them was a drummer boy who could not have been more than twelve. The guerillas approached and the musicians all waved their white handkerchiefs in surrender.

"Kill 'em all," one of the rebels ordered. "They didn't show us mercy, we don't show them mercy."

One of the musicians, his face bloated with grief, dropped to his knees begging to be spared. He still spoke as a bullet caught him in the chest. Another musician, his hands in the air and his eyes following the barrel of the enemy's gun being raised to his head and the explosion spattered a fragment of his brain to the grassy coffin below. The other musicians screamed, but they were quickly silenced by gunfire. The captives died where they were, some still clutching their handkerchiefs foolishly.

The drummer boy turned and took off running. A guerilla chased after him, cussing when his first two shots missed. The third one found its target and the boy fell face forward in the meadow.

The insurgents whooped like savages as they set fire to the bandwagon. One of them suggested stealing the instruments, but the other argued they wouldn't want to carry them back. After congratulating themselves on a job well done, they regrouped before riding off.

Tinker pulled himself up from what he hoped was only a nightmare, his heart pounding as if demanding to leave his chest. He ran toward the burning wagon and the musicians sprawled nearby. One man held a bugle in one hand and a handkerchief in the other. Another died with his mouth partly open as if he were frozen in the middle of his words.

Visions of a burning Lawrence, Kansas flashed before him….

Tinker would never forget that horrendous August morning. Fires all around. Was he in hell? He had just looked up to see flames gutting the second floor of the town's Allen Farm Implement and Hardware building, where the Republican newspaper offices were. He was still staring at it when a frightened boy grabbed his shoulder. "I've gotta get home," the boy had said. "Find out how my parents are doin.' Maybe both of my brothers are there already. Or maybe they're dead."

That sound! A boy begging to be saved. Tinker snapped out of his thoughts when he heard the moans of a youngster lying further away from the smoldering bandwagon. "Help me," the lad cried. His one arm was draped over his snare drum, his other was bloodied and lay limp at his side.

Tinker knelt next to him and caressed the boy's nest of chestnut hair, all in disarray, just like this massacre. "I'll get yah an ambulance, son. I'll get yah fixed up."

"Why did they shoot me?" the boy moaned. "All I ever did was play my music."

Yeah, Tinker thought, *dat be all my friend Lazarus do 'fore he done got killed by a man who hates negroes. Like dis here boy, Lazarus done never get no chance to be a man.*

"I'll help yah," Tinker said. But the boy's head slumped to one side. "Hey, friend," Tinker said, "doan do dis t'me." He pressed his ear on the lad's chest. So silent, so quiet. Ever so quiet.

"No!" In his rage, Tinker rose up. Bodies everywhere. Bloody mounds of flesh strewn across the meadow, scattered across the land like manure or like the grass and the weeds— forgotten. He punched both fists into the sky. "Lawd, stop dis here war. Stop dis here killin'!"

He gazed at the young drummer boy's death mask and recalled again his own father's warning: *Die smart; don't die stupid.*

Tinker cried, burying his face in his hands, gasping for breath between sobs, dredging up more sorrow from the pit of his soul.

"Looks like I got myself a nigger!" a coarse voice roared.

Tinker looked up. A bearded man on horseback grinned back while training a Winchester at him. "You make one bad move, boy, and I'll empty this gun on you. Y'hear?"

Chapter 14

Otto looked himself over in the mirror and glanced in Superintendent John Defrees' direction. "Are you sure I look presentable?"

"You look fine," Defrees said with a reassuring smile.

"I cannot tell you how delighted and honored I am that you've asked me to show President Lincoln our facilities."

"It made perfect sense to me. You certainly have a good grasp of our operation. Besides, you will enjoy meeting the President. I can assure you he is not at all the way the press has written about him."

Otto nodded. Defrees would certainly know that. Prior to his appointment to the Printing Office two-and-a-half years ago, Defrees was a delegate to the National Republican Convention. As such, his advice was sought by many Republicans, including Abraham Lincoln.

The receptionist entered the room, her eyes sparkling with excitement. "The Presidential party is here, Mr. Defrees."

Otto reflected on Defrees' comment that the President was not at all the way the press has written about him. After following the superintendent to the reception room, Otto cleared his throat and ran his fingers through his hair before entering.

Standing by the doorway, he paused, blinking in surprise at how tall, thin, and awkward Lincoln appeared. The President, accompanied by two Union officers, bent to kiss the hand of one of the ladies working there and then faced Defrees. "It gives me great pleasure to see you again, John," Lincoln said. "During these troubled times, I seldom get an opportunity to visit old acquaintances."

Defrees noticed Otto approach. "Mr. President, permit me to introduce you to Otto Heller. Perhaps you recall my telling you about his heroism."

Lincoln's thin lips formed a courteous smile as he faced Otto. "Indeed, I understand you helped rescue more than thirty-one slaves as a conductor for the Underground Railroad. Impressive."

Otto's face warmed from the unexpected compliment. "Thank you, Mr. President, but I was only echoing my father's philosophy. He was an ardent follower of Henry Thoreau, who believed that when unjust laws exist, one should not be content to obey them."

"That is well put, Mr. Heller. Unjust laws should never be respected. Fact is, I wish I would have issued that Emancipation Proclamation much sooner than I did. I only delayed the inevitable because of my wish to preserve the Union at any cost."

"Well, Mr. President," Defrees suggested, "shall we get on with your visit?"

Lincoln nodded and the superintendent started the tour with the wetting room on the first floor. It contained troughs and equipment used for wetting the paper prior to use, followed by a hydraulic press that took out the creases "I don't know if I agree with this process," Lincoln said, grinning. "If pressure can remove wrinkles, why is it that I still have mine?" His gray eyes sparkled at his own joke.

After showing the President the Ink Room, where oil and lampblack were mixed, Defrees took him to the press room. "Here you will see," he shouted above the din, "Adams bed and platen presses and Napier cylinder presses, all steam-powered, that are capable of producing 100,000 sheets of printed material every day."

Lincoln smiled again. "I'll have to ask Congress to cut down on legislation so we can stop cutting down all those unfortunate trees."

Such quick wit, Otto thought. *How was the President able to find humor in life with the pressures of trying to heal a divided nation?* While Otto tried to imagine the enormous weight that this extraordinary man carried on his shoulders, Lincoln took him aside and shouted above the din of the machinery, "I understand that your dear wife also works here at the Printing Office. Not in this noisy area, I assume."

"No, Mr. President. Penelope works in the binding room on the third floor. She folds printed sheets by hand along with two hundred other women."

Lincoln's tired gray eyes met Otto's. "I understand she was with you during the recent Lawrence massacre and that she had witnessed the senseless killing."

"Mr. President, how did you know about that?"

Lincoln smiled briefly but there was a sadness in his eyes. "I follow every aspect of this conflict."

Otto bit his lower lip. *Perhaps Senator Lane had told him.*

Lincoln tugged his beard as he turned to gaze out the plant window for what seemed like a long time. "I admire them," he finally said. "I truly do."

Otto cocked his head. "Who, Mr. President?"

"Why, the women, of course. Sometimes I wonder who has made the largest sacrifice in this war—the men who fight or the women who suffer while their men fight."

*****

The next day
Atlanta, GA

Jane Millicent opened her mouth as wide as a cup and sang with gusto—apparently not caring if she was the loudest member of True Baptist Church. She would bellow out "My voice rises to God" while emphasizing the deity with a "God-ah" flourish. Or she would sing, "My voice rises to God" and roll all the r's with her tongue.

Nellie tugged Mrs. Millicent's sleeve after leaving the church with Sara. "I likes the way yah sing, Miz Jane."

"Why, thank you, Nellie. You have a very nice voice yourself. How did you learn to sing like that?"

"From my momma. But I not see her no more."

"I know what it is like when you lose someone you love."

Sara glanced at her aunt. Jane Millicent never talked about her husband, whom she had lost at Gettysburg. Yet she carried on as if she were contended. *Perhaps Jane Millicent is a better actress than I.*

99

"Good morning," Sara said to two neighbor ladies glaring at Nellie and then at her. "Is anything the matter?" she added. But the ladies walked briskly as if a snake was on their trail.

"They are just busybodies," Jane Millicent said. "Pay them no heed."

Fortunately, Sara thought, *those two ladies were in the minority.* Most of the congregation accepted the fact that Nellie was no longer a slave. But before she took her seat in her aunt's carriage, one woman—a prostitute no less—had the audacity to approach Sara and inquire about Nellie. "Why isn't that colored lady at home," she asked, "doing chores instead of attending Sunday services?"

"I will have you know," Sara replied, "that Nellie does have chores to do. She sews uniforms for our soldiers and prepares food for the men guarding our city. And she spends Sundays praying for them. Maybe she ought to spend her Sundays instead praying for your soul."

Sara had no use for women who sold their bodies for money. God will burn all of them in Hell.

"Don't be so judgmental," Jane told her during the drive home. "After all, Jesus loved sinners."

"But I'm not Jesus."

Mrs. Millicent shrugged off Sara's reply, and after dinner, took her usual nap. Sara knitted and watched Nellie through the corner of her eye. The seventeen-year-old moved her lips as she held the *Atlanta Daily Intelligencer* in her hands.

"Nellie, what is it you are reading so intently?"

"It say here that General Bragg took over Lookout Mountain and laid siege to the town of Chattanooga. What does 'siege' mean, Misses Toby?"

"It means that the Confederates surrounded the town."

Nellie smiled. "Does that mean we can go back home now?"

Sara wished it were true. "The Yankees haven't left. I think Bragg intends to starve them out. But until the enemy is totally removed from that area, I don't think it would be wise to return."

Nellie tossed the newspaper aside and went to the bookshelf. She ran her finger over the spines of the books. "It ain't here," she said.

"What's not there?" Sara asked.

"The books Jessica used to read ain't here. She like *Leaves of Grass* and *Uncle Tom's Cabin*. Told me once she wanted to write more'n anythin'. I miss her so much. I'm not ever gonna see her again, am I?"

"Nellie, that's not true."

"Jest like I never gonna see my momma again."

Sara knew Nellie was probably right about her momma, who was recaptured at the bank of the Missouri six years ago, although Nellie made it to the safety of the Radford family.

"Don't give up on seeing Jessica again," Sara said.

But Nellie, her arms folded, raised her eyes toward the ceiling. "If only Sissy would return, she could tell me when I'll see her."

"You're a young lady now, Nellie. It isn't proper to believe in angels anymore."

"I know. A lot of things ain't proper no more after you grow up."

Sara was about to correct her English again when a thought struck her. "Oh, Nellie, I do have some encouraging news for you."

Nellie cast a doubtful glance. "Good news?"

"Yes, indeed. I received a heartening letter yesterday from Mr. Toby. I meant to tell you about it earlier."

"Tell me about what?"

Sara went to her desk and pulled out an envelope which she had opened yesterday. "Here it is," she said, opening the letter while taking a chair next to Nellie. "Let me read you the part that you will find interesting." Her eyes scanned the letter until she came to the proper paragraph. Here it is... 'I know Nellie would be interested in learning that I had come across a soldier named Lieutenant Matt Lightfoot with the Eighth Kansas when I was in Chickamauga. He was accompanied by two male nurses, other wounded men, and a female nurse named Mary Delaney. Interestingly, Miss Delaney was the one who had treated my injuries in a hospital three months ago. But even more interesting is that Lieutenant Lightfoot knows Jessica Radford.'"

101

Nellie, her hands to her mouth, squealed in surprise. "Jessica? Where is she?"

"Be patient, dear," Sara said, "I'm coming to that. The letter says 'It seems he not only knows Jessica Radford but he knew her parents as well. The night her parents were murdered by bushwhackers was the same night these evil men kidnapped Nellie.'"

Sara took a deep breath. She had already decided to skip reading aloud the next sentence about how the Radfords were killed—possibly even burned alive in their cabin. *It must have been horrible for Jessica to have discovered the charred bodies of her parents and find poor Nellie missing. Thank the Lord, if Roger had not brought Nellie out of captivity by purchasing her from her kidnapper, Nellie would still be a slave.*

Sara glanced at Nellie, who was thirsting for every word. "'But all this while," Sara continued, "'that we took care of Nellie, the poor girl ached to find the only sister she ever knew—Jessica. Now, through Matt, we know where she is at.'"

Nellie's eyes gleaned from excitement. "Where?"

"In Washington, D.C. Matt gave Roger Miss Radford's address." Sara skipped a few lines and added, "Oh, you will find this humorous, Nellie. Roger said that he had to don a Yankee uniform from one of the dead soldiers in the field so he could take them to a military hospital in Rossville. He had not realized that he wore the uniform of a colonel when he entered the Federal hospital until every soldier saluted him. He somehow managed to find some nondescript clothes and find his way back to the Seventeenth Tennessee."

Sara expected Nellie to be laughing, but she wasn't. "When can I see her again?" Nellie asked.

"When this d—" Sara stopped. This was the Lord's Day. "When this war is over, Nellie. That's when."

*****

November 1
Chattanooga, Tennessee

102

Lieutenant Matt Lightfoot grew accustomed to the daily rebel gunfire from Lookout Mountain. The Confederates were just as stubborn in commanding Lookout Mountain, Orchard Knob, and Missionary Ridge as the Union was in refusing to be starved into surrendering. Today was the first good piece of news he had heard in weeks—the success of the Cracker Line operation that opened up a new supply line for the Union. Until now, rations had been drastically cut back for everyone, including the wounded. But Mary Delaney somehow managed to sneak in hardtack or dried beef on the pretext of visiting him to check on his recovery.

"You need your strength, lieutenant. Just eat," she'd whisper.

"Where are you gettin' this? You're not givin' me your own rations, are you?"

"Shh. Never mind," she'd say and disappear.

Bored after spending almost five weeks in bed since his surgery, he used his knife to whittle away on a small maple log. He carved only a part of Lincoln's head when Mary entered the tent. She smiled slightly as she twisted her apron with nervous fingers.

"I have received word," she said, pausing long enough to look about the crowded tent, "that you will be rejoining your unit."

"I expected I would be."

Mary grabbed more of her apron to twist as she came closer. "I really believe you have already served the Union well, so there should be no need for you to risk your life again."

"You've got to know," he whispered, "that I must be there for the others."

Mary nodded. "Somehow I knew you would say that."

Matt struggled to get dressed, and Mary helped him. He tossed his wooden sculpture into his haversack and made his way out of the tent, being careful not to step on any of the sick and wounded lying on dirty blood-stained sheets covering the straw-covered ground. Mary followed him out.

"You were fortunate," Mary said, "that the musket ball that struck you missed vital organs. Had it been a Minié ball, you might not have survived. Such ammunition shatters bones and cartilage. I've seen men with such wounds in the chest that did not survive."

"Yup, Miss Delaney, I'm truly fortunate. I'm especially thankful for your kindness these past few weeks." He changed his gait to a trot and headed toward a pair of white oak trees. Slanting at opposite angles, these trees formed a peculiar vee against a moonlit backdrop of Missionary Ridge.

"Where are you going in such haste?"

"I've some urgent business to take care of by those trees yonder."

"I am happy we could talk candidly, now that we are finally alone."

"Shucks, I'm as delighted as a jaybird." He leaned against a tree with both hands and stared at her. "I've noticed you lost a lot of weight, and I'm leanin' towards the idea that you've been sharin' your meager rations with me."

She smiled, but said nothing.

"Miss Delaney, I will need some privacy."

"Yes, of course," she said, giggling as she turned and moved a step away.

The incessant chatter of night crickets was accompanied by a splashing over dry leaves. Matt quickly enveloped the embarrassing sound with a question. "Miss Delaney, now that General Grant has assumed command of Army of the Cumberland, have you heard any rumors about when he might take some action here in Chattanooga?"

"No. I am unfortunately not privy to the thoughts of our commanders. But I assume we will be on the offensive soon. From what I understand, Grant is a strong-minded man who does not sit around for weeks doing nothing. And I think Lincoln was rather impressed by his victory in Vicksburg."

"I'm hopin' Grant will break the siege so we can finally get on with this war."

"Yes," she said quietly. "Hopefully, yes."

Even though Mary's back was still turned to him, Matt sensed her anxiety from the way her head was bowed. He took a step toward her.

"Mr. Lightfoot," she asked, possibly sensing his nearness, "have you heard from Jessica?"

"Nope. Last time she wrote she said she moved to Washington with the Hellers. I wrote her at her new address, but I suspect the mail had a hard time gettin' through because of the rebel blockade."

She turned toward him with an uncertain smile. "Do you still intend to wed her?" Her eyes betrayed a curious misgiving, as if she already knew the answer.

"Yup, but I don't know if she has similar intentions. Why do you ask?"

She looked away. "No particular reason."

Matt sensed that she would not want to talk about it further. He walked with her in the cool stillness of the night, debating what he should say to her, when she broke the uncomfortable silence.

"I don't know how much longer I will want to serve as a nurse here. It has been rather wretched seeing all these men suffer. I fear by now I might have become immune to all this misery."

"I hope you don't quit. I owe you a heap of thanks for savin' my life when I was wounded."

"Anyone would have done the same."

"Not so. Another nurse would not have stood up to that rebel lieutenant as you did."

"Please, Mr. Lightfoot. You are causing me to blush from all this praise."

"Have I convinced you not to leave?"

Mary's eyes turned serious. "I don't know. Truth is, I was going to resign until I heard from Colonel Martin that you had reenlisted. I thought when I saw you again that you—" She stopped herself from going on, grimacing as if she were sorry she had said as much as she had.

"Please continue, Mary," Matt said after her long pause.

105

"—that you had no future interest in Jessica. I must go, Mr. Lightfoot, it is getting late."

Matt buried his hands in his pockets, not sure what to say as she started to walk away. He glanced up at the dots of white piercing the dark sky. A pale moon hid under a cloud layer as if retiring for the evening. The night air carried the faint sounds of soldiers laughing near a campfire.

If only Mary knew of those many hours he had spent in recovery—desiring her.

Chapter 15

From his position on Lookout Mountain, Lieutenant Roger Toby could make out the house with the aid of binoculars. How often Sara would gaze in this direction from her kitchen window and tell him this mountain reminded her of Mount Sinai. That's where God lived in the Bible, she would tell him, and that was the same God who watched over her here, from the mountain. And when the cloud formed over the top of the mountain, He was still watching.

But God—if there even was one—was not watching any more. Their home was probably desolate by now. Sara did say in a previous letter she intended to move to Atlanta to be with her aunt. But did she?

Putting away his binoculars, he made his way to his tent. He eased himself onto a cut log that served as a chair and re-read what he had written to Sara thus far. Dipping his pen in ink, he went on to finish it...

> *Darling, I have recently been transferred to the 19th Tennessee, and that occurred because the Army of Tennessee is being reorganized. So now I am reporting to Colonel Francis Walker, who is serving under a brigade commanded by General Otto Strahl, under Stewart's Division. Wonderful to know that General Stewart is also opposed to slavery. But Sara, I still cannot accept the notion that slavery is the issue in this war. I happen to be fighting for our independence from the Union—a cause that is both honorable and just.*
>
> *I have been getting this strange feeling that the Federals are preparing for a major offensive. I strongly hope General Bragg moves down to Lookout Valley, the Tennessee River, and to the roads leading to Bridgeport and wipes out the enemy. Bragg ought to realize the importance of this.*

Anyway, I digress. I realize you are not inter-
ested in military matters, so I'd rather confine this
letter to talk about you and Nellie. We need to
somehow bring Nellie to Jessica when this war is
over. I know how much Nellie misses her, and while
I am happy to bring them together, I will miss
Nellie—as I know you will too.

I sure wish we can achieve victory in short or-
der. Then we would have our dreams to look for-
ward to, wouldn't we? For me, it's returning to the
banking business, and for you, the theater as an
actress.

I am addressing this letter to you at Aunt Jane's
address since I assume you are now living there.
Having not yet received a letter from you, I do not
know your situation, but I hope and pray that eve-
rything is going well for you.

With all my love,

Roger

Roger put his pen down and went back out to look at the
valley below. A thin layer of clouds had formed and obscured
his vision of the town.

He knew that if Rosecrans were still in command of the
Army of the Cumberland, he would not be as concerned. After
all, Rosecrans had suffered a serious loss at Chickamauga, and
some of it was due to his incompetence in causing a gap in his
line that allowed Longstreet to charge through the Union de-
fenses. But General Grant was to be feared. He was a military
man who wasted no time in executing his strategy. Surely he
would take advantage of any weakness that Bragg showed...and
Bragg had certainly showed it by not translating the Chickamauga victory into an aggressive assault on Union fortifications
in Chattanooga.

The clouds below the mountain began to thicken.

Chapter 16

Penelope, holding the envelope with one hand while stirring the stew in the pot with the other, sensed Jessica's curious eyes upon her.

"Did the mail come today?" Jessica asked, placing the johnnycakes on a large plate.

"Yes, it did." Penelope's attention shifted from the envelope to Otto seated at the table. The way he frowned back at her told her not to say anything to Jessica about it. "I had been reading a letter Otto had shared with me." She returned the envelope to her pocket before removing the stew from the burner.

"Anything important?"

Penelope mopped her brow with her sleeve. "Why—ah, no—just business matters, that's all." She moved toward the table and glanced at Jessica. "What did Uncle George say to you in his letter? You mentioned he had written. How did he know where to address it?"

"I must confess that I wrote to him first. When Matt told me he was now with the 31st Ohio, I thought he'd appreciate hearing from his niece—even though he never respected my convictions concerning a woman's role in society."

"As my ex-husband, George never accepted me for who I was either. By the way, did he happen to ask about me?"

"Actually, he apologized for the ignorant way he had behaved because you have negro blood in you. He wished there was some way he could make it up to you for all those wasted years."

Penelope thought a moment. *Wasted years—that was a good way of describing it. He was embarrassed to be seen with me in public. Didn't even want any children for fear they might turn out to be black.*

Penelope ladled the stew into bowls. "Anything else?"

"He also apologized for the cruel way he behaved whenever he'd be with Nellie." Jessica cocked her head in curiosity. "What was he referring to, Penelope? Nellie never mentioned anything about that."

"He'd call her a stupid nigger-girl. And he'd get upset over the smallest things with her—like her insistence on holding his hand when he took a stroll outdoors." Penelope shook her head. "As far as I'm concerned, his apologies aren't worth anything. Did he say anything else?"

"Yes, he described how brutal the Chickamauga campaign was and he assumed he'd now be in Chattanooga—provided he didn't get killed in the meantime."

"My dear wife," Otto said, chuckling, "perchance he is expecting sympathy from you."

"Well, he won't be getting any from me," Penelope said, taking her seat at the table. "Let's change the subject. I would like to talk about you, Jessica."

"Me? About what?"

"You've been working very hard these past few weeks, with all the cleaning, the marketing, the housework, and children. I recall you telling me a while back that you hoped to see 'Catching an Heiress' and 'The Manager's Daughter' appearing at Ford's New Theatre. Since these are playing tonight, perhaps you'd want to take the evening off and go to the performance."

"Thank you, Penelope, but it would be unseemly for a lady like me to go off by herself in the evening."

"Jessica makes an excellent point, you know," Otto said, passing her the johnnycakes. "Perhaps we should all go. The children have never seen a live performance. It would be good for them to have the experience."

Emma's and Mitzi's faces both brightened. "May we go, mama?" Mitzi asked. "I've never seen a play. Neither has Emma."

Emma twisted her mouth with lively curiosity. "What's a play?"

"That's where people pretend they're somebody else," Jessica said. "It is like the time I pretended I was a man and fought in the war. Something similar to that."

Otto laughed. "That was more like an insanity spell rather than a play."

"Well, I don't regret doing it," Jessica said, "and I would do it again."

"May we go to the play?" Mitzi asked again.

Penelope sat down and put the cloth napkin on her lap. "I am very tired this evening, my child. I would not be able to enjoy myself if I did go." She hated saying this because she knew the children wanted her to go. But lately, she became increasingly fatigued. Her work at the Printing Office didn't seem to be that strenuous, but her body ached and all she wanted to do when she came home was relax.

"Otto, why don't you accompany Jessica and the children, and I'll stay home tonight."

"Darling, are you sure?"

"Yes, of course. I have some knitting to do and want to get caught up with my reading."

An hour later, Penelope sat by the window and watched them depart. Jessica appeared to be in good spirits as she walked with Otto to the waiting carriage. The children got in first and Otto assisted Jessica by offering her his hand. She accepted it with a gracious smile, which bothered Penelope. Jessica was never one to accept the assistance of a gentleman when exiting or entering a coach. And her face seemed to glow when Penelope suggested that they go without her.

Don't be absurd, Penelope told herself. Jessica has never given her any reason to suspect there was an amorous relationship between them.

Penelope reached for a copy of yesterday's *Washington Evening Star*. There was an article about how the South was starving. But while it went on about how food shortages would make it a dreary winter for Southerners, the article emphasized the hardships that Union prisoners faced because of the scarcity of food and clothing.

Penelope turned the page to an article about yesterday's great celebration at Gettysburg, which included a parade, music, and speeches. According to the *Star,* the Honorable Edward Everett "delivered an eloquent address," a dirge was sung by the Union Glee Club of Baltimore, and then President Lincoln delivered a dedicatory address. There was no commentary about the President's address, which surprised her, because Lincoln's words appeared to be powerful—especially "It is for we, the living, rather to be dedicated here to the unfinished work that they have thus far so nobly carried on." It made Penelope uncomfortable that she and Otto did not suffer like those poor folks in the South.

She was also struck by the words: "…that we here highly resolve that these dead shall not have died in vain, that this nation, under God, shall have a new birth of freedom."

Freedom made her think of Tinker, because it was all he had talked about when he departed for Fort Leavenworth last August. But now what would become of him?

She reached into her dress pocket for the envelope and removed the letter. It was from an officer with the Second Kansas Colored in Fort Smith Arkansas. Although Otto shared the news with her when he saw her at the Printing Office, he asked her not to tell Jessica about it until he had a chance to talk to her about it himself. He told her he knew Jessica would be terribly upset, and he wanted to prepare her for the shock.

Penelope took a deep breath and read the letter again.

Dear Mr. Heller:

We have had a difficult time reaching someone who might have known one of our missing soldiers, but after a considerable search, we learned that you are acquainted with Private Tinker. We regret to inform you that on October 6 of this year near Fort Blair in Kansas, Private Tinker fought bravely in battle but was now missing in action. One of the wounded men claims he saw Tinker abducted by one of Quantrill's men. Unfortunately, we cannot ascertain whether he was subsequently slain.

We apologize for the delay in delivering this information to you, but we had a hard time in discovering your whereabouts after the devastation of the town of Lawrence where you had formerly resided.

112

Please be assured that we will inform you promptly if we learn further details about Private Tinker's whereabouts.

Sincerely,

J. H. Gilpatrick
Major, 2nd Kansas Colored Infantry

Penelope felt her body stiffen as she read the letter for the second time. *Tinker, you deserve better than this.* Closing her eyes, she thought about that time in Lawrence when she allowed Tinker to hide in the storeroom because he had deserted his regiment. He did not want to face a prison term or a possible hanging. So he hid so he could be free. *Now that you've returned to fight, you've lost your freedom.*

The letter floated to the floor as she sank her head into the palms of her hands. *Mr. President, you referred to "a new birth of freedom" at the Gettysburg cemetery. But at what price?*
*****

Chattanooga, Tennessee

"Please cease saying that I've saved your life," Devin Alcott told Salem, who was holding a drum decorated with a large eagle displaying its wings against a background of stars and stripes. "I did what anyone would have done that day by carrying you off the field and finding you a surgeon."

"Well, I still be grateful to yuh," Salem said.

"I'm delighted you're going to join the band. Lazarus used to play a drum like yours."

"Yeah, dat Lazarus be a good boy from what I hear. Dat Lieutenant Lightfoot say he die a hero, like my brother, Ishmael."

"How have they been training you to use the drum to signal troop movements?"

"I'm learnin' real fast, Devin. Dey meeting me again to go over signals. Looks like maybe they gonna move soon."

113

"I think you're right. After a while you can feel it in your bones, and you just know it's going to happen."

Devin removed his fife from his knapsack and stared for a moment at a ripple of land that loomed ahead. Missionary Ridge. He wondered where it got that name. A missionary was one who spread a new doctrine. Maybe it'd be fitting if they fought there and spread a new doctrine of freedom.

"Wanna play somethin' t'gether?" Salem asked.

"How about 'Just Before The Battle Mother?' It's a great song as you're marching into battle."

"I don't know dat one. How does it go?"

"I'll sing the last part of the song, and then I'll play it." He sucked in some air and sang at the top of his voice:

"Hark! I hear the bugles sounding, 'tis the signal for the fight,
Now, may God protect us, Mother, as He ever does the right.
Hear "The Battle Cry of Freedom," how it swells upon the air,
Oh, yes, we'll rally 'round the standard, or we'll nobly perish
there.

"Farewell, Mother, you may never press me to your breast again;
But, oh, you'll not forget me, Mother, if I'm numbered with the
slain."

A smile broke over his face like a sunrise. "Now here is how it sounds on an instrument. It will sound a lot better than my vocal chords." He put his fife to his mouth and started to play. After a few minutes, Salem tapped his drum—first with hesitation, missing the beat, then playing it better.

"I gots to work on it some more," Salem said.

"Yes, but it does not have to be perfect. When you're out there on the battlefield with bullets flying all around, no one's going to bother to tell you that you didn't do it correctly."

Salem laughed. "Dat's right." He put his drum down. "I wanna ask you somethin'. How come you talk so educated-like? You sound like a college boy."

"I had too much education in Canada. It's not good when you have a lot of book-learning and you fight in this war. You see a lot of mistakes, and you end up wishing you were the one giving the orders instead."

Chapter 17

November 23
Chattanooga, Tennessee

"It appears we are in excellent position to advance," General Ulysses Grant told his aide-de-camp, Lieutenant-Colonel Horace Porter. Grant swept his gaze through his field glasses from the base of Missionary Ridge on the left to Chattanooga Creek on the right. It was all well-fortified and equipped with artillery. Especially Fort Wood, which lay between Chattanooga and Missionary Ridge—where rebels had most of their strength.

"You're correct, sir," Porter said. "Now we just have to wait for the clouds to lift."

"That is one thing we can't control," Grant said with a slight smile. But he hoped to control the outcome of this battle. He had his men in place, as planned. Sheridan's and Wood's divisions had formed their line at the foot of Fort Wood. Palmer, with the XIV Corps, southwest of that line, supported Sheridan with a division and had another division under Johnson—hidden well in the trenches. It was like a chess game, with the pieces lined up, knowing your strategy up front, but realizing it might have to change if he threatens you. The only way to win this one, however, was to divide and conquer.

He dreamt about his wife Julia again last night. She was back in Galena, Illinois, begging him not to go when she heard about the Fort Sumter attack. "What about your children? What about me?" President Lincoln was there, waiting for him in the coach, calling for him. Grant joined the President and some other men in the carriage. A burst of gunfire. One of the men slumped over. "Dear God," Julia screamed. "They killed him!"

Grant awoke in a cold sweat from that dream. If it was a foretelling of his death, he was not afraid of it. Dying was a part of living. But he feared what it would do to Julia. She followed

116

him in most of these battles, remaining safely near the scene of action. She had always talked about how she wanted her life to be one long summer of sunshine, flowers, and smiles. But she did not understand this war. And she would not be able to live with herself if he failed to survive this conflict.

He searched in darkness for a partly-full bottle of brandy in his tent. He finished it before the sun rose in the morning.

"The clouds have lifted!" Porter yelled.

"They have indeed," Grant replied. "Our sacred duty has begun."

The booming of cannons from Fort Wood and other points on the line signaled the start of the advance. Rebel pickets fell back upon the main guards. The first cries of death from musketry fire arose.

Grant surveyed Orchard Knob, bursting with gunfire. "May God be with us today."

*****

At the sound of the bugle, the picket line of the Eighth Kansas advanced quickly toward Orchard Knob. Matt saw it was a circular mound with a line of rebel breastworks running over it. It was nothing more than an isolated hill that lie between Chattanooga and Missionary Ridge, but apparently the brigade commander did not think he was likely to overtake it. Orders were for the Eighth to serve as a reconnaissance mission—to engage the rebels in battle, to learn the strength of their force, and to await the arrival of the main line of battle.

A swirl of activity changed all that. As more troops from the Union divisions formed in front of the breastworks, Captain Conover ordered his men to help distribute a fresh supply of ammunition. Matt had been worried about running out of ammunition as he thought it would have been impossible to resort to bayonets, with the rebels so firmly entrenched in their breastworks.

As he wondered when the main line of battle would come to Orchard Knob, he heard Captain Conover screaming at him. "Lightfoot! Assist the other companies in doubling the picket reserves on the skirmish lines."

117

Matt rounded up his men to the advanced skirmish lines and was astounded at the size of the Union lines now fronting what he had previously thought was an insignificant hill. *Was this going to be the main line of battle? I thought the plan all along was to capture Missionary Ridge.*

The brigade bugle sounded. Several officers in the distance yelled "Forward!" and the regiment bugles all responded in turn.

*****

Being in the rear, Devin Alcott could not see the breastworks, although he knew from a study of the topography that they were approaching Orchard Knob. "Salem," he said to the drummer next to him, "be ready to pound that drum when the bugle sounds. Don't worry about getting the beat right."

Salem looked too nervous to smile. "Yeah, Devin, I do dat."

"Don't let yourself get scared, Salem. Trust in the Lord."

"I do trust in da Lord, but I don't know if He hear me sometimes."

"With all the noise we're making, He hears us all right."

The brigade bugle sounded, and Devin did not even wait for the regiment bugle to follow suit. He began playing "Just Before The Battle Mother" and glanced over to Salem, staring straight ahead and who still held his drumsticks rigidly.

"Salem!"

Salem quickly glanced to his left at Devin and began to beat his drum, unevenly at first, not at all in tune with the melody. But as the troops marched briskly, and as the flag bearer ahead yelled "Chickamauga, Chickamauga!" Salem got in tune.

The troops were now yelling, screaming like demons, rushing toward the scene of action. Devin and Salem rushed with them.

Devin ran, puffing, his heart racing, too out of breath now to carry a tune. But as Salem ran alongside him beating the drum, Devin gave him a thumbs up.

Salem grinned and pounded his drum even harder.

118

*****

General Braxton Bragg knew he'd slaughter the Federals if they dared to make an advance against Missionary Ridge. The rugged, natural features of the ridge would certainly deter them from making a direct assault, and he saw no need for constructing defensive positions on the heights.

He wished the other generals who served under him, especially Polk and Longstreet, would show proper respect for his orders and did not threaten to countermand them. After all, he had a distinguished career in the Mexican War and showed considerable success at Shiloh and Chickamauga, did he not? He knew these Yankees. They would retreat like whipped dogs once they realized they faced insurmountable odds in trying to climb the ridge or scale the mountain. What his fellow officers did not realize was the advantage of time. Let those foolish Northerners make their mistakes so he could take advantage of them.

But what was happening now on Orchard Knob? He looked again through his field glasses. Earlier, it appeared that Union troops had marched out and formed in a line of battle. *Those foolish Yankees were engaged in another worthless parade.*

Suddenly they opened a volley upon the Confederate pickets and began their charge with whoops and yells.

"What in blazes is happening?" Bragg shouted to Major General John Breckenridge. "What are those fools doing down there?"

"Looks like a frontal assault on two of our Alabama regiments, sir."

"For that worthless piece of land? For that trivial, insignificant hill?" Bragg searched through his field glasses, looking for the whereabouts of General Anderson. "Where the hell is our commander for Hindman's Division?"

"Don't know, sir."

"We only have about six or seven hundred men down there. They have thousands."

119

"Nothing we can do about that, sir. Too late to send for reinforcements. Perhaps Anderson should order Manigault, the brigade commander, to retreat."

"It's hopeless!" Bragg screamed, placing his hand on his forehead. The migraine headache he had experienced earlier had suddenly returned.

*****

Matt felt foolish giving the Sunday sermon yesterday to General Willich's brigade. What a hypocrite he was, preaching about morality when he, himself, did not abide by God's laws. It was appropriate that it rained that day, because he felt like crying to the Lord to forgive him. Those sensual desires he had for Mary gave him comfort while he was in the field hospital. There was nothing around him but pain and suffering, and at the time he convinced himself that the Lord would not deny him a few pleasures of the mind, imaging what it would be like if he could be close to her.

The regimental bugle sounded, and it took a few seconds for Matt to realize he was in a battle zone. "Lightfoot!" Colonel Martin snapped. "Don't delay. Engage your men immediately to move further up toward the breastworks."

"I will, sir," Matt replied. He waved on the men and they charged toward the rebel pickets, shouting "Remember Chickamauga!" while loading and firing as rapidly as possible. Matt followed men from the 35th Illinois toward the rebel rifle pits. Some of the Confederates died where they were, others dropped their weapons and ran for Missionary Ridge. One of the rebels tripped over a fallen log and Matt rushed toward him, Matt's carbine pointing at the man's head. The rebel, lying on his back, his eyes bulging with fright looked up at Matt. "Don't take me prisoner," the soldier said, his voice trembling. "Mah two brothers died in one o' your stinkin' prisons. Just shoot me. Ah don't care."

Matt cocked his rifle.

Chapter 18

"I'm already drowning in paper," Otto told Superintendent Defrees at the Printing Office. "Now you are telling me to begin preparation for *The Congressional Globe.*"

"I'm sorry," Defrees said with an understanding smile, "but blame the 28th Congress for that."

Otto figured there was no point in complaining. Congress needed to have its official proceedings published. Which would have been fine if he had no other obligations. But work on *The Congressional Globe* would be in addition to his other duties in the collection, typesetting, and printing of other Senate and House documents, the executive and judicial departments, and the Court of Claims.

The Federal government is one huge paper mill. Maybe the South will win the war just by observing us sinking into a sea of paper.

"Meet me in my office in an hour," Defrees later told him. "I received some excellent news and have cause for celebration."

Shortly afterwards, Otto opened the door to the superintendent's walnut-finished office and saw five men engaged in conversation. The managers of the press, composing, binding, and folding room ceased their excited chatter when Defrees caught Otto's attention.

"Join us, Mr. Heller," Defrees said, his face blossoming into a huge grin. "As I have already informed the others, I received this off the telegraph wires last evening," he explained, holding an announcement in his hands. "We gave the Confederates quite a scare yesterday afternoon, winning a victory at Orchard Knob in Tennessee. Grant made it his headquarters as he contemplated his next move toward Lookout Mountain and Missionary Ridge." He nodded to a servant at the doorway, who brought in a tray of glasses and a bottle of port wine.

"This is cause for celebration," he said, smiling as Otto and the others helped themselves to a glass of wine. Defrees raised his glass. "A toast to Chattanooga. May our victory there erase the memory of Chickamauga forever!"

*****

The next day
31ˢᵗ Ohio Infantry
Chattanooga, Tennessee

Major George Radford felt like a slab of ice when he awoke at sunup, even though he slept in his wool uniform. Shivering outside his tent, he waited impatiently for his coffee to heat up.

A whippoorwill chirped its melodic up-and-down chant soon after the major began thinking about his niece Jessica. He laughed to himself as he recalled the folklore attached to that bird call—that an unmarried woman who heard just one call of the whippoorwill meant that she would not get married for a year. From what Jessica said in her letter about her weighing the possibility of marrying Matt, maybe that bird was telling George it would be a while before Jessica allowed herself to be wed. He hoped the superstition was wrong. Jessica needed a man to settle down and quit trying to do things that only men should do—like running businesses or fighting wars.

His letter was still in his haversack, and he hoped Jessica would share it with his ex-wife Penelope, who might be surprised by the secret he revealed to her. *Sometimes we do a certain thing because it's the right thing to do.*

A bugle sounding reveille brought George back to the present reality of the pending battle. He took a swallow of coffee and tossed the rest out before hastening to his tent.

He slipped on his haversack, checked his cartridge box, and grabbed his Henry repeating rifle, holding the .52 caliber weapon like a welcome companion. He could fire six aimed shots with it before a rebel armed with a musket could fire off a single one. It helped him get through the Chickamauga

122

campaign unscathed, and it would certainly be his best friend at the base of the ridge this morning.

He hoped the Army of the Cumberland would be able to continue their momentum from yesterday. General Hooker had easily repulsed General Stevenson's Confederate troops at the north slope of Lookout Mountain. Today would be different, however. General Bragg's men were strongly entrenched above formidable Missionary Ridge, and it would take a miracle for the Union to overtake it. If the Union was fortunate, they might succeed in securing the base of the ridge, but what then? The rebels could pin them down from above. What could Generals Thomas and Grant possibly have in mind?

Radford was thankful he was not a general. "I'm just going to kill me some more rebels," he said to himself as he rushed out of his tent to assist the captain with roll call. Minutes later, he joined Lieutenant Colonel Frederick Lister, his commander, to coordinate the planned attack on the rebel breastworks at the bottom of Missionary Ridge.

With Colonel Lister by his side, Major Radford called the troops together. "The breastworks are yonder," he shouted, pointing toward Missionary Ridge. "That's our target. The rebels have the ridge heavily fortified, so we stop at the breastworks and clear the rebels out of there. Buglers will direct our positions as we advance. Understand?"

The colonel gave the official order: "Forward Thirty-first." The men, moving in even rows, yelled back: "Charge! Onward! Get them yellow dogs!" As they moved forward, their steeled faces were resolute in their pursuit, their relentless quick-time pace moved like a river, and their bayoneted muskets and rifles stabbed the sky toward the ridge in the distance.

Union cannons boomed from Orchard Knob as the Thirty-first Ohio followed two assault lines in the direction of the Confederate breastworks. Return fire from the rebels was relentless.

It would be more difficult to advance than Major Radford thought. He had not gone more than fifty yards when rebel firing from the breastworks intensified. It would be a foot at a time all day, he thought, as he moved a little and stopped, moved a little more and stopped.

A group of some twenty soldiers reached the rebel breastworks at the foot of the summit to Mountain Ridge. Leading the charge was a corporal who carried the colors of the Thirty-First. The Union soldiers ahead of Major Radford gave a yell as they leaped into the trenches. A shell exploded at the color bearer, but a private leaped up, preventing the flag from touching the ground.

George Radford's heart pounded like the brutal beating of a battle drum. Death. The smell of it was acrid gunpowder. The sight of it was blood splattering the blue jerseys of his fellow soldiers. George trembled and murmured the refrain to the Battle Hymn:

> *"Glory! Glory! Hallelujah! Glory! Glory! Hallelujah!*
> *Glory! Glory! Hallelujah! His truth is marching on."*

Someone once told him the music kept him from forgetting his fears and remembering what he was here for. *His truth is marching on. His truth is marching on.*

George shouted as he jumped into the trenches. Others in his regiment did the same. The rebels were there with fixed bayonets. Behind those Confederates were other rebels on higher ground aiming their weapons at different regiments from the Army of the Cumberland who now charged.

Enemy cannons boomed from the ridge high above, but their shots sailed well over everyone's heads. At the breastworks, grunts of anger...deep moans of pain...cussing...a scream from a soldier shot in the face by a Minié ball.

A Confederate battery to the left swarmed toward the Thirty-first. A new round of fire ensued. George felt a pain in his left arm, but kept charging. He and the others in his regiment pushed the rebels beyond the breastworks.

George looked down at his arm and thought it was curious that his sleeve was soaked with blood. "Don't feel a damned thing," he muttered.

He was still staring at it when he felt one sharp pain in his chest, followed quickly by another. As his body crashed to the hard, cold soil he thought he saw the face of someone he knew.

"Forgive me, Penelope," he whispered before he closed his eyes forever.

*****

The men of the Army of the Cumberland were like savages, cursing, guns blazing, their eyes flashing with demonic fury as they charged the rifle pits. Lieutenant Roger Toby, on Missionary Ridge, blinked in disbelief at their ferocity.

His pulsed quickened. *Victory was at hand.* "Rush on, get 'em, yaw laggards," Roger yelled at the Confederates nearest him. He ran down the slope of the ridge waving on the others to do the same. But as he watched his men hide behind trees and commence firing, Roger's finger froze at the trigger.

"Damn yaw, Lightfoot," he murmured. "Yaw no blood brother of mine."

But he was. Because of Nellie, damn it, they were almost like blood brothers. And Roger had almost killed his brother.

Routine. This is supposed to be routine. "Like doing a drill," a major once told him. "Once you've gone through the training shooting at rocks, you do it again, shooting at the enemy. Routine."

Roger loaded his weapon and took aim. He had a job to do. Forget Lightfoot.

That damn music filtered through his ears and his hands shook. Someone in the band was playing "The Bonnie Blue Flag."

Hurrah! Hurrah! For Southern rights hurrah!
Hurrah for the Bonnie Blue Flag that bears a single star.

Stop it! It reminded him too much of Sara. An outdoor band had played that Southern fighting song back in February of 1861, in Columbia, her home town. They were newlyweds, kissing as they sat on the grass, staring at the bonnie blue flag of South

125

Carolina waving in the breeze. He wanted independence from the Union as much as she did. But he forgot about the price.

He took careful aim at the Union men below.

> *First gallant South Carolina nobly made the stand,*
> *Then came Alabama, who took her by the hand;*
> *Next quickly Mississippi, Georgia and Florida,*
> *All raised on high the Bonnie Blue Flag that bears a*
> *single star.*

The voice returned to chide him…

— Never forget, Roger, that you're fighting for the independence your people so richly deserve.

Roger looked into the far distance and rotated his head from side to side, as if to shake the voice away…..

> *Hurrah! Hurrah! For Southern rights hurrah!*
> *Hurrah for the Bonnie Blue Flag that bears a single*
> *star.*

Roger hummed the sweet music that brought him back to South Carolina. But then the voice returned, demanding an answer…

—You're part of the fighting machine, are you not?
— But what about that boy reaching for his handkerchief?
— Casualty of war. That's all, lieutenant.
— And what about my "blood brother" Matt Lightfoot?
— Stop it! You are part of the Confederate Fighting Machine.

He turned his attention to the bottom of the ridge and began firing. He had a mission to do and his hallucinations were just getting in the way of accomplishing it.

*****

While he waited for orders after forming a line of battle, Matt wondered if that frightened rebel he could have killed

126

was now in the process of killing someone else. But Matt knew why he had to let him go. He knew what it was like to experience raw fear. In an earlier battle, he had begged another Cherokee soldier for mercy…and received it.

Colonel Martin waved his sword in the air after the buglers in General Willich's brigade gave the signal to advance. Union cannon fire exploded, ripping through the sky, whitish-gray smoke rolling like thunder. The enemy reciprocated in kind, and Lieutenant Lightfoot waved his men on toward the breastworks. "Double-quick time, boys!" he yelled, running in zigzag fashion toward the rifle pits near the foot of the bridge.

He glanced to his right and saw a negro racing alongside, a fife in his left hand and a carbine slung over his right shoulder. "Soldier," Matt asked, panting, "don't I know you from somewhere?"

"Yessuh. Salem, suh."

The name Salem hung in Matt's mind as he dropped to the ground to load his weapon. He knew that man from somewhere, but where? It did not matter. He pushed himself up and ran further, fell to one knee, fired, and ran again. All the while, the negro had kept pace with him, playing the "Battle Cry of Freedom." Behind him a boy rat-tat-tatted his drum and an older man carried the colors of the regiment.

Matt soon lost sight of the band as the men from different regiments in the brigade dissolved into a large body of fighters. The Forty-ninth Ohio…Thirty-fifth Illinois…Sixty-eighth Indiana…Fifteenth Wisconsin…Eighth Kansas. They were all one now, pursuing the rifle pits, dislodging the enemy in hand-to-hand combat. Some of the enemy took flight. Matt refrained from shooting them in the back, but others in the brigade had no such reluctance. Matt would have preferred to take them prisoners, but how would that happen? The enemy was up on the ridge, looking down at them, like peasant hunters waiting for birds to rise for the kill. If the brigade retreated to their former positions, they would certainly be visible targets.

This was a dilemma. What did the grand plan call for once the foot of the ridge was secured? They could hold for reinforcements, but what good would that do? They would still be down here, looking up at the enemy.

While Matt awaited further orders, cries of "Remember Chickamauga" went up from a number of the enlisted men. They immediately began climbing up the ridge, first just a few of them, and more after that, and more after that. The side of the ridge was alive with Union skirmishers climbing their way up, moving from tree to tree, screaming "Chickamauga." Their yells sliced through the air, heavily laden now with gunsmoke and cannon fire.

"What the hell is going on?" Matt said aloud. "Who gave the insane order to climb up the ridge?"

Failing to get anyone's attention, Matt looked about and saw Colonel Martin gazing up at the ridge, a look of disbelief apparent in his eyes. *Were the men acting entirely on their own?*

Amid the shouts, Matt heard that music again. A fife and drum played "Battle Cry of Freedom," and Matt searched for the source. There he was—that negro boy he had seen earlier. The boy's eyes met Matt's, and he stopped playing long enough to smile back at him.

Matt knew that boy from somewhere. He wished he had time to explore his memory. Moving up ahead, allowing others to rush past him in their eagerness to overtake the enemy, Matt gazed in wonder at the troops and how they took it upon themselves to make the climb. Perhaps this was their only recourse. They could not have stayed down here for long, trapped between the mountain and the open field. But the rebels atop the ridge would not be able to lower their cannons any further, so perhaps the only sensible direction for these Federals was to the top, to meet the enemy head on.

The "Battle Hymn" continued to play. Matt knew the words well. *While we rally 'round the flag, boys, rally once again, shouting the Battle Cry of Freedom.*

The fife ceased playing in the middle of the chorus. All that could be heard now were the victorious shouts of the charging Army of the Cumberland and the explosion of musketry.

Matt stopped and looked to the rear. There were several men down, but there was one boy in particular that caught his attention. It was that same boy—that colored fifer.

After dropping down to one knee, Matt put his face close to the boy's. "Salem!"

Salem stirred, his sad eyes trained on Matt's. "I die a hero. Like mah brother."

"Your brother?"

"Ishmael."

Ishmael? Matt knew Ishmael and did not need to search his memory to recall that tall slave hung for crimes...

Before Ishmael was about to be executed by the Union military, he had pleaded with Matt. "I don' want my brother Salem to know the bad thing I done."

"I'll come up with somethin' to tell him," Matt said. "I'll ask my commanding officer not to reveal anything about this to him."

"I shore 'preciate that, Reverend. I want yuh tah give him mah rifle." He pointed toward the corner of the tent. "It be there with mah other things."

Groaning, Salem lifted himself up, his lips quivering. His moist eyes were dark pebbles of sadness as he handed Matt his rifle. "I not need this no more."

"Hang on," Matt said. "I'll try to find a surgeon."

"No, suh. You take this here gun."

Salem closed his eyes. A curious smile encircled his dead face, as if he had gotten his wish to die like a hero.

Matt held Salem's rifle in his hands and saw the engraving on the stock: FREDUM. Trembling, Matt opened his own haversack and removed a framed daugerotype Jessica had once given him.

He grasped Salem's lifeless hand and bent its fingers over the picture of John Brown.

Chapter 19

Jessica told the coachman not to wait for her. As he rode off, the horses' clip-clopping beat a steady rhythm through an overcast and cold Sunday morning. With a hand clutching her valise, she walked briskly toward the end of Seventh Street. Mr. Heller told her that the gentleman she sought might be there at the Campbell Hospital at the north end of the city, as he had been spending many hours there. But there was no guarantee.

It didn't matter to her. If he wasn't there, she would find an inn where she could warm herself and read her poetry. Or perhaps she'd read the newspaper, although she had already learned about the Union victory in Chattanooga. The news failed to elate her, as it would have given her satisfaction only if the victory would have assured her that this dreary, long war was finally drawing quickly to an end.

She wondered if her recent acquaintance Kate Chase Sprague, was right about Lincoln's inability to bring the war to a rapid close.

"Mr. Lincoln is a stubborn fool," Kate had said a while ago. "He believes he could pacify the South by offering them a general amnesty if they would surrender. The President ought not be so close-minded and obstinate regarding the need for total Confederate surrender. I believe my father is far more qualified for that office. Salmon helped get the Republican Party motivated, went on to establish an effective banking system, and even gave Mr. Lincoln sound military advice. If anyone ought to be President during these dire times, it ought to be Salmon Chase, do you not agree?"

Wanting no part of politics, Jessica pretended to agree with her. What she really hoped to find was someone who was likeminded as herself, who believed in the colorful tapestry of words for their own sake.

130

Jessica hoped that the gentleman she sought was here to-day. She had a lot to share with him.

She walked briskly toward the military hospital, a collection of long, narrow buildings constructed of rough boards. As she came closer, she saw a smaller building off to one side that had said "Administration Office" on it and headed in that direction. Just as she was about to open the door, a man dressed in a major's uniform exited.

"May I be of assistance, ma'am?"

"Yes. I am looking for a gentleman who frequently visits here. His name is Whitman. Walt Whitman."

The major pondered for a moment and directed her to a center building, which served as a dining room and kitchen. When she arrived there, she saw Mr. Whitman seated at a table with a mug of coffee and writing. He looked no different than he did when she saw him last. His beard was longer, but his blackish gray hair was still unkempt. He also appeared a bit uncomfortable with the azure neck cloth he wore with his faded blue shirt.

His attention remained on his writing as she stood across from him in the otherwise empty room. She had to ahem twice before she caught his attention.

Squinting at her as if the sun was in his eyes, he looked puzzled. "Do I know you?"

She placed her valise on the table. "We met back in September. Mr. Heller introduced me to you."

"Oh yes, I remember. You have aspirations to be a writer. Would you have a seat?"

She placed her valise on the bench and sat next to it. He resumed scribbling.

"A poem of yours?" she asked.

"I beg your pardon."

"Were you writing a poem just now?"

"I had some preliminary thoughts on one. Would you mind if I read what I have so far?"

"I would be delighted."

He looked down at his paper and cleared his throat. "Aroused and angry," he began, "I thought to beat the alarum,

131

and urge relentless war." He paused, looked at her for a moment, and continued: "But soon my fingers failed me, my face drooped, and I resigned myself…" He took a deep breath and sighed. "…to sit by the wounded and soothe them, or silently watch the dead."

There was more written on his paper, but he flipped it over. "I could not have written that three years ago. What I have seen here and at other hospitals sickens me to the core of my soul, and I had to express my disgust in words. Even then, I don't know if I painted my grief accurately." He closed his eyes for a long moment, and Jessica felt uncomfortable by the silence.

He opened his eyes and appeared disoriented for a moment as he stared back at her. "What circumstances have come about to bring you, Miss…Miss…? I apologize; I seem to have forgotten your name."

"Miss Radford. Jessica Radford. I came because I had completed several different poems, and I wanted to learn what you thought of them. I cannot tell you how much you have inspired me with *Leaves of Grass*, and I—"

"What sort of poetry have you written?"

"Oh, on various subjects." She opened her valise and removed a sheath of papers. "Here is one I wrote about the sunrise. And here are others I've written about a child's wonderment concerning a flower in bloom and how a book opens new adventures to us. Which one would you like to hear me read?"

"None of them."

Jessica drew back, her mouth open in disbelief.

Whitman leaned forward. "What else have you written?"

"Well, I have a portion of my novel. It's called *A Slave Only Once*. I had been working on it during my carriage ride here. Are you interested in hearing about it?"

"What is your novel about?"

Jessica, not expecting Mr. Whitman to ask about her novel, hastened to put her thoughts together. "Well, it's about a slave girl who grows up and finds hostility among white people, even after she becomes free. I'm thinking it could be the

132

first of two books. In the second novel, she gets an education, marries a former slave, rises to power, and fights for others against this racial bias. Yet, she is still disliked—even more so now that she is influential."

"Why did you write *A Slave Only Once?*"

"Because I've seen the tragedy of slavery. My parents, before they were murdered, adopted a little negro girl who was brought to our door by a man with the Underground Railroad. I've also felt the pain of a former slave, a man named Tinker who fought for the Union because he wanted to free others and now, after engaging in battle, he is missing—perhaps even dead." Jessica took out her handkerchief and dabbed her eyes.

"So your novel serves as a template for your own life?"

"Of course not." *Doesn't Mr. Whitman fail to understand that it's not about me? It's about people like Nellie and Tinker.*

Whitman closed his eyes for a brief moment, and when he returned his gaze, his lips curled into a slight smile. "Which of these do you feel most passionate about—a sunrise, a flower, a book, or slavery.?"

Jessica was surprised at the question. "I don't understand what you mean, Mr. Whitman."

"I mentioned to you earlier that I could never have started this piece I am now writing about the wounded and dying if I had not personally experienced the immense pain these men had suffered. You, apparently, have experienced the pain that these slaves have endured."

"I see what you mean."

"Shall I imply by that your decision then is to write about the evils of slavery?"

"Yes, but I want to do more than just write about it."

"You can, you know. Perhaps you can join an anti-slavery organization and give lectures to make others aware of the inhumanity of slavery."

"I don't think women would be accepted as public speakers."

"It doesn't matter. In *Leaves of Grass* I've written 'I am the poet of the woman the same as the man, and I say it is as great to be a woman as a man.'"

133

"That may sound noble as a poem, Mr. Whitman, but it bears no semblance to reality."

Whitman leaned back in his chair and dissected her with his intense stare. "Mr. Heller informed me that you actually fought in the war as a man and risked your life. Now here you are, telling me that what I wrote bears no semblance to reality?"

Jessica felt her face warm from embarrassment. "But I wouldn't even know how to go about—" She stopped herself short. Maybe she would find out. The image of Kate Chase had just come to mind. If anyone would know how to go about doing anything, it would be Kate.

Mr. Whitman rose from his seat. "I must excuse myself, Miss Radford. There are many ill and wounded men I need to attend to this morning."

After he left, she thought about his suggestion. She would have to do more than *write* her passion. She would have to *speak* it as well.

*****

The next day
Leeburn, Georgia

"Dey got me workin' by mxin' up gunpowder," Joshua told him in the dining hall of Myers Munitions Works. "I hates dat. It gets in the air and you gots to breathe it all da livelong day. Sometimes I thinks if'n I's ever to smoke me some 'baccy, I would light up like a damn firecracker." His yellow teeth flashed as he laughed. "You sho'nuff lucky dey got you workin' yonder in da storage bunker."

"I doan feel so damn lucky," Tinker said, feeling his muscles tense at the injustice of it all. "Doan yah know Lincoln freed slaves in da South with dat there Emancipation Proclamation? You free. I free. We all free."

Joshua laughed. "Dat don' mean nuttin' heah. Why would Massa make us free? Lincoln ain't his boss."

"Not right. Jest not right. I be a free man."

"You gots papers, Zeke?"

134

"My name not Zeke. Slave mastah give me dat name. My name is Tinker."

"Don' matter a whit what yer given name is. If dey wansta call you Zeke, dat's what dey gwine call you."

Tinker shook his head. "I jest want out o' here. Dat's all."

"Like I say, if'n you's got dem papers showin' dat you is free, dass all you gwine need."

"I didn't have 'em with me at da time. Dey be in my haversack."

"Well, dem sojers can't take you as a slave if'n you is free."

"It wasn't soldiers who done take me. It was bushwhackers like Quantrill."

"Don' know dat name," Joshua said, cocking his head to one side. "You don't sound like you from Georgia. Whereabouts you hail from?"

"Kansas. I be a free man, and I shouldn't be here at all." He took his time eating his potato. "Dese here rebels, they come and steal me away from the battlefield."

Joshua's large brown eyes widened. "Oh, you a sojer?"

"Yessuh, a Yankee. Been fightin' at Fort Blair in Kansas back in October. Dey come'n steal me away to Atlanta and put me on da auction block. The mastah who buy me say I be da strongest buck he done ever see. Well, I only be on his plantation for a month when da rebel troopers, well dey come by and offer him a bounty so's I can work outside da plantation."

"So dey done bring you here?"

"Yeah. They tell me da 'federacy needs me to work in dis here munitions plant. Dat's how I got here." Tinker bent over to whisper into Joshua's ear. "But I ain't plannin' on stayin' here none either."

"Can't escape from here," Joshua said, lowering his voice. "Dey got dogs dat hunt you down. When dey bring you back, dey make life hard fer you. Once they kill a darkie climbin' the fence. Left his body hang dere over da fence for two days so we kin all see it. Made him an example."

Tinker thought about this in the evening when he entered the barn to sleep with the other slaves. With this being a military unit, with those fences, and the guard dogs, and the soldiers with

135

weapons-it would be a lot harder to escape from this place.

But so what? He wasn't afraid to die, although he could remember how his father had warned him: "Die smart; don't die stupid."

This wasn't dyin' stupid. He'd be risking his life for the cause of freedom. His only regret was that he would not be holding Charlotte in his dying arms if it came to that.

Dying only good if da woman yuh love be by yer side.

*****

Washington, DC

When two military couriers arrived at the Heller house while she was teaching mathematics to the children, Jessica felt the blood drain from her face. "Are you Miss Jessica Radford?" one of the men asked, in a cool, military-like tone of voice.

She shook her head, unable to speak.

"Telegram from the United States Army," he answered, handing it to her.

After she closed the door, her hand shook as she held the telegram. The anger screamed in her head—*Matt Lightfoot! I had warned you about reenlisting.*

Emma ran over to her, tugging at Jessica's dress. "Miss Radford, aren't you going to open it up?"

"Don't you want to see what it is?" chimed in Mitzi.

"No," she answered. "Not right now."

She dropped the envelope on the table, too ill to open it.

Chapter 20

December 5

Dear Ms. Radford,

    Pardon me for my effrontery in writing to you without having previously been acquainted, but I feel compelled to introduce myself. I am the spouse of Roger Toby, who is currently serving with the Army of Tennessee. My husband wrote that he had encountered a Union nurse named Mary Delaney and a lieutenant named Matt Lightfoot with the Eighth Kansas on the eve of a battle near Chickamauga, Georgia. Roger noticed the lieutenant wore a curious medallion about his neck, and upon closer examination, saw it was the same medal that Nellie once owned. She is living with us not as a slave but as a free woman, and she talks about you all the time. Perhaps there is some way that we can meet so I can bring Nellie over to you. Given this war, it would be difficult for me to do this, but perhaps we can remain in communication nonetheless.

    While Roger and I have lived our entire married life in Chattanooga, I had to abandon it and take Nellie with me to Atlanta. Thus I left my beloved home prior to the unwarranted Federal occupation and am now residing with my aunt. You may be able to reach me here in Atlanta at the address I've posted on this envelope.

    I trust that this is your correct address, which Miss Delaney had provided me through her talk with Roger. When you are able, I would appreciate hearing from you further on this matter.

Sincerely,

Mrs. Sara Toby

Jessica folded the letter hurriedly and put a finger to her moist eye. *Oh Nellie!* She took a deep breath. *Nellie, dear Nellie, at least I know you are safe in Atlanta.*

Even before this letter arrived, Jessica knew Nellie was living with the Toby family because she had gone through the wounded lieutenant's haversack. There, she had discovered a letter indicating that Nellie was alive and living with him and his wife Sara. Ever since then, Jessica knew Nellie was safe, but until now, she didn't know how to reach her. Now she had an address.

But how was it possible to see her now? There was a huge gulf between them. A wall that sliced the nation with angry men on each side who were willing to kill each other for the sake of "honor" and "country."

*****

"I've lost weight," Penelope admitted as Jessica helped lace her corset, "but I think working long hours reduced my appetite for food."

"Why even bother with a corset," Jessica asked, "if you and I are simply going to the market this morning?"

"Mr. Heller is taking me to a piano recital when he returns from work today, and I don't wish to change again."

"Well, getting as thin as you are you won't even need that silly corset. Anyway, I'll meet you downstairs while you finish dressing," Jessica said. "You'll want to wear your cape and gloves. It's quite chilly outside."

After Jessica left, Penelope wasted no time in dressing. She had hoped Jessica would not have said anything about losing weight. There was a problem, Penelope was sure of it, but she did not want to worry Otto about seeing a doctor to discover why. It was not only her weight loss but she noticed she became increasingly exhausted at the end of each day.

The snow fell in large clumps as Jessica accompanied her to the stable next to the house. "I enjoy snow," Penelope said, somewhat out of breath, "but I only appreciate watching it through a window and not lumbering through it. If Mr. Heller

138

were not consumed with all of that printing concerning the official proceedings of Congress, I would have had him help me with my other chores."

"Does he enjoy his line of work?"

"He never told me he disliked it. But I suspect that some-day he'll want to have his own publishing company again."

"Would you want me to hold the reins?" Jessica asked, when they came to the carriage.

"Yes," she said, chuckling, "I'll just sit next to you and complain about the weather."

As they made a turn toward "H" Street, four Union officers on horseback slowed to allow a passerby to cross.

"I hope," Penelope said, "that these soldiers aren't on their way to deliver some person tragic news about a loved one."

"I feel the same." After a moment, she added, "I suppose you feel it was impudent of me to be delighted to learn that the telegram I received was about my uncle's death rather than Mr. Lightfoot."

Penelope shrugged. "Not at all."

"I do feel badly about Uncle George. Never thought about him being killed in the war."

"George Radford was a good man, in a way. He just never understood how to make a wife happy."

"Although," Jessica added, "he did show an amazing act of kindness in that final letter he had sent you."

"You mean about having arranged to donate all of most of his assets to Nellie? Yes, I suppose so."

Jessica placed a thoughtful finger to her chin. "Why do you suppose he did that? He never cared about Nellie."

"And he did mention to me once that he didn't under-stand why your family would adopt a negro child as their own daughter."

Jessica frowned. "But then why would he want to name Nellie in his will?"

Penelope thought about all those times during her marriage to George when he exhibited his disdain for negroes. Knowing she was mulatto, he told her of his concern that their children might be born black. Maybe he had a premonition about his

139

death and wanted to change his legacy by giving most of what he owned to a young black lady.

"I guess we'll never know," Penelope answered.

*****

As executor to her uncle's will, Jessica knew she needed to see an attorney, but with the war still on, it would be difficult to bring Nellie to Washington. But why mention any of this to Sara? It would be so much better to give Nellie the good news in person—when she saw her again. Maybe when this war was over, she would have a grand reunion not only with Nellie, but with Matt, Mary, and all her friends.

Matt! She wished she had not written that earlier letter to him. What was she thinking? She felt like one of her characters in the novel she had written—unable to make up her mind. Wanting to be understood had less to do with him than it did with herself. She did not want to rule out the possibility of marriage, and she regretted not telling him that she simply needed more time.

Returning to the letter she began writing, Jessica went on—

Matt, I hope this reaches you in time. I regret that previous letter I had sent you telling you I have no desire to marry you. That was foolish patter on my part. I only wrote it because I had been angry with you for reenlisting without consulting with me first. And I had harbored the awful thought that perhaps you were still in love with Mary. I should have torn up that letter and never sent it. I don't mean any of those things I said, my darling.

I received a telegram from the military that gave me quite a fright, as I naturally assumed it bore tragic news about you. Of course, it is heartrending that my Uncle George was killed in action, and I do grieve over his loss. But in a way, it was fortunate that I assumed the worst about you, because it made me realize how much I do miss you, and it would cause me undue

140

anguish to realize that you were yet another victim of this diabolical war.

I think of you quite often, Matt. I hope that you have not changed your mind about seeing me again. My feelings for you are tender, and it is my fondest wish that you visit me at Christmas so we can rekindle all of those joyous moments we've shared in the past. I wish you were here in my presence rather than in my imagination as I write this letter. Again, please tear up that previous letter I had written you. I deeply regret ever having written it.

Thank you for all your tenderness and care, and I remain yours affectionately,

Jessica Radford

*****

December 8
Chattanooga, Tennessee

"I really must return to my tent," Mary said. "If anyone sees us together like this, sitting on the bank of the river and looking at the moonlight, there might be talk."

Matt held a stick in his hands as he watched the moon rippling like a pale yellow bed sheet over the water's surface. "Well, I don't give a cotton to what people say anymore. I asked you here because I wanted to tell you somethin' important, and if I don't get your permission to be candid with you, Miss Delaney, I will explode. I swear I will."

Mary's long curls stroked her round, petite face, and she moved her hair away from her eyes. "What is it, Matt? What has agitated you tonight?"

"I received a letter from Jessica this mornin'."

"You did? What did she say?"

Matt snapped the stick in his hand and muttered something inaudible. The pain was too great and he couldn't express it.

"Are you going to tell me or not, Matt?"

141

"Jessica told me that she had no interest in marryin' me."

"What?"

"Yup, she gave me all kinds of reasons for her decision. She didn't appreciate the fact that I once owned slaves and don't think it is wrong to do so. And I didn't tell her about my reenlistin' until I was ready to leave."

Mary took his hand and gently squeezed it. "Oh, Matt, I'm so sorry for you."

"You're leavin' the regiment next week, aren't you?"

"Yes, I've already given the colonel my intention."

He turned toward her and brought his face close to hers. "Do you recall that one evenin' when I asked if you'd make love to me?"

"Oh, dear Matt, I do," she said demurely, squeezing his hand again.

"Shucks, Mary, I can imagine that right now you're blushing."

"The dark of night hides many things, does it not?" She released his hand. "Are you certain Jessica is no longer in your heart?"

What could he say? That he still loved Jessica, even though she had rejected him. If so, what was the point of his love? "You are quite special to me, Mary. I feel a special closeness to you."

"And I have always felt close to you, Matt. Closer than any man I have ever met."

"Would you walk with me?" he asked, getting up.

"Of course." She rose and walked with him hand-in-hand down a grassless wagon trail.

"Matt," she said, spinning around to face him, "Sometimes I have dreadful thoughts about you getting killed, and it pains me that we would have never consummated our relationship."

Matt felt his old desires for her returning. Stop, he told himself. He was a minister of God. When he studied theology, he memorized *1John2:17*: "...the world with its lust is passing away, but he who does the will of God abides forever." He needed no one to remind him that such an affair would be a grievance against the Lord. Hadn't he sinned enough by having imagined

142

making love to her while he lay in the hospital tent these past few weeks—envisioning how warm and tender her body was as he held her close to him, how she laughed when he stroked her soft skin, how she sighed when he consummated the act—when he was finally one with her? Now she was here, truly here and not in his imagination, suggesting her willingness to offer herself to him. He still loved Jessica, but Mary was here for him. Perhaps this would be the last time for him to experience such joy.

He placed his arm about her waist. "Where can we be truly alone tonight?"

"My tent is yonder," she said in a whispered tone, "but you will have to be quiet. I am not certain the colonel would appreciate an officer sharing shelter with a female nurse."

"Yup, I understand," Matt said. "Maybe I ought not put you in an awkward position."

"Don't be foolish, Matt. We just have to keep our voices low."

They undressed in the comforting darkness of her tent, and Matt's heart raced in anticipation at the thought of having her. "Sure wish we didn't have to be secret like this," he said, lying on the cot while she covered him with the warmth of her naked body.

"Under the circumstances," she said, with a happy lilt to her voice, "we have no alternative."

"Shucks, Mary, I've never known such a wonderful woman as you."

"Not true, Matt. You've known Jessica."

"She'll only be a memory now."

"Do you still love her?"

Matt avoided her stare. *What a question. How could I deny I still loved her—ever since we met in Lawrence two years ago? I would never again know such a woman—one who was not only attractive, but who had a burning appetite for life and the determination to live it to the full.*

"I don't wish to talk about Jessica any longer," he said. "As far as I'm concerned, I want only you."

"And you have me. I am yours," she sighed, pressing her softness against him.

143

Matt tried to imagine what it would have been like if she were Jessica and they were on their marriage bed. No war. No worry over being killed the next day. Only a sweet honeymoon…perhaps children…a home…a bright future.

Yet here was Mary, a woman of remarkable understanding and kindness. And as he basked in her warmth, he knew he had never asked if she loved him because he feared the answer would be "yes." Then what would he say in return—that he loved her too? Would he need to lie to her?

"I love you," she whispered.

He groaned as he felt his passion erupt deep inside of her.

"Oh, Mary," he said, knowing that was not the response she wanted from him.

*****

Washington, DC

By eight o'clock, Penelope retired for the evening after putting the girls to bed. While Jessica sat on a chair in the study looking through her manuscript, Otto placed another log in the fireplace. "Looks like General Longstreet decided to give up Knoxville and let the Union have it," he said, returning to his seat on the davenport.

"I had not heard about that," Jessica said, glancing up.

"It's true. Apparently, Longstreet learned that Sherman was approaching Knoxville with 25,000 men and Bragg decided to retreat. I imagine Lincoln must be well pleased with that information, coming on the heels of a Union success in Chattanooga. I don't see how the Confederates can not possibly win this conflict." He paused a moment as he looked at her. "What is that you've written?"

"A novel."

"May I see it?"

"Certainly." Jessica, holding her manuscript, vacated her chair and sat next to him. "I want to mail this to a publisher but I'm not sure who might be interested in it."

"Hmmm, *A Slave Only Once*. Interesting title. Allow me to look at that." He took the papers from her and scanned them.

Jessica inched closer to him and touched his sleeve. "*A Slave Only Once* is a novel about an escaped female slave who has a young daughter still being held in bondage by her slave master. Although she is later reunited with her daughter—who suffers from a mental disorder—she finds no one willing to hire her or treat her fairly even after her emancipation from slavery."

Otto flipped through a few more pages. "How much of yourself went into your main character?"

"You don't understand. This is not about me. This is a novel concerning a woman's emancipation from slavery."

"But I *do* understand. You are a white woman, but you yourself are not free. Is that correct?"

Jessica flushed. "You are very perceptive, Mr. Heller."

"I must say you are a very talented writer. But, of course, I have told you that before."

"I know," she said, placing her hand lightly on top of his, "but I enjoy hearing it anyway."

"Have you written the entire book?"

Jessica was surprised he did not pull his hand away from hers. "A goodly portion of it."

Emma's voice emanated from her bedroom, and Jessica got up. "Excuse me, Mr. Heller, but I'll find out what she wants."

Jessica returned, holding Emma's hand. "She can't go to sleep," Jessica said, "and she wants you to tell her a story."

"Come here, my child," Otto said, putting the manuscript to one side and directing her to his lap. "Did I ever tell you the story about the little slave girl who used to see angels?"

"No, Papa," Emma said. "Did she really see angels?"

"I think so. One angel in particular. But no one ever believed her. So when she grew up, people told her to stop believing in them and then she stopped seeing them."

"I may have seen an angel once," Jessica said.

Emma's eyes lit up. "Really?"

145

"I saw someone. Maybe it was an angel, maybe my imagination. But what I saw was a young black girl wearing a white gown. She had this soft voice too."

"What did she say?" Emma asked.

"Oh, child, this is foolish talk." She gave Emma a playful poke. "As far as I'm concerned, *you* are my little angel."

Emma giggled.

Otto looked up at Jessica. "I know a publisher who might be interested in reviewing your manuscript. If you will entrust me with your book, I will send this to him. Perhaps my influence in publishing might be of some assistance in this matter."

"Oh, Mr. Heller," Jessica said, bending down to hug and kiss him. "Thank you very much."

Emma giggled again. "Miss Radford, are you in love with Papa?"

Chapter 21

December 12
Dalton, Georgia

My dearest Sara,

I cannot believe this war is not over. By now I thought we might have gained our independence from Federal tyranny. Hope this does not distress you, but I do not know when I will be able to see you again. This pains me to say this as I cannot endure even another month without you. I had hoped to see you this Christmas but was not able to secure military leave.

This is disheartening. Events here at camp have deteriorated. The South has suffered a humiliating defeat in Chattanooga. I fear that the Union will make this town a base of operations. How could this have happened? How can I maintain my hope for eventual victory? Perhaps the Yankees will make fatal blunders that will help us gain our momentum.

Anyway, I am thankful you did not remain in Chattanooga but took the initiative to leave before those Federals took over the town. No telling what atrocities they may commit on our helpless citizens.

If possible, please send me a pair of stockings and a scarf since the nights are cool here. However, I realize that you are undergoing hardships of your own, given your deteriorating supplies of necessities. I hope your aunt remains in good health and that you and Nellie are able to have some semblance of Christmas joy without me. As soon as I am granted leave, I will visit you. Both you and Nellie will be always in my prayers.

With all my love,

Roger

*****

December 16
St. Louis, Missouri

Mary Delaney pushed her way past civilians and soldiers at the crowded train depot. Women chatted about Christmas presents, others wondered aloud as to whether St. Louis would get enough of a snowfall to permit sleighing, two children held open an issue of *Harper's Weekly* and pointed to an illustration of a rotund man full of merriment named "Santa Claus," and the voices of soldiers punctured the air with their enthusiasm in getting an extended leave for the holidays. With all of this talk surrounding her, Mary wondered if the people had forgotten that the war was still being waged in different parts of the country.

There was only one chair left at the train depot's restaurant, and she had no choice but to share a table with a Union officer. The man, whom Mary could see was a major, pulled out her chair for her. "Traveling alone?" he asked.

"I was mustered out of the Kansas Eighth yesterday and I'm returning home."

The major raised an eyebrow. "Mustered out of the Kansas Eighth? I don't understand."

Mary waited until the server filled her cup with tea. "I was a volunteer nurse, and I've seen enough bloodshed and suffering that it's a pleasure to be returning to a civilized society."

"Where are you headed, if I may ask?"

"Lawrence, Kansas." It sounded empty when she said it. There was no one there for her. Jessica was now in Washington, Matt was still back in Chattanooga, and she had been gone so long, she had lost track of her other acquaintances.

"That is a coincidence," the major said. "My sister and her husband moved there last month. They were surprised to find significant building activity there. I understand that Lawrence is completing a bridge across the river and the Union Pacific is planning to lay rails there. Looks like they plan to give Quantrill

148

a strong message that the townspeople won't be defeated by the likes of him."

Mary ignored him, but cracked a smile as she ate a slice of apple she had been served. Jessica used to remind her of those days long ago when she used to pick apples from the Radford orchard when visiting Jessica. Mary liked apples so much—whether whole, dried, or baked in a pie—that Jessica used to call her "Apple Mary."

"Did I say something humorous?" the major asked.

"No, not at all."

Mary's smile faded when she wondered why Matt never told her he loved her. Was he too shy, afraid about the possibility of rejection? Or was he still in love with Jessica even after he was scorned by her?

*****

December 24
Washington, DC

Devin Alcott found he wasn't able to sleep well on the two-day train ride to Washington, D.C., what with the uncomfortable seat, clickety-clack of the rails, and the noisy chug of the engine. However, Lieutenant Lightfoot, who accompanied him, slept throughout the night. Devin had to wake him when the train pulled into the station.

"We're here, lieutenant."

"Mary, please understand," he mumbled, his eyes half open.

"Mary? Who's Mary, lieutenant?"

An embarrassing smile crossed Matt's lips when he stared at Devin. "Never mind. I apologize. I must have been dreamin'" He looked out as grayish-black clouds from the engine played against the window.

Devin got up and stood in the aisle waiting for him. "As I mentioned to you earlier, I wish I could stay in Washington for more than a day, but I must continue on tomorrow on my way to Quebec."

149

Matt followed him to the end of the car and waited for the porter to retrieve the luggage. "Where are you going to be stayin' here in Washington?"

"The Willard."

"The Willard Hotel? That's the most famous—and expensive—place in the city. I hear even Lincoln stayed there at his first Inaugural. How can you afford it?"

Devin picked up his bag at the same time the porter handed Matt his luggage. "I told you that my Canadian parents are wealthy. They've paid for my room weeks in advance."

Matt hailed a coachman. "I suppose they're relieved that you have finally been mustered out of the service."

"Yes, but they still don't understand why I felt the need to fight on foreign soil for the freedom of slaves."

When the coach arrived at the Willard, Devin asked if Matt would join him for a cup of coffee. "I appreciate the invitation," Matt said, "but I'm goin' straight to the National Hotel. There's a young lady I'm rather anxious to meet."

"Oh? Would that, perchance, be a lady named Mary?"

"Nope," he said, with a nervous stammer. "Someone else."

*****

Sitting in a cushioned chair in the hotel lobby, Matt examined the wood carving he had made for her. This was his best effort yet, and he hoped Jessica liked it. He reached inside his coat. Her most recent letter was still there. Jessica has surely complicated matters, he thought, by first sending him a letter telling him she had no interest in marriage and then sending this one, where she had appeared to be open about the matter.

Soldiers in his outfit used to joke about the changeability of women, how they might say one thing one day and something completely different the next. But he never thought Jessica was like that. She was a self-assured woman who formed her own ideas and didn't like to change them. So why did she reverse her thoughts about him?

This evening, Devin would join him at the Hellers for supper. He told Matt how much he appreciated the invitation

150

and looked forward to meeting Matt's young lady—whatever her name was, he had said, teasing.

Matt strolled outside to empty his mind of Mary while awaiting Jessica's arrival. But how could he ever forget Mary? That special evening he enjoyed with her in her tent was impossible to erase. Her skin was soft, her caresses angelic, and her whispers soothing in the darkness of her tent. How was he to know Jessica was going to complicate matters like this?

He caught a glimpse of Jessica two storefronts away, hugging a young negro woman standing next to a one-legged negro man about her age dressed in a Yankee uniform. The man tapped his cane against the brick-paved walk as he shook his head.

Jessica caught Matt staring at her and waved at him. She shook the soldier's hand in parting and smiled as she made her way to Matt.

"It has been a long time," she said. She held out her hand and he kissed it.

"Yup, it sure has." He watched the two negroes Jessica had been conversing with disappear into the crowd. "Do you know those two colored people?"

Jessica frowned. *You can sometimes be an insensitive boor, Matt. They are people, not colored people.*

"No," she answered, "but I would like to. The lady's husband was wounded in Chattanooga last year. Although he has now lost one of his limbs for the Union cause, he is still treated with disrespect here in Washington. He is not even allowed to vote. That is indeed revolting."

"Nothin' we can do about that, Miss Radford."

"I disagree with that," she said, raising her voice an embarrassing notch. "If we all took a stance against such an atrocity, we would change people's attitudes toward the colored."

Matt decided to swiftly change the subject. He handed her his latest wood carving. "This is for you."

"This is very good," she said, turning the object around in her hand. "You may become another Leonard da Vinci some day. But why a bust of Abraham Lincoln?"

151

"Because you talk about him all the time. Been callin' him our savior for the abolishment of slavery."

She eyed him suspiciously. "You say that as if you don't believe it."

"Shucks, it's been a while, hasn't it, Jessica? I mean, since we saw each other. How are you enjoyin' life here in Washington?"

"I'm not quite sure. I don't quite fit in society circles. The upper echelon here don't enjoy mingling with bourgeois such as me."

"That's their loss." He took her arm. "Shall we go on to visit the Hellers?"

"We could do that later. Has your friend Devin arrived?"

"Yup, and he'll be joining us for supper tonight."

"That will give us plenty of time to talk." She gazed about the busy lobby of the hotel. "Somewhere in private, of course."

"Where would you like to go to be alone?"

She leaned close to his ear. "I was thinking of visiting in your room, here at the hotel."

"Jessica! That'd be highly improper."

Two or three people glanced in Jessica's direction. "Lower your voice," she said softly. "I'm not suggesting anything immoral. It's simply a place where we can be private."

Matt agreed and went upstairs first to wait for her in his room. He sat on the bed and put his head in his hands. Why did he even bother to come here? Mary had already left for Lawrence when he received Jessica's second letter, and now he felt obligated to both women. No, not obligated...in love with. Dare he say it? Yes, in different ways, he loved them both. Jessica's great beauty, intelligence, and sense of independence. Traits his mother had. But then there was Mary's generosity and warmth.

Do not ignore your heart, his father used to say. "There are times your heart knows the answer that your mind does not."

Matt thought about writing Mary a letter, but what would he say? That he was going to Washington, D.C. to visit with Jessica? Perhaps Mary need not know. Not yet, anyway.

There was a light rap on his door.

Matt let Jessica in. "I hope no one has seen you standing there."

"Why, Matt, you've invited me to a hotel room before. Don't you remember?"

Indeed he did, Matt recalled. On the morning of the Quantrill raid, he had taken Jessica with him to the City Hotel in Lawrence to escape the marauders.

"That was different," Matt said.

She sat next to him on the bed, but he moved a foot away.

Jessica laughed. "Don't worry. I'm not going to try to seduce you. I do feel I need to apologize again for telling you I had no interest in marriage."

He took her hand and ran his finger over it. "Shucks, Jessica, I've never stopped lovin' you. You must know that by now."

He looked at her intelligent, sapphire eyes. There was only a hint of softness in them, and Matt wondered if her feelings for him were as strong as his were for her. But he was somewhat reassured by her loving smile and the way she brushed up against his shoulder.

"I didn't want to give you the impression," she said, "of your believing that I was not interested in your marriage proposal."

"Dear Lord!" He dropped down to one knee at the foot of the bed. "Does that mean you'll marry me, my sweet Jessica?"

"I may not be as sweet as Mary Delaney."

Matt wanted to add, "but you are," but he couldn't say it. Mary was exceptionally sweet. He remembered his conversation with her as if it were yesterday...

"As far as I am concerned," he had whispered to Mary that night in her tent, "I want only you."

"And you have me. I am yours," she said sighing and pressing her softness against him.

153

"Well," Jessica said with a pleasant lilt to her voice, "have you lost your tongue or are thinking about my question?"

"You haven't yet answered mine, dear Jessica. Will you marry me?"

*****

Devin made it to the Heller residence by six o'clock that evening. When Penelope opened the door, he introduced himself and presented her with a bottle of wine. "I'm not a connoisseur of fine wines," he said, pointing to the label, "but I assume 1860 had to be a good year because we had no war then."

"Why thank you, Mr. Alcott. Matt Lightfoot told me all about you. Won't you come in?"

Penelope led him to the living room where Matt and four others whom Devin did not recognize, were gathered to meet him. Lights from candles above the fireplace brightly lit the room, while a Christmas tree adorned with garlands stood in the corner and near a piano. A wooden bust of Mr. Lincoln graced the top of the piano.

"You obviously know Mr. Lightfoot," Penelope said, "and the gentleman next to him is my husband, Otto Heller. And here is Miss Radford."

Devin took the hand Jessica offered and kissed it. "A pleasure to meet you, Mary. Mr. Lightfoot mentioned your name on the way here."

Matt's jaw dropped open while Jessica raised a curious eyebrow. "Mary?" she said. "No, my name is Jessica. Mary is Mr. Lightfoot's other friend."

Matt glared at Devin for a brief moment and turned an apologetic face toward Jessica. But she laughed lightly as if the mistaken identity provided humor to the occasion. "Mr. Alcott, you will be interested in learning that we've already met."

"We have?"

"I was Private Walter Brontë with the Eighth Kansas."

"What!"

154

"Yes," she said, lowering her voice to a baritone level, "and if my hair was cut short and I wore your Yankee uniform, I would be he."

"It can't be. How did you get away with it?"

"It was not easy. I can assure you of that."

"Oh-h-h," Devin said, chuckling, "I had heard there was a `woman in our ranks who had been mustered out of the regiment, but I didn't know it was you. I just assumed Private Brontë had been killed in action. No wonder Private Brontë never answered my questions as to whether he had a young lady back home."

Jessica laughed. "Obviously, Mr. Alcott, he didn't know whether you were referring to me or to my friend Mary Delaney."

"I've already met Ms. Delaney," Devin said. "She had been a nurse with the Eighth Kansas. Wonderful woman."

"Indeed," Jessica said, her lips forming a wry smile.

"I've asked Miss Radford to be my bride," Matt added, grasping the fingers of her hand. "She wants to wait until I'm mustered out of the regiment this year before making any commitments. Isn't that correct, dear?"

She studied him for a moment. "That is what we've agreed upon. This will give us time to make certain we will make a decision we won't regret later."

"If the two of you become betrothed," Otto said, "we'll have to find another nanny for our children."

Devin noticed the two little girls staring up at him. The younger one's mouth was ajar, as if she had never seen a negro before. The older one spoke up first. "Is it true, Mr. Alcott, that you play music?"

"Yes, and he plays beautiful music," Jessica said, dropping Matt's hand and moving over towards Devin. "Perhaps you could entertain us, while Mrs. Heller and I set the table for supper."

Penelope and Jessica left for the kitchen while Otto encouraged Devin to play the piano. "What would you like to hear?" Devin asked, after trying some of the keys to see if it was in tune.

155

"Mitzi is learning how to play the piano," Otto said. "She's good at it for her age."

Devin turned to face the two girls. "Which one of you little pumpkins is Mitzi?"

The older girl smiled back. "That's me. I'm nine. And this is Emma. She's the baby in the family."

"I am not. I'm already six."

Mitzi, with begging eyes, looked up at her father. "Can I please sit next to Mr. Alcott and watch him play?"

Otto nodded his approval and Mitzi squealed excitement as she took her place next to Devin.

He played the piece, and the second time he played it, everyone joined in singing:

"*When Johnny comes marching home again,*
Hurrah! Hurrah!
We'll give him a hearty welcome then
Hurrah! Hurrah!
The men will cheer and the boys will shout
The ladies they will all turn out
And we'll all feel gay,
When Johnny comes marching home."

"I know a Christmas carol," Mitzi said, her fingers on the keyboard. "Want to see me play it?"

"Of course," Devin said. "Which one is it?"

"'It Came Upon the Midnight Clear.' I like that song because that's where they tell everyone to be quiet and hear the angels sing."

"Let's hear you play it then." Devin put a finger to his lips. "But we'll all try to be quiet so we can hear the angels sing."

Mitzi's mouth formed the words to the song as she ran her fingers over the ivories with confidence. When it was over, Devin turned to Otto. "I really think Mitzi ought to be encouraged to play. She has a good ear for music."

Otto smiled. "If you ever decide to live here in Washington, Devin, I would be pleased to have you give her lessons."

Jessica clapped. "I think that is a splendid idea."

"I don't believe that would be a wise thing to do," Matt said. A silence covered the room and Matt coughed, apparently embarrassed by the surprised stares he received. "What I mean is, I think the colored people have a different sense of music. I've heard their spirituals, and the music is superb but it is quite different than the kind we enjoy."

"Mr. Lightfoot," Devin said, folding his arms across his chest, "I also play Mozart. Would you consider that black music?"

Jessica was livid as she spun in Matt's direction. "What is wrong with you, Matt? Just because you owned Tinker at one time, you think every negro talks, thinks, and sings the same way."

Matt's face turned red. "I'm sorry. I didn't mean to appear biased, but the races do come from different cultures, and each culture has its own gift."

"And your's should be to keep silent," Jessica added.

Chapter 22

December 24
Atlanta, Georgia

By six o'clock that evening it was already dark and Nellie took rapid steps along the Chattahoochee River toward Mrs. Millicent's home. *I sure wish she could be here wid me. First time I gotta go by myself.*

Of course, she could not blame Sara, who was acting in a Christmas play at church tonight. Mrs. Toby liked to act and this was her chance to play the starring role as Mary. Sara Toby would have walked with her tonight if she could.

"I wish you didn't have to work those long hours as a seamstress," Sara had told Nellie, "because I fear for your safety." However, these were hard times for Atlanta. Nellie's work would bring in extra money.

"Be fortunate someone will hire you for wages," Sara had also said.

"Why?" But Nellie already knew the answer. *Why should they hire a free negro when they might be better off owning a slave?*

Nellie figured she had better do what Sara told her. Be quiet, no matter what they said about her. But it was not easy. Just today, a white man in his fifties spotted her busily engaged in sewing a garment.

"Martha," he had called to the white woman who was the plant overseer, "since when did you start hiring nigger slave girls?"

"She's not a slave girl, Mr. Whitcomb. She belongs with that trashy white woman, Sara Toby, who's living with Jane Millicent on Baxter Street. Imagine, Mrs. Toby takin' in a nigger and not only claimin' that the colored girl is free but callin' that girl her daughter!"

Nellie found if difficult to remain silent. If only she was back in Washington with Jessica. Someone told her once that Washington was about 650 miles away—probably only a three-day journey by rail and stagecoach. But Sara told her that for a Southern woman to travel to Yankee territory was risky and that Nellie would just have to wait for an opportune time to be reunited with Jessica.

Nellie resigned herself not to think about that right now. She reminded herself that as long as she was in Atlanta, Mrs. Toby needed the extra money. Still, Nellie wished she had the angel medallion which Jessica's pa had given her. She always liked to read the inscription that said God has given His angels charge over her. Now she unsure as to whether that was true anymore. She had not seen Sissy, her guardian angel, for six months now, and she might never see her again. When Nellie mentioned this to Sara a few weeks ago, Sara told her that she had outgrown the "need" for an angel.

To make her point, Sara reached for her aunt's Bible. "Let me read you something," she said. She turned the pages rapidly and stopped when she got to the passage she was looking for. "Here it is. It's a letter from Paul to the Corinthians: 'When I was a child, I spoke like a child, I thought like a child, I reasoned like a child. When I became a man'—or in your instance, a woman—'I put an end to childish ways.'"

She beamed a smile at Nellie. "So you see, you've outgrown the need for an angel."

Maybe Mrs. Toby was right. *I be eighteen in three months 'n women like me don't need no angels.*

No matter how awful Atlanta was right now, Nellie figured today's Christmas Eve had to be a lot better than the Christmas Eve she experienced six years ago. Back then, she and her momma had stolen a small boat and made it across the wide Missouri river. They were still in a slave state when they reached the Missouri shore, but momma kept telling her that everything would be fine. She even told her that Sissy would help her.

"She make shore you be free," she told Nellie. "And you will, no matter what."

When the slavers caught up with them, Momma ordered Nellie to run like the devil. "Doan stop, child. Keep a-goin'."

"But Momma," Nellie screamed, "don't leave me here. I need you."

"I gwine be back, my child. I swear, I gwine be back."

Those were her last words. *She said she gwine be back, but she not be back. Maybe by now she's already dead.*

Nellie took a handkerchief from her pocket and dabbed her eyes. Two passers-by, a young white man and woman clutched arm-in-arm stared at her for a moment before resuming their conversation. The dim light of a streetlamp caused an eerie shadow from barren wintry trees to fall on the path. The pale moon surrendered itself to a dark cloud that gradually hid it from view. The only sound the nearby river made was the rippling of water over the wheel of an old mill.

Turning right at Baker Street, Nellie thought she saw large shadows moving in the distance, in the treeless distance. Was she imagining things?

In a low, almost whispering voice, she sang a tune she learned when she was about to be sold off at a Memphis slave auction. Maybe the words would give her courage…

> *"Slavery chain done broke at last, broke*
> *at last, broke at last,*
> *Slavery chain done broke at last,*
> *Going to praise God till I die."*

She kept on walking, faster this time. The shadows moved again. Getting closer. Nellie stopped, her heart pounding.

"Sissy, help me," she said, her voice straining. "If yah still be around, help me. Please!"

A figure raced toward her. No, *two* figures. Men. Two white men. "Hey nigger-girl," they jeered. "Come here, nigger-girl."

Nellie screamed, but she was too stunned to move. A man grabbed her arm. "She's a pretty little lady, ain't she, Clayton?"

"Yeah, Ted, she sure is."

"Hey, nigger-girl," Ted grunted as he ripped the front of her dress, "let's see if the rest of you is black."

160

Nellie continued to scream as she flayed her arms, but Clayton grabbed them like a vise and yanked her toward the ground. "Feisty little bitch, ain't she? Hey, Ted, what's wrong with you?"

"I don't know," he said, his voice quaking as he remained motionless, his rough hand no longer massaging her bosom. "I feel like someone's watching us."

"That's stupid," Clayton said, "ain't no one here." He looked up anyway, and his mouth dropped open. "Oh my, God!"

Ted looked up too. "What the—" His face was chalky and he stumbled, picked himself up, and stumbled again, running as if he were being chased by a rabid dog. Clayton followed him, cussing as he ran.

Nellie, clutching the remnants of her dress, saw what they saw. But as she stared at the bright light coming toward her, she was not afraid.

1864

Chapter 23

January 5
Lawrence, Kansas

Dearest Matt,

I received your letter yesterday and was thrilled that you wrote to tell me you were thinking of me. It is unfortunate that we still do not have a telegraph line here so I could more speedily correspond with you. You mentioned about the dreadful cold you are experiencing in Strawberry Plains, Tennessee, and I am sending you, with this letter, a pair of wool socks. I had started knitting them when I was still with the Eighth Kansas.

I am surprised at the extent of building activity here in Lawrence, just three-and-a-half months after that horrific Quantrill raid. Poor John Speer never did find the body of his son Robert, but I admire his fortitude in reestablishing the Kansas Weekly Tribune. Work is also underway to extend the rail line through Lawrence, and I understand the project might be completed by the summer. The bridge across the Kaw will also be finished, and we will no longer depend solely on the ferry to take us across. It is unfortunate that we did not have conveniences such as a telegraph, bridge, and railroad at the time of the raid as we might have avoided this tragedy.

My home here had been destroyed and I am sharing a house with a family. While I am barely able to eke out a living by waiting on tables at an eatery here, my brother Joseph has a friend who has recently returned after serving with the 23rd

Missouri and is now a physician with Pavilion Hospital in St. Louis. I have corresponded with Joseph to see if his friend might be able to find me a position there, but I will have to advise you on that.

My Christmas Day was less than cheery without you, but I understand the demands of the military. I still think about that special moment we had together, and June will not come soon enough for me when you will be discharged from service and we can be together once again.

Love,

Mary

*****

January 18
Dandridge, Tennessee

A chilling rain fell and Lieutenant Lightfoot's wet uniform clung to his skin as he rode his horse alongside an extensive Union wagon train.

"This cruel weather and rain are bad enough," he shouted to another lieutenant, "but the disgrace of a retreat from the enemy is far worse."

The other lieutenant, with rain pouring down his face, just waved his agreement. Matt rode on through the mud, the icy rain slashing his skin like tiny whips as he watched men sloshing, ankle-deep through the muck. Their wet faces were as bitter as their anger. Every few yards, it seemed, wheels of one or more of the wagons would get stuck in the mud and some of the troopers had to push them out.

Matt could not believe that a council was called last night to order a retreat. He was convinced they could have held their ground, given the determination of the men and sufficient ammunition to repel the enemy. Why did General Sturgis even bother to make it as far as Dandridge—only to give up on his objective of controlling the East Tennessee and Virginia Railroad? Besides, Union scouts should have discovered that General Sturgis's cavalry would be met by rebel reinforcements.

Nonetheless, the order passed down to the Eighth Kansas that it was to serve as a rear guard. But the cold, chilling rain made travel difficult. By his reckoning, Matt figured that they had traveled only six miles and it was already noon.

"Form battle lines!" a major shouted, pointing to our rear.

Matt turned around to see a rebel cavalry force forming, apparently preparing for an attack. Immediately, two Union regiments formed, one on either side of the road, and lined up for battle. Matt fell in behind them, readying himself for an enemy charge. None came, although the rebels launched several long range volleys of cannon in their direction.

After waiting several minutes for an attack, Colonel Martin, in charge of the brigade, ordered his men to continue their retreat. Matt took up his former position and moved on, occasionally looking behind him to see the enemy in the far distance.

In the evening, the brigade went into bivouac some six or seven miles from Strawberry Plains. After starting one of the fires at camp, Matt sat down on a cracker box to eat his meal. He shivered in the cold but he was glad Mary had sent him the wool socks. She was a kind and generous woman, and that was why he was unable to tell her about his impending engagement to Jessica by letter. Mary deserved to hear from him in person, and he would visit her when his enlistment was over in March. She had mentioned about the possibility of moving out of Lawrence, so he hoped he would hear where she would finally settle down.

Damn this war, he thought. *Maybe the Copperheads— those Northern Democrats—were right by favoring a negotiated peace and putting an end to this conflict. Didn't President Lincoln realize that this war has been going on far too long already?*

*****

February 9
Washington, D.C.

The afternoon sun burst its jubilant rays through the clouds, and Abraham Lincoln, peering out the window of his office, hoped this was a good omen. All he ever wanted to do as President was to preserve the Union, but the duration of this war and the growing number of deaths—on both sides of the conflict—bothered him. He never assumed to be a military man, dictating the planning of campaigns and how they should be executed, although he became involved in the war's overall strategy. What he needed, however, was a general who would take full responsibility for military decisions and act upon them. As President, he would give that general all the assistance he needed.

Until recently, he had no such commander on whom he could depend. Men like Meade, McClellan, and Halleck disappointed him greatly. But with the promising victories at Gettysburg, Vicksburg, and Chattanooga, he finally felt confident that he discovered the right leader—an unassuming but competent man named Ulysses Grant.

Lincoln's personal secretary, John Nicolay, entered the President's office to remind him that it was time to leave for his appointment. Lincoln thanked him, but when Nicolay mentioned that the carriage was ready to take him there, Lincoln simply shook his head and pointed to his walking stick.

Matthew Brady's photographic studio was about a mile away from the Executive Mansion, and Lincoln walked, holding the hand of his ten-year-old son Thomas. A bodyguard and an artist named Francis Carpenter, who would offer advice for the official poses, accompanied the President to the studio. Lincoln turned to young Thomas. "Everyone needs to refrain from riding when they can stroll on a beautiful day such as this, especially Presidents who allow themselves to be indulged with carriages. Look—even the sparrows are promenading on the ground today."

Meeting Lincoln inside the studio was a man about forty, with a mustache and a pointed beard and dressed in a broad-brimmed hat, linen topcoat, and black trousers. "This is Matthew Brady," Francis Carpenter said. "And the gentleman next to him is his assistant, Anthony Berger, the photographer who will assist Mr. Brady."

Berger nodded politely while Brady extended his hand to Lincoln. "It is indeed an honor to meet you, Mr. President."

"I believe the honor is mutual," said Lincoln. "Not only have you won a top prize at the New York World's Fair nine years ago, but I've seen your excellent daguerreotypes taken of several battles. You have literally brought the war to the doorsteps of our citizenry."

Matthew Brady returned a grateful smile, while Mr. Berger stooped to shake the boy's hand. "This must be your son, Thomas."

The boy pulled his hand away and ran through the studio. Mr. Berger chased after him.

"We call the boy Tad," Lincoln joked as he watched the pursuit. "Some folks believe we named him after a tadpole because he is such a slippery fellow, but we really named him after my father."

"Well, Mr. President," Brady said, "please come to this part of the studio for your sitting. I know you are quite busy these days, so this shouldn't take up too much of your time."

"I appreciate that." Lincoln strolled to his assigned chair in the sitting room and his lips formed a playful smile. "I sense there may be a bit of a problem in having my picture taken. Newspaper cartoonists have already sketched my portrait as a court jester and buffoon. But here we are, about to confuse the public by showing them yet another person."

*****

February 13

"It appears about time for me to take to the podium and introduce you," Otto told Jessica in the meeting room of the National Hotel.

Jessica nodded and surveyed the room, counting only eighteen people in attendance, including Kate Chase Sprague, who helped her set up this meeting, and some woman named Elizabeth Cady Stanton, who claimed to be the founder of an abolitionist group called the Women's National Loyal League.

A large banner with the boldly-printed words "No Slavery Anywhere" hung over the front wall of the room while bunting decorated each of the other two walls. The people, sitting in groups of two or three, were still involved in conversation when Otto took to the podium.

"Ladies and gentlemen," he began, "I want to thank you all for coming here tonight. I realize that most of you do not know me, but my name is Otto Heller and, when I lived in Kansas, I was actively involved in the Underground Railroad movement. I risked life and limb to the cause because our nation's laws were unjust at that time. Henry Thoreau, in one of his lectures, raised the question of civil disobedience. He asked whether, when unjust laws exist, we should be content to obey them. My answer is and always shall be 'No'."

After a few more introductory remarks, Jessica took the podium. Her knees shook and she held the sides of the podium to keep her hands steady. Three men in the front row sat with their hands folded, glaring at her.

"The reason I am here," Jessica said to the audience, "is to inform you that the President's Emancipation Proclamation is only a modest beginning to the true emancipation of slaves in this country. It did not free slaves in areas other than the rebel states. What we need, and it will likely take a constitutional amendment to do this, is to outlaw slavery throughout this country."

An unshaven man in the front row rolled his eyes and stood up. "You have no business speaking to us like that, woman. This sort of discussion is reserved for men. Besides, if slavery is outlawed what are we gonna do with all those free niggers?"

"I concur," the second man said. The third man jumped up and began shouting his agreement.

168

"Since when," a woman in the audience shrieked, "I say, since when is public speaking only a man's prerogative?"

Jessica recognized Elizabeth Cady Stanton as the woman who had just spoken up. Mrs. Stanton waved an angry finger at the man. "Women are slaves in this day and age just as negroes are!"

"Please!" Jessica cried out. "Please, can we have some sense of decorum and decency here? I am only telling you that the slavery issue is not dead. The South is not heeding Lincoln's Proclamation. Why should they? But once this war is concluded, we will have this slavery issue facing us. It won't disappear. How are we going to deal with it?"

"We'll just send those niggers back where they belong," one of the men shouted. "Yeah," another yelled. "I'll take 'em back to Africa myself." Suddenly, the room erupted in several loud conversations.

Jessica's muscles tightened. *How would they feel if they themselves were slaves being taken back to Africa?*

The room erupted in noise. Even women such as Kate and Elizabeth engaged the men in a shouting match. Jessica felt a headache coming on.

Otto took her arm as she left the stage.

"I'm sorry," she said, "but I can't do this."

"Don't let these imbeciles sway you," he said. "They have lost their reason."

"I don't care. Please take me home, Mr. Heller. I beg of you, take me home!"

Minutes later, Jessica sat next to him in the back of the coach, her head on his shoulder. The pain of failure still ached, but Mr. Heller was always a comfort to her. She had felt a certain reassurance in his presence, but she wished she could feel that way with Matt. Her concern was he might say something intolerable or embarrassing to her. Yet for some unexplained reason, she still loved him. Or did she? The thought did cross her mind that perhaps she wanted to marry him just to put an end to this sinful temptation she fought against when she was alone with Penelope's dear, sweet husband. Marriage would finally make a respectable woman out of her.

169

"I'm sorry," she said to Mr. Heller, pressing her head against his strong shoulder. "I've made a complete fool of myself."

He stroked her hair with the broad palm of his hand. "No you haven't, dear Jessica." He dabbed her wet eyes with her handkerchief. "Remember what Whitman said in one of his poems... 'The conductor beats time for the band, and all the performers follow him.' You don't abandon the orchestra just because a few players don't understand the music you are teaching."

Chapter 24

After a careful search of the cupboards, Nellie found a slice of bread. Cutting away the green mold from the center, she wished she knew where the food was hidden. "We're all hungry," Sara had told her this morning, "but you must understand the Yankees are cutting off our supply lines, and that includes food."

Nellie was glad she had saved some of the old *Harper's Weekly* magazines that Sara was going to use for fuel. *Least if I can't eat, I can read.*

While Jane and Sara were out visiting their neighbors this Sunday to collect money for the war effort, Nellie looked at the cover of the August 17, 1861 edition of *Harper's*. It showed an illustration of a large number of people rushing down a wide road, and the headline, "Stampede of Slaves from Hampton to Fortress Monroe," caught her attention.

"The Southern worker, black and white," the article said, "held the key to the war, and of the two groups, the black worker raising food and raw materials held an even more strategic place than the white." Nellie sighed.

This be true of her momma, Nellie thought. *Momma be a good worker, but all that her Massah want was cotton. More cotton. Bales of it. Money. It bring in lots o' money.*

Today was Valentine's Day. It was supposed to be a special day when people close to each other expressed their love. But she loved her momma and probably would never see her again. Yet, she hoped someday to see Jessica. She remembered that long talk she had with Jessica nineteen months ago....

"I've always liked this spot," Jessica had said to her, getting off her horse. "Gives me peace of mind just listening to the water rippling down the stream."

171

*I joined her at the bank. "We used t'go fishin'
here, you'n me. You remember? Done never catch
nothing."*

*Jessica nodded. "Pa told me later there were
no fish there. Made me think there were bass and
pike and all kinds of fish in that creek."*

"You mean your Pa tol' yah a lie?"

*"I wouldn't call it a lie," Jessica said. "He just
wanted us to believe in things."*

Nellie tossed the copy of *Harper's* to the table. *There ain't
nothin' wrong in believing,* she thought. With the way things
were going, Nellie figured that believing in something, in anything, was the only thing people could do these days. There
was nothing else. As the wall clock facing her continued its
loud ticking, Nellie stared at it and imagined it saying "believe, be-lieve, be-lieve." *Yes, I still believe,* Nellie thought. She
had quit believing in Sissy, her special angel. But last month,
when two white men had her in their grasp, about to rape her,
they suddenly let her go. At first, she wondered what had
caused them to release her....

*I now saw what those evil men saw. A tall
man dressed in white and sittin' on a white horse.
I rubbed my eyes 'cause I couldn't believe it. Could
it be? No, it be only a man who done dress up like
an angel. He say he be on his way to a Christmas
pageant. "Do not fret, Nellie," he had said, gazing
at her with warm, kind eyes. "I am a Christian
soldier, and I will see to it that you are properly
taken care of."*

Nellie shrugged when people told her it was a coincidence. They said she was just fortunate a compassionate soldier happened to arrive at that very moment to save her. It
had nothing to do with angels. But Nellie wondered about
that. That light from his lamp whiter than anything she had
ever seen from any lantern. And how did that stranger know

172

her name? No, she did not care what anybody thought. As far as she was concerned, Sissy had sent him to her.

*****

April 3
Atlanta, Georgia

Roger Toby sat on a tree stump near the door of Jane Millicent's house waiting for Sara, Nellie, and Jane to arrive. Church bells tolled the Sunday service, reminding him of the time in years gone by when Ma used to push him off to church. Pa would take them all in a mule-driven wagon, cussing all the way because he had no desire to go.

After Ma died, Pa quit going to church and Roger failed to see much value in it, although his friends told him he would be a better man if he had some religion in him. It wasn't true as far as he was concerned. When he first got married, he got mixed up with Nasha, a pretty slave girl Pa had on his tobacco plantation. But Sara never found out—thank God—and since then, he had emerged as a successful banker.

Then the war came and changed him in a way he did not want to be changed. Killing was easy at first. With every dead Yankee, the Confederacy was closer to gaining its independence. But then—damn it to hell—came the Union victory at Chattanooga. Shouldn't have happened.

He slammed his fist against the palm of his hand. *Bragg, yaw lost the war for us. Gone. I see no sunrise for the South. How do yaw expect me to go on fightin' like this? Where are our victories?*

He creased his tired eyes with his fingers. *Nothing gives me pleasure anymore. Not even the sight of dead Yankees on the battlefield.* Ever since he confronted Lieutenant Lightfoot in Chickamauga—knowing that if he had killed him, he would never forgive himself—he felt different about the enemy. If he could leave his regiment today, he would. But he had nine months to go, and the days until he would be mustered out of service were inching along like a stubborn mule.

Roger was startled out of his thoughts when he heard the neigh of horses and the abrupt halt of a carriage. "Oh Lord, I

173

am so happy to see you!" Sara exclaimed, throwing herself at him.

"I've looked forward to this day," Roger said, swinging her around and kissing her. He turned to stern-faced Jane Millicent, who promptly told him not to try to lift her up also—or else.

"Then what about this other beautiful lady?" he said, touching Nellie by the shoulders. "My yaw sure are turning into a little princess. I bet some young lad is going to snatch yaw away as his bride."

Nellie turned to Sara with a questioning glance.

"Mr. Toby means you're old enough to get married," Sara explained.

"I reckon so. I'm eighteen already."

"I bet yaw destined to break some man's heart someday," Roger said.

Nellie turned to Sara again for an explanation.

"He means you are such a wonderful young lady, some man will probably fall in love with you."

Nellie giggled.

"Incidentally," Roger said, "I didn't forget yaw birthday."

He waited until they were all seated for dinner before he gave her his present. "Actually," he said, reaching in his pocket, "it's a present yaw gave me." He pulled out a medallion and handed it to her. "This was a present yaw gave me two Christmases ago. Remember?"

"I do," she said, her smile widening as she held the chain and medallion in her hands. "Did it save you from harm?"

"I don't know if it saved me at all, Nellie. But this medal moved around almost as much as I did. A man named Tinker whom yaw know had it first. That's why it has a dent in it. Then he gave it to Matt Lightfoot, and he gave it to me. But it rightfully belongs with yaw."

"I probably don't need to wear it anymore. Mrs. Toby says angels don't exist."

"I wish they did exist. Who knows? Maybe they do."

"Roger," Sara said, "don't fill her head with such foolishness."

"Define foolishness for me," Roger said.

174

"You know very well what I mean. Being absurd, lacking good sense."

"Well, then this war is utter foolishness. I sure wish it was over by now. All this senseless killing with nothing to show for it. Wives cryin' for their husbands and mamas cryin' for their children." Roger paused, noticing Nellie shaking her head, her back turned away from him.

"What's wrong?" Roger asked.

"Nothin.'"

"Something's the matter. What is it, young lady?"

She turned a sad face toward him. "I miss my momma very much. You tink maybe she be alive?"

*****

The same day
Washington, DC

Lincoln clasped his hands together, leaning his elbows on his desk, as Kentucky Governor Thomas Bramlette concluded his remarks. "So, Mr. President," he said, "I must protest the recruitment of colored regiments in our state. Not only is there not a need for this action, but you are exercising your own personal moral judgment in this situation, overstepping the bounds of your sworn oath as President. That is all I have to say."

Lincoln studied the other two men in the room. Former U.S. Senator Archibald Dixon nodded his head in approval while Albert Hodges, the editor of the *Frankfort Commonwealth* was busily scribbling notes. Bramlette's flushed face told Lincoln that the governor was passionate about his convictions. Perhaps a year earlier, Lincoln would have agreed with him. But events had changed since then. This war had to be won by the Union, and if it took more colored troopers to win it, then that must be so.

Leaning back in his chair, Lincoln sighed. "Gentlemen, I realize that I had shifted from my policy of not interfering with my stance on slavery in my inaugural address to my later position of emancipation." He looked at each man as if expecting a comment. "But," he continued, "I have also taken an oath to preserve,

175

protect, and defend the Constitution of the United States. To this day, I have done no official act in mere deference to my abstract judgment and feeling on slavery. Had I even tried to preserve the Constitution to save slavery, I could not do so by permitting the wreck of government, country, and the Constitution all together."

He leaned forward again, resting his elbows on the desk and pressing his bearded chin against the knuckles of his hand. "But what I am also saying, gentlemen, is that I am against slavery, and if slavery is not wrong, then nothing is wrong."

*****

April 11
Charlottetown, Prince Edward Island
The Province of Canada

> *Dear Mr. Heller,*
>
> *I apologize for taking this long to write back to thank you for your kind hospitality at Christmas. It was a comfort meeting with you and Mrs. Heller, as well as Matthew, Jessica, and your two adorable children. It is a shame that Mitzi and Emma can not be shielded from the fear and turmoil of battle. Incidentally, this war now being waged among your states in America has had a profound impact on Canadians as well. There has been discussion on this side of the border that it may pose a military threat to us (which I discount), but this is helping mount support for unification of colonies in Canada. Interestingly, I believe the Colonial Office in Britain favors such a reorganization since Britain would find it less costly to maintain, compared to working with individual colonies.*
>
> *But I do not wish to bore you with the politics here. Suffice it to say, I am still searching for a position with an orchestra here but am having no success. I have considered emigrating to America once your war has been settled, in favor, I hope of an ultimate Union victory.*

Per Mitzi's request, I am enclosing a photograph of me at home playing the violin. I am also enclosing sheet music for Beethoven's "Ode to Joy" from his Ninth Symphony, and I think she will find it challenging, but I am sure she will be able to master it. I was quite impressed with Mitzi's musical abilities, and I think she should be encouraged to pursue a musical career, if that is her goal.

Sincerely,

Devin Alcott

Chapter 25

As the music from the 27th Michigan Volunteers filtered through, John Nicolay peered out the window of the Executive Mansion. "Mr. President, an extensive crowd is gathering on the lawn."

"No doubt," Lincoln replied, "they believe the newspaper accounts prematurely claiming a victory in the Wilderness conflict." He wished the stories were true and yearned to know more about the outcome of Lieutenant General Grant's campaign through the dense wooded terrain in Virginia. But Grant had forbidden newspaper correspondents the use of the telegraph for conveying military intelligence. And this meant that not even he, the President and Commander-in-Chief, could avail himself of daily news dispatches from Grant. Fortunately, Mr. Wing, a newspaper correspondent returned from Grant's campaign two days earlier and told Lincoln about Grant's personal message to the President—that Grant says there will be no turning back in his campaign. According to Mr. Wing, the battle was progressing favorably.

Lincoln took a moment to listen to the band outside. "John, that is as fine a performance as the Marine Band two days ago. Perhaps I will repeat the message I gave at that time—to give three cheers for Major General Grant and all the armies under his command." Without waiting for a response, he took up his pen and signed the letter he had just written in reply to a lady from Pennsylvania who was concerned about his health and personal welfare.

"With all due respect, Mr. President," John added, "with the encouraging news you received from the New York Tribune correspondent, perhaps a few additional words to the crowd are in order."

"You may be right, John," Lincoln said, raising his lanky body from his chair. "I will give a brief address at the portico."

Lincoln gathered his thoughts together. Grant was a fighter, a commander unfamiliar with the word retreat. Lincoln recalled telling him that all he, as President, ever wanted was someone who would take responsibility for military campaigns and act. As of four days ago, the Union had not given any ground to the rebels. But by now, has the Union suffered a dreaded loss of life? Have Generals Grant and Meade been stopped in their drive toward Richmond?

No, Lincoln told himself, he would not let the people sense his own uneasiness. He stopped at the portico and stared out at the crowd. The band struck up "Hail Columbia," and Lincoln waited until it was over, reading the anxiety on people's faces…a woman holding a youngster with each hand, an elderly man leaning on his cane, a young man in uniform clutching the hand of a lady who may have been his sweetheart. Faces wanting answers. Lincoln wished he had them.

"Fellow citizens," he began. "I am very much obliged to you for the compliment of this call, though I apprehend it is owing more to the good news received today from the army, than a desire to see me. I am indeed very grateful to the brave men who have been struggling with the enemy in the field, to their noble commanders who have directed them, and especially to our Maker."

The faces in the crowd were teary-eyed, hopeful, some smiling through their pain and others looking as solemn as statues. But they leaned on every word he uttered, and Lincoln wished he had the same confidence in this war and in General Grant that he tried to deliver to the crowd. "I commend you," he concluded, "to keep yourselves in the same tranquil mood that is characteristic of that brave and loyal man. I have said more than I expected when I came before you. Repeating my thanks for this call, I bid you goodbye."

*****

May 14, 1864
Crab Orchard, Tennessee
near foot of Cumberland Mountains

179

The morning sun glistened on the tops of the Cumberland Mountains and the mist surrounding them began disappearing when the courier brought much-anticipated mail to the Eighth Kansas. When his name was called, Matt received one letter, which he assumed was from Jessica until he opened it. It was from Mary.

Dearest Matt:

I wanted to tell you I have left Lawrence, Kansas after a tearful goodbye to some of my friends there. My visit with John and Elizabeth Speer was especially painful. After their two sons were murdered by the Quantrill raiders almost nine months ago, they are rebuilding their lives, and John is continuing to publish the Kansas Tribune. Elizabeth tells me that they never did locate Robert's body so they could give it a decent burial. Other Lawrence families are still grieving the loss of their loved ones, but they are using their faith in God to help see them through this ordeal.

I must also tell you that I've taken a nursing position with Pavilion Hospital in St. Louis. In addition, I am involved with the Mississippi Valley Sanitary Fair to help raise funds in order to provide medical care for soldiers and freed slaves.

It was fortunate that Willard, a friend of my brother Joseph was now working as a physician and was able to secure gainful employment for me. I think you would enjoy Willard's company. He is quite attentive and considerate of my needs and has a delightful sense of humor.

I pray that you will be safe from danger and that we will have the opportunity to see one another again. I have not received any correspondence from you, and I worry that perhaps you are ill and cannot write.

Yours truly,

Mary

Matt felt like a fool in not having written as regularly to her as he did to Jessica. He could not continue this charade much longer, yet he postponed telling Mary about his intention to wed Jessica. While he was not officially engaged to her, he knew that when he was mustered out of the service, he would see Jessica again and they would make plans for their wedding.

He put the letter in his pocket and stared at the mountain. The orders from Major General Sherman were for the Eighth to serve as an escort to a pontoon train to Chattanooga to support Sherman's move toward Atlanta. But ascending and descending one of these mountains would be excruciating, requiring every ounce of energy they had.

Just like it would require every ounce of courage for him to write that letter to Mary and tell her he could not see her again.

*****

May 19
Washington, DC

While waiting for Penelope in the visitor's reception area of the U.S. Printing Office, Jessica came upon an earlier issue of the *Congressional Globe* and scanned it for any mention of the Fort Pillow, Tennessee butchery. According to last month's article in the *New York Times*, not only did the rebels overrun the Federal fort, despite a Union surrender, but they apparently massacred almost three hundred colored troops and killed several negro women in cold blood.

A shiver ran through her body and her mind reeled. *Could this possibly be true?* She had no way of knowing, but she closed her eyes at the thought that it might be. Perhaps the initial public outcry in Washington might have pressured Lincoln and the Congress to take action over any atrocities. She scanned through the *Globe* and came across only a short statement about it:

> *Resolved, That the Joint Committee on the Conduct of the War be, and they are hereby, instructed*

181

to inquire into the truth of the rumored slaughter of the Union troops, after their surrender, at the recent attack of the rebel forces upon Fort Pillow, Tennessee, and also whether Fort Pillow could have been sufficiently re-enforced or evacuated, and if so, why it was not done; and that they report the facts to Congress as soon as possible.

Jessica frowned after learning there would only be an investigation but no action. Perhaps the matter would have to rest until the end of this nonsensical, fruitless war.

Just then, Penelope entered the room and Jessica tossed the publication on the table. Penelope's smile seemed forced, and her forehead was etched with thin lines of worry. "It's wonderful that you could join me for a light dinner today," she said, holding Jessica's hand for a moment. "I'm glad that we have some time together before you need to pick the children up from school."

"Is everything all right?"

"Everything should be more than fine," Penelope said, lowering her voice to a whisper, "I received a promotion today. I am now supervisor of the Folding Department."

"Congratulations."

"Truth is, I was amply warned that this is an unusual step because men have traditionally held supervisory positions. But Otto convinced Mr. Defrees that I had greater qualifications for that position than any of the men who were vying for that title."

"That is great news."

Penelope's frown deepened. "I am not sure of that."

"What do you mean?"

Penelope looked about to see if anyone was nearby, and then pulled out a slip of paper. She handed it to her.

"An anonymous person," Penelope said, her eyes twitching with fear, "left this note on my desk."

Jessica gasped in reading the note. It was a simple statement:
If you want to live, resign.
*****

May 21
Spotsylvania County, Virginia

"This would be a suitable place to hold a war council," General Grant told General George Meade as they approached a two-story brick building that he recognized as a church. "Let's have our staffs rest here."

Meade halted the troops and commanded them to dismount.

"Today is Saturday," Grant said, "is it not?"

"Yes sir."

"Good. Then we won't be in danger of disrupting services. Have the men carry out church benches and group them in a circle beneath those shade trees yonder. I don't know about you, but I could use a rest."

It was noon when the officers sat, three or four to a bench, and talked to each other. "Our next position will be Guiney's Station," Grant said to Meade, pointing to a map held by another officer. "Then we make our way toward the North Anna River. I may have Burnside and Wright strike the enemy from different positions once we cross the river."

"General," Meade said, "isn't Guiney's Station the location where General Jackson died last year?"

"It is. I knew Stonewall Jackson both at West Point and in the Mexican War. He was a good man, a good soldier. But he made a tragic mistake in deciding to fight against his own country."

Brigadier General Babcock interrupted the conversation just then. "A photographer would like to take a few pictures of you and your staff. May I grant him permission?"

"Yes," Grant said, laughing under his breath, "but shoot him if he turns out to be a rebel spy."

He turned to Meade after Babcock left. "Photographers and journalists can be a nuisance sometimes."

"I agree. Especially when they publish an unkind account of you in the Wilderness Campaign, calling you a butcher."

Grant got up and paced before the bench. Certainly, Hancock's Second Army Corp, Warren's Fifth Army, Burnside's Ninth

Army, Sheridan's Cavalry, and Hunt's Artillery performed well in the Wilderness Campaign. But an estimated 17,000 men were lost—including General James Wadsworth, a fact which deeply touched the President. Whole regiments, such as the 20th Massachusetts, were ripped to shreds, while Grant pushed on. Stubbornly.

He stopped in front of Meade and placed a heavy hand on his shoulder. "These journalists are sadly mistaken," he said. "I grieve for every man who gave his life for the cause. I most assuredly do."

*****

May 22
Baltimore, Maryland

"I would say that altogether we have well over 350,000 by now," Elizabeth Cady Stanton said as she tallied the signatures that Jessica helped to obtain yesterday and today for the Women's National Loyal League.

"I only managed to get about two hundred," Jessica said.

Stanton placed Jessica's signed petitions in a large envelope. "No need to apologize, Miss Radford. I realize that getting even that many can be difficult. Ladies in my league have been at this for a year now, but we are still considerably short of our goal of one million that we can lay at the feet of Congress."

"Mrs. Stanton, when I ask even regular churchgoers to sign a petition abolishing slavery everywhere, some of them look at me as if I were a lunatic. 'Don't you know,' they say, 'that the President issued the Emancipation Proclamation to do just that?'"

"That's because some people are poorly educated. They don't realize that the Proclamation only abolished slavery in Confederate states. As far as I'm concerned, Lincoln's antislavery policies are not going far enough."

"Well," Jessica said, rising from her chair, "I have a train to catch for Washington. I wish you every success in your endeavor."

184

Stanton got up as well. Her smile warmed her broad, friendly face as she extended her hand. "Thank you for your help. By the way, have you heard any news from the publishers about your novel?"

"Not yet," she said, shaking Stanton's hand, "but some people tell me my novel would be a good addition to Harriet Beecher Stowe's *Uncle Tom's Cabin* as far as having an impact on the slavery issue."

"It may well be." Stanton regarded her for a moment. "Miss Radford, do you feel as passionately about women's rights as you do the rights of slaves?"

"I suppose I do."

"I spearheaded a women's rights convention sixteen years ago in Seneca Falls, New York. While our efforts have been mollified due to this war, I'd like you to consider meeting some friends of mine."

Before Jessica could respond, Elizabeth Stanton handed her a card. "Just write to me when you can. We need more women with your ambition."

"I appreciate the invitation," Jessica said. But after they parted, Jessica returned her attention to her novel. The people she wanted to meet at this juncture were other writers, not more rights advocates. Later as she settled herself in a railroad car with a newspaper, an article caught her attention. It was about the death of novelist and short story writer, Nathaniel Hawthorne. His passing was a disappointment as she had contemplated visiting him some day to tell him how much she admired his writing. She was especially taken by *The Scarlet Letter* about an illicit love affair in Puritan New England. Poor Hester! She had to wear the scarlet "A" (for adulteress) because she refused to reveal that her lover was a young minister. Yet for Jessica, Hester was a true heroine. The public be damned. If she chose to have an affair with a man, whose business was it of society to scorn her?

She knew, deep inside, that she enjoyed Matt's company. When her Pa introduced him to her four years ago at her high school graduation picnic in Lawrence, she was impressed by his appearance and friendly manner. Even today she could envision him as that lanky, dark-haired man in a checkered shirt and dark trousers, wearing a straw hat at a jaunty, devil-may-care angle, and holding a long-stemmed pipe. He looked odd to her, the way his harsh Indian features clashed with his friendly smile. But when he kissed her hand, a prickly feeling raced through her arm.

Matt had a certain charm about him, the way he respected her as a lady. He had a creative touch, as evidenced by that wooden carving of Lincoln he had given her. But there was also a certain ruggedness about him, and she could imagine how, if they were married, he would always be there to protect her from any danger.

But he was also self-willed and stubborn just as she was. What if she discovered later that her ideals conflicted with his? What if he objected to her growing obsession with the slavery issue? Would he argue with her about his belief that freed slaves and white folk should not mingle with one another? What if she did not care to be a Methodist or have any religion for that matter? Would she be, nonetheless, irrevocably bound to him in marriage?

Matt would make a decent woman out of her, from society's perspective at least. She ought to consider it. Yet it would not erase how she still felt about Otto. Nothing could erase that.

Chapter 26

June 9
Baltimore, Maryland

At the Republican National Convention, Lincoln waited for Henry Raymond, the chairman of the National Union League, to finish his talk. Although he would be nominated for reelection, Lincoln did consider it a strong possibility that he would not actually *win* reelection. He had people even in his own cabinet, men like Salmon Chase, his Treasury Secretary, who continued to oppose him. Mr. Chase was like a needle pinching the skin, stressing that the war had been unduly prolonged. Even some of Lincoln's previous supporters wanted to distance themselves from his stance on emancipation.

Only a week ago, the President recalled, liberals such as Elizabeth Cady Stanton and other displeased Republicans held their own convention in Cleveland to protest both the conduct of the war and his imbecilic policies as President. They had planned to nominate, instead, John Frémont on an independent party ticket. But although the Ohio convention folded and prominent newsmen such as Greeley withdrew their support for Frémont, he, Lincoln, felt the opposition in his own party could hurt his reelection chances. A lot would depend on how the tide would turn before November.

Surveying the crowded room, where some five hundred delegates nominated him for reelection, Lincoln wondered if they had doubts about his chances of a second term. Reports had filtered in from Cold Harbor, where General Grant's massive assault on rebel entrenchments six days earlier resulted in an estimated 12,000 men who were killed or wounded. So many had already died. He felt the chilly harshness of reality in the last thirty days in which the Union suffered some 54,000 casualties—almost the size of General Lee's entire army.

Perhaps the naysayers were right. Unless there was some decisive turnaround prior to the election, Lincoln knew he would be a one-term president. But what could he do—go along with the foolhardy beliefs of that traitorous Ohio governor, Clement

Vallandigham, who was pushing a "let-us-make-peace-at-all-costs" philosophy...a man willing to give a good portion of the United States to the Confederate States of America just to make peace? No, Lincoln told himself, he would never do that.

Amidst scattered applause, the President came to the podium and looked at his audience with tired eyes, eyes that begged for sleep. He struggled with his thoughts, aware of a restless mind that nagged him about the uncertain outcome of this war, a mind that tried to be a solid wall against the complaints of his demanding wife. But his mind also grieved at the spiraling number of inconsolable widows, while agonizing at a future election he could surely lose.

Lincoln nodded to the chairman taking his seat before returning his attention to the hundreds of delegates in the room. "Gentlemen: I can only say, in response to the kind remarks of your chairman, as I suppose, that I am very grateful for the renewed confidence which has been accorded to me, both by the convention and by the National League. I am not insensible at all to the personal compliment there is in this; yet I do not allow myself to believe that any but a small portion of it is to be appropriated as a personal compliment."

He leaned forward, pressing his hands against the podium and glancing about the room. "The convention and the nation, I am assured, are alike animated by a higher view of the interests of the country for the present and the great future, and that part I am entitled to appropriate as a compliment is only that part which I may lay hold of as being the opinion of the convention and of the League, that I am not—" he looked down for a second and returned his gaze to the audience— "that I am not entirely unworthy to be instructed with the place I have occupied for the last three years. I have not permitted myself, gentlemen, to conclude that I am the best man in the country." He smiled for the first time during the pause that followed. "But I am reminded, in this connection, of a story of an old Dutch farmer, who remarked to a companion once that 'it was not best to swap horses when crossing streams.'"

*****

June 11, 1864
Charlottetown, Prince Edward Island
The Province of Canada

Dear Miss Radford,
 I hope you won't consider it too forward of me to be writing to you, but I know you have an appreciation for the fine arts, so I thought you might be interested in something I have created. It's a musical composition entitled "The Pain of Freedom," The composition is included with this letter, and I thought perhaps you can see if Mitzi might play it while you sing the verses.
 It is dreadful sitting back here in Canada and reading the negative press about the War Between the States. Some people here cannot understand why slavery should even be an issue there, but they fail to understand that the war is not only about slavery, as you already know. The loss of life on both sides of the conflict is incredible and has gone well above the loss of America lives suffered in the War of Independence from the British as well as the War of 1812—combined.
 While I am glad to have at least participated on the Union side, I don't know if the Union is engaging in this conflict with the attitude of minimizing casualties. I can only point to the recent battle in Cold Harbor, where estimates of casualties for both sides combined exceeded 25,000. That is a population larger than the majority of your towns. Yet your General Grant continues to move forward. I have a difficult time understanding that ideology.
 Pardon me for going on about the war. I did want to write to you to tell you that at some time in the future I would like to visit with you as well as Mr. and Mrs. Heller and their children. I understand from my last correspondence from Mr. Heller that your novel, A Slave Only Once, will be published. Congratulations! I expect to be

one of your earliest customers when it becomes available.

Meanwhile, I hope Mitzi continues her lessons on the piano. I am glad that you have placed the framed daguerreotype of me playing the violin in her room so that perhaps it will serve as an inspiration for her.

My best wishes to you and to the Heller family.

Sincerely,

Devin Alcott

*****

June 12
Alexandria, Virginia

During his long train ride toward the nation's capital, Matt had time to think about his plans for the future. He had spent years in the seminary studying to be a Methodist minister, and he would continue to preach, God willing. Although Jessica attended Catholic Mass with Penelope and the children every Sunday, he wondered about her faith. Would she be open to becoming a Methodist and raising their children in his religion? Jessica rarely discussed religion with him. But she ought to know he would be willing to take a second job if he had to supplement his meager clergyman's salary. He would see to it that she would never have to worry about money.

But her foolishness about the slavery question bothered him. It wasn't that he had no feelings for the negro. When a brave colored soldier named Salem died in his arms on the Chattanooga battlefield last year, Matt cried. Poor Salem died believing that his brother Ishmael died a hero, but Matt never told Salem the truth.

Why was Jessica so obsessed with the slavery issue? After all, Jesus never condemned the idea of owning slaves. And some slaves were, in fact, treated well. He himself had always been kind to Tinker, hadn't he? Besides, if Jessica is hell-bent on changing slavery laws in this country, there were men in

190

responsible positions who could do this more effectively than she or any woman.

But Jessica was not just any woman. That was what he admired about her. She had the strength of her convictions, a rare thing for a woman. His mother also had that trait. She supported her husband while convincing him that her suggestions were irrevocably his own ideas. It worked out well. Perhaps it would work out well with Jessica, if only she would not be so fiercely independent.

Matt smiled. *Marriage would certainly change that.*

As the train rolled into the station, a Union officer raced down the aisle declaring the arrival in Alexandria. After waiting for his turn to disembark, Matt followed a long line of soldiers, some of whom had their faces covered with bandages, and others who were missing an arm or a leg.

The platform was a teeming blur of returning soldiers, anxious wives, and excited children. Hugs, kisses, and screams of delight abounded everywhere and somewhere in the distance, a military band played. Matt looked about for Jessica, but it was only after he pushed his way past the throng that he saw her. Not only her, but Otto, Penelope, and the two Heller children as well. They waved back at him, and Jessica hurried toward him, her arms open in greeting.

"Oh, Jessica!" he said, kissing her. "I've missed you so!"

"And I as well. I have some splendid news to share with you later."

"News?" Matt's heart raced. *She plans to announce our engagement.*

"I have a carriage waiting for us," Otto said. "It's only a six-mile trip to Washington, but I thought we might all partake of some fine food at a restaurant at the waterfront here."

Matt sensed that whatever news Jessica had to share would be postponed. The conversation at supper became a monotony of words. Jessica said little, but Mitzi and Emma went on and on about their friends at school, Otto talked about the possibility that Lincoln might not win reelection, and Penelope mentioned her promotion to supervisor at the Printing Office.

191

"And," Otto said across the table to Matt, "that threat my dear wife received over her promotion is no longer of concern. Apparently, it was someone's notion of a cruel joke."

Matt nodded as he ate his string bean and tomato salad. This was not how he imagined his homecoming. He had hoped to be alone with Jessica. If she had made her decision about marriage, why was she not saying anything?

Otto leaned forward, a smile crossing his lips. "You haven't heard a word I've uttered, have you?"

"Shucks, I apologize," Matt said. "I've not been able to sleep well on the train."

Jessica returned her water glass to the table. "Goodness, Matt, I almost forgot to tell you about the most exciting event of my day."

"Exciting event?" *Was she going to announce their engagement?*

"Yes. Mr. Heller informed me this morning that I will be a published author. Baker, Reiter, and Johnson have agreed to publish *A Slave Only Once* and they will be sending me a contract. This is tremendously exciting.!"

Matt's face fell but he quickly transformed it into a pleasant smile. "Why, congratulations, Miss Radford. Excellent news."

"If it weren't for this dear, kind man," Jessica said, looking in Otto's direction, "I would never have been strongly considered. You must be a highly persuasive gentleman, Mr. Heller."

"Nonsense. You must take all the credit, Miss Radford. You write beautifully."

"She always has," Matt interjected. "I used to ask for her advice when writin' my sermons."

"Do you plan to find a ministerial position here in Washington?" Penelope asked, cutting the meat on her plate.

"Don't know. Haven't really decided where I might want to establish permanent residency." He turned his head toward Jessica. "There are many factors to consider. Isn't that true, Miss Radford?"

Jessica smiled, but it seemed forced. "I would agree with that."

The next day
St. Louis, Missouri

"I never imagined I would have such reliable transportation to the hospital every day," Mary said as Dr. Willard Hamilton stopped his shay at the livery stable.

He turned the reins over to an attendant and offered her his hand while she disembarked. "Well, my dear Miss Delaney, I have many talents. Would you care to know the others?"

"No," she said, smiling, "I am a bit too timid to ask."

He laughed, making short raspy throat sounds while he held her hand. "I will wager you have a delightful sense of humor, Miss Delaney."

"It is difficult these days with so many men being slaughtered."

"It is senseless, especially when you see boys as young as fifteen being killed. And for what purpose?" He released her hand when she made it up the steps to the main door. "I apologize for my anti-war sentiments. I am sure you are not interested in my droning on about the inept war that the President is waging."

"I try to avoid politics when I can. I have seen far more bloodshed than I should have. A friend of mine named Jessica Radford has as well. In fact, I must write to her."

"Yes. Perhaps you can invite your friend to our house and we can discuss our various war experiences."

"I shall do that."

"I must say, Miss Delaney, in the short time you've been a nurse at this facility, you have received many compliments from the hospital staff as well as from patients. I assume, naturally, that you have developed a good bedside manner from your experiences with regimental field hospitals."

"Indeed I have." The image of Matt Lightfoot, suffering from a chest wound, came immediately to mind. She wondered why he never answered her last letter. Did their time together in her tent convince him she was not a moral woman? No, not Matt. He was a gentleman. But perhaps he had been killed....No! She could not live with that horrible thought.

"Is there anything the matter?" Willard asked. "Did I say anything to cause you discomfort?"

"No, not at all."

"I assume then, that we are still planning on attending the concert this Saturday?"

"Yes, I will look forward to it." *And I will also look forward to seeing you again, Matt. Why don't you write?*

Chapter 27

Lieutenant Roger Toby spotted Joseph Cross, a regimental chaplain, seated on a cracker box outside his tent. The chaplain's head buried in the palms of his hand, his elbows pressing against his knees, he looked up. His tear-streaked face surprised Roger.

"We lost a great man today," Cross said.

"I don't understand."

The chaplain winced, his eyebrows arched in disbelief. "My Lord! You don't know what happened just a little while ago?"

"No, I was in my tent writing a letter to my wife. I heard the explosion of shells. They were rather close."

"See those men coming down the side of the mountain?" He pointed to a rocky ridge that overlooked Marietta, Georgia. "They're carrying the remains of General Leonidas Polk. He had been observing, along with Johnston and Hardee the Union troops some three hundred feet below." He took out a handkerchief and dried his eyes.

"General Polk was killed?" Roger asked, disbelieving.

"Yes. Enemy artillery fire began at that moment. Johnston and Hardee took cover, but a shell crashed directly into Polk. He died instantly." He rose and walked to a table in his tent. "Copies of this work were found in the general's pocket." He held up a bloodstained copy of *Balm for the Weary and Wounded* by Reverend Quintard for Roger to see. "He was going to give Johnston, Hardee, and Hood each a copy."

"I understand General Polk was a religious man," Roger said.

"And a good man. They are taking him to Marietta where they will find a suitable coffin. I understand that right now, General Johnston is composing a eulogy. We will miss him terribly."

Roger had only recently become familiar with *Balm for the*

195

Weary and Wounded and knew two stanzas from it by heart....

> *If on my aching, burdened heart,*
> *My sins lie heavily,*
> *Thy pardon grant, Thy peace impart*
> *Good Lord, remember me.*

> *If trials obstruct my way,*
> *And Ills I cannot flee,*
> *Then let my strength be as my day;*
> *Good Lord, remember me.*

Roger knew there could be no God. *If He existed, where was He when all these good people were being slaughtered?*

"Are you a religious man, lieutenant?" Quintard asked.

"Absolutely not."

*****

June 19
Washington, DC

Matt found himself lost in thought as he stood with Jessica in church to sing "Amazing Grace." John Newton, Matt reflected, navigated a slave ship and had experienced a narrow escape from death before he wrote those immortal lines: "'Tis grace hath brought me safe thus far, and grace will lead me home." But what did he—Matt—do after his own narrow brush with death on a Chickamauga battlefield? He had a sinful, passionate moment with Mary. He lacked the courage to tell her he did not love her and he did not answer any of her letters.

His life was a lie, not even telling Jessica, when she asked him, where Mary was now living. His only hope was that Jessica would not learn the truth and that she would say yes to his marriage proposal after he traveled with her to St. Louis. Once she was finished meeting with her publisher there, she

196

would do what she hinted she might do—settle down in a new environment—hopefully, with him for a lifetime.

Jessica gave him a gentle squeeze of the hand when the hymn was over. She looked even prettier than she was when he first met her. Her azure eyes had the blueness of a fresh lake, and her smile was mature, like a woman who was sure of herself and less concerned about what others thought of her. Even though they had never consummated their love, he could still recall that night in Lawrence where he held her naked body against his. She was a delight, but her face lacked a certain softness and innocence. Perhaps her fanciful ideas had been replaced by the cruel reality of this war.

"Matt," Jessica said when they left the church, "I'm pleased that you've agreed to accompany me to St. Louis."

Matt grinned. "Shucks, I couldn't very well have a nice lady like you travelin' alone during these perilous times."

Jessica took her seat in the carriage. "I don't know if any of those rebels would have the courage to tangle with a wildcat like me. I still have my .44 Colt revolver and am not afraid to use it."

"I know, and I've also seen how well you handled a musket in Tennessee. Of course, you were some gentleman soldier named Walter Brontë at the time."

"Have I ever told you how I chose that name?"

"Nope. Don't believe you have."

"I arrived at 'Walter' from Mr. Whitman's first name and 'Brontë' from Emily Brontë—an excellent novelist. If I had to do it over again, I would probably assume the name Stowe, for Harriet Beecher Stowe. Did you know that when she met President Lincoln two years ago he told her 'so you're the little woman who wrote the book that started this great war.'?"

"That'd be nonsense. No book can start a war. Besides, this conflict did not begin over the slavery issue."

"Perhaps, but I believe it's going to end that way. I think the end of slavery will result in other problems. The novel I'm having published is about a former slave who fights to break the bonds of bigotry."

197

Matt nodded as if he agreed with her, but his mind raced to change the subject. "I'm in the process of carvin' you another statue. I hope you like it."

"You don't have to carve me any more statues, Matt. I still admire the bust of President Lincoln you've given me. Mr. Heller has it prominently displayed on his piano."

"Didn't you say Mr. Heller was the one who helped you find a publisher?"

Jessica's eyes brightened. "Indeed. He is one of the most generous and thoughtful men I have ever met. And I daresay, while he is an older gentleman, he is still quite dashing."

"Shucks, Jessica, I'd be jealous if he weren't already married."

"Jealous?" She laughed lightly. "That is a most ridiculous notion." But she enjoyed his comment. *He truly loves me if he's envious of my affection for another.*

Once the train pulled from the station, Jessica busied herself with reading. She looked up, and noticing the bored look on Matt's face, she invited him to read a copy of her manuscript.

Matt took her sheaf of papers, rifled through them, and stared back at her. "Aren't you concerned about losing this while you are traveling?"

"I used carbonated paper that allows me to copy it on a thin paper sheet underneath my original."

"That is indeed interesting. How did you discover this?"

"Mr. Heller told me about it. He also showed me a drawing of an invention—a typewriting machine device that would do away with writing by hand. Isn't he a marvelous man, knowing all those things?"

"He is a marvelous man to be sure," he said, his voice cracking.

"I hope you will enjoy reading my manuscript, despite any residual feelings you might have about slavery."

Matt deliberated whether to try to convince her that he no longer felt that slavery was acceptable. As far as he was concerned, negroes should be free but his concern was what would happen once they integrated with polite society. He started to go through her manuscript as she opened a book she had been carrying.

Matt skimmed through the pages. *This is pure fantasy. A former female slave would not rise to such a height of power in our society. Didn't Jessica realize that once negroes were set free that they would be lost without a slave owner who gave them a certain sense of security?*

They sat in silence for a long while. Finally, she turned toward him, showing him her copy of *Confidence Man* by Herman Melville. "This is his latest novel. His critics were very hard on him, but I wanted to see why for myself. Perhaps they find it difficult to understand."

"Speaking of that, Jessica, I hope you won't take offense if I tell you that I had difficulty with my reading of your most recent novel."

Her eyes narrowed. "Difficulty? In what way?"

"Your hero in this story is a freed slave. After the war's over, she goes into politics and becomes a United States Senator. That could never happen."

"Why not?"

"I reckon that after this war is over there'll be an intense struggle between the negro and the white man. The negro will have to overcome obstacles in education, employment opportunities, and recognition as equals in all areas of society."

She gave him a look of disbelief. "Doesn't the Bible say that with God *all* things are possible?"

*****

June 22
St. Louis, Missouri

Matt and Jessica took adjoining rooms with a connecting door, and after supper they spent time in her room playing chess. But Matt found it difficult to concentrate, staring at her bed and chasing away thoughts about how he would have forbidden pleasures with her later tonight. He closed his eyes. *God, be merciful to me, a sinner.*

199

"You are probably three moves away from being check-mated," Jessica said, looking back at him with a triumphant smile.

"Shucks, I've never been good at this game."

She moved another piece. "I know. Mary told me you weren't good at games." She cleared her throat. "Incidentally, have you heard from her?"

Matt bit his lip and stared at the chessboard. "Yup. We've had some correspondence."

She moved her rook. "Check." She leaned back in her chair and Matt could sense her staring at him. "Do you recall that night we spent in Lawrence at an outdoor concert? We sat on the grass as the band played 'Home Sweet Home' and we made a promise that I would forget all about John Howell, that soldier I had met long ago. And you promised you would forget about Mary Delaney. Remember?"

Matt moved his knight three spaces over. "I remember."

"Have you had affectionate thoughts about her?"

Matt swallowed hard. Mary's words returned again to haunt him:

> Mary allowed him to enter her tent in Chatta-nooga and she snuggled up close to him. "I don't wish to talk about Jessica any longer," Matt had told her. "As far as I am concerned, I want only you."
>
> "And you have me. I am yours," she sighed, pressing her softness against him.

"Checkmate," Jessica said, with a suddenness that alarmed him until he realized it was only a chess game he had lost.

*****

Jessica looked at herself one more time in the mirror. The red merino shirt she wore coordinated nicely with her black crinoline skirt, clothes that she bought last time she went shopping with Penelope. Her blond hair was parted in the middle and tied with a red ribbon in the back. She squeezed her lips together to see if they would turn a bit more red. Yes, she looked fine for this morning's meeting with the publisher and editor at Baker, Reiter, and Johnson.

She had also made a decision last night after Matt complained about the fact that he respected her too much to have relations with her at this point. He blamed it on his Christian training that taught him about the importance of postponing such intimacies until marriage. But Jessica wondered if it was mere coincidence that he encountered this problem only after she began talking about what a wonderful woman Mary was. Matt became crestfallen and had the look of a man who had been caught stealing.—or cheating. Did he already have those "forbidden" intimacies with Mary?

Jessica felt a chill race through her body when she thought of marriage. Her parents often used to argue with each other, sometimes telling each other they were sorry they ever got married. Of course, she was fond of Matt, a handsome man with Cherokee features, self-assured but maybe too much so. He would be a good provider and told her on more than one occasion that he would like to raise a large family. She enjoyed the romantic moments they had, and maybe she would discover that marriage was good for her. Perhaps being in a stable home and having certain responsibilities, she would grow to appreciate married life. But she knew herself too well. She needed her independence. And she needed freedom to do all she could to help the downtrodden, without any man trying to convince her not to.

Marriage to Matt? If only she didn't feel so rushed into a decision of that magnitude.

When she entered the hotel dining room, she saw him tapping his spoon against the table. "Are you composing a new drumbeat?" she asked, grinning.

He rose from his chair, his face turning a shade of crimson as he dropped his spoon to the floor "Miss Radford! You look wonderful."

"Thank you. I wanted to wear something proper for my meeting this morning."

The server came by just then to take their order. Matt ordered coffee, fried eggs and toast, but Jessica asked for just coffee. "I'm too excited to eat," she said. "The editors are going to discuss manuscript revisions and ideas for a possible cover design."

"While you're gone, I'll be visitn' the Trinity Methodist Church. I'm also goin' to explore other opportunities in this town. Maybe I'll even inquire about livin' arrangements for you and me here."

Jessica twisted her table napkin. How was she going to handle what she would say to him tonight?

*****

After leaving Jessica at the stone building housing the publishing office of Baker, Reiter, and Johnson, Matt had the coachman drive him to the riverfront. He paid the driver and walked to the riverfront. There, staring out over the Mississippi, he could visualize himself as a small boy whose Cherokee father told him that running waters held deep secrets of the earth. "That is because the Great Spirit abides in these waters," he would say, "and when your soul is troubled, these waters will bring you in harmony with the Spirit." Matt still believed in the Great Spirit—altered to fit the Christian version of God. Now, when he looked upon the blackish-blue water splashing against the huge metal walls of an ironclad warship below, he hoped the Great Spirit would help him cope with his uneasy soul. He had completed his service with the military, but would he now find his happiness? "Someday you will meet a strong woman, a good woman," his father had once promised.

Matt hated himself for not telling Miss Delaney about his plans to marry Jessica. He should have corresponded with Mary, but all the while he was afraid of hurting her feelings. Surely, Mary deserved to know the truth and he really ought to tell her tonight.

He reached into his pocket for her home address.

*****

"This is quite embarrassing," Willard Hamilton said, grinning as he lay on her davenport while she applied liniment to his bare

202

ankle. "My foot must have caught in the stirrups when I dismounted."

"It looks like a fairly bad sprain," Mary said, lightly rubbing the swollen ankle.

"Indeed. I am sometimes so careless, I'm not even aware of what my limbs are doing as I talk. Imagine what would happen if the hospital discovered their leading surgeon was clumsy."

Mary laughed and the curls of her autumn-red hair bounced against her forehead. "Well, we will just have to keep it a secret, then, won't we?"

"Indeed we will. Just as we must keep it a secret that I am in your boarding house right now and am having a delightful time enjoying the pleasure of your company."

"Dr. Hamilton, you are making me flush with embarrassment."

There was a sudden rap on the door. "I wonder who that might be," she said, getting up. She opened the door and froze.

"Mr. Lightfoot! What in God's name—?"

He handed her a bunch of daisies. "Sorry for showin' up like this unexpectedly, but I was in town and I thought I would visit with you."

"Well—ah—please come in."

Matt took two steps into the parlor and stopped when he saw a man with neatly-combed brown hair and trimmed mustache. He was dressed in white jean pants, blue coat, and with bare feet extended over the arm of a davenport. He smiled back at Matt's bewilderment. "Are you another one of her suitors?" he joked.

"Oh shush," Mary said. "Don't mind my friend Willard Hamilton. He's a notorious jokester."

Willard simply grinned.

Mary gave Matt a quick peck on the cheek. "Thank you for the flowers." She paused a moment, as if hesitating to bring up a delicate subject. "I thought you had died on the battlefield. I haven't heard from you in a long while."

"I want to apologize for that," Matt said. "I do need to offer you an explanation, but I—" He took another glance at Hamilton.

"If you plan on courting this fine lady," Hamilton said, grinning "you will need to wait your proper turn."

Matt shifted from one foot to the other but kept his eyes on Mary. "Shucks, I guess I should have come at a more convenient time."

"Nonsense," Hamilton said. "I was just leaving." But no sooner had he moved his ankle than he grimaced in pain.

"You're not leaving anywhere just yet, Dr. Hamilton," Mary said. "I've got to apply a little more liniment and wrap a bandage tightly aroundt it."

Matt went to the door. "I'm sorry, Miss Delaney. Forgive me for intrudin' on you and your friend."

"It's not an intrusion. Where are you staying?"

"At the Pacific House Hotel."

"When will I see you again?"

"I—I don't rightly know. I really must be goin'. It was a pleasure meetin' you, Mr. Hamilton."

"Don't leave just yet," Mary said softly, but it was too late. Matt bounded down the steps and was headed for a waiting coachman.

"Who was that?" Hamilton asked.

"A friend." Mary forced herself to keep from crying. "Just a friend."

Chapter 28

Jessica reread the last line of Mr. Heller's telegram: "The children and I need you."

She stuffed the message into her pocket and pushed open the door of the publisher's office only to be greeted by the stifling heat of a St. Louis summer. No point in even thinking about making her permanent home in this town. The children needed her. The nanny Otto had hired was incompetent.

The telegram was welcome news as she had vacillated about where she wanted to live. "You will love it here," Matt had insisted, "with much to offer in the way of culture and accommodations."

But the children—she'd miss them, and she'd miss Otto as well. "The children and I need you."

How could she move to a strange town? There was something intriguing about living in Washington, where the one man who inspired her could make a difference in the outcome of the slavery issue. After all, she had promised herself she would do what she could to help win Mr. Lincoln's reelection.

Besides, it was different for Matt. He had no roots, and he was looking for a permanent place to settle as well as a new ministry. He also thought about something she didn't want to think about at the moment—marriage.

Later that evening, Jessica was in her room, fastening the buttons of her simple blue patterned housedress with bishop-cut sleeves and wondering what to tell him about her decision. He promised he would meet with her here at six before going out to supper, but Jessica wished she had more time to consider what she would say to him.

It was exactly six o'clock when he knocked on her door, and Jessica welcomed him in. "I hope you don't mind that I dressed in simple attire for our supper tonight."

He kissed her and beamed an uncertain smile back at her. "You look wonderful in anything you wear, Jessica."

She looked at herself in the mirror. "How was your day?"

"Wonderful. Met with the pastor of a church in town. Tells me he knows a pastor in a new church who is lookin' for an assistant. I plan to meet with him soon."

She sat on the edge of the bed. "That is good to hear. I am happy for you."

"If I take the position, I'll have to supplement my income by takin' another job. But that shouldn't be a problem. It is only important that you and I be happy together."

Jessica patted her hand against the mattress. "Come here, Matt. We need to talk."

Matt's uncertain smile disappeared into a look of concern as he eased himself next to her. "What is it, darling?"

"You must know that I am fond of you and have been for quite some time. But I—I just—" She exhaled deeply. "I simply cannot agree to marry you."

A muscle twitched in Matt's face and his hand grasped her arm. "What are you sayin', my dear Jessica?"

"Matt, I'm returning to Washington. I'm needed there. Otto and the children need me. I've made friends there. Here in St. Louis I know no one."

Matt's face brightened. "Fine. We can get married in Washington, then. It doesn't matter to me where we live."

Jessica shook her head. *This was not going to be easy.* "Matt, I have made up my mind. I cannot commit to marrying you."

Matt leaped from the bed. "What are you saying? That you're not sure? That you need more time to think about it?"

Jessica struggled for the right words. "You want a woman whom you could cherish. A woman who would be satisfied being at home, raising children. A woman who kept her place in polite company. I'm not that kind of woman, Matt."

Matt raised his finger at her. "Now hold on! How do you know what I want? Maybe all I want is to have you by my side. Maybe I just want to be with the woman I love every day."

"Your problem is you envision things the way *you* want them to be and not the way they truly are."

His eyes burned with anger. "Yup, I do. I'm always lookin' at the way I want them to be. But let me tell you this, Jessica— you are too independent for your own good. The Lord knows I've tried to cater to your every whim. I've tried agreein' with you. I've kept silent while you went on your jaunts to hold an anti-slavery talk and while you made decisions I didn't agree with. If you loved me, you would occasionally respect my opinions and try to understand my point of view about everything. I hate to disillusion you, but you don't always have the right answers."

Jessica took a quick step toward him and faced him with her own anger. "I have one right answer this evening, Mr. Lightfoot. I was going to take the train back to Washington tomorrow and have supper with you tonight. But frankly, I've decided to leave tonight!"

His face softened and he placed his hands on her shoulders. "Do you love me, Jessica?"

She looked away. "I can't say the words you want me to say, Matt. I like you, and in some ways, I even admire you. But love—love is far too strong a word."

Matt dropped his hands and a despairing grayness crossed over his face. "So you don't love me, is that it?"

She looked at him for only a second longer, then turned away. "I will need to start packing my things."

Matt dropped to the bed and put his face in his hands. She thought she heard him sob, and it stunned her. She had never seen him weep before. She sat next to him and cradled him in her arms, all the while thinking that this was the same man who fought so bravely in the war, the man who was proud of his Cherokee heritage. But now he was a stranger, a man lacking the strength and courage she assumed he always had.

"I beg you, Jessica, please don't leave. If you go, I have nothing. I am in great despair."

"I will write to you," she promised.

"I'll go back to Washington with you."

"Whatever for? I'm not marrying you, Matt."

They said little after that. But later, as they rode in the carriage en route to the train depot, they kissed, and she wanted to say that somehow, despite everything, she still loved him, but she found it impossible. He'd press her to change her mind.

No, she had to leave. Yet she realized she would be taking an awful memory back with her, the memory of him standing near the carriage, waving slowly back at her as she looked out the window, his face like that of a man condemned to be hanged.

The train hissed and chugged and pulled away and, as she sat by the window, she closed her eyes. That night she dreamt about the first time she had met him at her high school graduation party in South Park in Lawrence, Kansas....

"Your pa," he had said, "tells me you like to write. That true?"

"I do, Reverend Lightfoot. I find life fascinating; I want to write about everything."

"Young lady," he said, "let your heart be your guide—not only in writin', but in life."

Jessica awoke from her dream in the dark of night, the clickity-click-clack, clickity-click-clack monotony of the rails urging her to go back to sleep.

But she couldn't.

Chapter 29

July 10
Leeburn, Georgia

"Nonsense," Jane said as she stopped the wagon when they reached the hotel with a "Women's Relief Society" banner draped over the entryway. "I'm not afraid of those Yankees. I'll kill every one who dares try to touch you or me."

"Well I'm rightly concerned not only about my safety but Nellie's as well," Sara said.

"I not be afraid of no Yankees," Nellie said, thinking about the Radfords, whom she used to live with in Lawrence, Kansas. "They nice people."

Jane frowned back at her. "Some are and some ain't. Y'see ordinary Yankee folks are different than those Federals who fight in this war." She stepped down from the wagon platform and waited for Sara and Nellie to disembark. "No telling what they might do. But like I say, I ain't afraid of 'em at'all. C'mon and help me unload the wagon."

Nellie grabbed a bundle of clothing while Sara and Jane struggled with carrying a large container of food and medical supplies to the door. "Why we must have half of Atlanta's contributions to the war effort in this box," Sara said as she and Jane dropped it on the hotel porch.

"It only appears that way," Jane said, opening the door of the hotel. "These are just some of the items our generous neighbors gathered for us."

The hotel lobby was a sea of assorted merchandise—socks, jackets, pants, boots, coffee, bandages, quinine water, medicinal plants, hardtack, potatoes, dried beef, and whiskey. Two women were picking out certain items and placing them in bags. Another woman stood at the counter, working on a ledger while Jane, Nellie, and Sara threaded their way through a small path leading in that direction.

Jane Millicent leaned on the counter and waited for the other woman to finish scrawling in her ledger. When the woman looked up, Jane told her about the packages she left on the porch and that she had come all the way from Atlanta.

"We appreciate your generous contribution to our Confederate soldiers," the woman said. "They need all the supplies they can get." Her eyes wandered over to Nellie but then returned to Jane. "Maybe she and your other slaves can bring in the materials on the porch."

Jane clenched her jaw and the muscles in her neck tightened. She took a deep breath and returned a forced smile. "Nellie here isn't able to exert herself because of her condition and we don't have any other slaves."

The woman at the counter looked again at Nellie as if she didn't believe that excuse. But then she glanced at Jane again. "I'll have those brought in. Where are you women headed?"

"We understand there is a fine restaurant about six or seven miles up on Granger Road," Sara said. "We might partake of dinner there before we head back for Atlanta."

"Pleasure meeting you," Jane said coldly to the counter woman. "We must be on our way."

Jane turned to leave, but the woman called her. "Ma'am, perhaps you can do me a favor and drop off something on your way. If you're going on Granger Road, you can take this parcel to Myers Munitions Works. It is only about a half mile past the restaurant." She lifted a box to the counter. "This contains cartridges that several donors have given us., and I would be much obliged if you could deliver this personally to Grover Myers, the owner of the plant. He will likely combine this with his other loads going out to a Confederate garrison."

Jane took the box and left in a huff, with Nellie and Sara trailing behind. "Imagine," Jane said, loading the box in the wagon, "thinking that Nellie was my slave."

"Now you can understand," Sara said, taking her seat on the wagon platform with Nellie, "what I had to go through with people always calling Nellie my slave girl."

Jane Millicent broke the long silence that followed. "Have you heard from Roger lately?"

"The last letter I received from him was a brief one where he said they were camped somewhere near Rome, Georgia. I suspect they are anticipating an eventual attack by that das-tardly Union commander Sherman. But he didn't say much about the plans for the Army of Tennessee. Maybe they don't rightly have any plans seeing as how Bragg led his troops to defeat in Chattanooga."

"True, but I have a lot of faith in General Johnston," Jane said. "He'll drive those Yankees back where they belong. You'll see."

Nellie hummed a negro spiritual as she watched the dust gathering behind them like a gray smoke as the horses lum-bered on. She did not care anything about the generals or about the battles. All she wanted was to see Jessica again. And she wouldn't be able to do that until this war was over.

"Here we are," Jane said as they approached a three-story brick building that displayed the name "Myers Munitions Works" near the entrance. "I'll drop that box off and then we'll find a restaurant for dinner."

"I'll go with you," Sara said, emerging from the wagon. "I'm rather curious as to how this plant is helping fortify our armies. Come along, Nellie."

A short stocky man with curly hair and dressed in jeans and gray homespun shirt stood in the spacious office, studying a large map on the wall. He smiled and bowed slightly when the three women entered. "Here," he said, rushing to help Mrs. Millicent with the box, "let me assist you." He placed the box on a desk. "What brings you ladies to our plant?"

When Mrs. Millicent explained this was a box of ammuni-tion from the Women's Relief Society to be delivered to Grover Myers, the man thanked her and smiled broadly. "Well, I'm Mr. Myers, the plant owner." He glanced down at himself. "Hope you don't mind my informal attire, but I make frequent trips through the plant. By the end of the day, I end up with soot on my clothes."

"What do you make here?" Nellie asked.

"Is she your slave girl?" Grover asked Sara.

Sara pressed her lips together and looked away.

"The young lady's name is Nellie," Mrs. Millicent said, her voice measured but raspy. "She's eighteen and lives with us."

211

The man stared at Nellie for a brief moment and returned his attention to Sara. "To answer your slave's question, we make all sorts of ammunition for the Confederacy, mainly gunpowder, artillery projectiles, and breechloading cartridges. We also make some spherical shot as well."

Mrs. Millicent took a step forward. "Perhaps since we came all this way, you could grant us a tour of the facilities."

Grover ran two fingers over his beard-crusted chin. "It'd be a bit out of the ordinary, but seeing as how I don't believe you're spies for the Yankees, I guess I could accompany you about the grounds."

The four of them strolled outside, and Nellie paid scant attention to Grover's description of how they had to take extreme caution in making gunpowder and how the casings for the shells were formed in a foundry in another building. She yawned as they neared the supply depot.

Grover pointed toward a shed adjacent to a railroad track. "We got two white folk and a Nigra workin' there." He then gestured toward a waiting railroad car. "Actually," he sneered, "that Nigra there does more work than the two white folk put together. He loads and unloads most of the rail cars himself and then I send him back to the warehouse to group the shells while the white men count the inventory and give me a report. Good worker, he is. Name's Zeke."

Nellie saw a large shirtless black man, his back toward her lifting a crate and placing it on a large cart. He turned slightly in her direction and resumed working. Beads of perspiration clung to his muscular back and his soaked jeans gripped his strong legs.

"Zeke!" Grover called out. "C'mon here and tell these nice folks what sort of work you do here."

The negro turned around and walked toward them. "Yessuh." He smiled at Sara and Jane, but his face froze and his eyes widened when he saw Nellie. "Dear Lawd!"

"What's the matter, Zeke?" Grover said. "You look like you seen a ghost. Tell these people what you do and then get back to work."

The slave swallowed hard, his eyes riveted on Nellie.

"Speak up, boy," Grover ordered. "What's wrong with you?"

Nellie put a hand to her mouth. *Tinker? It couldn't be!*

The negro turned his attention to Sara and Jane, but Nellie was certain she saw his eyes glisten. "Well, I go to da factory every mornin' and I—I—" He dropped his head and sucked in some air. "Pardon me, ladies, I'm not feelin' all dat well right now."

"Well, suh, what I can say is dat I go to the factory every mornin' and I—I—"

"Go back to what you were doin', Zeke. I'll go show these ladies more of the plant."

Nellie stayed where she was, watching this man called Zeke dragging himself back to his chores like a wounded dog. There were a few stripes across his back, not fresh ones, and Nellie knew he must have had a whipping some time ago.

"Nellie!" Sara shouted back at her. "What are doing there? Come join us."

Nellie looked back at Sara, who was only about twenty yards away. "I've got to go to the bathroom. Can I meet you back in the office?"

Sara agreed but told her not to wander about and to head straight for the office. Nellie approached the negro, who had his back turned to her as he pushed a cart full of boxes toward a rail car. She wondered if she had been mistaken. Could it have only been someone who looked like Tinker? There was only one way to find out. She looked around to be sure no one else was around.

"Tinker!" she shouted.

The negro spun around, his face awash with tears. "Oh Lawd, Miz Nellie! Is dat you?" He stretched out his arms and she ran to him and let him hug her.

"Tinker, I miss yah so much it hurts."

He put her hands down gently and a weak smile creased his face. "Yuh a good friend, Nelle, 'n I miss yuh too. How come yuh here in Georgia?"

213

Nellie explained how she and Sara had to leave Chatta-nooga to live with Aunt Jane in Atlanta. "I think about yah a lot, Tinker."

"Me too." But he also thought a lot about Charlotte. After all these months, he could still not forget her sweet kisses.

"Why do yuh love me, Charlotte? I'm jest a good-fer-nothin' colored man."

"Don't put yourself down like that, Tinker. You're the bravest and kindest man I've ever known."

"You're my first woman," he said, beginning his rhythm as she lay on the wool blanket outdoors.

"I hope someday to be your only woman."

Tinker felt embarrassed when he caught Nellie staring at him. It was almost as if she were reading his most private thoughts. "Miz Nellie, when can I see yah again?"

"I dunno when. Sara and her aunt talk 'bout goin' to Bir-mingham to escape the Yankees. But if I go wid them, I may not see yah ever again." She began to cry.

"Shhh. I got an idea." He brought his lips close to her ear and whispered. "I been plannin' to 'scape from dis here place anyway. Maybe I can take yah wid me."

Nellie's eyes widened. "When? How?"

"Depends when you can get here."

Nellie thought a moment. "Maybe next Sunday 'bout three. Sunday be da best day."

"Sunday good for me too. Plant shut down on Sunday."

"Sara don't make me go to church no more. So when they go to church, I can take the horse they let me ride and come here to see yah."

Tinker scratched his chin. "Between here and da restau-rant half-mile down the road dere be a water wheel. And dere be a ditch nearby and lots o' trees on both sides. If yuh hide in the ditch, no one kin see yah."

"I gwine to be there for yah."

Tinker looked up just as Grover, Sara, and Jane ap-proached. His tortured face scanned the ground beneath him

214

before he returned his gaze to Nellie. "Look, yah best be gettin' along now."

Nellie gave him one more squeeze. "I miss yah, Tinker." She ran toward Sara, refusing to look back to see his pain because the pain in her own heart pierced her like a knife.

*****

Washington, DC

Jessica sat with Mitzi and Emma in the bedroom, trying to sound casual as she was about to read them a story, but the conversation in the next room concerned her. She moved herself nearer to the closed door so she could hear better.

The whispering between Otto and Penelope came in waves, interrupted by "Lower your voice, my dear, the children may hear."

"But it's the children I am most concerned about," Penelope was saying, her voice rising.

"Please don't be alarmed," Otto answered in a hushed tone. "But you must understand we need to take precautions. Our forts, you realize, are only being protected by unorganized, inexperienced defenders."

"So we're to prepare to vacate Washington," Penelope said, lowering her voice. "Is that what you're saying?"

"What I am saying is that we need to prepare for the worst. The Confederates have already made it to Baltimore and are headed this way."

"Perhaps the President will order General Grant to Washington to secure our defense."

"Perhaps. If it isn't too late."

"I'll start packing some of our things."

"Miss Radford," Emma squeaked, "are you going to read us a story or are you going to listen to mommy and daddy?"

Jessica moved away from the door and forced herself to smile as she sat next to them on the carpeted floor. "I'm going to read you both a story."

215

Mitzi stood up and moved the curtain away from the window. "Are we going to have to move? I see people outside loading their wagons like they are going to leave town."

"That's a decision Papa has to make. Now please sit down." *The rebels were coming*, she thought. If *they occupied the city, would they harm any of the civilians?* She didn't care about herself; she had a gun. It was the Heller family she cared about. What would happen to the family?

She opened the book, eyed both of the children, and placed her hands on the pages to stop herself from shaking. "Now, what story would you like me to read to you?"

Chapter 30

The next day

President Lincoln's carriage stopped at Fort Stevens just as a Union shell fired against the Confederate position. Mary Todd Lincoln insisted on remaining in the carriage while the President got out, returning the salute of an officer.

Lincoln looked about at the number of troops manning the guns and others barking orders or carrying out messages to their commanders. The officer who had greeted the President escorted him to the fort.

"It appears that that obstinate, pain-in-a-pig's-belly rebel, General Early, wants to wake up our town today," Lincoln quipped. "But I think our guns will wake him up as well."

"Yes sir."

"Is General McCook overseeing operations here?"

"Not presently, but Major General Horatio Wright is over yonder," he said, pointing to a young man with a short, pointed beard and ringlets of tufted hair. He stabbed his finger northward as he talked to another officer. Just then Wright happened to notice the President and hurried over.

"Mr. President," he said after saluting, "it is an honor for you to be here."

"I am relieved to see that the lead elements of the VI Corps have arrived from the Potomac."

"Yes sir. We're planning to send a division forward to attack, and I was just in the process of coordinating it."

"Very good, Horatio. I followed your actions at Cold Harbor. The VI Corps waged a costly, difficult campaign, but you helped the Union hold its position."

He grinned broadly at the compliment. "Thank you, sir. Would you care to get up on the parapet and watch our maneuvers?"

Without giving it another thought, Lincoln agreed and was escorted to a low wall where he could see the battle. "Please, sir," Wright said, following him there, "you will be putting yourself in danger. I didn't realize you would take my offer seriously."

"Nonsense, Horatio. I ought to know first hand how this battle is progressing."

"Don't do it, sir, or I will need to have you forcibly removed."

Lincoln ignored him and stood up, his long frock coat flapping in the breeze. After someone handed him a spyglass, he watched as Union troops drove the Confederates away from their positions in front of the forts. He heard the zing of flying bullets, one hitting the wall to his side. A cannon roared. More flying missiles. Another near miss. One soldier near the President screamed as he was shot in the leg.

All of a sudden, a voice called out to him, an angry, sputtering voice: "Get down, you damn fool, before you get shot!"

Lincoln got down immediately, shocked that someone had the audacity to address him in that manner. He took cover but poked his head up every so often to see more of the action.

"Are you all right, sir?" one of the men asked him.

Lincoln grinned. "Yes, but that man who shouted at me just then—is he a Democrat?"

"I don't know his politics, Mr. President, but that man's name is Captain Oliver Wendell Holmes."

"Well, Captain Holmes ought to be congratulated for speaking his mind. We need more men like that in our government."

*****

St. Louis, Missouri

Using a small chisel, Matt played with the details of the face of his statuette until he felt he had it right. It would have been far easier for him to work from a daguerreotype, as he had with the Lincoln figure that he gave Jessica, but there was no picture of Nellie when she was eleven years old. He had only his memory to go on, the way she looked when he first met her in Lawrence more than six years ago. Her large eyes, her blameless expression, her pudgy face, and the way she smiled at him with innocence and curiosity.

He had delayed going to the Pacific House Hotel today to send a telegram because it was the same hotel which he had vacated the day Jessica had left him. But he would have to go. He needed to shut out the memory of that night when she decided to take an early train back to Washington. She refused to marry him, and he didn't hold out any hope that she would ever change her mind.

He had to forget about her. Soon, he hoped, he would be appointed pastor to a new church, but in the meantime, he would have to be content with work he obtained as a sawyer for a lumber mill in town. The hours were long, the work strenuous, and the pay barely enough for him to pay for food and rent. There was no work today, however, and at least he'd be free to send his telegram to straighten out certain financial matters since his move from Washington.

He went up to the telegraph office inside the hotel. After he wrote out his message, the clerk looked carefully at the name. "Are you Matt Lightfoot?" he asked.

"Yup, that's me."

"Just a minute please." He disappeared and conferred with the man at the registration desk. "Just as I suspected," the clerk said upon returning. He held two letters in his hand. "This hotel has messages for you."

"May I see those?" Matt asked, holding his hand out.

"Yes, of course. Here are two letters addressed to you."

Both messages were from the same person. Mary Delaney. She wanted to see him if he were still in town.

After paying for his telegram, he took a chair in the reception area and opened the letters. Mary Delaney! He had almost forgotten about her. She still needed an explanation as to why he had been reticent in replying to her letters while he was still serving with his regiment. He had no reason to avoid seeing her now—now that Jessica had shredded his heart into tiny bits.

But the least he could do would be to see Mary again. She had saved his life at Chickamauga. But what did he do in return? Take advantage of her. If she never forgave him for that, he would understand.

It was twilight when he went to call on Miss Delaney. He told himself he would simply apologize and leave. If that gentleman friend of hers—what was his name?—Willard Hamilton was there, he would tell her anyway. She and Mr. Hamilton had their own lives to live.

He knocked on the door, and when there was no answer he waited. In another minute he'd knock again, and if she weren't in, he would leave. He wondered what was the purpose of him being here anyway. One thing he wanted to avoid was a nasty scene where she might tell him how despicable he was for not writing. Maybe somehow she even knew about his intentions to marry Miss Radford, and that would certainly inflame the situation.

He knocked again and was about to turn on his heel and leave when the door opened.

Mary smiled slightly at him but she also frowned as if she were annoyed at his presence. Her hair was tied in a chignon and she wore a red garibaldi blouse and patterned skirt. "Matt Lightfoot! I thought you'd never want to see me again."

"Why in the world would I not want to see you again?"

"Because," she said, inviting him in, "I didn't get any reply from you at the hotel, and I was told you had checked out. I assumed you must have left St. Louis and never received my messages."

"I'm still in town," he said, his eyes searching the room. Willard Hamilton was not there and Matt sighed in relief. "I sure hope I'm not disturbing you."

"No, of course not. Have you partaken of supper?"

"Yup, I sure have, thank you."

She eased herself on the davenport and invited him to sit next to her.

"I really won't be stayin' long, Miss Delaney. But it bothered me that I had not responded to your kind letters."

"There is no need to apologize. I know how terribly difficult it is for men on the battlefront to concentrate on writing letters when they are under the stress of battle. I know what that is like."

"Do you miss the regiment?"

"Yes, but I am in a different situation now and attempting to make a new life for myself."

"Yes, indeed. I see you have found a new male companion."

Mary looked puzzled for a moment. "Oh, you mean Dr. Willard Hamilton? He's our hospital surgeon. I really wouldn't call him a male companion as such. He is a good friend." She inched herself closer to him. "What has happened to you since you were mustered out of the Eighth Kansas?"

"Looks as if I will be the pastor of a new church. Meanwhile, I've taken a job with Jason's Lumberyard."

"That's only a block away from the hospital where I work." He said nothing in reply, and she fidgeted with her hands before placing them on her lap. "Well, what brought you here to St. Louis?"

Matt took a deep breath. Should he tell her about Jessica, that she accompanied him on his trip to St. Louis? No. What would he say? That he fully intended on marrying Miss Radford and setting up a home here in town? There was no point to it.

Mary pursed her lips and she looked down at her folded hands. "And what about Jessica? Have you seen her?"

"Yup, I sure have and she is fine."

Mary's face changed into a scowl and she rose up in a huff. "Is that all you have to say about my friend?"

Matt's heart pounded. Somehow she knew more than he had assumed. He now wished he had never come tonight. "What do you mean?"

"I took a buggy ride past the hotel when I saw you and Miss Radford enter the building. Why did you not tell me on your previous visit that she was in town? She's my good friend, and I would have loved to meet with her."

Matt swallowed hard. "I assumed Miss Radford would have told you she was coming to St. Louis."

Mary's emerald eyes burned into him. "How could she have told me that? You're the only one who knew I had moved. Is she still here in town?"

221

"She returned to Washington, D.C. and is living with the Hellers."

Mary put a hand to her forehead. "Why did you keep Jessica's trip a secret from me?"

Matt got up and headed for the door. "I had no intention of upsettin' you when I came. Perhaps I should leave."

"I thought you and I had something special. All this while it appears you have been romancing Jessica. You could have at least told me at the outset that you didn't love me." She started to sob. "Or is it—is it—that I am now soiled merchandise in your eyes?"

"Please, Miss Delaney. I never wished to hurt you." He touched her arm but she pulled it away.

"I don't want to see you ever again. Do I make myself clear?"

"Yes, but—"

"Never again," she said, opening the door. "Goodbye, sir."

*****

July 17
Leeburn, Georgia

Tinker knew he should not have been so definite with Nellie about telling her he was going to escape from the plant today. There was a guard posted at the front entrance, and there was a high wall which would be difficult to scale. No slave to his knowledge had ever made it out to freedom.

But there had to be a way. There just had to. His thoughts of freedom and of meeting Nellie this afternoon were shattered when Grover unexpectedly saw him at the plant.

"What are you doin' here on a Sunday, Zeke?" he asked. "Don't you go to church like the rest of the workers?"

Tinker thought quickly. "Doan feel all dat good, suh. Maybe da Lawd will 'scuse me for missin' services."

"Well, since you're here, I want you to prepare and serve tea and toast for me and a guest of mine."

"A guest?"

"That's right. The Major and I will be in my meeting room at the plant," Grover said. "I wish to make him as comfortable

222

as possible as we have important business to discuss. I could use your help."

"Yessuh," Tinker said, and he followed Grover to the kitchen, wondering how this was going to affect his rendez-vous with Nellie planned for this afternoon.

The Major and the plant manager entered the room ad-joining the kitchen while Tinker searched for the canister of tea and loaf of bread.

"You are not putting your full effort into the Confederate cause," the Major began, his voice booming.

Tinker moved closer to the door, hoping to pick up the rest of the conversation.

"What do you mean?" Grover retorted.

"What I mean," the Major said, "is that we expect your plant to work at full capacity. Armaments are more crucial now than ever before."

"But we've got our plant running five-and-a-half days a week as it is. We must allow a half-day on Saturday for repairs and maintenance. Sunday, of course, the plant is shut down for the Lord's day."

"Knowing it is being done to aid the Confederate cause," the Major said, "the good Lord won't mind if you work on His day."

Tinker had to restrain himself from laughing as he put the water on the stove for tea and got the cups and saucers. *I thought the Lawd daon take no sides.*

The two men went on to discuss production volume for everything the plant made. Tinker lost all interest in the con-versation and was ready to enter the room with their tea when the major began talking about Confederate strategy.

"*We've got Sherman coming down our throats,*" *the Major said, "and you can help us stop him.*"

"*How's that?*" *Grover asked.*

"*Well, we have an informant that told us the Yankees will be splitting into three columns—one headed by Thomas, one by Schofield, and the third by McPherson. We have reason to believe*

223

*McPherson will be essentially following the rail-
road from Decatur to Atlanta and his column is
the weakest of the three and very vulnerable to
attack."*

*"I'm not a military man, Major. None of this
means anything to me."*

"Well it should. Let me show you a map."

There was a pause as the paper was being unfolded. The
Major cleared his throat.

*"See right here is Peachtree Creek," he said.
"The Federals are headed in that direction. We
believe if you bring several wagonloads of arms
to this point right here, closer to where McPherson will be, by Tuesday evening, we would be
ready for a major assault on McPherson's left
flank. We believe we will be able to destroy
McPherson and cause confusion with the other
divisions. If we receive the ammunition in time
and synchronize this attack, we can destroy the
morale of Sherman's army."*

"Excuse me, major," Grover said, "but I probably should
discover why our tea is taking so long. Zeke!"

Tinker picked up his tray containing the tea cups, tea pot,
and toast and carried it to the meeting room. "Sorry, suh," he
apologized, placing the tray on the table.

"That's quite all right," Grover said. He turned to the Major
and smiled. "This here is Zeke, our best worker. Never com-
plains and always does what he's told."

"Thank you, suh."

"Oh, Zeke," he added, searching for something on his
belt, "I need to get my latest inventory log sheet in the warehouse office. The major and I are trying to figure out what we
could ship out to him tomorrow." He handed Tinker a ring
with keys on it. "The large bronze one is the warehouse key."

"Yessuh."

"The log sheets are in the ledger just inside the door. Understand?"

"Yessuh."

Tinker could not believe his good fortune. After returning to the kitchen, he leaned on the counter, biting his lip, his pulse racing. *Yah gotta think this out. What d'ya need? Matches. Yes, matches.* He searched the cabinet for matches. They got to be here. They got to be somewhere. He looked further and found them hidden in a small box near the silverware. He grabbed three matches and hurried out the door.

That safety fuse coil he hid last month…a jute cord wrapped around a core of fine black powder and coated with lacquer to protect it from water…yeah, that coil he buried in the ground, just outside the underground bunker. Never thought he could use it 'cause he never done could figure out how to get into that bunker. But one of these here keys might do it.

He knelt on the ground, trying to remember exactly where he buried it. That coil just had to be here somewhere.

A large boot stomped inches away from Tinker's fingers. Tinker looked up at the face of a guard. "What d'ya think you're doin'?" the guard demanded.

Tinker took a deep breath and exhaled slowly, his heart beating like a wild drum.

*****

Atlanta, Georgia

As soon as Sara and her aunt left, Nellie took a pen and wrote a brief note:

> *Dear Mrs. Toby,*
>   *I hope maybe you won't be too angry but I am going to see Tinker. He gonna take me with him when he leave the factory today. I go with him and we gonna find Union army somewhere. I got my*

225

free papers with me and maybe soldiers will help me get to see Jessica in Washington.

I feel very bad about going because you be so good to me. But I got to see Jessica and don't know when this here war will ever be over. Besides, Tinker is my friend and I know he take good care of me.

I got my angel medal with me and I know you don't believe in angels but I do. I know Sissy will take good care of me.

All my love,

Nellie

Nellie left the note on the table and packed sausages, potatoes, peas, and crackers into a saddlebag Sara bought for her just two weeks earlier. "Now that you're riding every day," Sara had told her, "you'll need to have something to carry your things in." Of course, the mount wasn't hers. It belonged to Miz Jane, and just about everything else in this house belonged to Miz Jane.

She felt guilty about taking the mount, whom she nicknamed "Victory," with her. But Miz Jane had two other horses and a wagon, so she would not miss Victory. Yet, Nellie knew that stealing was a sin, so she promised herself that once she got to Washington, she would somehow see to it that Miz Jane got paid for it.

Nellie deliberated whether she also wanted to take Sara's .31 caliber Remington pistol. Sara had taken it with her from Chattanooga and carried it with her everywhere—except to church. "Mind you," Sara once told her, "without this at my side, I'd be afraid to go anywhere."

But Nellie took it anyway, realizing that Jane Millicent still had a rifled musket. Miz Jane knew how to use it, once bragging about how she shot a deer from the kitchen window. "They be safe with the musket," Nellie said to herself, although she wished that doubts about their safety with one less weapon would quit nagging her.

By noon a light drizzle began to fall, but Nellie ignored it as she saddled up Victory. Sara and Miz Jane would be coming soon, so she thought she had better leave the outskirts of town by another route. She passed two mule-pulled wagons, covered with white canvas, coming toward her. Some of the shops were already deserted with "closed" signs posted on the windows. *Maybe people leavin' town.* She wondered when Sara and Miz Jane would leave for Birmingham like they talked about. The Yankees could be here any day, but she wasn't afraid of Yankees, feeling as if she were one herself when she used to live in Kansas. But maybe Sara had a right to be afraid. How would they treat Southern women? She had heard stories about some bad things that happened to them, but maybe they were just stories. *Sara, I'm gonna miss yah. I'm so sorry I hafta leave like this, but I just hafta.*

She passed by a train depot made out of brick, with huge half-circle openings ready to swallow trains as they entered. But there were no trains now. There was no telling what rail lines were still working and which were not because of this war. The only way Sara and Miz Jane could leave now, Nellie thought, was by buggy or wagon. And she had seen several of them on the road already.

She began singing the Glory-Glory-Hallelujah refrain from the "Battle Hymn of the Republic." *Yeah, this here war will be over 'n all this cryin' 'n weepin' 'n men gettin' killed, that's all gonna go away. I just gotta believe in the Lord.*

A barking dog suddenly ran in front of Victory and the horse reared. Nellie held the reins more tightly but Victory dashed off into a full gallop anyway. "Stop it!" Nellie screamed. Victory ran swift and furious, like a runaway train. She yelled at him to stop. About a half-mile ahead of her was a building. It was at the end of a dead-end street. A two-story brick building and Victory was headed right for it.

Nellie trembled at the thought that this might be her last hour on earth.

227

Chapter 31

The guard accepted Tinker's explanation about searching for a lost coin. It was a flimsy excuse, but when the guard learned Tinker was on official business, he escorted Tinker to the warehouse and watched him get the inventory sheets Grover wanted.

Tinker pretended to be on his way to back to the main office, with Grover's ledger in his hand, but when he noticed the guard was out of sight, he returned to the area where he felt he remembered burying the coil. Fortunately, the ground was soft and he was able to dig it out with one of the keys.

But he wasn't sure about the door to the bunker. He tried the metal door, one key at a time. Tinker cussed to himself. *One of dese here keys got to fit, it jest got to.* But nothing worked and Tinker was down to his last key, thinking all the while that maybe Grover didn't even have it on the key ring.

The last key worked! Tinker said a quick prayer and opened the door. There was just enough outside light for him to see one of the gunpowder bags and he quickly forced one end of the coil inside of it. He closed the door and ran the cord out—five feet, ten, twenty,—where was the end of it? Must be over fifty feet because he was almost near the warehouse door when he ran out.

His hand shook like a leaf blowing in the wind as he searched for a match. Did he lose the matches? He kept searching. Finally, he remembered sticking them in his shoe. He took one out and struck it against the hard cover of Grover's ledger. Someone told him that this fuse could burn at a steady rate, but he had no idea how much time he had to run once he lit it.

The fuse sparked as he lit it, and immediately he took off running. He tripped over a box and slid against a post. He shook his head and got up, running, looking behind him to see if anyone was following him. Suddenly someone grabbed him by the shoulders. He spun around. It was Grover.

"What took you so long? You got that inventory?"

Tinker noticed the gun in Grover's holster. Grover once bragged that he had personally shot and killed two men with it. Tinker looked back at the warehouse. Time was moving on. Minutes, maybe seconds left. And it wasn't just the gun that frightened him this time.

Grover grabbed the ledger Tinker forgot he still held in his hand. "Give me this! What is wrong with you Zeke? Are you turning into a stupid nigger?"

"No suh. Sorry suh."

"Let me look this over." He scanned the records, mumbling some of the numbers. "Hmmm. This doesn't check out with what I know we've got. Give me those keys, Zeke. I'm going to have to do another box count on paper cartridges."

Tinker handed him the keys and started to leave.

"Hey, boy," Grover called. "Where the hell do you think you're going?"

"Goin' back, suh."

"No, you're not." He pulled out a sheet of paper from his coat pocket. "I want you to go with me. I want to be sure we've got all the boxes I told him we have. The Major's waiting."

Tinker felt beads of sweat on his forehead and his heart beat like a bass drum. "But suh—"

"But what? Come on, get movin', Zeke!"

Tinker sauntered behind Grover, who turned around and told him to hurry.

"Sorry, suh."

When Grover got to the door of the warehouse, he looked out toward the bunker at the faint glimmer of sparks. "What the hell!" He sprinted toward the bunker. "Damn you, Zeke! Come here!"

But Tinker sprinted for the exit, running in a zigzag fashion. *Oh Lawd, help me!*

Grover shouted for him to stop. The gun went off. Tinker, screaming from a searing pain that hit him somewhere in the leg, fell face forward. He pushed himself up, a thousand stings clawing at him. He ran again, anticipating the second bullet which he was sure would be fatal. But it never came.

Instead, a roaring blast came from behind him, like the sound of a dozen Parrot Cannons going off at once. The heat from the explosion scorched his back like dreadful sunburn. He got up again and limped his way out to the front of the plant. He turned around to watch the black fireball, like a dark, smoking mushroom, grabbing at the sky.

The force of the blast knocked over part of the fence near the gate. Tinker hobbled toward the road. He hoped Nellie would be there for him at the ditch down by the windmill. He had to get out of here and ride to safety in a hurry or else he'd be a dead man.

Chapter 32

July 18
Atlanta, Georgia

Dear Roger,

I have some distressing news, and I wish you were here to give me comfort. Nellie has gone and has left me a note telling me she was running away with Tinker. Yesterday afternoon, I rode over to Myers Munitions Works in Leeburn where Tinker had been working as a slave. But the plant had been destroyed by fire and some Confederate soldiers were asking passersby if they had witnessed any suspicious activity prior to the explosion. I had to leave the vicinity, not knowing whether or not Nellie and Tinker may have been killed in the devastation.

I fail to understand why Nellie left Jane and me in such despair. As it is, I am undecided whether to wait for Nellie's possible return to Atlanta or to go ahead with plans to leave Atlanta for Birmingham. Aunt Jane has been feeling rather ill lately, and a long trip like that would cause a strain on her health. Everything has been so unreal I sometimes think I am acting in a cruel play, but when I realize this is truly happening to me, I yearn for those simple and innocent years of yore.

Of course, I realize you have your own concerns and that you are doing all you can to protect Atlanta from a Yankee invasion. The only recourse I have now is to pray for Nellie's return, Aunt Jane's health, and your safety.

Please let me know if there is anything I can send you in terms of food or clothing. Hopefully, *you will return soon and God will help us get through this ordeal together.*

With all my love,

Sara

****

July 19
Marietta, Georgia

The rays of morning splashed across a wide expanse of rocky bluffs and dense pines, bursting in green, while white Union tents dotted the rest of the landscape like large moths eager for action. Tinker sat alone at the far edge of the Yankee camp, trying to ignore the pain in his leg. It didn't matter, he told himself. At least he was alive.

He finished his fried eggs and biscuits and was just about to leave the table when Private Bonneville of the Wisconsin 21st called out to him. "Tinker, you are sure damn lucky. I could have shot you right then and there last night. If it weren't for that negro woman riding that mount, I would have."

"I know," Tinker said, getting up on a wooden crutch. He remembered how worried he was yesterday when he made it to the ditch near the windmill and Nellie was not there. When she finally did come, Nellie helped him on her mount and rode off toward Marietta. He was convinced the Confederates were on his trail, so he shot at what he thought was the enemy, out to capture him. Turned out it was Private Bonneville, who shot his rifle into the air, ordering him to halt.

"Yah don't understand," Tinker said. "Yah was not dressed like a Yankee 'n I thought you be a slave catcher or maybe a rebel. I would rather die than go back to slavin'."

"I understand."

"With all due respect, suh, I doan think yah do."

Private Bonneville gave an irritating scowl at first, but then his face softened. "I heard all about your incredible escape. How's the leg?"

232

Tinker looked down at his heavily bandaged lower leg. "The surgeon said I be lucky. The ball hit my calf, went through muscle, but didn't hit no bone. Not sure dey got to amputate. Dey is lookin' for signs of gangrene." Without waiting for the private to answer, Tinker excused himself and limped with his crutch, looking for Nellie. He found her at the far end of the camp, cleaning the Remington pistol she had let Tinker use yesterday.

"Mighty glad you came, Miz Nellie. Doan know how I'd get away if you didn't show up."

"Almost had an accident with Miz Jane's horse on the way here. It got scared by a dog or somethin'. Anyway, lucky thing someone helped me get the horse to stop."

"I guess we all be lucky."

"Except for that leg of yours."

"I kin still get around. Da surgeon he done give me dis here what he call a deluxe underarm crutch. He say it once belong to a captain. He say da captain doan need it 'cause where he be down in da earth, he doan need no crutch."

"I pray that yah don't hafta go where the captain is. I need yah, Tinker."

But Nellie knew she had another need—to somehow let Sara Toby know she was all right and not to worry. There was no way to reach her. Nellie searched for the medallion around her neck but it was gone.

"Doan you remember?" Tinker said, observing her frustration. "Yuh gave it to da chaplain, who tol' yuh he was gonna send it t' his little girl fer comfort in case she worries 'bout him."

*****

Washington, DC

The afternoon sun formed a golden glow against the window shade in the master bedroom of the Heller house. The long hollow chime tubes of the tall walnut clock in the corner indicated that it was three o'clock when Jessica entered the room, carrying a tray containing a bowl of chicken soup and some crackers.

"Penelope, you've had little to eat," she said, "so I made this for you."

"Thank you. I've not had much of an appetite today."

Penelope raised her body to a sitting position to accept the tray. "You've been so good to Mr. Heller and me, I don't know how to thank you."

"Do you miss not working at your own business like you did in Lawrence?"

"I do," she said weakly, "but I enjoy working with Otto. We have much to discuss at the end of the day, and we—" She coughed once, paused, and coughed again.

"Maybe I should contact a doctor."

"There is no need. It is probably just a stubborn cold. When will your book come out, Jessica?"

"In August. I'm expected to make trips to several cities for autographing parties the publishers is arranging."

"That must be thrilling. I am so happy for you."

Jessica raised the window shade halfway up. "I hope the book will give me a platform on which I could talk about the need for a constitutional amendment to abolish slavery."

Penelope glanced at the window. "Some people are saying that Lincoln is in error in making the abolition of slavery a condition—" She coughed again. "—a condition for establishing peace with the South. It doesn't appear he will win reelection with that conviction."

"If a Democrat wins the presidency on a proslavery platform, we are doomed," Jessica said, taking the tray after Penelope motioned she couldn't eat the soup. "If I need to, I will campaign for Mr. Lincoln myself."

Penelope attempted to laugh, but she coughed instead. "Jessica, you should have been a man."

"I've already fought like one in this war. Might as well be one." She was about to leave with the tray when Penelope called out to her. "I understand you and Mr. Heller are going to a poetry reading this Saturday."

234

"Why, yes. Walt Whitman promised to give readings from a new but unpublished work called *Drum-Taps*. I will also be presenting readings of poems by Wallace and Lytle. It will be quite an affair."

"You and Mr. Heller share the same interests when it comes to the fine arts. I feel dreadfully left out at times."

Jessica bit her lip. Had it been that obvious? She and Otto had gone to two plays and a concert and had recently been spending some time together discussing the second novel she was writing. Neither Otto nor Penelope had ever said anything before to her about the possible impropriety of any of this. Was Penelope hinting at the unseemliness of those situations?

"Penelope, I—"

Penelope's laugh fluttered like a butterfly. "I'm delighted that Mr. Heller can share his knowledge and interests with you. With me, on the other hand, I tend to have more of a business personality, if there is such a thing. Actually, Otto and I were discussing—" She coughed and cleared her throat. "We were discussing the possibility of investing in a general store which I might run. But this war is making it difficult for us to make decisions. Why just a few weeks earlier, it seemed as if the Confederates were going to seize this town."

"I had better tend to the children," Jessica said, leaving with the tray. Maybe it was a mistake for her to return to Washington. She could have married Matt and become a respectable wife and mother. Instead, she was living in the same house with a man she wished were hers and not Penelope's.

*****

St. Louis, Missouri

Hodgkin's Sawmill, which rafted both long leaf pine and cypress logs, had some heavy contracts with the military, and Matt found himself working longer hours than he cared to. But it paid him more than four dollars a day, and he was able to save some of it to help supplement his income when he became a pastor of a new church. In a way, he felt his work was

Biblical because, after all, didn't Jesus' earthly father Joseph, also work with wood?

He had thought about writing to Jessica, but what would he say? It was difficult just to be friends and assume that nothing of a deeply emotional nature had passed between them. So he would conclude by tearing up any letter he started to write to her.

Working hard was one way to rid his thoughts about Jessica. After work, he would join the other men for a beer and then go to a restaurant for supper. After that it was time to sleep and look forward to another work day. The monotony of it all....

Later tonight he would take a walk along the river, perhaps go to the park, and think about his plans for the future. So today would be just like any other day, but his intuition disagreed with him on that. "More boards, Matt," his supervisor called out, and Matt placed several boards on a long table, after first prying them loose from the skidding tongs that held them. He measured the lines for the cut carefully, then moved a board to the waterwheel-powered band saw.

He had wasted some boards today because of uneven cuts, and he felt the pressure of his supervisor scanning his work. Matt could not afford to lose his job because of poor workmanship. Slowly, he fed the board to the band saw. From the corner of his eye, Matt saw a fire break out at the other end of the mill. He turned to look, and suddenly he felt an enormous pain emanating from his left hand. The board was drenched in blood. Matt was too shocked to scream.

The supervisor wrapped up his hand in bandages and got him into an ambulance. Matt felt like such a fool with all of the attention he was getting for his own stupidity. Fortunately, the hospital was nearby and Matt was impressed with how quickly they got him into the only empty bed on the hospital floor.

The last thing Matt remembered was the doctor telling him he was going to use chloroform. Then the darkness set in.

"Couldn't save the thumb, Mr. Lightfoot," a familiar voice called out to him.

236

Matt opened his eyes. A blurred vision of a figure hovering over him soon became a woman dressed in white, with curls of autumn-red hair framing her round, petite face.

"That chloroform really put you to sleep," she added.

"Mary!" Matt exclaimed, unbelieving. "Mary, what are you doin' here?"

A smile widened her lips. "I work here, Mr. Lightfoot. I'm a nurse, and when I learned about your accident at the mill, I told the doctor I would tend to your needs."

He recalled how Mary Delaney tended to his needs as he recovered from a chest injury incurred in the Chickamauga campaign. Her quick action in shaming that Confederate lieutenant into escorting the Union ambulance had saved his life. And her providing him with food when supplies were scarce helped him gain his strength during recovery. How could he ever forget her kindness?

"Mary, I'm so sorry," he said, thinking about how upset she was with him the last time they met.

She sat on the edge of his bed, her face turned away from him. "I was rather hoping I would see you again. I should not have been so harsh with you."

"Shucks, Mary, it's I who should apologize, not you. I've been so thoughtless."

She faced him with a smile. "Let's start anew, Matt. I want to forget about any ill feelings I might have had about you. In spite of your affectionate feelings toward Miss Radford, we can still be friends nonetheless."

"Yes, we most definitely can still be friends."

*****

July 20
Marietta, Georgia

Four uniformed Union officers were seated at a long table when Tinker and Nellie entered the cabin at five o'clock, as requested. "Please come in," the colonel said, rising from his seat. The late afternoon sun filtered through the window of the kitchen, which was now the makeshift headquarters of the First Brigade.

Tinker removed his cap and took three cautious steps toward the table and Nellie followed behind him. "You want to see me, suh?"

"Yes indeed," Colonel Hobart said, all smiles. "Major Fitch here, in command of the Wisconsin 21st, told me your story yesterday about the munitions factory being sabotaged. Congratulations."

"Yes," Major Fitch added, "we checked it out and indeed there was a Confederate plant destroyed in Leeburn. It seems there was an explosion in their warehouse and a passerby described a negro about your build limping down the road after that occurred. Looks like that could have been you."

"It definitely be me," Tinker said.

"We also took note of the other information you gave us," Colonel Hobart said. "It appears that the enemy had been planning to attack Thomas' army as it crossed the creek and he planned to do it with some massive artillery that never arrived—due in large measure to your destruction of their plant. We owe you a debt of gratitude for your efforts, Tinker."

"Thank yah, suh."

"We've also received a telegram from the Second Kansas Colored," the major said, "verifying you were among the missing in the Fort Blair massacre last October. Apparently, according to what you've told us, you had to undergo the ordeal of becoming a slave again, although you had been a free man."

"And he got hurt bad," Nellie said, her face wrinkled in agony. "Real bad."

"I know," the major replied. "We'll see to it that he gets the best of care. We plan to take him to Armory Square Hospital in DC. You told us you know a family living there."

"Yessuh. The Hellers. But I also need Nellie here to help care for me. She help save my life."

The colonel thought a moment. "I think we can arrange transport to the capital for your friend Nellie as well. What do you think, major?"

"That should not be a problem. We can get him up to a railroad depot in Nashville."

238

The colonel's gaze lingered a moment on Tinker. "That was a very heroic effort on your part, and it may result in saving Union lives. I'm going to make a recommendation to Stanton at the War Department that you be a recipient of the Medal of Honor. It would be unusual to award such a medal to a negro soldier, but this is turning out to be a very unusual war."

"Thank yah, suh."

"No, thank *you*, Tinker. I wish I had more men like you on our side."

Chapter 33

August 3
Alexandria, Virginia

The first thing Nellie did when she got off the train was to run to Jessica waiting at the platform to give her a giant hug. "Oh, Miz Jessica, I happy to see you again."

"It has been a long while," Jessica said. "Twenty-two months, in fact. It might as well have been twenty-two years."

Tinker, leaning on a wooden crutch, grinned as he stood behind Nellie. "Doan I get a hug too?"

Jessica embraced him. "Of course you do, Tinker." She noticed his bandaged leg. "Did you get that in the war?"

"Well, not 'zactly. It be a long story, Miz Jessica."

"We could talk about it on the ride back to Washington. I have much to share with you."

"So do we," Nellie said with a knowing smile.

Jessica had the coachman drive to the corner of King and Pitt Streets and stop in front of a three-story brick building. "That's the Marshall House," she said. "Soon after the war started, the innkeeper raised the flag of the Confederacy on the roof of his hotel. But a Union officer named Colonel Ellsworth was killed by that innkeeper when he removed that flag. President Lincoln grieved over the loss of Ellsworth, a close friend of his."

"Lincoln is good man," Tinker said. "I hope he still be President next year. He help make us free."

"I know, but the way things are going for him, I doubt he'll be reelected."

During the ride the talk drifted into a discussion of the war, but Nellie knew she would not be able to contain her excitement any longer. "Can I tell you my good news now, Miz Jessica?"

"I have good news for you as well, Nellie. But tell me yours first."

Nellie went on to tell about how Tinker blew up a Confederate ammunitions factory, got hurt in the process, and was able to give a Union regiment some good intelligence.

Tinker leaned forward in his seat. "Dey gonna give me da Medal of Honor. But dey say dey gotta go through lots o' different folks fer dat. Fact is, dey even gonna contact the War Department."

"That's wonderful news.," Jessica said. "I didn't know they would be willing to give an honor like that to a negro soldier."

"Well," Nellie said, "that's what they say they gonna do. What good news you got for me?"

Jessica pursed her lips in thought. "Do you remember my Uncle George?"

Nellie nodded. "I 'member he would call me a stupid nigger when I was younger 'cause I couldn't read too good. But he say I'm black, stupid, 'n quiet. He likes me bein' quiet 'cause he say some darkies talk too much. What happened to him?"

"He was with the 31st Ohio Infantry and died in Chattanooga."

When Nellie said nothing further, Jessica added, "He had nothing personal against you, Nellie. Uncle George always had a problem with negroes—which was interesting because he married Penelope, a mulatto. Although she wanted children, he didn't because he thought they might turn out to be black and it would cause him embarrassment. He probably felt guilty about that and the way he treated you. Maybe by turning a large portion of his assets over to you, he felt he could somehow make up for that. Anyway, I think you ought to know he was a very wealthy man."

Jessica frowned when she noticed Nellie's sad eyes. "What's wrong?"

"I feel bad he had to die in this here war. He not be that bad a man."

*****

August 6
St. Louis, Missouri

"These are beautiful," Mary said as she bent down to examine a cluster of False Foxgloves at Shaw's Botanical Garden.

"Yes," Matt said, "the Cherokees used these for medicines. My father was a great believer in using nature to heal our ills."

"Your father was a wise man."

"Much wiser than I. My foolishness cost me my thumb, and now the world will have lost a great sculptor."

"Nonsense. You can still learn how to carve beautiful objects with nine fingers."

"Yup, either that or learn a new hobby. Such as escorting you to the theater. I am indeed fortunate that you agreed to let me take you."

"Well," she said, accompanying him down the trail, "Willard had asked me a week earlier for dinner tonight along the riverfront, but he found he had to be at Alton this afternoon."

"I'm delighted that I chose to stay in St. Louis. It's a wonderful town. For instance, did you know that the library, founded eighteen years ago, is the oldest one west of the Mississippi?"

Mary laughed. "I will wager that you didn't know that a former slave named William Wells Brown, the first negro novelist, wrote his autobiographical slave narrative in St. Louis."

Matt smiled. "I wonder if Jessica knows that."

"I should write to her. I've tried several times, but can't get past the first sentence. I mean, after all that has happened—"

Matt touched her arm. "Mary, I cannot tell you how deeply I regret not tellin' you at the time that I was still seein' her."

She looked at him with a twinkle in her deep emerald eyes. "I know. You've already apologized to me a hundred times. Like you've said, we should start all over."

He ran his hand over her shoulder. "There's one thing that I've said back in Chattanooga that is certainly true today."

Her face shone with expectation. "And what is that?"

"It's you," he whispered, "whom I am most fond of."

*****

August 7
Birmingham, Alabama

> *My dearest Roger,*
> *I have just returned from church and have prayed devoutly to the Lord, but I wonder if He*

242

hears my prayers. Not only is the war going badly, but Aunt Jane passed on two weeks ago. She was buried behind her home with a simple grave marker. I haven't heard from Nellie, and I do not know whether she is still alive. To think of all that time we spent with her, providing her a safe haven, and now she runs away. It is diffi-cult for me to accept that she is an ungrateful wench. I suppose in her mind, she felt she was doing the right thing, but I think she could have at least discussed her plans with me before she embarked on her journey.

As you can see from the return address, I have moved in with the Jordan family in Bir-mingham to escape the ravages of war that have affected Atlanta. I don't think General Hood will be able to stave off the onslaught of Sherman's demonic troops, and for my own safety, I had to flee to a safer place of refuge. Do you remember the Jordans? They attended church with us in Chattanooga and had moved to Birmingham in 1862. I had been corresponding with them ever since, and I am so grateful for their kindness in allowing me to stay with them.

I should not complain about my own suffer-ing when I realize you might be on some battlefield trying to protect us from the Yankee onslaught. Please let me know how you are doing, and let me know if there is any possibility of you getting a leave to visit with me again. But since I am even further from you than before maybe that would not be feasible.

Oh Roger, why does Mr. Lincoln refuse to sit down with President Davis and achieve a com-promise that would end this terrible conflict? I understand that the opposition party is desirous of doing that very thing. Why must Mr. Lincoln be so obstinate in his demands of abolishment of slavery? I, too, am not personally interested in the existence of slavery, but if it will save further lives and bring an end to this devastating war, I think we should consider it.

My prayers are with you as always. Let me know if you would like me to send you any parcels.

My love always,

Sara

*****

August 9
Washington, DC

Tinker had the same dream again last night. He was with the Eighth Kansas and was leading a group of soldiers up a steep hill. Accompanying him was Jessica and Charlotte, and each of them held his hand.

The sky was blue, bluer than any lake or river he had seen, but the climb was difficult. It was a spring day, and he could smell the grass under his feet and hear the song of a whippoorwill. Jessica began to cry. "I'm tired of doing this alone," she said.

But Charlotte released Tinker's hand and her normally sad eyes turned into eyes of outright determination. "But I'll never tire of helping you, Tinker. Because I'm black like you, the world hates me as much as they hate you."

Tinker noticed a drum and a carbine lying against a white oak. He picked them both up and turned about. "Here, dis be yours, Lazarus," he said, handing the drum to a fifteen-year-old negro lad.

"I thanks yuh," the boy said and began beating his drum.

Tinker spotted a tall negro man dressed in a Yankee uniform and handed him the carbine. "And dis here," Tinker said, "be yours, Ishmael."

244

Ishmael turned the gun about in his hands and looked at the word FREDUM engraved on the stock. "Doan want dis no more," Ishamel said. "Already got my freedom."

"Yeah," Tinker said, smiling, "yuh and Lazarus both got your freedom. Yuh both die like heroes.."

Lazarus stopped beating his drum and glared at him. "I not die like hero."

"Me too," said Ishmael. "I not be no hero."

Lazarus and Ishmael disappeared and a strong voice called out: "That rifle be mine." It was Salem, another negro soldier, and he grasped the carbine with one hand while his other hand held a fife. "I take up the fight for all o' dem. I not 'fraid to die." But he was still speaking when a bullet whizzed by. Salem, his eyes wide with shock, stared at Tinker. He stumbled and fell, his body hitting the ground with a thud.

"Then I march on by mahself," Tinker said, picking up the carbine. He struggled up the hill, each movement upwards more painful than the one before. Finally he made it up to the top, and awaiting him there was Matt Lightfoot, his former master. Matt presented him with a medal for meritorious service to the Union. "You are a fine soldier," Matt said, "and I am proud of your achievements."

"I doan need no medal," Tinker said. "All I wants is to be da same like everyone else."

Jessica appeared and stood next to Matt. "Yes, he deserves equality."

"Not true," Matt said. "Tinker, you're not like the rest of us." He moved his arm in a wide span to reveal a large number of white men, women, and children gathered behind him. "Surely, you can't mean the kind of total freedom like we have."

"But I do, suh. Dat what I mean by 'freedom.'"

"That's foolish talk, Tinker. Here, take this medal and wear it proudly." He pinned the medal on Tinker's jacket and saluted him. "Outstanding achievement, Tinker."

"But I wants to be like all of you," Tinker shouted to the large group before him. "Dat be all I want."

"No!" the people shouted back. "That's not possible."

245

"Please!" Tinker begged.

Suddenly, a white man in the crowd flashed a pistol at him and threatened to kill him.

"Please!" Tinker repeated, just before the shot rang out.

Tinker awoke in his small boarding house room. It was still dark outside. He sat up on his cot, his heart pounding, relieved that it was only a dream. His pillow was wet and he didn't know if it was from tears of disappointment or from the sweat of his journey.

*****

August 12, 1864
Charlottetown, Prince Edward Island
Canada

Dear Miss Radford:

I hope you will forgive my impudence in writing to you but I read exciting news about the publication of your novel concerning slavery, and I applaud you for it. I have been languishing here in Canada, wishing I could be of more service to the cause of your abolitionist sentiments. As a result, I have decided that I would like to become a citizen of the United States. My father promised he would be of assistance to me in that regard in that he had been a military attaché to King George IV and still wields some influence with your Secretary of State.

Meanwhile, I would like to visit your country again and help support the abolitionist movement. Being both black and a foreigner, I know my influence would be rather limited, but perhaps I can work in the background in some way. I have an additional motive in eventually becoming a citizen of your country in that I would like to eventually find employment as a musician.

I suppose my experience as a soldier in your war and of seeing black heroes such as Salem and Tinker fighting so gallantly for the freedom of others has inspired me. I've read about a woman named Susan B. Anthony, who, five

246

years ago, urged her audience to "make the slave's case our own" and that "it is our own backs that are bared to the slave-driver's lash." That sums up how I feel about this injustice as well.

I am planning to be in Washington in two weeks. I will call upon you after my arrival to see if you might have time to discuss how I might be able to assist you in your efforts.

Sincerely,

Devin Alcott

*****

August 13
Washington, DC

"But I feel like singing today," Nellie said as she sat on the cot, next to Tinker.

"I'll play," he said, reaching for his harmonica, "but I doan feel like playin'."

"Do yah know '*Steal Away?*'"

"Shore do. Used to sing it back in Virginia when I used to pick tobacco. Don't have a good singin' voice, though. I'd rather play it 'n sing it."

"Are yah ready?"

Tinker nodded and began playing. Nellie sang the words in as loud a voice that she could:

> *"Steal away, steal away, steal away to Jesus!*
> *Steal away, steal away home,*
> *I ain't got long to stay here."*
>
> *My Lord, He calls me,*
> *He calls me by the thunder;*
> *The trumpet sounds within my soul,*
> *I ain't got long to stay here.*

247

Green trees are bending,
Poor sinners stand a-trembling;
The trumpet sounds within my soul,
I ain't got long to stay here."

"You sure got a mighty nice voice," Tinker said. "Maybe you should sing with dat man dat comin' here to see Miz Jessica. What's his name?"

"Devin Alcott?"

"Yeah, dat be him. Miz Jessica say he play mighty good."

"Maybe I do that," she said, rising from the bed. She looked out the window, her brown eyes searching for something. "Now that I got money, Tinker, we can do what we talk about when you and me come on the train from Nashville."

"Yah mean get married?"

"Yeah. Get married. Ain't that what yah tol' me?"

Tinker nodded. He had indeed told her that, but he wasn't sure why. Nellie was a good friend, but did people marry each other only because they were good friends? "I did tell yah dat I might want to get married. I like yuh, Miz Nellie. But I feel like a father t' yuh. I'm thirty-six 'n yuh is only eighteen."

"That don't bother me none. I'm sure I can learn how to be a good wife."

"Well, maybe so," he said, scratching his balding scalp, "but I gots to get me a job first. I already owe Miz Jessica rent for dis month."

She turned toward him. "Yah don't need a job. The money that Mr. Radford left me in his will is 'nough for yah 'n me to live on for a long time."

Tinker took a step back and dug his hands in his pockets. "Not good fer yuh to support me. I gotta get a job. Maybe I can do blacksmithin' like I used to do with Mr. Forester back in Lawrence."

She moved toward him, her head hung low as if she were expecting bad news. "I love you, Tinker."

He took her by the shoulders. "You will always be my sweet, little Nellie."

But I loves yuh like a father'd love his daughter. I don't know if I kin love yuh like a husband. Still think of yuh as the little girl who sat on my lap while I read her stories. Hard t' think o' yuh now as my wife.

A black woman who could have been his wife four years ago came to mind. Charlotte was someone he would never forget, the way her long black hair fell in a long, loose curtain when she stooped to rinse her face in the creek...how her large eyes sparkled with enthusiasm when Tinker invited her to a party hosted by his former master...her long-lipped encouraging smile when he read to her...and her tearful good-bye when she said she needed to travel to Illinois to see her mother who had taken ill. "But I will return," she promised. "I love you very much, Tinker, and I always will."

But she never returned. *I should've asked her before she left. I should've asked her. Maybe she would've come back.*

"Say you love me, Tinker," Nellie insisted.

He blinked and turned to face her. She was like a puppy, eager for his attention. *Child-woman. Who are you child or woman?*

"Sweet Nellie," Tinker said as Charlotte faded from his mind, "I love you."

If he said it often enough, he figured it'd be true.

Chapter 34

Jessica had to do something about getting the War Department involved. It had now been more than six weeks since Colonel Hobart had told Tinker about his being a recipient of the Medal of Honor. Jessica first turned to Otto for help. Given his influence with Lieutenant Pond of the Third Wisconsin Cavalry, Otto heard from someone with the Wisconsin 21st who informed him that the paperwork for Tinker's medal was probably languishing somewhere in the War Department.

"If dey don't wanna give me dat medal, dat's fine," Tinker had told Jessica. "I don't need a medal to tell me dat I done good."

"I'm sure if you had been white," she answered, "you would have had your medal by now."

"There ain't nothin' yuh can do 'bout it."

"Yes, there is." She left Tinker and sent Kate Chase Sprague a telegram asking to meet with her. *If anyone had any influence with those ne'er-do-wells in Congress, it would be Kate.*

Jessica spent the morning finishing a chapter of her second novel, entitled *Black and Proud*. Her agent told her that while her St. Louis publisher elected not to pursue this new work of hers, a Chicago publisher expressed interest in it, and Jessica felt pressured to undergo a daily writing regimen. After a hasty meal, she rode to the National Hotel and looked for Kate in the dining room. Kate was easy to find, with feathery headdress and red silk dress with pagoda sleeves trimmed in black.

Seated at a table near the window, Kate was apparently oblivious to Jessica's presence, chatting with a clean-shaven, well-dressed gentleman standing at the table. Jessica coughed to get her attention.

"Why, Miss Radford," she exclaimed, smiling widely. "I'm so glad you could come. Permit me to introduce Senator Benjamin Wade."

The senator bowed slightly and extended his hand. "Pleased to meet you, Miss Radford."

"Senator Wade," Kate explained, "is popularly known as a 'radical' Republican. He sponsored a bill that would administer the affairs of southern provisional governors in southern states—which Mr. Lincoln promptly vetoed."

The senator excused himself, and Jessica waited until Kate finished her diatribe against the President. "But enough of that," Kate concluded. "I am delighted to see you again. What do you think of this hotel? Did you know that Henry Clay died in this very hotel twelve years ago?"

The server took their order for tea and scones and left. "Kate," Jessica said, with sharpness in her voice that surprised her, "I came to see if you could help me get in touch with Stanton and the War Department."

"The War Department? Whatever for?"

Jessica explained the situation concerning the delay over Tinker's Medal of Honor. "I realize that your father has a strong dislike of the President ever since Lincoln accepted Salmon's resignation. Yet, I know your father and Mr. Stanton have been good friends."

Kate nodded, and after a long pause said, "Yes, it is true what you say about Salmon and Edwin Stanton. "Actually, it was partially due to Mr. Stanton's recommendation that my father received the appointment as Secretary of the Treasury. But now that he is no longer in that position, I just don't—"

"You wouldn't be doing this as a favor to Mr. Lincoln," Jessica interrupted. "You and your father have always agreed that the negro question should not be avoided."

"Indeed. And yet Mr. Lincoln, in his earlier years as President, would have been willing to forgo the negro question for the sake of preserving the Union. It took him two years before he finally decided to issue the Emancipation Proclamation, and I suspect his motives were political rather than based on any moral principles."

251

"Mrs. Sprague," Jessica said, feeling her own patience thinning, "for the sake of human rights and human dignity, for the sake of a negro who had risked his life for the Union cause, would you please see if there is anything you can do to bring this to the attention of Mr. Stanton? That is all I am asking."

The tension in Kate's face eased and she grinned as she looked back at Jessica. "You are a most persistent young lady," Kate said, "and I am afraid you will wear me down if I don't agree with you." She paused a moment. "Very well. I will speak to my father about this and see if he can persuade Mr. Stanton to look into the matter."

*****

September 15

Having missed work yesterday, Penelope told Otto she was feeling better and thought she had hid the bloodied handkerchief from him. But he found it on the bed when he insisted on fluffing up her pillow.

He showed her the handkerchief. "My God! Penelope! What happened?"

"It is just a little blood, Otto," she said in a choking half-whisper. "I will be fine. I really need to attend to my work at the Printing Office." She attempted to get out of bed but Otto gently but firmly made her lay back.

"I insist on having a doctor pay you a visit today. I believed you at first when you said you may have had a bad cold, Penelope. But I doubt that very much." He placed his hand on her forehead. "You have a fever and look how damp the pillow is. "

Penelope coughed several times in succession as she tried to talk. Finally, she turned her head to one side. "I wish I would not tire so easily," she said, straining. "I might be able to perform my tasks more readily if I did not tire so."

He sat on the bed and stroked her hair. "It is not normal for you to discharge blood like that, my dear wife. And you've lost considerable weight these past few weeks. Even Jessica

252

remarked about it and told me of her concern for your health."

"Well, if it would please you, then—" She coughed and gasped for her next breath. "—then you should send for a physician. But I hope someone who is capable can run the Folding Department."

"The Folding Department can go to the devil, Penelope. You should be focusing on your health."

Otto lingered for the doctor to appear, despite her protests that he ought to be at work. Thankful that Jessica kept the children occupied elsewhere, he waited outside Penelope's room after the doctor arrived. Then he paced the floor, the boards creaking beneath his boots. *Why was the examination taking this long?* After what seemed like an eternity, the doctor emerged from the bedroom, and Otto looked intently at him, searching for any sign of alarm on the physician's face. But the physician's countenance was frozen in a mask of surrender as he placed his black bag on the table.

"How is she, doctor?"

"Please sit down, Mr. Heller."

Otto, a shiver running through his limbs, took a chair. He pressed his hands against his knees to keep them from shaking.

"From what I have been able to discern," the doctor said with cautious slowness, "it appears that your wife has consumption. She will need bed rest, and I suggest making her as comfortable as possible. Use cold cloths to keep the fever down. I will prescribe some medicine, but beyond that there is not much I can do."

Otto grabbed the doctor's sleeve. "Will she—? Is she—" He couldn't get himself to say the dreadful word.

"Papa!" a child's voice cried out.

He turned and saw Mitzi and Emma staring back at him. Their sad faces told him they already knew the answer.

The children. I had forgotten about the children. How will I cope with their misery if Penelope passes on?

*****

Lawrence County, Tennessee

My Dear Sara,

    How can General Sherman be so brutal? He not only took over control of Atlanta, but he forced our citizens there to swear allegiance to the Union or else leave the town. Many of these families became refugees and left behind their homes and possessions. Protests from Confederate officials fell on deaf ears. Sherman, that devil, said that "war is war and not popularity-seeking." How inhuman!

    In times like these, however, the basest of human natures rises to the surface. I remember you telling me that man's blackest desire in Shakespeare's tragic plays was to kill another if murder indeed helps him achieve his goals. I have witnessed that on a grand scale in this conflict. But maybe Shakespeare is right. By now, I have found it easy to kill without a forethought about the men I have sent to their graves.

    General Hood is determined to win this war, but I don't see how that is possible with the great losses we have already suffered. I see no end in sight, and the only thing that keeps me from losing my sanity is knowing you will be there for me when this is finally over.

    It is devastating that you have not heard from Nellie or know of her whereabouts. We should hope for the best in these dire times. I long to see you and I am happy that you are safe in Birmingham. If I can get another leave of absence, I will try to arrange to see you.

    My prayers and my thoughts continue to be with you, my dearest!

Sincerely,

Roger

Roger waved the letter in the air to dry off the ink, folded it, and put it aside. Then he extinguished his oil lamp and listened to the lonely sound of crickets in the blackness of the night just outside his tent.

And he thought of Sara. She was a good woman, loyal and patient and God-fearing. *My longing for you increases with each passing day.*

*****

Washington, DC

Edwin Stanton, his long white-and-black beard running over his cravat, adjusted his spectacles as he stood alongside Abraham Lincoln and John Nicolay on the lawn of the Executive Mansion. A regimental band played "When Johnny Comes Marching Home Again" to a crowd of people, including four who stood near the President.

Lincoln leaned toward Stanton and whispered, "Mr. Stanton, that is excellent news about Sheridan. I'm sure that in a very few days, General Jubal Early will not be able to use the Shenandoah as a gateway to attack Washington."

"Things are going well, if I must say so," Stanton replied. "The election may be turning the corner in your favor. And this award presentation to a negro soldier shouldn't hurt your chances at all."

"The election is only one concern I have. My other is that negroes who have fought and died so nobly for the cause deserve all the respect they can obtain."

The band stopped playing and John Nicolay announced that ten members of a Maryland regiment were going to march in place in front of the Stars and Stripes while the band played "The Battle Hymn of the Republic." Lincoln surveyed the crowd consisting mainly of women, children, and soldiers wounded in battle. They stood at attention, but their faces were tired, perhaps weary from this war, and Lincoln sensed their pain, having lost close friends in the conflict himself.

After the band finished playing, Edwin Stanton was introduced to say a few words prior to the presentation of the

255

Medal of Honor. The people clapped while Stanton took a megaphone and asked that Private Tinker come forward.

"Tinker," Stanton said, reading from a short note he had written, "you have served your country well. I, as Secretary of War, wish that every man serving in this conflict would exhibit the same courage that you have exemplified. For your gallant and noble deed in destroying a munitions plant vital to the Confederates and in passing on helpful information to the Wisconsin 21st concerning rebel maneuvers near Peachtree Creek in Tennessee and in fighting so valiantly at Fort Blair in Kansas, it gives us pleasure in presenting you with this Medal of Honor."

People applauded while Tinker took a few cautious steps forward and shook hands with both Stanton and Lincoln. He waited while Mr. Stanton pinned the medal on his frock coat.

"Any words you'd like to say, Tinker?" Lincoln offered.

"No suh. I is too nervous, and I ain't a good talker neither."

"Folks tell me the same thing about myself," Lincoln quipped with a smile.

As the band played "The Battle Cry of Freedom," Lincoln half turned as if he were about to leave, but Jessica moved toward him, blocking his path. "Mr. President," she said, "I just want to thank you for taking yourself away from your other tasks and doing this today. It will mean a lot not only to Tinker but to negroes everywhere."

Lincoln tipped his hat. "Why thank you, ma'am. I understand you are the author of an interesting novel about a negro woman who experiences true freedom."

"Yes, Mr. President."

"Indeed. You were mentioned in the newspaper, and I was intrigued by the premise of your book. It appears to be a rather curious story, and I aim to read it sometime—perhaps after this conflict is over and Mary and I take a vacation." He scratched his chin and a small smile crept over his face. "You know, I joked with Harriet Beecher Stowe about my suggestion that her *Uncle Tom's Cabin* had started this war. Maybe your novel will induce Congress to pass an amendment that will outlaw slavery forever."

"I do hope so, Mr. President. It is my fondest wish."

*****

Nine days later

The interior of Holy Trinity Catholic Church smelled of incense and beeswax as the priest conducted a Funeral Mass in Latin. The rain pounded the stained glass windows outside as if demanding to get in. An altar boy held the Missal for the priest, who poured out obscure words from a language no longer spoken, but pronounced them in a way that added to the eeriness of a casket draped in black in the aisle.

Jessica recalled reading how, after the Second Battle of Bull Run, the Union requisitioned this church for use as a hospital, with boards laid atop the pews for flooring and the Sanctuary used as an operating room. *Death permeated the walls of this church then, and death permeates those walls now.*

The memory of what had happened only three days ago returned. Otto had left for the Printing Office and asked Jessica not to wake Penelope. "I haven't seen her sleep this peacefully for some time," he had said. "Usually she coughs incessantly the first thing upon arising. So please try not to disturb her."

But Jessica became suspicious when Penelope had not stirred by noon that Saturday, so she went to wake her and found her dead. Jessica instructed the children to stay in their room and then raced across the street to get a neighbor to ride to the Printing Office and inform Mr. Heller. The children were curious why their mother was not getting up today, and Jessica had the unpleasant task of telling them that their mother had died.

Emma, her face drenched in tears, swung her small fists at Jessica's legs. "Not true. She's not dead. She's not!"

"We all have to die sometime. Didn't your father tell you that?"

Emma screamed, pressing her hands against her ears. "But not my mommy. Not her!"

257

Jessica waited until Emma dropped like a limp doll on the floor and had stopped crying. "Emma, your mother is very happy where she is right now." But even as Jessica mouthed the words, she wished she knew that it was true. She had never considered herself religious, blaming it on the fact that her parents had always argued about religion.

Otto arrived early from work and called for her from the next room. Jessica paused before entering. How did he handle the news? But she found him at his desk, writing furiously on a sheet of paper, and he did not look up when she approached him.

"Miss Radford," he said, still scribbling, "I would like you to take these messages to the telegrapher at the depot and be sure these telegrams go out tonight. I've written to my friends in Topeka and Lawrence, and I think you should send messages to Miss Delaney and Mr. Lightfoot as well." He looked up at her briefly, his lips forming a straight line, his eyes fixed like flint. "I'll be making arrangements for the funeral and other matters. Now hurry, don't just stand here looking at me. What is wrong with you?"

"Nothing, Mr. Heller, I was just—"

"Just what?" he growled. He reached in his pocket and counted out several dollars. "This should take care of it. Now go and take these notes with you."

Later, when Jessica saw him standing outside, staring at something in the distance, she approached him. "I feel terribly grieved," Jessica said. "She was such a good woman."

"I don't wish to discuss it, Miss Radford."

"But—"

"Are you deaf, woman? I said I don't wish to discuss it."

It was like that every day—even today, as Otto watched the Funeral Mass with a hard stare. His countenance was a shield that conveyed a rigidity of spirit and a businesslike attitude over it all.

Jessica was nonplussed at his behavior. *Does he realize what had happened? What was going on deep inside? Was he*

258

in denial of her death? Did he know the end was coming for her and was already prepared for it?

Mary was seated across the aisle from Jessica, while Tinker and Nellie were seated several rows back with other negroes who were attending the ceremony. Jessica was delighted that Tinker wore the Medal of Honor on his blue uniform, even though he did so reluctantly. He did not want to bring attention to himself, but Nellie had convinced him he would be wearing it in recognition of all the other colored soldiers who had died in this war.

"Jessica," Mary had said earlier, "you must feel especially distressed about Penelope's passing. She was such a dear, sweet, lady. I only regret that Mr. Lightfoot could not be here to offer his condolences."

"And how is Matt getting along these days?"

"Wonderfully. He will soon become pastor of a new church in St. Louis."

Jessica wished she could be more direct with her about Mary's interest in him. *Was there any?* Instead, Jessica asked if he had any other plans.

Mary just smiled and excused herself. Jessica watched her meet with others outside the church. *Mary, what are you hiding from your best friend?*

Jessica avoided her after the funeral and focused her attention on the children seated behind her. Emma and Mitzi were staring glumly out the carriage window. Jessica struggled for words of comfort she might give them, but finding only emptiness inside her own soul, she turned away and kept her silence. The weather had not accepted today's grief, for not only had it stopped raining as the carriages made their way to the cemetery, but the sun brightened and warmed the landscape.

Otto, looking out the carriage window, suddenly turned to Jessica seated next to him. "Penelope is quite a lady, isn't she?"

"*Was*, Mr. Heller, not *is*. Penelope is dead."

At first his face betrayed puzzlement, but then it reshaped itself into a look of grudging acceptance. "I mean she *was* quite a lady. She was quiet but she had an impressive mind." He continued to talk after they left the carriage and followed the priest to the gravesite. "I've never met such a courageous lady," he said, oblivious of the others in the party staring at him. "Did you know," he said to Jessica, "that she saved a dozen men escaping from the Quantrill raiders in Lawrence? She even saved *my* life that day."

Jessica nodded, discomforted by the people staring at them—including the priest, who with an open Catholic prayer book in hand, was waiting to start.

"She was indeed brave," Otto said. "Why, when that man stuck a gun in her face and asked her where all the men are disappearing, do you know what her answer was?"

"Mr. Heller," the priest called out, "we are ready to begin now."

Otto continued as if he weren't interrupted. "Her answer was 'You may shoot me if you will, but you won't ever find out where the men are.' That is the kind of lady Penelope was."

People in the crowd whispered to one another, but Tinker came to the rescue with words that finally quieted Otto. "This be Miz Penelope's special day," Tinker said, "and she needs fer yuh to be quiet."

After the priest read from the Bible, he mentioned that Nellie would sing a farewell piece. Nellie, wearing a plain black cotton dress, folded her hands in front of her and gazed at the casket while Devin put a fife to his lips.

Nellie looked at Jessica for only a moment. Then she returned her attention to the casket as she sang:

> *"Farewell, vain world, I'm going home,*
> *where there's no more stormy clouds arising*
> *My Savior smiles, and bids me come,*
> *where there's no more stormy clouds arising."*

Otto cried in loud sobbing, throaty sounds, startling Jessica because this was the first time she had seen him cry with such choking tears. She clasped his hand, and he turned to her with a stunned look on his face as if he suddenly realized she was truly gone.

As Devin played the fife, Nellie continued singing:

> *"Sweet angels beckon me away,*
> *Where there's no more stormy clouds arising;*
> *to sing God's praise in endless day,*
> *where there's no more stormy clouds arising."*

"Oh God, no!" Otto cried out, rushing toward the coffin. He threw his trembling body on it. "Oh my dear, sweet Penelope!"

Chapter 35

The steam whistle shrieked and the train jerked forward. Mary Delaney, pressing against the window, smiled at Jessica, who stood on the platform waving a gloved hand back at her. As the grayish smoke from the engine began obscuring the faces of the well-wishers at the depot, Mary leaned back in her seat, thankful to finally be getting back to St. Louis where she belonged.

But this morning's news about General Price heading north through Missouri, ostensibly on his way to capture St. Louis, unnerved her. When she finally arrived in town, would she expect to find the city in Confederate hands? The latest information being telegraphed was that as of yesterday, Price and his troops had engaged Union pickets as the rebels bore into Ironton, some ninety miles south of St. Louis. Beyond that, there was no further information.

Mary rested her knitting on her lap and tried to busy herself with the shawl she had started when she arrived in Washington. Back in St. Louis she had a quilt she needed to resume work on, a quilt containing remnants of clothes of her friends, including those who once lived in Lawrence, Kansas but had since either died or moved on after the Quantrill raid.

When done, the quilt would show two clasped hands against a background of blue and gray, which Mary thought would represent the ultimate friendship with the peoples of a divided country. Matt agreed with her and told her that her quilt—which she had begun during the Perryville campaign—could also represent other things.

"I suppose you are correct," Mary had said to him. "If I had asked Jessica for her opinion, she would say it would be the eventual equality between the races."

"But Jessica is simply not realistic about such matters," Matt replied.

Mary wanted to ask if he still loved her, but dared not. Matt was such a difficult man to truly know, and she had no desire to be hurt again.

Unfortunately, Jessica had pressed her for an answer before she departed for St. Louis. Jessica's question still resonated in her mind:

"Mary, are you and Mr. Lightfoot seeing more of each other?"
"Yes, we have become good friends."
"Are you more than good friends, Mary?"
"Jessica, it was my understanding that you have no interest in marrying Matt. Is that correct?"
"Yes, but I mean—" Jessica looked flustered. "Oh, I don't know what I mean."

Mary resumed her knitting, conscious of the hypnotic sound of the rails and the occasional blast of the train whistle. Yesterday's events came back to her in a flash. Particularly how Jessica had expressed her appreciation for Mary's attendance at Penelope's funeral...

"It was wonderful of you to come to my parents'
funeral when you did," Jessica had said. "I needed a
friend and you were there."
"I'll always be here for you. You know that."
"Yes," Jessica said, choking. "I do."
"And I am so glad Matt survived from that serious
wound he received?"
"Serious wound? Matt never told me about that.
Why would he hide that from me?"

Mary put her knitting away and closed her eyes. She should have never mentioned about Matt almost dying from his battlefield wounds. She didn't realize Jessica never knew how likely it was that Matt would not survive.

*****

October 1
Washington, DC

Tinker, dressed neatly in regulation Union trousers, blue shirt, military vest, and dark blue frock coat, smiled nervously at Nellie, adorned in a light blue cotton dress with ruffled sleeves. He took slow steps toward the altar, glancing sideways at the small group—including some soldiers from a colored infantry—who attended the wedding ceremony. Now that he had a job waiting for him, he could support her—even though she already had a generous inheritance. Devin Alcott, who also attended the wedding ceremony, had teased him about it earlier. "Tinker, you've got a job and a lady who loves you," he said, laughing, "so your days as a carefree bachelor have drawn to a close. But now you'll be a happily married man."

Tinker was not convinced of that. Was he making a mistake by marrying a girl-woman?

Leaning on his cane, Tinker glanced at Nellie as they stood before the minister. Soon he and Nellie would walk out here being Mr. and Mrs. Tinker Longfellow. That would be his official last name. "You can't go around in this world known only by one name," Otto had told him....

"Tinker, men like to call each other 'Mister This' or 'Mister That.' What will you call yourself?"

After thinking about it for a moment, Tinker said, "How 'bout 'Longfellow'? I like 'Song of Hiawatha,' so maybe dat be my name—Tinker Longfellow."

He smiled when Nellie caught his stare. She looked so sweet in her dress, so much like a lady. Too bad she had been so brutally violated by the man who had kidnapped her from the Radfords. Tinker wondered whether her tragedy would now affect her ability to be intimate with him as her husband.

"Yah tol' me yah had a surprise for me," Nellie said to Tinker before the wedding. "What is it?"

"It's gonna have t' wait."

Nellie literally danced down the aisle when the ceremony was over. Tinker had never seen her so happy before. "I aim to love yah till the day I hafta go to the Lawd," he had added to his vows. "I hope yah don't go back to the Lord until I tell you it's fine," she answered, lighting up the room with her big smile.

"Tell me where you aim to work, Tinker. Is it fer a blacksmith shop here in Washington?"

"No. It ain't a blacksmith shop and it ain't in Washington. It's in Chicago. We gonna leave next week for a new place to live."

Nellie frowned. "Chicago?"

He expected Nellie to be surprised. He had been when he received the news last week. Illinois Governor Yates in his letter told him that because of his heroism in the war, that he, Tinker, would have a job working as a coal tender for the railroad in that city. "Don't worry about anything," the Governor wrote, "I'll be sure you are treated fairly."

"Chicago?" Nellie repeated, her round face forming a scowl. "That mean we hafta be away from Jessica 'n Mr. Heller 'n the chillen?"

Tinker nodded, but he cracked an encouraging smile. "Doan worry none, Nellie. Chicago's a big town, a nice town. You'll see. You'll like it."

But Tinker wasn't convinced himself. What about these "black laws" that Mr. Heller warned him about just yesterday? Mr. Heller said he heard about it from an Illinois Senator. They were "discriminatory," he said.

"What dat mean?" Tinker asked.

"It means you might be making a mistake going there."

*****

October 9

Otto insisted on Jessica accompanying him and the children to Mass today, as he had done every Sunday since Penelope's death. "I don't understand," he said, waiting for her as she alit from the carriage, "how you could be raised with a Methodist father and a Catholic mother and not want to attend either church."

265

"Frankly, "Jessica said, "when my parents were alive they argued constantly about religion. They couldn't even agree on baptism, and hence I was not even baptized."

Otto's dark wooden eyes sprung to life as he stared at her. "Not baptized? Surely, you must consider the consequences of that, Penelope."

Jessica frowned. "Penelope?"

His face flushed from embarrassment. "I'm sorry. I meant to say 'Jessica.' When you get used to someone for so long, it is difficult to forget that you—" His voice trailed off.

"I know. Come on children," she said, helping Emma from the carriage. She turned to help Mitzi.

"I can get off all by myself," Mitzi insisted.

Jessica stifled a laugh. That girl will probably end up being a stubborn, independent lady just like herself.

During the Communion service, as she sat next to Emma and Otto while Mitzi went to the altar rail, Jessica pondered whether she ought to write Matt a letter to let him know how she was doing and to see if he'd be interested in communicating with her. Her publisher asked her to visit several cities in promoting her book, and St. Louis was one of them. If she did go, she wanted to see Matt again—but only if the feeling was mutual.

And she thought about Otto as well. After Penelope's death, Otto acted like a whipped dog, like a man whose dreams had been crushed and now he was just going through the ordeal of survival. Usually, he would come home after work, read a newspaper and eat supper without uttering anything except responding to questions Jessica or the children might have. After his meal, he'd walk outdoors and return, ready for bed.

Devin joined them for Sunday dinner, as usual, and Jessica looked forward to his company. At least it provided a diversion from the boredom of her workweek. He brought with him a violin, which he claimed was hand crafted in Saxony.

"It had been my father's instrument," Devin said, feeling the black-stained beech fingerboard and the beech sound board. "It was one thing he hesitated to part with when I told

266

him I was immigrating to the United States." He put it in his violin case and took a seat by the window.

Mitzi parked herself on his lap and looked up at him, smiling sweetly. "Would you please play something for us, Mr. Alcott?"

He smiled back at her. "I'll do better than that, my child." He arose, lifting her up in his arms. "I'll have you play with me."

Mitzi laughed. "That's silly. I don't even know how to play the violin."

"But you do know how to play the piano, young lady." He sat her on the piano bench and mussed her hair with his hand. "Your father tells me you play Beethoven's 'Ode to Joy,' impressively so I will play it with my violin while you accompany me on the piano."

A nervous Mitzi made a miscue as she started playing but soon got into the music, and the combination of piano and violin seemed to come together flawlessly. Jessica was unaware that she had been humming the tune while they played until the piano and violin both stopped.

"I'm sorry," Jessica said with an embarrassing smile, "but that music carries me along and makes me feel as if I'm on gossamer wings."

"I've never heard you use that expression before, dear Penelope," Otto said, glancing toward Jessica. "As a matter of fact, I didn't know you cared much for Beethoven."

Devin stared at him but Jessica was getting used to Otto's occasional name slip by now, so she brushed it aside with a joke. *Maybe over time*, she thought, *even Otto's subconscious mind would accept Penelope's death.*

*****

Dear Matt,

Mary Delaney gave me your address in St. Louis, so I hope you don't mind my effrontery in writing to you like this. I have felt badly about my behavior ever since I left St. Louis. Thus, I would first like to apologize to you and hope you understand that I am sincerely sorry. With all the other pressures I felt I was under, I could not focus my energies on the prospect of marriage—although contrary to what I may have told you, I have never ruled it out as a possibility.

My publisher has included St. Louis as one of the towns where I am scheduled to speak. If I do go there, I would like the opportunity to see you. Mary tells me that you are the pastor of New Hope Methodist Church, and I congratulate you. I know it is something you have always wanted.

I am still in the throes of writing Black and Proud, my second novel, but it is becoming increasingly difficult to find the solitude I need to write. The children, as well as Mr. Heller, need me more than ever, but for my own sanity I will have to arrange for another nanny when I am away on my trips.

I have had the distinct pleasure of meeting Mr. Lincoln during a ceremony in which he presided where Mr. Stanton awarded Tinker with the Medal of Honor for Tinker's heroism. Mary told me she would provide you with details of Tinker's exploits resulting in this award, but I only mention this in passing to tell you how impressed I am with President Lincoln. He is a humble and unassuming man, despite his high office and is greatly appreciative of negro contributions toward the preservation of the Union.

I must close with my fondest wish that you think of me at least occasionally in your heart. Please write when you have the opportunity.

Sincerely,

Jessica Radford

Chapter 36

It was a two-story brick house that would have to serve as New Hope Church until the building could be occupied next week. Pastor Matt Lightfoot stood before fifteen people seated on chairs, exchanging conversations in the large parlor, grateful they showed up for his first service. He cleared his throat to get their attention, and the chatter soon died off.

"Before we begin our service, I want to thank you all for coming," he said. "Today is my debut as your pastor, so I trust you will let me know if I fall short of your expectations." He glanced down at a paper he hoped he would not have to discuss, but he had no choice. "Unfortunately, by Special Order Number sixty-two, issued by General Rosecrans, I'm obligated to ask you to take an oath of allegiance to the Union, so that I can file it with the Assistant Provost Marshall."

The people resumed their individual conversations, which were now punctuated with ire. One tall, elderly man rose up. "With all due respect, Reverend, since when does our government have a right to dictate anything concerning church members?" Bursts of agreement shot up from different people in the room.

"I feel as outraged over this requirement as you," Matt said, "but you must recall what happened to the Pine Street Presbyterian Church in this town."

Matt still cringed at how Reverend McPheeters, the Pine Street Church pastor, was treated because of his belief that his political views should be of no concern to his congregation.

"The government has no right to interfere with us," a woman cried out. "Our allegiance is to the Almighty alone."

A younger gentleman sided with Matt. "Pastor Lightfoot is correct in reminding us about Pine Street Church. We don't want to lose Reverend Lightfoot like the Pine Street Church lost Reverend McPheeters, do we?"

Only two people left after that, refusing to take the oath of allegiance. Still, the ordeal left Matt angry. Loyalty of a particular government had nothing to do with loyalty to God. *What we feel personally about the morality of this war should have nothing to do with our belliefs.*

He reflected on that later when he reread Jessica's letter. How was she able to cope with all those anxieties of hers without an assurance that somehow God would help her see her way through it all? He thought about that question for a while. He also wondered why she had requested to visit him in St. Louis. *Wasn't the matter settled?*

*****

October 28
Washington, DC

> *Dear Mrs. Toby,*
>
> *I had meant to correspond with you earlier, but with the press of other matters, it had escaped my attention. I wanted you to know that Nellie was wed earlier this month to a negro gentleman named Tinker. They are residing in Chicago as Mr. and Mrs. Tinker Longfellow at 75 West Juniper Street. You may wish to write to them at that address, and I am sure they would enjoy hearing from you. Nellie had told me that she had written to your Atlanta address but has not received a reply from you. Perhaps you have moved, and if so, I hope that this letter finds you at your new location.*
>
> *I want to thank you for taking such good care of Nellie, whom I consider a flesh-and-blood sister. Regretfully, this war has made it difficult for us to meet, but I hope we meet someday and become better acquainted.*
>
> *Respectfully,*
>
> *Jessica Radford*

Jessica sealed the envelope and busied herself with setting the plates on the table.

"Is Papa joining us for supper?" Emma asked, taking her seat next to Mitzi.

Jessica looked at the mantel clock for the fifth time since she prepared supper. Seven o'clock. *He had never been out this late before.* "I don't know. Probably not."

"Where is he?" Mitzi said, her eyes searching Jessica for an answer.

"Don't fret about it. You girls can eat now and Papa will have his supper later."

Jessica excused herself and went to her neighbor to ask if she would watch the children. Jessica had to search for him. *What could have happened to him? Had he fallen ill and is being unattended to? Had he suffered a tragic accident? Did he wander somewhere in his continuing despair over the loss of Penelope?*

He had complained this morning that he had not had any sleep the previous evening. He was silent at breakfast and didn't bother to say goodbye as he left the house. She scolded herself for not insisting that he stay home today.

The Printing Office was locked when she arrived, so she walked back toward the stables, tightening the shawl about her neck. The sun had already set almost two hours ago, and it was unseemly for a woman to be walking alone in the semi-darkness of a street lit by gaslight. She passed by brick buildings and walled-in interior yards, and she stopped at the entrance to a tavern where loud noises filtered through to the street. Peering through the window, she saw it crowded with men, some holding steins in their hands and laughing and others puffing away on cigars. Jessica assumed that Friday night was probably one evening when men felt they could lose their inhibitions and celebrate, even if their wives were home worrying about them.

Just like I worry about Mr. Heller, she fumed. She thought she heard his voice and looked in the window again. Sure enough, there he was, sitting on a stool, waving his free hand at the barkeep while drinking with the other.

No sooner had she entered the smoke-filled noisy room when men called out a crude greeting to her as if she were some common prostitute. Jessica ignored them and headed straight for Mr. Heller.

Otto looked at her with bloodshot eyes, mumbling incoherently as he attempted to get off his stool. "Miss Radford, join me for a toast," he said, slurring his words.

The alcohol from his breath made her wince, but she tried steadying him by grasping his shoulders, but he nonetheless slipped to the floor. He laughed as he looked up bug-eyed at the ceiling. "Things sure look different from here."

"Please get up, Mr. Heller," Jessica said. "You are acting like a buffoon."

"A buffoon?" he snorted. "Now what sort of talk is that for a lady of your station?"

As two men helped him to his feet, Jessica pulled on his sleeve. "We must leave now, Mr. Heller. But I do not think it wise for the children to see you in this condition."

"What condition?" he said, rolling his eyes as if he were unaware of his surroundings.

The barkeep, a slender man with thinning brown hair came to Jessica's rescue. "He is not fit to go anywhere like this," he said. "There is a small house behind this tavern. A friend who had been using it is away, and I could let him rest there."

Jessica could see no other alternative. Were she to take him home in a chaise, she would have to somehow get him to the house and explain Mr. Heller's embarrassing condition to her neighbor and his children.

She nodded her approval and followed the barkeep as he escorted Mr. Heller to a one-room house. He dropped Mr. Heller on the bed and removed his boots. "Perhaps you could have someone come by in the morning and take him home," the barkeep said.

Jessica thanked him for his kindness, and after he left, Jessica noticed a pen and paper on a small desk next to the bed.

272

She was about to go to it and write him a note before leaving when Otto pushed himself up in bed. As he turned to her, his eyes were half-open, his face contorted as if he had been crying. "Thank God, you're here," he said. "I need you. I feel so alone."

"Just try to get some sleep."

He slinked back into the bed and began to sob. "Jessica, don't ever leave me."

The man is delusional. How could he beg me not to leave him when he had always pretended to be indifferent to my affections while Penelope was still around?

She sat on the bed facing him and stroked his head. "Just try to get some rest, Mr. Heller. You will feel better in the morning."

Otto sat up at once, placing his hands on her arms. "No. Don't go, Jessica. Please don't go."

Jessica took out a handkerchief from her dress pocket and mopped his damp forehead. Here was the man she had always admired. He always knew what to do, never worried about what others would think, brought slaves to safety, and always supported her—whether it was about her disguising herself as a man to fight in the war or whether it was her novel, which he helped get published.

He began unbuttoning the front of her dress. "I need you tonight," he mumbled. "I want you."

"What are you doing!" She grabbed both of his hands and forced them down.

"But I love you," he said, looking up at her with pleading, bloodshot eyes. "I have always loved you, my darling."

These were the words she had wanted to hear from him. But not this way. Not words uttered by a man who smelled like a distillery.

She pressed on his collar bone, forcing him to lay back on the pillow. "You need to get your rest, Mr. Heller."

His eyes were partly closed, but his lips were moving and his words wandered like broken fragments of a hoarse whisper,

273

interrupted by a choking spasm. "I want to make love to you. I need you so much, my precious."

She mopped his forehead again. *Drunken fool!* But as she looked at him, she wondered about her own feelings. Matt and Otto were so different. Yet Matt was a man she could feel passionate about if she ever let herself feel that way. He always wanted her. There was no struggle for his love. But with Otto it was different. His resistance to her affections in the past made him all the more attractive, even though she had always felt it was sinful.

"I hope you feel the same way about me when you're sober," Jessica said as she covered Otto up with a blanket.

Chapter 37

If the preacher is going to continue talking about his opin-ion that all this suffering is God's will, Sara Toby reflected as she left the church, *I'm not going back any more.* Once she had a beautiful home, friends, financial support, and a hus-band with whom she shared a bed. But now, she did not even know whether Roger was still alive since receiving his last let-ter a month ago. And Nellie was gone as well, somewhere. Yet the preacher has the audacity to say that all these things— including her daily suffering—that all these things are God's will?

Last night she had the same dream again—that she was to star in a play in which a Yankee soldier confronts Roger and laughs as he butchers him with an axe. Her role in the play was to watch as a horde of Union soldiers trampled over his body. After she escapes toward the river when the men began to charge her, she finds herself in the water, sinking all the while into her watery graveyard. Just then, she fixes her face upon one kindly man in a white gown and red sash who reaches to pull her out. She sinks fast and tries in vain to grab his arm.

Even during her waking hours, she felt as if she were drowning. The Jordans, the people who had invited her to live with them, had defaulted on their house payments and de-cided to move on to another Alabama town.

Sara could scarcely believe that she was now homeless and totally without any means of support. The only posses-sions she had were a horse and a musket which Jane Millicent bequeathed her when she died. But she had long ago sold the horse, and the only practical use she saw for the musket was to hunt her own game.

Someone had to hire her. But there was no work here. Not at the grocery, not at the livery stable, not at the mill, not anywhere. Now, down to a slab of cheese and two slices of bread, which a local church had provided her, she began knocking on the doors of houses. Finally, one homeowner reluctantly offered her a job as a laundress and scrubwoman. But that only lasted a week.

"Sorry, ma'am," the woman said when Sara begged her to stay on. "My slave is back with me now. Don't need your services."

She was right, Sara admitted. People who had slaves could get those tasks performed without having to pay with highly inflated Confederate notes.

After being turned away from a hotel, where she begged for temporary shelter, she sat on the wooden steps leading to the inn. "God, why am I going through this?" she asked, gazing up at the white speckled night sky. "What is the purpose?"

"God's not up there," a chuckling voice spoke.

Sara looked up to see a gentleman in a gray frock coat and tall hat, tapping his cane against the step. "Permit me to introduce myself."

He stated his name which Sara promptly forgot, but she stood up to face him when he mentioned services that he required. "What sort of work?" she asked her heart thumping at the thought of being employed again.

"Why, to pleasure me this evening," he said, smiling broadly.

She slapped his face, but he only laughed, holding a gold coin to her face. "This can be yours, ma'am. Just for the askin'."

Her pulse quickened. She thought of screaming for help, but there was no one around.

"How dare you! I am not a trollop," she said, glaring at him.

He flashed the coin at her again. "I have ten excellent reasons why you should bed down with me, ma'am. And if you want more, I know other gentlemen willing to pay the same."

The sight of a ten-dollar gold piece amazed her. Without listening to the "no" screaming inside of her, she accepted the offer, arguing with herself that she had no choice.

Later, as he undid the stays of her corset, she realized this would be the acting role of a lifetime. But after he removed her chemise and touched her naked skin, she shivered. Closing her eyes, she forced herself to imagine that none of this was real...that her pretense at enjoyment was simply another role she had to play...that she was no longer Roger's loving and devoted wife. Sara Toby was someone else, someone waiting by a kitchen window at her old home in Chattanooga, staring out at Lookout Mountain, recalling how Roger would tell her it was the fist of God, daring any intruder to climb its steep slopes.

"Surely, this cannot be your first time," the man said, easing her down to his bed.

Lookout Mountain. The fist of God. Roger. The thoughts from her past needled her. "It's my first time with a stranger."

"Are you married?"

She closed her eyes. "No," she said, her voice quivering. The slopes of her life were indeed steep. The image of Roger somewhere out there, fighting and maybe even dying, for a cause he believed in came to mind, while she slipped deep into the mud. And then another image—their honeymoon in Georgia. How Roger worried about being gentle with her because it was her first time.

The stranger kissed her on the curve of her neck. "You are a remarkable woman."

"No, I'm not," she said, her words tiptoeing through her conscience. "I'm not remarkable in the least."

"I beg to differ with you," he said. "You are worth every dollar I've paid."

She tried to imagine he was Roger as she synchronized the rhythm of her body with that of the stranger's. *Oh, Roger, my darling. Please know how deeply I regret this!*

*****

November 8
Chicago, Illinois

It didn't take long for Tinker Longfellow to realize that his Medal of Honor award and his service in the military amounted to little when it came to recognition from his coworkers. He had not heard the term "nigger" used much while he served with the Union, but he heard it almost daily, usually behind his back, as he did in his work….He was told he should be happy in being with the Chicago & North Western Railway. One of the men who knew William Butler Ogden, the railroad president, met him the day after he arrived and told Tinker all about the railroad. How it started the first trains in and out of Chicago, how the railroad had merged with other railroads in Wisconsin and Illinois and was on its way to becoming a major east-west link for the rest of the country.

Tinker couldn't figure out why the other workers ignored him. But Nellie suggested it was probably because they were jealous. They resented the fact that he only got the job because Governor Yates had some influence with Ogden.

"Jest don't tell folks where you lived before," Nellie had said.

Tinker had to admit she was right. He was aware of Illinois's "Black Laws" which forbade the immigration of blacks into the state. It would be best if no one knew where he lived before.

Still, he resisted her warnings about not stirring the waters and getting involved with any activities opposed to the Black Laws. He knew he should have told her that he had met with John Jones, a leader with the Wood River Colored Baptist Association. "We are supposed to be free men," Jones had told him, "but are we free? No! We can't vote, we can't mingle with white folk, and we can't even go to school to get an education."

"I kinda felt dat when I got here," Tinker said. "But I thought it might be me, dat maybe they jest don't like me."

"Got nothing to do with you, Mr. Longfellow," Jones said. "Got to do with the color of your skin."

Tinker didn't believe him. The people just needed to realize who he was. But when he showed up at a voter registration table a week ago, he was asked to leave the premises. Not only did he not have a right to register to vote; he had no right to even be there with the white folk who were registering. "But I'm a soldier. Gots me a Medal of Honor 'n everythin'. I should be 'llowed to vote."

"I don't care if you're the King of England," the clerk snapped back. "You have no right to be here. Now please leave before I call the authorities."

Tinker hung his head. *Mr. Jones be right. My Medal of Honor mean nothin' to nobody. My service t' my country mean nothin'.* He wished he could be more like Nellie and take things in stride.

"I don't care if'n you 'n me pay taxes," Nellie told him. "Yer jest gonna stir up trouble. Let things be."

She was right. All he could do was let things be. Tomorrow's paper would have the results of today's national election. He could only hope people did the right thing and voted for Abraham Lincoln.

*****

Washington, DC

Ward Hill Lamon felt a sourness in his stomach as he watched the election returns being telegraphed in. It appeared that President Lincoln was on his way to a second term of office, and he wished he could rejoice in the victory with others. But how could he? With the prospects now favoring Lincoln's reelection, Lamon now had an even greater concern for the President's safety.

Lamon leaned his tall, heavy frame against a supporting pillar in the Executive Mansion. He recalled having to persuade Lincoln to allow him to be his personal bodyguard, in addition to being the U.S. Marshal for the District of Columbia. Lincoln still lamented about being persuaded, back in February of 1861, to arrive unannounced in Washington prior to his inauguration. Allan Pinkerton and his detectives, along with Lamon, had convinced Lincoln of a planned assassination attempt in the wake of strong anti-Lincoln sentiment in Baltimore. Lincoln's clandestine train ride in the night resulted in ridicule and Lincoln had regretted listening to Lamon.

Although a Southerner himself, Lamon knew it would not bother his conscience if he had to use a pistol or Bowie knife

279

to protect the President from any Southerner who dared try to harm Mr. Lincoln. He only wished that the President was more concerned about his own safety. In 1860, while he was in his Illinois chamber in Springfield, Lincoln told Lamon of an eerie vision he had experienced while looking in a mirror. Lincoln mentioned seeing a double image of himself—one being a vibrant image and the other taking on a ghostly pale white. He told Lamon it concerned him a little. It seemed to convey the possibility that he would not complete his second term as President. But later, Lincoln dismissed the whole idea as an absurdity.

Well, Lamon, reasoned, it was not absurd to think that someone might want to kill Mr. Lincoln. Surely, the President must be aware of the presence of his enemies. And now that the President has been reelected, the anger of his enemies may have escalated into action.

Lamon waited until the President retired to his bedroom and then, armed with his pistols and Bowie knife, stretched himself on the floor, just outside of Mr. Lincoln's door. *If someone wants to kill Mr. Lincoln, they'd first have to get by Ward Hill Lamon.*

The light through the cracks of the bedroom door disappeared, and Lamon sighed deeply. With one hand on his pistol held over his chest, he closed his eyes but listened for the sound of intruding footsteps before passing off into sleep for the night.

*****

The next day

Devin Alcott had mixed feelings about the offer he received as music instructor for the School of Practice for U.S.A. Field Musicians at Governor's Island, New York. It would involve two hours of class instruction and four hours of music practice every day for young drummers and fifers. A former officer with the Eighth Kansas had recommended him to the school, although Devin had other plans. Now that he had become a U.S. citizen, he thought he would have an easier time

280

finding a job as a musician in Washington or Baltimore. But such was not the case, and Devin began to wonder whether it was the fact that no such opportunities existed or whether his skin was the wrong color.

He took out his pen and finished his letter to Tinker and Nellie…

> *Maybe after this war is finally over, I will be able to return to what I want to do more than anything—to play music. I hope to visit with both of you, but with that draconian Illinois law you've described to me, I don't believe now would be a good time to do that. Hopefully, politicians will recover their sanity about blacks and whites and allow me to live anywhere I choose and with whomever I choose.*

> *Perhaps one or more of the boys whom I will instruct in music at Governors Island will some day become a serious musician. The Lord knows that I certainly intend to be one.*

Chapter 38

Washington, DC

Jessica didn't know what to make of Matt's letter. Picking it up, she read the one paragraph that puzzled her…

> *I have accepted the fact that you have decided not to marry me and to live your own life. I understand how my persistence may have driven you away from me. But now that I have had the opportunity to be separated from you all this time, I think you made the right decision. I have another love I am pursuing, and it has taken up much of my attention. I certainly would welcome seeing you again, but this time it would be in a wholly different light than before.*

Wholly different light than before? Did that mean he no longer loved her? And what about "another love" he was pursuing? Was he referring to a new romance or his ministry?

She crumpled his letter and threw it in the trash. If only Matt would be more like Mr. Heller, she would have had no difficulty in accepting his marriage proposal. Mr. Heller had a kind heart for others, and his past devotion to Penelope and his deep concern for the emancipation of slaves resonated with her.

She recalled how one evening she had gone to the kitchen for a cup of water and heard Penelope giggling and Otto's subdued command to lower her voice. The sounds emanated from the bedroom, and Jessica put her ear to the door…

"Oh, Otto, how wonderful!" Penelope whispered. "Please do not stop."

The repetitive squeaks of the bed were the only sounds Jessica heard next. How she despised Penelope at that moment!

That woman had Mr. Heller all to herself and there was nothing Jessica could do about it.

But the next day and every day thereafter, whenever Jessica entered their bedroom to change the sheets and clean the room, she could only look about her in disgust. Life had surely cheated her of the happiness that could have been hers. It was not fair. Not fair at all.

But now when she looked at this same bed, she fought the tears that insisted on rising to the surface. This was no longer a marriage bed but a bereavement bed. It seemed as if it were only yesterday when she discovered Penelope sprawled on that bed, with a death-face smile that told the world she was finally at peace.

Jessica wished *she* had that peace. Perhaps Otto was right in suggesting that she consider being baptized. Everyone she knew had religion, and maybe that was carrying them through life. Had she been a Christian, she perhaps would not have been so desirous of his love while he was still married to Penelope. But his lusting for her, his overtures for love that Friday before last, would only have meant something to her if he were sober. But since that time, she never broached the subject of his attempted seduction and neither did he. Did he remember what had happened that evening and was too embarrassed to bring it up?

Unlike before, he talked more about events at work when he returned home. The only time sadness crept over him was at mealtime when he would glance at the empty chair, Penelope's chair, in the dining room.

Tonight he seemed even more relaxed than usual. The children had already gone to bed and Otto put aside the newspaper he had been reading. "Are you all packed for your trips to Chicago and St. Louis for your talks and book signings?"

"Yes. And, of course, you know that our neighbor will be watching the children while I am gone."

He furrowed his brow with eyes that were haunted by an inner pain. "The house will be empty without you."

"You won't be alone, Mr. Heller. You have the children to keep you company."

He nodded and resumed reading his paper. "It is wonderful news about Lincoln's reelection."

Jessica leaned back in her chair. "Yes it is. He took all except three Union states. I pray that this means a quick end to the war. I'm still hoping it will also mean an end to slavery."

"I suspect others are beginning to agree with that opinion," Otto said. He paused a moment and put his paper down. "Even Mr. Lightfoot."

She stared at Otto for a moment. "I hope he has. I wonder how he is getting by these days."

"It's a pity it didn't work out between you two," he said, rising from his chair. "You are an incredible woman, Miss Radford, and any man would be blessed to have you as his wife."

Would you, Mr. Heller, be blessed to have me?

"I have always enjoyed your company, Miss Radford, and now that Penelope is gone, I—" He stopped in mid-sentence and shook his head. "Never mind, I'm just tired. I must retire to bed now." He walked toward his bedroom door.

Jessica rose and went to him as he reached for the door-knob. "Mr. Heller, may I ask you a personal question?"

"Why, yes. What is it?"

"This is rather difficult for me."

"We've always been good friends, Jessica. I won't be offended by whatever you ask."

"That night you were intoxicated and I was in the room with you. Do you recall what happened?"

"Why, I—" He hesitated, looked briefly at her, then looked away. "I recall trying to take advantage of you, and for that I am terribly sorry."

"But don't you remember? You told me that you—" She struggled for the courage to finish what she had started to say. "—that you loved me, that you had always loved me."

His eyes were downcast, and he looked weary and defeated. "I don't know what I said, Miss Radford. Again, I must apologize for my rude behavior." He opened the door to his bedroom and turned to her. "I wish I could say I love you,

Miss Radford, but I am incapable of loving another woman again—not after Penelope."

Jessica nodded, but a thought flooded her mind—

We don't have to love each other to need each other, Mr. Heller. Do we?

Chapter 39

This was the third consecutive Sunday that Sara had not attended church services. Instead, she strolled along the river, thinking about those days in Chattanooga when she and Roger would spend an afternoon fishing. He'd row her out to the middle of the Tennessee River and they'd stare up at Lookout Mountain...

> *"Think I can climb it?" he asked.*
> *"I dare you," she laughed.*
> *"I'll climb it if you first swim across the river."*
> *"You devil. You know I can't swim."*

But she could act, and Roger attended every one of her performances in Chattanooga. The war had shattered all those memories. Now Roger was out somewhere in Tennessee fighting although he told her in his last letter he had no will to fight. The South was lost.

I'm lost too. I only hope I am able to face Roger when he returns.

Jessica's letter informing her of Nellie's new residence in Chicago sat on her desk for days, and Sara tried more than once to write to Nellie. She had to tell Nellie how heartless it was to run away like she did. But she also wanted to tell her how much she loved her.

Sara wrote the next line...

I dread Roger's return because of what I had done.

Sara glanced at the man sleeping in her bed and wished it were Roger...

I cannot relate to you the horror of what I have had to go through, having sunk so low that I—

"I cannot tell her that!" she moaned, grabbing her trembling wrist. She tried reaching for the ink bottle, tipping it

286

over, and letting its contents drip over the letter like black blood.

*****

Ten days later
Franklin, Tennessee

Major General John Schofield breathed a sigh of relief when his two Federal infantry corps managed to slip past Hood's Army of Tennessee last night near Spring Hill. He assumed that his mission would be to continue north past Franklin and into Nashville to join up with General Thomas. Once there, the Union would have the strength to crush the rebels.

But he had also expected that Thomas would have sent the pontoons Schofield needed to cross the Harpeth River and bring his wagonloads of supplies over. The pontoons were not there early this morning, so he was surprised by Thomas's first telegraphed message that gave him permission to cross the river and retire to Nashville. Before Schofield could react to this message, a second one came in instructing Schofield to protect his wagon trains and take a position in Franklin.

But Hood was on Schofield's heels, and the Union general had no intention of engaging with Hood at this point when it was likely that Hood's troops outnumbered his. What was the point of battling the rebels at Franklin anyway? Decorated for his services at Wilson's Creek in 1861 and recognized for effectively commanding several departments in Kansas and Missouri, Schofield had set his focus on helping Thomas defeat the rebels near Nashville. He had to. He was determined to attain the status of Phillip Sheridan, another general who was the same age as himself—thirty-three. Sheridan exhibited excellent leadership at the Perryville, Stones River, Chickamauga, and Chattanooga campaigns. Schofield needed Nashville, and with the strength of Federal forces there he could be assured of certain victory. He had no interest in a potential Pyrrhic triumph at Franklin.

"Order the men to rebuild the parapets," Schofield, said to Generals Cox and Wagner, as he pointed to a map. "We will

287

need a continuous and extensive line of breastworks, from east of the Columbia to Franklin Pike to the Harpeth. We'll need to work fast and work hard. Dig in our artillery behind the breastworks and lets point those guns south at Hood's advancing forces."

"How will we get our supplies across the river?" Cox asked.

"That is a fair question. I will have to leave you in charge of fortifications while I go see what we can do about our river crossing."

*****

By noon, having made his headquarters in an orange brick farmhouse owned by the Carter family, Schofield was glad that the breastworks were completed. An inner line of entrenchments had also been dug some sixty feet south of the Carter house and in line with the farm office and smokehouse.

He walked outside and took a deep breath, taking in the nostalgic smells of fallen leaves, burnt ash, and wet hay. In his home state of New York, he might have been bundled up at this time of the year, protected against the sharp frost of an early winter. Now that dinner was over and horses fed and saddled, he had to wait for Hood's next move. Knowing Hood personally from his West Point days, Schofield felt that Hood would probably not act as rationally as other officers. Hood, in his estimation, was not an able commander, preferring instead to operate on sheer determination rather than careful, calculated planning.

Schofield wished he did not have to tear down those barns as well as the timbers from Carter's cotton gin so that the Federals could use the timber for head logs in building their entrenchments. But, he had to agree with General Cox, that the hill on which the Carter estate rested was a key to the defense in front of Franklin. This would be a pivotal area where Schofield's forces would have to be when and if Hood made a charge against the Federal line.

Schofield would have preferred that the large number of people residing at the Carter house, including twelve young children, would have left their home in lieu of the impending battle. But they had elected to stay, fearing that they would have no home to come back to when they returned. He took assurance in that possibility that these folks could be spared since they did have a rock-walled cellar below the house. When and if the shooting started, they could take refuge there.

A little girl about six years old in a black cotton dress stood on the porch when Schofield turned to reenter the house. She clutched a rag doll and her face was streaked with tears.

"What's your name, little girl?"

"Ruth Carter." She made a face at him. "I don't like those men over here. Leave us alone!"

"I'm sorry," he said, stooping down to her level, "but we are expecting an attack. We need to be here."

"But I don't want you here. Leave us alone."

"Believe me, child, I would if I could. I really would." He got up and watched as the girl ran back, sobbing, almost tripping over a soldier sleeping on the porch. Children are the major casualties of hatred, Schofield thought. Just like in the Bible. *Herod murdering the Israelite sons in Egypt...Rachel crying for her children...Suffer little children.*

*****

Lieutenant Roger Toby instinctively reached in his coat jacket to touch her letter. It was the only part of her that he had, and just feeling the letter made him realize that she was real, that she would be waiting for him when he returned. The rest of this war was not real. The Confederate soldiers on both sides, stretching on as far as the eye could see, were not real. It was as if he were but a spoke in a wheel among an enormous number of wheels, and he would move only because he had to, because the wheels were all moving and he had to move with them. He had longed for Southern independence from the Union, but somewhere during the war—probably at Chattanooga—he was convinced that the cause was lost. Nashville was strongly fortified by the Union and Sherman was cutting a swath eastward toward the seaboard of Georgia.

What was left for the Confederate States of America? Nothing but a dream, a futile dream.

Roger could not believe his ears. Someone had just now asked what time it was and another answered that it was about four o'clock in the afternoon. But what difference did that make? The day, the time, the year—it was meaningless. All unreal. The only reality was that Sara was back in Birmingham, saving herself for him, praying for his safety, crying for his return.

What was the point of General Hood's decision in forming a skirmish line some 200 yards in front of the Union lines? If it was because Hood wanted to redeem himself for Schofield's narrow escape at Spring Hill, then this was folly. If it was because Hood felt that the Union army would retreat to Nashville, what good was that?

Roger was just one spoke in a wheel…among many wheels, driving forward.

A regimental band began playing "The Bonnie Blue Flag," and the song brought tears to his eyes.

> *Hurrah! Hurrah! For Southern rights hurrah!*
> *Hurrah for the Bonnie Blue Flag that bears a single*
> *star.*

Sara came instantly to mind: her warm, blue eyes, her teasing smile, her tears when he said goodbye to her when he returned to his regiment.

Remember how you sat with me on the grass three-and-a-half years ago? It was in Columbia, and we were newly married, I held your hand, and I kissed you. We shared our thoughts as we stared at the South Carolina flag together. I was the only man you ever loved, the only lover you ever had or will have until the day I die.

"Keep your men in line!" a major ordered. "Damn those Yankee boys!" another shouted.

Suddenly a volley of solid shot, grape, canister erupted from the enemy lines. "Charge!" Roger screamed, mechanically—as if it were someone else who had just issued the order. He pushed on, waving the men forward. Stumbling, he, picked himself up, and fell again. The Union soldiers were in retreat and the Confederates, in the thousands, like devils swarmed after them. The Union breastworks were in the distance, but since the retreating Federals were becoming dispersed with the rebels, the Union could not fire for fear of killing their own men.

Roger spotted an orange-brick farmhouse up ahead, but men in blue were rushing toward the house from the north, screaming, guns blaring. "Fix bayonets!" came an order from somewhere down the Confederate line. Roger trudged on, the battle now breaking into a wild melee, the most vile language being shouted by both sides at each other.

Minié balls thundered against the side of the house, but Roger made it to the backyard. A Minié ball grazed his side and he slid to the dirt. He heard a young child, a girl about six in a black dress, screaming at a Union soldier who had grabbed her arm and appeared to be very drunk.

Instinctively, Roger pushed himself up and slammed the butt of his rifle against the Yankee's head, causing the Federal to fall into a heap on the dry ground. The girl looked at Roger for a moment, her parched lips forming a thin smile, and then ran into the house.

Roger fell back to the ground, exhausted and weakened from the Minié ball in his side. He crawled on his belly toward a small wooden shack that he felt might have been the owner's slave quarters. He looked up to see men on both sides clawing, punching, and stabbing each other. One Confederate grabbed a shovel from the ground and slammed it against the face of a Yankee. A Federal officer plunged a knife into the eye of a rebel solider. The cannon fire, musketry, canister, screams of the wounded, and cursing grew to a crescendo. Grayish-black smoke covered the area like a shroud.

Roger felt a heavy thud on his backside. He jerked his head back when he saw it was the body of a fallen comrade. Bodies began piling up around him, two or three high. Cries of the wounded. Agonizing cries. He felt nauseous hearing them.

He crawled from under the body atop his and pushed himself closer to the slave cabin. A young man in a blue uniform, perhaps his own age sat with his back against the wall, muttering, "Please don't kill me, please don't kill me." His eyes were wild, and blood gushed from his right leg. He froze when he saw Roger reaching for his weapon.

"No, don't!" the man begged. "Please don't!"

Roger pointed his weapon at the man's head, but his pleading face was too difficult to observe. Maybe he could look askance while he shot him.

The voices in Roger's head grew louder....

— *You're part of the war machine, Roger.*

— *But we've got a man here, pleading. He could have been me, begging to be saved.*

— *Does not matter, lieutenant!*

— *But this young man, what about him?*

—*Casualty of war, lieutenant. Do your job.*

Roger looked at the terrified man, still begging for his life. "I've got to do this," Roger said, and he clicked his weapon, but it didn't fire.

"Damn it to hell!" Roger yelled, tossing his gun into the air. He stumbled back toward the yard, tripping over the bodies of soldiers, picking himself up, and stumbling again. A shell exploded nearby, sending him reeling backwards, falling on a layer of bodies.

Lights pierced the smoke-laden sky...white lights resting on the soil, now surrounded him. *No, not lights. Angels. Yes, winged angels.* Their young faces glowed, and their gowns shimmered in white. The ground was covered with these heavenly creatures tending the wounded and dying. Roger blinked. It was as if the soldiers had become statues, holding silent guns, in a field now ablaze with angels of mercy, all chattering soft words of comfort.

Roger thought he also saw the face of Sara, but her image was dim, just as the whole world seemed to be growing dim. Then all turned black.

*****

December 9
Birmingham, Alabama

Sara pretended to be aroused as the man brought his rhythmic excitement to closure and exploded deep within her. It had been six weeks since she had started on this road—first feeling as if she were drowning in the mud of a pigsty, but now, as she expanded her clientele and learned to use her acting talents to the full, she began to relax. The money had been easy and her professional encounters with men were not unpleasant. Besides, she knew all about Roger's betrayal during the first year of their marriage. She never told him that she knew he had been having relations with that black slave girl Nasha. What she was doing was necessary; she was doing it to survive. He had done it for pleasure.

Her gentleman caller got dressed and dropped a gold coin in her hand.

"Thank you," she said, rolling the coin with her fingers.

"Terrible tragedy about the South," he said. "I mean the Army of Tennessee losing six generals at the Franklin battle. Six o' them, mind you in one battle. One o' them was Cleburne. Smartest and best general we ever had."

Sara winced. Roger's last letter said he was headed toward Franklin. Since then, she heard nothing from him. Did he survive? *Oh dear Roger, please come back.*

"Are you feeling well, ma'am?" the man said as he approached the door.

"I will be fine." She wished it were true.

"Well, I must be going. Dinner engagement."

After he left, Sara got up and went to the window to watch the busy traffic below. She took her time getting dressed and was about to boil water for tea when there was a knock on the door. Thinking it was her last customer who might have returned for some reason, she opened the door with a ready smile. But she was taken aback when a uniformed Confederate soldier greeted her with a telegram.

Sara frowned. "For me?"

"Yes, ma'am."

After the soldier disappeared, Sara opened the telegram, her heart beating rapidly as she thought the worst might have happened to Roger. She breathed a sigh of relief when the telegram told her that Roger was alive but had been recovering from wounds incurred in battle. He would eventually be transported to a Confederate hospital in Birmingham.

She wandered to the bedroom and removed a framed photograph of Roger from the dresser drawer. After placing Roger's picture on the dresser top, she turned to look at the bed.

That expensive silk sheet she had bought earlier was now soiled and wrinkled.

1865

Chapter 40

"This calls for a celebration," Otto Heller said when he returned home from the Printing Office. "They say that there was a thunderous explosion of cheers on the House floor, with men embracing each other. There was even a burst of cannon fire on Capitol Hill to announce the big event."

"What big event?" Jessica asked, putting a pot on the stove.

"The Constitutional Amendment to abolish slavery. The House of Representatives voted 119 to 56 in favor of it."

Jessica shrieked with excitement and ran to hug him. "At last! It was a long time in coming."

"I knew you would be thrilled," he said, holding her in his arms. "Of course, it won't actually take effect until the states ratify it, and that may take a while." He released her from his embrace and took a chair at the table. "At least, we are finally on the right road."

"We probably have Mr. Lincoln to thank for that," she said, putting the plates on the table.

"How are the children doing?"

"Mitzi's teacher says it is rare for a ten-year-old to have such a gift for music."

"Devin deserves a lot of credit for encouraging her. Have you heard from him?"

Jessica placed the forks and spoons on the table. "Yes, I received a letter from him last week. He says he's actually enjoying instructing boys in fife and drums at Governor's Island. But he still has plans to find a job as a musician once this war is over."

"And how are *you* doing, Jessica? You haven't said much about your trip to St. Louis."

What could she say? That Matt was not home when she called on him? That perhaps he was deliberately avoiding her? That Mary was friendly, but evasive?

296

Jessica forced a smile. "As I have said, the trip was fine. I signed a number of my books. Some folks in the audience didn't care for my speeches about racial equality, however. I guess if the amendment passes, we'll still have a long way to go. I should call the children to supper."

"Never mind. I will do that, Jessica." He left the room and returned with Emma and Mitzi.

"Emma, tell Miss Radford what you learned in school the other day," Otto said, grinning at his seven-year-old.

"It's a game where you take pieces of countries and then you put them together."

Otto turned toward Jessica. "They're called dissections. It's something that a British mapmaker invented. A map of the world is drawn on hardwood and then cut into pieces. The children learn their geography by putting all these parts together."

"Sounds interesting," Jessica said, placing the cornbread in the center of the table. "Perhaps they ought to do one of the United States and see how those parts fit together after this war is over."

"I'm rather curious how that's going to work myself," Otto said. "I think Mr. Lincoln will stay the course on healing wounds rather than on punishing the South. But it's not a very popular position by any means."

*****

The next day
Chicago, Illinois

Nellie Longfellow looked a bit concerned when she and Tinker arrived at the Joneses house on Edinah Street. "Do yah think Midnight will be all right while we're gone?"

Tinker rolled his eyes. *She think of her black terrier like if it be her own chile. Always worryin' 'bout that lil' dog. Yet she doan want no chillum of her own.*

"Yeah," Tinker replied, "dat dere dog will be all right. You worry too much 'bout the wrong things."

297

"Well, I worry about yah gettin' involved like yah do tryin' to get the state to change their Black Codes. Don't want no trouble."

"Good thing you come tonight. Maybe yuh see fer yerself what a nice man dis John Jones is."

Nellie shook her head in amazement as she stared at the large brick home. "This here Mr. Jones 'n his missus must be doin' mighty fine fer themselves."

"Mr. Jones got rich from his tailoring shop he started almost twenty years ago."

"Well, I sho am impressed."

Tinker laughed. "Maybe someday I get rich too 'n we have an even bigger house." No sooner had he knocked when the door opened. A somewhat stout man with dark hair running down to the edge of his cheeks smiled. Tinker noticed that Nellie seemed surprised, and he could only guess it was because John Jones, who had been rebelling against the Black Codes of Illinois, was light-skinned and not black like Tinker.

After a cordial introduction, John invited them to the living room, where a lady with flowing dark hair, wearing a dark blue dress with white ruffles, stood up from her chair.

"This is my wife Mary," John said. "I owe a lot to her. Without her support, I don't think I would have accomplished half as much as I have."

"My husband insisted I meet yah both," she said to them. "He's been to a couple of your meetings and likes what yah have to say."

John took a seat across from Tinker and Nellie while Mary went to get the coffee. "Tinker tells me that you know of someone who had rescued slaves through the Underground Railroad."

"That's right," Nellie said. "I was one of them slaves he rescued. The man's name is Otto Heller 'n he's livin' in Washington, DC with that author-lady, Miss Radford."

John raised an eyebrow. "Jessica Radford? I read somewhere that she will be coming to Chicago soon to talk and sign books. Since the abolitionist critics already panned it, I will definitely look forward to reading it."

298

Tinker smiled. "Dat Miz Jessica is some lady."

"Mr. Jones," Nellie said, "my husband tells me you been workin' with the Underground Railroad bringin' slaves to freedom."

"In a way I have. You see, this house and my shop on Dearborn were used as stations when conductors passed negroes through to Chicago. When John Brown managed to bring eleven slaves to Chicago on his way to Harper's Ferry, I invited him to this very house."

"That so?" Nellie asked.

Tinker was sure, the way her eyes got glossy, that Nellie was thinking about the brief time she saw Mr. Brown in Lawrence, Kansas, only months before he made that raid on Harper's Ferry.

Mary entered and, after pouring everyone a cup of coffee placed the coffeepot on a ceramic dish and joined in the conversation. "Speaking for John," she said, "I suppose you could say it had something to do with his mother being a negro and his father being a stubborn German who didn't believe in slavery."

"True," John added. "I should also say that being a light-skinned mulatto, white folks just assumed I had no negro blood in me. It helped open a lot of doors for me."

The conversation then went into specifics about the letters that had been written to the state legislature demanding a repeal of the Illinois Black Laws and his personal efforts in organizing blacks and whites against such restrictive legislation. "And I want to thank you," John said, glancing at Tinker, "for delivering handbills to folks inviting them to participate in our efforts."

Nellie's face wrinkled, and John noticed it immediately. "What's wrong, Mrs. Longfellow?"

Nellie still couldn't get used to being called "Mrs. Longfellow," and it took a moment before she realized he was addressing her. "I'm just worried about white folks gettin' angry with us," she said. "Don't wanna cause no trouble."

"There's a lot of injustice here, Mrs. Longfellow," he replied. "We've got to help make this a better place to live.

299

We've got to demand the right for better education. We don't even have basic rights, like the right to vote, even though we pay taxes like everyone else."

"He's right," Tinker said. "I'm a decorated war hero 'n it don't mean nothin' here. I hafta worry every day 'bout keepin' my job."

"Maybe this is one way of losin' it," Nellie said, "by gettin' into things we ought to stay clear of."

Tinker found it useless to change Nellie's attitude as they rode back to her residence. Maybe tomorrow they could talk about it more.

He started undressing when he came to the bedroom, but was shocked by Nellie's scream from the backyard of the house. "What is it?" he shouted, running toward the back door. But he didn't have to wait for her answer. Near a small dog-house that Tinker had built, Nellie was kneeling by the black terrier. The dog's neck had been slashed and a hand lettered note was attached to one of the animal's legs:

Go Back To Africa. Next Time This Will Be You.

*****

February 12
Washington, DC

Jessica had a front-row seat with Otto in the gallery overlooking the House of Representatives. The House floor below as well as this gallery were filled to overflowing, and Jessica noticed there were some negro men in the crowd. She rather expected it. This would be the first time that a negro would speak in the halls of Congress.

Kerosene lamps emitted an orange-yellow glow to the entire scene. The smell of old leather and cigar smoke filtered through the atmosphere and the buzz of excited chatter filled the room.

Otto leaned his head in her direction. "I'm delighted we could get a neighbor to watch the children."

"This is a rather historic occasion for emancipated slaves," Jessica said.

He took her hand and squeezed it gently. Jessica turned to him and smiled.

The gavel sounded the call to order, and after some preliminary remarks, Schuyler Colfax, the House Speaker, introduced Reverend Highland Garnet. After a mixed applause—some clapping with enthusiasm and others barely bringing their hands together—Reverend Garnet, a 40-year-old negro man wearing a black suit and vest took the podium.

He leaned forward. "Matthew 23:4 says 'For they bind heavy burdens, and grievous to be borne, and lay them on men's shoulders, but they themselves will not move them with one of their fingers.'" Garnet surveyed the audience and went on to parallel the hypocrisy of the Scribes and Pharisees of Jesus' day with some of today's legislators in Congress. "Yes, they stand in the most sacred places on earth, and beneath the gaze of the piercing eye of Jehovah, the universal Father of all men, and declare, 'that the best possible condition of the negro is slavery.'"

Jessica closed her eyes for a moment, recalling the letter she received from Devin just yesterday. He wasn't a slave and had never been one. Yet Devin described the abuse he had taken from a fellow instructor, a white fellow instructor. Abolishment of slavery was not the end of the problem, but just the beginning.

"Great God!" Garnet continued, "I would as soon attempt to enslave Gabriel or Michael as to enslave a man made in the image of God, and for whom Christ died. Slavery is snatching man from the high place to which he was lifted by the hand of God, and dragging him down to the level of the brute creation, where he is made to be the companion of the horse and the fellow of the ox."

Jessica's mind wandered as he spoke. At first, she chided herself for not doing enough to help the cause of slavery. Then she wondered if she ought to consider resigning her role as a nanny for Mr. Heller. She needed more time for writing. After all, her Chicago publisher announced that *Black and Proud* would be coming out soon, and they encouraged her to submit another novel for consideration. As a result, she had given serious thought to moving to Chicago in order to be more accessible to her new publisher. She also would be more accessible to Nellie and Tinker as well, two people whom she had always cherished.

She looked again at Mr. Heller. When she told him in October that she loved him, his only answer was that he wished he could say he loved her too, that he was incapable of loving another woman like Penelope.

Not true, Jessica thought. She would always remember his words that evening....

"But I love you. I have always loved you, my darling."

If only...if only he would have whispered that to her when he was sober.

*****

The next day
St. Louis, Missouri

Matt unloaded a box of provisions at Benton Barracks, a Union encampment five miles north of St. Louis, before joining Mary waiting for him at the wagon. "I sure see what you mean about this bein' a busy place," he said. "I'd have thought with the end of this war in sight, there'd be fewer soldiers awaitin' deployment, not more."

"If you find that incredible," she said, "you ought to take a tour of the military hospital here. The last time I came, empty bed space was virtually non-existent."

Matt nudged the mules forward and the wagon creaked and groaned its way down the road. "I count myself fortunate that my only noticeable injury is a missin' thumb—and that is due only to my sheer stupidity."

Mary straightened the ruffles of her dress. "A missing thumb is nothing. You should have been here at Benton last year. I've seen men from the Second Missouri Colored Infantry who died from gangrene after their feet or hands were amputated."

"Mary," he said after a long pause, "you've spent the good part of this war sacrificin' your time and attention to the wounded and dying. It seems you are always off somewhere doing somethin' for someone else."

"Aren't we supposed to be compassionate?"

He pondered a moment. "Yup, that's true. But what does Mary Delaney want out of this life?"

She stared at the buildings they passed, letting the question sink in. "I'm not sure," she said. "I suppose I'd like to settle down some day and raise a family, but—" She paused long enough to laugh. "—but I'll consider it after I complete that quilt that's been taking me forever to finish."

Matt brought the mules to a halt and turned his full attention to her. "This part about 'settlin' down' that you mentioned. It's somethin' I wanted to do myself, but only with the right woman."

"Maybe someday you'll find her," she said, laughing lightly.

He put his hand over hers. "Shucks, Mary, I've already found her, and I have been such a fool to not have known it earlier."

Mary flushed. "Matt, I don't know. I—"

"I've told you months ago when we were alone in Tennessee that I was fond of you. But I need to retrieve that statement."

Mary's eyes teased him. "Are you saying you are *not* fond of me?"

Matt smiled. "I'm sayin' I'm more than fond of you. I love you more than any woman I have ever met. I've been a fool not to realize this."

"Matt, I don't know what to say."

"Just say that you love me."

Chapter 41

Sara held her head high as she walked arm-in-arm with Roger from church toward their buggy. She felt indeed fortunate that her husband, blinded in both eyes from an exploding shell, was unable to see those reproving stares of these townswomen. It seemed as if the entire town knew about her lifestyle. Not only had her attempts to land a part in a church play or in the choir failed; no one would sit near her.

"I have always looked forward to being home again." Roger said, limping as he waved the long cane that he held in his right hand.

"I have as well," she said, guiding him toward the buggy seat. For a while, the Christian Home for the Blind, located in Jason, a day's jaunt from Birmingham, had taken care of him. But now he was home for good. Although she had promised to be his "eyes" for him, the strain of constantly waiting on him, of providing him with the opium pills he needed to kill the pain in his side and leg, had worn her thin.

Earlier, as she sat in the pew next to Roger, listening to the minister drone on about the importance of keeping God's commandments, she let her mind drift to happier times with Roger. She missed her home in Chattanooga and those evenings when she would act out a part from a play and Roger would have to guess the role and the name of the play. Once they attended a picnic where they encased their legs in flour bags and had to outrace each other by hopping. On other days, they would just watch the sunset from their porch.

Those times were gone forever. Now, he would retire to bed after arriving from any travel. She would read to him a bit, but then he'd need the opium and she would dress his wounds. A doctor at the hospital had told her he might be delusional at times, and it was probably due to his pain. It would explain why Roger kept talking about angels he saw near a farmhouse in Franklin and how he was no longer afraid to die.

"It may be weeks, if not days," the doctor added. "We've done all we could for him."

If only she had Nellie to keep her company. When Nellie ran away and the South experienced one defeat after another, and when she was on the brink of starvation once she came here to Birmingham, she had had to question the Lord's "mercy." The Lord did not even bring back the same husband she had married.

Still, "mercy" was the only thing Roger seemed to want to talk about. "There were beautiful angels all over that field," he would say. "They had such loving, warm faces, faces that seemed to glow, and with the fighting going all around them, they were showing mercy to the dying."

Sara was always tempted to tell him he had been hallucinating, but did not wish to upset him.

"Why don't people believe in angels?" he would ask. Later he would scream in pain, and she would give him opium pills. "Aren't these pill harmful?" she once asked the druggist. "If he needs them to obtain relief, give them to him," the druggist replied.

Roger failed to realize how much he was torturing her by his incessant discussion of "angels" on the battlefield and how he felt closer to God now that he was blind. He'd make her read Bible scripture and discuss it with him.

"How will yaw manage making the payments?" he once asked.

"Never mind about that." How could she tell him she had an appointment with a wealthy merchant this week? "I will manage, Roger. Don't fret about it."

"Yaw are a truly remarkable woman," he said, squeezing her hand. "I am so happy to have married yaw."

"Have you been keeping up with the news?" she asked, anxious to change topics.

"Somewhat. I declare those attendants at the Christian home only read to me the kind of news that won't upset me."

"Well, I hope this won't upset you, but the Yankees have recently captured our South Carolina capital."

Roger groaned. "I rather expected that to happen, the way this war's been mismanaged." His lips quivered, struggling for words. "Columbia...your home town...where I had first met yaw...where I proposed marriage to yaw. It's now forever changed."

She thought about all those men she had lain with before Roger returned. "Yes, forever changed."

*****

March 3
Washington, DC

In lieu of President Lincoln's Second Inaugural Address slated for tomorrow, Otto Heller had the day off. Since the children were in school, Jessica felt this might be the proper time to tell him about her decision.

Otto told her he wanted to do some marketing in the morning, so it wasn't until eleven o'clock when he returned. He was beaming like a happy sunrise. "Jessica, I am so glad we could have some time alone today. I've got something to ask you."

"We should talk, Mr. Heller. There has been something on my mind I wanted to discuss with you as well."

"Allow me to go first," he said, holding her by the shoulders. He took a step back, still smiling, his eyes searching every inch of her. "I don't know the proper way to go about doing this and I'm probably going to end up appearing rather foolish."

Jessica frowned. She had never seen him so animated before.

"Jessica, I need you."

She moved her face closer toward his. "I need you as well, and since the children are away, perhaps you and I could—"

He placed his finger on her lips. "Please don't misunderstand my intentions. That one night was a mistake which I have long regretted."

"A mistake?"

306

"Don't take offense, Jessica." He reached for something in his pocket. "I've given this a great deal of thought, and I hope you would agree to be my wife." He opened the small box in his hand and showed her the ring. "This is for you."

Tiny flecks of light sparkled off the diamond. Jessica was speechless. This was not at all what she expected to hear. "But you told me that you would never be able to love anyone but Penelope."

"That may be true. But I am quite fond of you, Jessica. I couldn't imagine spending the rest of my life without you. And the children love you too. In a way, they consider you their new mother. I've hesitated asking you this because I had been rather hoping that you would be baptized a Catholic. My faith is very important to me."

"I know. Your bedroom has more religious art on the walls and dresser than any church I've been to."

He laughed slightly, but turned serious again. "I am hoping you will say 'yes.'"

She took a seat on the davenport. "Yes to being baptized or yes to marrying you?"

"Ideally, both. But if not, then just say you'll marry me."

"This is so sudden, Mr. Heller." She had earlier prepared to tell him she would be leaving him and his children and moving to Chicago, to be closer to Tinker and Nellie, as well as her new publisher.

"I fully understand you will need more time to consider it," he added, as if reading her thoughts. "We share similar interests. However, if you are not overly fond of me, perhaps you might think of our marriage as a relationship of convenience."

Marriage as a relationship of convenience? She always imagined she would marry someone she truly loved. What was it that La Rochefoucauld, that seventeenth century French writer, said about love? *In their first passion, women love their lovers. In the others, they love love.* Was that true about her? Did she truly love him, or love what he had done—rescuing slaves, supporting her decisions, such as disguising herself as a man to fight in the war or making antislavery speeches? Or perhaps, as a writer, she was just in love with "love."

Otto dropped down next to her on the davenport. "You look serious, dear Jessica. Did I say anything to cause you concern?"

She leaned her head on his shoulder. "Not at all. I was just reflecting."

Who was this man, Otto Heller? Memories flooded her mind like a waterfall...How he introduced her to Walt Whitman, influenced a publisher to seriously consider her novel, attended a theater play with her, and brought her flowers when she was not feeling well. Overall, he was a kind and generous man.

But did she truly love him? She recalled another maxim by La Rochefoucauld. *True love is like ghosts, which everybody talks about and few have seen.* Her head spun, feeling pressured to give him an answer.

"Jessica," Otto said, bringing his face closer to hers, "I will try to make you very happy."

Studying his pleading eyes, she was relieved he offered her more time to consider his proposal. Matt's image—and the tender way he had said he loved her—kept getting in the way.

Chapter 42

April 5
The "River Queen"
near Richmond, Virginia

At bedtime, Abraham Lincoln smiled to himself as he reflected on the day's events. Yesterday was Tad's twelfth birthday, and what better way to celebrate than by walking with him through the fallen rebel capital. Some newly freed slaves dropped to their knees before him, chanting "Glory, Hallelujah," but President Lincoln asked them to stand up. "Kneel only to God," he said, "and thank Him for your freedom."

With a satisfying sigh that Grant was on the verge of complete victory and the war would soon be over, he drifted off to sleep....

He found himself in stillness, a blackness not unlike death itself. Sobbing. He heard the sobbing of many people. What were they crying about? This was a happy time, a time for rejoicing, not sadness. He saw himself leaving his bed and wandering downstairs. The sobs grew louder but there was no one in sight.

Where are these folks who are crying? He wandered from one room to the next. No one. And yet the sobs, the wailing, the misery continued. He kept walking until he finally arrived in the East Room. Entering it, he saw a catafalque, and on it was a corpse wrapped in funeral vestments. Soldiers, acting as guards, stood nearby while a huge crowd gazed mournfully at the corpse.

Lincoln looked about, confused. He grabbed the sleeve of one of the guards. "I demand to know who is dead here."

The guard looked at him with a face broken apart with sorrow. "The President. He was killed by an assassin." The wailing grew louder and Lincoln burst out of his dream.

He sat up at once, his heart pounding madly. It was only a foolish dream, he told himself. Still, as much as he tried, he could not return to sleep.

April 11

The man with dark curly hair and a mustache arching over his thin upper lip shifted from one foot to the other as President Lincoln made his address to a large crowd outside the Executive Mansion. He knew it would be difficult to listen to a man he hated, especially now, two days after General Lee surrendered at Appomattox. Still, he wanted to hear what this bastard had to say.

The lights from the Executive Mansion illuminated the faces of a mostly enthusiastic audience as the tall, gaunt figure read from his speech. One man held a light for him while Lincoln's young son Tad stood at his side.

"Some twelve thousand voters in the heretofore slave-state of Louisiana," the President continued, "have sworn allegiance to the Union, assumed to be the rightful political power of the State, held elections, organized a State government, adopted a free-state constitution, giving the benefit of public schools equally to black and white, and empowering the Legislature to confer the elective franchise upon the colored man."

A page of his speech fell to the ground and Tad quickly picked it up.

The mustachioed man with dark curly hair shook his head. "This means nigger citizenship, and I won't allow it," he muttered to his friend. "How dare he make such a statement!"

Lincoln leaned closer to his notes as if having difficulty reading them in the glow of the lamp held before him. "The colored man too, in seeing all united for him, is inspired with vigilance, and energy, and daring, to the same end. Grant that he desires the elective franchise, will he not attain it sooner by saving the already advanced steps toward it, than by running backward over them?"

The mustachioed man, John Wilkes Booth, his face snarling with disgust, turned again to his friend. "That is the last speech he will ever make."

Chapter 43

Otto, suffering from what he described as a flu-like chest pain, refrained from accompanying Jessica to the theater this evening. Since she had purchased four tickets in advance, she gave one to her neighbor and hired a chaise to take herself and the two children to the play.

While Emma appeared to be content that she was going out, Mitzi was popping with questions about the forthcoming performance.

"The leading actress in 'Our American Cousin'," Jessica explained, "is a lady named Laura Keene. She's a British actress who has been doing light comedy in this country for thirteen years. I understand she is quite good."

Emma stared out the carriage window and into the foggy night. "Too bad Papa can't be with us. Doesn't he like to see plays too?"

"He wanted to," Jessica said, "but he's not feeling well. He probably caught a bad cold."

"Are you going to marry Papa?"

Mitzi grinned. "I hope so, Miss Radford. Papa gets lonely sometimes."

"I know he does," Jessica said. She never told Otto she had inadvertently read an excerpt from his journal describing his struggle in wanting to make love to her but wishing to avoid sin. "But Mitzi, you need to realize that this is an important decision."

Jessica had heard of women who were never inclined for marriage for whatever reason, and she feared she might be one of them. But Mr. Heller's suggestion that their marriage—should she agree to it—might be viewed as a relationship of convenience, was an idea that greatly eased her mind. She could enjoy his company, and he could be an asset to her in her writing career, so why the concern about "romantic love?" Perhaps she would follow the footsteps of Jane Austen, who,

311

in her novel *Persuasion*, created a heroine named Anne Elliot who "learned romance as she grew older—the natural sequence of an unnatural beginning."

Still, Matt's face loomed large in her mind whenever she thought of the prospect of marriage. *Oh Matt, I've destroyed the bridge between us. Please let us build it again.*

Once inside Ford's Theater, Jessica followed a woman who directed her and the children to their seats. The interior of the theater was awash with candlelight and people chattered excitedly to each other like chickens in a henhouse.

"It's crowded tonight," Mitzi said. "There are more people than there were the last time you took us here."

"That's because the President is expected to attend." She pointed to a special area to the right and above the stage that was decorated with silk flags and a painting of George Washington. "See that place over there? That's called a state box, and that's where the President will be seated when the play starts."

She handed the children their programs and stared at the empty red rocking chair in the state box. Just last month she had attended Lincoln's second inauguration. March 4 was a dreary day, with rain coming down in torrents and the wind howling through the streets…

There seemed to be no end to the rain. There was mud everywhere, even on her new red moiré skirt that she had purchased from a Baltimore clothier. Her shawl was drenched in water and her boots looked as if she had been wading through a pigsty. The wide avenue near the Capitol was lined with people, not only on the sidewalk but on balconies of public buildings. Flags fluttered in the gale and in the midst of all of this, a parade pushed though, a parade of cavalrymen, musicians, firemen, regiments of soldiers carrying guns, and dignitaries wearing red scarves and white rosettes. It was well past noon when the President appeared from behind the columns of the portico and Jessica caught a glimpse of her favorite poet, Walt Whitman, looking up at the sky. Jessica followed his gaze. A tiny cloud hung in the heavens just above the portico. Just then the sky brightened with sunshine, and Jessica hoped this was an omen that would bode well for the President and the future of the country—especially for former slaves like Tinker or even black men who were never slaves, like Devin Alcott.

Jessica felt someone elbowing her. "Miss Jessica, look—the play is about to start." Mitzi's eyes danced with excitement. "Are you paying attention?"

"Sorry, Mitzi, I was thinking about Mr. Lincoln."

"Isn't he coming?" Mitzi asked, noticing the empty state box.

"He's probably delayed. He'll be here."

*****

Having left the Herndon House after discharging his instructions to his three fellow conspirators, John Wilkes Booth walked back to the National Hotel, where he had been staying. He trusted Lewis Powell, a muscular man who was both brutal and strong-willed to carry out the job of killing Secretary Seward, but Booth was far less confident about George Atzerodt, who had protested the idea of his murdering Vice President Andrew Johnson, saying "I enlisted to abduct the President of the United States, not to kill." Booth had to threaten Atzerodt to do it, and while he finally agreed that he would, Booth wished he had time to find someone with the courage and will that Atzerodt seemed to lack. Booth had confidence in David Herold, his third conspirator, but, unfortunately, Mr. Herold had the mind of a boy and was not very bright, although he knew the streets of Washington. Herold would probably do well guiding Powell toward Seward's house tonight.

Booth came down to the hotel lobby and gave the clerk his keys. "Are you going to the theater tonight?" Booth asked him.

"No, Mr. Booth."

"Well, you should. There will be some fine acting there tonight."

As he walked briskly to the theater, Booth congratulated himself on being able to plan the necessary details on such short notice. It was only this morning when he learned that the President would be attending this play. Still, he was able to arrange

313

with someone to procure a small bay mare from a livery stable and take the animal to his stable at the rear of the theater. After the players were done with their rehearsal in the afternoon, he went to the President's box and bore a peephole in the door directly behind where the President would be sitting. After cutting a mortise in the outside brick wall of the building, he fashioned a simple wood doorjamb to prevent anyone from entering the box from the outside.

About fifty yards from the theater entrance, he heard the sound of horses' hooves and the bouncing of wheels on the cobblestone pavement. The President's carriage had arrived. Booth glared at the tall, gaunt figure of Lincoln emerging, followed by his wife Mary and another couple.

Booth checked his pocket watch. Eight-thirty. A little over an hour-and-a-half from now it would 10:15 p.m. That was the agreed-upon time where all three of his men would simultaneously complete their assigned duties. He went backstage and watched the first act with disinterest. Just before intermission, he entered the lobby and checked for the presence of any presidential bodyguards. None. Finally, he went to the back door and asked Edman Spangler, a stagehand and a family friend, to hold his horse for him. Booth would have no time to waste once the deed was done.

*****

The band struck up "Hail to the Chief" when Lincoln arrived, and Jessica and the two children stood up with the rest of the audience and clapped. The President, carrying his tall silk hat in his hand, slowly climbed the stairs leading to the dress circle and his box. Lincoln moved to the box rail and accepted the applause with a gracious smile and more than one dignified bow.

Jessica tried to get her thoughts back to the play that had been interrupted by the President's appearance. She knew the storyline for "Our American Cousin"—about an American bumpkin who went to England to claim his inheritance while he is being pursued by a female fortune-hunter who wants him to marry her daughter. But now that the President was

314

here, she found her mind drifting to that time the President awarded Tinker the Medal of Honor. When Lincoln held her hand as she was introduced, she felt shivers in meeting a man who had done so much for emancipation of slavery. But he seemed so frail, his hand so thin and cold, his eyes kindly yet tired, that she wondered if—now that the war was finally coming to a close—he would get the rest he deserved.

*****

Nine o'clock. Booth's stomach churned. He wished he didn't have to wait. He crossed underneath the stage leading to an exit and to Tenth Street and finally, Taltavull's Star Saloon. His mind spun. The South was losing the war, if it had not already. But if he could only carry this out, he could throw the entire country into open revolution.

"Your usual brandy, Mr. Booth?" the barkeep asked him when he took a stool.

"No. Whisky and a glass of water, please."

"A lot of excitement will be going on with the President being here, Mr. Booth. Are you watching the performance?"

Booth returned a sour face, his silent rebuttal burning in his mind. *No, you fool, I'm going to be in it tonight!* Brutus, he thought, had to kill Caesar to prevent him from becoming a tyrant to his country. In the same way, he needed to prevent Mr. Lincoln from becoming the brutal tyrant of this land. And the South had to be avenged for the evils that the Union had brought forth upon them. This country was formed for the white man, not for the negro, but Lincoln does not will it to be so. The President therefore must be stopped, and he would stop him. God has ordained that he would have to be the instrument of Mr. Lincoln's punishment.

The second scene of the third act began. Booth knew that near the close of this scene there would only be one actor on stage, only one person who might try to restrain him when he ran on stage.

10:12 pm. Time to move. He checked to be sure he had his small, muzzle-loading derringer in his trouser pocket and a large hunting knife in his jacket pocket. A Lincoln attendant was

315

seated near the vestibule box. Booth handed a card to him that assured the attendant that Booth wanted to briefly visit with the President.

Then Booth dropped down one step and opened the door. Closing it behind him, he placed a wooden bar against the door, anchoring the other end in the mortise cut he had made earlier.

Harry Hawk, the lone actor playing the part of Asa Trenchard, was in the center of the stage. "Don't know the manners of good society, eh?" Hawk said in his role as Mr. Trenchard. "Well, I guess I know enough to turn you inside out, old gal...."

Quietly, Booth, derringer in one hand and knife in the other, approached the President.

*****

Mitzi laughed along with the audience and clapped when they clapped, obviously enjoying the performance, but Emma's eyes were half-closed. Maybe when she's Mitzi's age, Jessica thought, she'll enjoy a performance like this. Jessica looked up and caught a glimpse of the President, leaning forward, his right hand supporting his chin while he rested his arm on the balustrade.

Just as she turned away, she heard a sharp popping sound, but had no idea what it was because at that moment the audience was laughing at a comical line uttered by Harry Hawk, the lone actor on stage. Suddenly, a woman shrieked. Jessica looked back up. Mrs. Lincoln was leaning out of the box, screaming, "The President is shot!"

Jessica rose from her chair, as did others in the audience, and as the President's wife continued to shout hysterically, a man leaped from the box. As he did so, he caught his foot on a flag draped over the box, and plummeted to the floor of the stage. He got up, brandishing a large knife and roaring "Sic semper tryannis," a Latin phrase Jessica knew meant "Thus it shall ever be for tyrants." Then the man ran into the wings of the orchestra, slashing the orchestra leader and hobbling quickly off behind the set.

316

A man in the audience screamed "Booth!" and others in the crowd picked up the cry: "Booth! Booth!" Jessica, still on her feet, felt as if she were in some unreal dream. Emma and Mitzi both screamed in terror. Jessica picked Emma up and tried to console her, although she didn't know what to say. People were yelling and cursing, the entire audience in bedlam.

With every muscle in her body rattling, her head fighting a headache, and a stomach that churned in displeasure, Jessica pushed her way through the crowd. People were smashing seats, cursing, groaning, and crying. A terror-stricken crowd stampeded toward the exits and Jessica fought not to lose sight of the children. It seemed like forever before she made it to the misty darkness outside. At that point, several men were helping carry the body of the President across the street.

Mitzi tugged on Jessica's dress, her eyes wide with fright. "What happened?"

Jessica looked back at the girl as if not comprehending the question. Lincoln's words from his second inaugural address haunted her:

"With malice toward none, with charity for all, with firmness in the right, as God gives us to see the right, let us strive on to finish the work we are in, to bind up the nation's wounds."

"What happened" Mitzi repeated, pulling harder on Jessica's dress. "Is the President dead?"

"I don't know," Jessica said. "But God help the negro race if he is."

Chapter 44

Having returned to Brooklyn in late March to visit his brother George and to oversee production of *Drum-Taps*, his latest book of poetry, Walt Whitman was stunned by the news. He read about Mr. Lincoln's death in the morning newspaper, and the tolling of church bells fit in with the darkening morning sky and his depression. He passed on breakfast and dinner, and told his mother he was taking a walk.

After taking his pencil and notebook with him to the docks, he noted that the thin black clouds in the sky were "like great serpents slowly undulating in every direction." Shops were closed, flags of ships flew at half-mast, and the faces of people bore "a strange mixture of horror, fury, tenderness, and a stirring wonder...."

He dropped down to the soft grass—grass, the very thing that inspired his first book of poems—and wept bitterly.

*****

Chicago, Illinois

Tinker had little to say to Nellie after he read the news. "Gonna go fer a long, long walk," he moaned.

"Where to?"

"Doan matter," he said, and he disappeared out the door, closing it abruptly behind him.

Nellie took the news of Lincoln's murder bitterly, as if her best friend had died. She remembered how Lincoln smiled when he bowed slightly and took her hand when she was introduced. She was touched by his gentle manner and wondered at the time if he showed a special kindness to her because she was negro. All she had heard about Mr. Lincoln was that he did not come from a privileged family. Fact was, he lived in a lean-to in the backwoods and his mama died when he was only nine years of age. With no money and no influential backing, he taught himself law and had all sorts of

318

jobs—field hand, store clerk, rail splitter. He was a nobody just like she or Tinker were nobodies, and maybe that's why he came to the cause of slavery. She didn't believe those folks who said he did everything because of politics, saying the right things, doing the right things.

But what did it matter now anyway as to what she believed? She tore the sheets off the bed and put them in a washtub. There were other chores, like putting water on the stove and lighting a fire. But all that would have to wait until later.

On the table was one of the pamphlets put out by John Jones: *The Black Laws of Illinois and a Few Reasons They Should be Repealed*. She had helped Tinker distribute them on the streets of Chicago, despite the hostile looks she received from some. Tinker had convinced her that he was right—freedom *was* worth fighting for. Last week, he lost his job with the railroad because of it, but he kept pushing on for repeal of the Black Laws.

Nellie bent down to pick up the pieces of a dish Tinker had thrown against the stove. Her body still shook from his rage. Did he take the gun? She raced to the bedroom dresser. Not there.

Fearing the worst, she left the boarding house searching for him.

*****

A stranger, a black man about Tinker's age, ran up to Tinker who was about to cross the road. He wrapped his arms around Tinker and squeezed him. "We done lost Father Abr'am," he sobbed. "We done lost him."

"I know," Tinker said. "I feels like we had Moses come down here a second time t' show us a new land."

The stranger, his eyes brimming with tears, looked up at him. "What gonna happen to us now? What gonna happen?"

"Doan know. Just plumb doan know." He looked across the road at two men strolling down the path. One of them, a man with a dark bushy beard, held a newspaper in his hands,

319

laughing. The other, younger and clean-shaven, was grinning broadly.

Upset that they found something humorous about this horrible day, Tinker jogged toward them, with the stranger following close behind. "It appears that this Mr. Booth did us a favor," the bearded man was saying, "and removed that tyrant from office."

"What!" Tinker screamed, pushing the man's face forward to the ground, the newspaper pages flying in the wind.

The stranger accompanying Tinker, raised his fist. "Traitor!" He pounced on the younger, clean-shaven man and began pummeling him. "Don't talk like dat 'bout my Father Abr'am."

The bearded man, his face red with outrage at the sudden attack, started to get up, but Tinker struck him hard on the nose. The man screamed in rage and fought back.

Soon a crowd gathered, and when the stranger told them those two men were traitors to the Union, they joined in by kicking and beating the pair. Minutes later, the police arrived, as did Nellie who rushed over to Tinker, now off to the side, wiping his bloodied face with a handkerchief.

"Tinker!" she cried. "What happened?"

"I doan like traitors like him, Nellie. He got what's comin' to him."

The police grabbed the two men that Tinker and the stranger had beaten and escorted them to a waiting wagon. A bystander threw a rock at the bearded man and the others shrieked obscenities.

"Tinker," Nellie yelled above the shouts of the crowd, her hands shaking, "what has happened to you? This ain't like you t' be like this. She brought her face close to his as she lowered her voice. "Where's the gun? Did you take it?

"I didn't take no gun. It's in the closet. But if I had it, I'd kill 'im. I swear I'd kill 'im."

"Tinker!"

He dropped to his knees and clung to her skirts, crying. "Old Abe, he be dead. God sent Moses to us, 'n we killed 'im."

*****

320

Governor's Island, New York

Devin Alcott read about the news before boarding a ferry that would take him to New York City prior to his taking a train to Washington. He could not believe it. *Had the world gone insane?* One of the newspaper writers suggested that Mr. Booth had shot President Lincoln because of Lincoln's interest in giving equal status to freed negroes. No one knew for sure since John Wilkes Booth had escaped, but there was some reason to believe that Mr. Booth had a strong dislike of colored people.

Devin closed his eyes. *You were right, Jessica. You predicted that the struggles for the negro would become more intense, even for those who—like me—had never been a slave. Why did I even bother to fight in this war if this was going to be the end result?*

He was glad he had already planned to leave New York for Washington. He needed to pay his respects to one of the greatest leaders he had ever known.

*****

Washington, DC

Jessica felt as if she had climbed to the Capitol dome, celebrating an end to slavery and an end to this horrific war—but now, with this news, she sensed herself falling, falling. The cold wind of deception and hatred blew through her hair. Falling, falling.

She studied the latest photograph of a tired President, his forehead creased with furrows, his eyes begging for rest. *Mr. Lincoln, were you able to laugh at the play? Did the hatred you sensed from a few prevent you from laughing? When you addressed an Indiana Regiment a month ago—when you said that whenever you heard anyone arguing for slavery, you felt a strong impulse to see it tried on themselves personally—did it fail to resonate with everyone? Now that you are gone, who will pick up the banner? Johnson, a Southerner?*

321

There was a heavy pounding on the door. "Miss Radford! Are you there?"

Jessica lifted herself from her bed and wiped the tears from her eyes with the sleeve of her dress. "I am here, Mr. Heller."

"May I enter?"

"Yes."

Otto's usually combed hair was mussed up, his clothes rumpled, and his eyes were nervous, darting about the room as if expecting something or someone to pop up unexpectedly. He stunk from the heavy odor of whiskey.

Jessica noticed the bottle in his hand and wrestled him for it. "Otto! I thought you had sworn off drinking ever since…ever since…."

The vision of him six months ago lying in a drunken stupor in bed rippled through her mind. It was the only time he had told her he loved her.

"What is wrong with you, Otto?"

He dropped down on a chair like a rag doll. "It had to be a Confederate conspiracy. Maybe the rest of Lincoln's cabinet are next. Why else would Booth take it upon himself to kill him?"

"I don't know," Jessica said, her voice straining. "The world has gone mad." She stomped toward the living room and sat at the piano. Her fingers struck the ivories with deliberate anger as she played the "Battle Hymn of the Republic." It was the same music a band at the Eldridge Hotel in Lawrence, Kansas had played in June, 1862, when she exited the stagecoach and waited for pa to pick her up. All sorts of ideas swarmed through her head back then. Enormous ideas of how she would help put a final end to the tragedy of slavery. But the man who was steering the ship to freedom was now dead.

Grabbing the carved bust of Lincoln from the piano top, Jessica stared at it for a moment. Matt had captured his likeness with precision, the way the stress of the long war had etched his face and the way his penetrating eyes marked his understanding of the pain of slavery.

She threw the object against a wall. "Why the hell did you have to die on me!"

*****

The next day
Birmingham, Alabama

No one except the local minister and two gravediggers showed up at the gravesite, but Sara was not surprised. She had been tainted with the ignoble scarlet letter "H" for "harlot" from her neighbors and friends. When Roger returned from the hospital two months ago, she tried to find decent employment. No one would hire her, and when she was pressed for payment of bills, she returned to her former profession.

At least Roger never learned of her shameful occupation, dying suddenly in the evening—about the same hour the assassin shot the President. She wondered if she might have caused Roger's death by increasing the opium dosage.

Thoughts of Roger haunted her. During his last days, she wondered if she had made a mistake by keeping him home. His delusions grew worse, and on the evening he died, he began talking incessantly about the angels all about him....

"They were there in Franklin," he had said, his voice becoming hoarse, beads of sweat glistening his forehead. "Now they are here—in this very house. They are so beautiful, Sara, and they—oh, hear them? God loves yaw—that's what they're saying. God loves yaw."

"He doesn't love me," she griped. "If He did, He wouldn't have let me—"" She stopped short of saying "He wouldn't have let me become a strumpet." Roger need not know what she did for a living.

He let out a profound moan, deep from his bowels, an unearthly cry of pain. This was the worst cry for help she heard and she ran to get his pills. "I can't take this anymore," she mumbled, as she emptied several pills into his hand.

Roger had died soon after she administered them. Later, the doctor told her not to blame herself. "He would have died anyway," he said, "and far less peacefully."

323

The gravediggers left after piling dirt into the hole where Roger's coffin had been placed. She felt a heavy hand on her shoulder and turned to look at the kindly face of the minister. "Shall we pray together?"

"No," Sara said. "I would rather be alone right now."

The minister left and although it wasn't cold, Sara tightened her cloak about her shoulders. *No point in staying in Birmingham any longer. Now that Roger had gone to his eternal reward, there was no future here. But just where will I go?*

Then she thought about Nellie. Sara missed her more now than ever. All these months had passed and she had never communicated with Nellie.

After kneeling on the grass, she closed her eyes and thought about what it'd be like to be sightless. Even if Roger had lived, would he have been willing to travel to Chicago just to *hear* and not see Nellie again? Yes, she'd have to send Nellie a telegram and tell her she was coming.

She rested the palm of her hand on his grave and looked up at the rain clouds drifting in from the east.

*****

April 21
Washington, DC

Jessica had not gone to the Capitol days earlier, when Lincoln's casket was placed on a bier beneath the rotunda, but Devin went. He informed her he would be leaving soon after, as he had been invited by the music director of Crosby's Opera House in Chicago to audition for a violinist's chair prior to learning about the tragedy. "It has taken all the joy out of me," he told her.

His departing words—"It has taken all the joy out of me"—when he left for Chicago three days earlier reverberated in her mind as she stood near the tracks of the railroad depot. There was no joy anywhere today as crowds pressed her on all sides while the cavalry proceeded in her direction. The deliberate pace of horses' hooves in the cortege punctuated the mixture of silence and sobs from the multitude. Officers barked orders and soldiers lifted the metal coffin containing the President's body. With systematic precision in their pace, they made their way to an ornate funeral car while another entourage of soldiers lifted the casket of Willie Lincoln. Jessica recalled reading that Mrs. Lincoln had insisted that their young son Willie, who had died three years earlier, be buried alongside his father in Springfield.

There was a long pause after the caskets were placed into position in the ornate funeral car near the rear. Union soldiers and dignitaries lined the track before the train pulled away from the station. Some of the colored troops could not resist sobbing, as if they had lost their own fathers. Through her blurred, tear-drenched eyes, Jessica watched as hardened, war-weary Federal officers and distinguished political leaders wept along with them.

The next stop would be Baltimore, then on to a number of other cities. Jessica could not pay her last respects while the body of Lincoln lay in state in Washington. She never forgot the pain of viewing the caskets of her murdered parents almost three years ago—and she never wanted to feel that way again.

But today she finally found the courage to say goodbye.

Chapter 45

April 26
Chicago, Illinois

By the time Sara arrived at the Chicago depot, she regretted having made the decision to travel that huge distance from Birmingham. Before she left, she was ordered to place black mourning crepe on her boarding house door and to remove a Confederate poster in her window. Then she was insulted by a Federal officer in Memphis who asked if, being from the South, she knew of any conspirators involved with the Lincoln assassination plot. Finally, a female passenger on the train wanted to know if she was loyal to the Union.

There was a photo of Abraham Lincoln in the *Chicago Tribune*, and she felt like tearing it up into small pieces. What a stubborn fool Lincoln was! He should have worked out some reasonable concessions with Jefferson Davis. But no! There were no concessions to be made as far as Lincoln was concerned. The South would never be allowed to break free from the Union and form its own country—this, despite the fact that the Constitution allowed the rights of states to secede from the Union. As far as she was concerned, it was regrettable that a bloody war had to be fought over a right that the Confederacy had possessed to begin with.

Well, Abraham Lincoln was no more. She was not thrilled that he had died in that tragic manner and felt badly for his grieving widow. That was something with which Sara could have empathy, having lost her own husband. She could not share in the joy that some of her Birmingham neighbors felt over Lincoln's murder. Abraham Lincoln was simply a misguided fool who should never have been President.

After the train pulled into the station, she hired a coachman to take her to a hotel that would be nearest to 75 West Juniper Street. The driver thought a minute. "Unfortunately, the only one that is closest to that address is the Monody Hotel on Wells Street."

"What do you mean by 'unfortunately'?"

The coachman laughed. "I guess you're new to the town, aren't you?"

"I've never been here before. Is it untidy or unsafe?"

"On the contrary, it is an elaborate and well-constructed hotel."

"Then enough of this ambiguous conversation. When we arrive, I'd like you to bring in my luggage and wait for me while I register."

"Yes, ma'am."

Sara was still mystified by the coachman's remarks after she signed the hotel register and asked a porter to bring her valise and trunk to her room. The Monody Hotel appeared to be well decorated, with plush red carpeting and adequate lighting, and the walls were paneled with varnished wood. Nothing seemed out of order. Only the hotel's unusual name perplexed her a little. Was not a monody a mournful ode recited by an actor in ancient Greece?

When she returned to the coach, she gave the driver Nellie's address, and settled in her seat. Unlike Birmingham, the buildings here were generally close together and were of all different shapes and sizes...shanties, tall office buildings, a church with a tall steeple, shops, nice residential homes, more shanties, and yet more shops.

The carriage pulled up to a two-story orange brick house situated between a four-story office building and a tailor shop. The street was unpaved, somewhat muddy from the previous rain, and Sara resolved she would have to have her new shoes cleaned and shined.

The driver helped her out the door. "You're not too distant from the court house," he said. "That building will be a very busy place in a few days."

"What do you mean?"

"Haven't you heard? Mr. Lincoln's funeral train will be arriving here at the end of the month."

"No, I haven't heard."

"Many folks are expected to come. He's one of our own, you know."

"How is that?"

"Lincoln was an Illinois man. We regard him as a blood brother."

Sara felt like telling him she had heard enough of this hero worship. It seemed as if the entire country was obsessed with this assassination. Surely, there had to be other pressing matters to discuss, such as how Andrew Johnson, the new President, was going to deal with the South now that the war had come to a disappointing conclusion.

After knocking three times on the door, Sara gave up and decided to try later. It was just as well. It'd give her time to unpack her things and see more of the town.

As she walked back to the Monody Hotel, it began to drizzle.

*****

Sitting at a table at the back of the restaurant, Tinker took another sip of coffee while cutting a hoecake with his fork. He wasn't hungry and hadn't been for days now. While Nellie was gone today working as a volunteer at the Soldiers' Home situated near the edge of the Camp Douglas prison, he spent the morning looking for work. Now that he had lost his job with the railroad because of his involvement in trying to repeal the Illinois Black Laws, he was devastated. Although he could read and write, the only jobs he could find involved low paying work that no one else wanted, such as hauling garbage to the city dump.

The restaurant was quiet, except for an occasional clattering of plates and quiet sobbing of a man dressed in a blue Yankee uniform. He held a forage cap in his hands as he gazed out the window. The leathered skin of his face had probably been witness to battles just as Tinker had been. Yet that man wept like a child.

Tinker, however, was more than sad. He was angry. Nellie had harassed him for days about his encounter with two men whom he had beaten eleven days ago because they mocked Mr. Lincoln. But the incident failed to get Tinker arrested. The police seemed to be satisfied that these traitors received the thrashing they did, and no charges were filed. Yet, he felt unjustly punished by Nellie who continued to nag him about this incident.

Tinker took another bite of his tasteless hoecake. He had made a mistake about getting married. He knew now that he only loved Nellie as a friend, not as a wife. Her fault-finding with him about little things—not wanting to attend touring shows and circuses, not getting involved in social clubs which newly-married couples joined, not wanting to read her poetry at night like he used to when she was a child—those little things added to his annoyance. Yet, despite her nagging, she seemed unconcerned about him being unemployed.

"Don't worry none 'bout findin' another job," she had said. "I got plenty o' money from the inheritance, 'n we be rich."

"I'm not gonna be one o' them leeches that lives off his wife," he said. "I gots my pride, y'know."

He couldn't help thinking about Nellie like a daughter. After all, she was half his age. Eight years ago when she lived in Lawrence with the Radfords, he would visit her. She was eleven then, and she'd sit on his lap while he read her a story and she'd give him a big hug and call him "Daddy"....

"I not your Daddy," he had told her.
"Do yuh love me?"
"Course I love yuh, chile."
"Then let's get married."
"Not dat kind o' love, Nellie. I ain't got dat kind o' love for yuh."

Tinker bit his lip. Nellie never did grow up. Back then she'd play hide 'n seek and stick ball. Now, as a grown woman, she still played games, like parading around like a soldier and saying "Look at me. I'm Miz Jessica, off to fight in the war" or she'd grab his undergarments and force him to chase her around the house for them. Or worse, she'd tease him incessantly when he was unable to perform in the marriage bed.

I didn't want a child, I wanted a woman.

A female voice jarred him from his thoughts. "Tinker?"

Tinker looked up at the face of an attractive mulatto woman in her thirties. Her skin was the color of pale coffee, her black hair was braided, and her thin lips formed a smile that beamed warmth.

"Charlotte?" He said her name so loud, others in the restaurant turned toward him.

"My word," she said, taking a seat at his table, "I had assumed you were dead."

Tinker frowned. "Now why on earth would yuh assume dat?"

"You didn't get any of my letters?"

"No. You mean yuh wrote to me?"

"I did. In fact, when I finally checked with the War Department in October of '63, I was told that you were missing in action." She placed her hand atop his. "Oh, Tinker, it is such a blessing to see you."

"What are yuh doin' here in Chicago, Miz Charlotte?"

"My father passed away recently. I went to an attorney to learn he put me in his will for a general store he owned in Tennessee. What about you, Tinker? How have you been?"

Tinker scratched his ear and smiled. "We gots lots to talk 'bout, Miz Charlotte."

*****

As Sara waited for a carriage to take her to Crosby's Opera House that evening, she noticed a brunette in a red dress standing next to her. The woman ignored Sara and looked about as if she were expecting a visitor.

A tall gentleman with a white goatee stopped in front of Sara and bowed slightly to her. His probing smile was so wicked she swore he could have passed for the devil himself.

"Are you expecting anyone, dear lady?"

She answered with a disinterested turn of the head, but sensing that it didn't discourage him, she riveted her eyes on his. "What on earth do you mean?"

"I mean," he said with a wink, "you are a most attractive woman. Would you be available for the evening?"

"How dare you. If you don't leave, I will call the authorities."

He tipped his hat in apology and moved on to talk to the woman in the red dress. He engaged in conversation with the woman for only a short while before he placed currency into the woman's hand. The two of them promptly returned to the entrance of the hotel.

Sara laughed to herself. So this is what the driver was trying to tell her about this hotel. This must be where trollops met their male patrons. She thought about those bygone days in Birmingham. Certainly she could do it again. It was easy; all she had to do was pretend. *No, that is not the actress I want to be.*

After paying $1.50 for an orchestra seat for Bellini's opera *Norma*, she counted the rest of her money. Nine dollars. The money that man gave the woman in the red dress could have been hers. *No, being needy was just the incentive I needed to look for serious employment—preferably the theater.*

Some of the women in the audience stared at her as she walked down the theater aisle, but Sara glared back at them. If they did not like this sumptuous green dress she wore, it was a pity. It was likely that they were gawking because she was not dressed in harmony with the mourning of a dead president. Well, if they challenged her, she could point to the mourning pin she wore as tangible proof of her loyalty—even though she was piqued at all this excessive devotion to a slain president she had never respected.

She searched through the pages of her opera book, hoping to find a narrative of *Norma*.

"Pardon me," a voice called to her.

A man seated next to her caught her attention. He was a negro gentleman, attired in a black waistcoat, boiled shirt, and purple cravat, and his young intelligent face was smiling back at her. She looked away. *Negro men generally didn't talk to Southern ladies unless they were spoken to. Were things different here in Chicago?*

"Ma'am," he continued, his intelligent face smiling back at her, "how familiar are you with Bellini's operas?"

331

"This is actually my first," Sara replied, hoping that would be the end of it so she could return to her opera book.

"If my audition goes well this Saturday," he said, "I will be attending quite a few operatic performances."

"Your audition?"

"As an alternate violinist. I used to be accomplished in that area before I put on a private's uniform and became involved with the saxhorn."

Sara didn't realize her look of surprise still showed when he added, "I take it you don't believe that a colored man can have such abilities."

"Well, no, I—"

"How thoughtless of me," he said, extending his hand to her. "Permit me to introduce myself. My name is Devin. Devin Alcott."

"And mine is Sara," she added. "Mrs. Sara Toby." She was about to say more, but the announcer came on stage to introduce the opera.

During the intermission, Devin approached her as she poured herself a cup of tea. "Did you know that Bellini's *Norma* was a disaster after its opening performance? Now it's regarded as a masterpiece."

"You evidently are very knowledgeable about music, Mr. Alcott. But I don't understand how a slave could have acquired such abilities." His jaw tightened and she instantly realized she had offended him. "I'm sorry," she said, "but I am puzzled."

His demeanor softened a bit and his lips curled into a soft smile. "Why don't we have a discussion about this later after the performance?"

She had never met a refined, well-educated negro before, and she looked forward to learning more about him. All sorts of questions entered her mind: How did he know so much about opera? How did he learn to play the violin? How could he afford to be so well dressed and occupy a seat in the most expensive section of the theater?

After she thought she had lost him in the crowd at the conclusion of the performance, she saw him again. He was leaning against the front of the building, watching the passers-by. "Oh, there you are, ma'am," he said, when his eyes met hers. "We're fortunate it's not raining; otherwise, it'd be a dreadful walk to our hotel, would it not?"

"*Our* hotel?"

He laughed and offered her his arm to escort her across the street. "Yes, the Monody Hotel. I've seen you there earlier today when you picked up your key, and later, as you stood alongside a hussy in a red dress near the hotel entrance. I am sure I can afford whatever price you would charge for your services."

Sara's face burned and she looked away. This negro displayed considerable effrontery in approaching her like this. Negroes deserved to be free. Still, they had their own special place in society. Back in the South, no black man, slave or free, would ever talk to a white lady unless she addressed him first. *The very idea of my pleasuring a colored man? Absurd!*

She shot an angry glance back. "You appear to be making an outlandish assumption, Mr. Alcott. I can tell you I do not appreciate it."

He maneuvered her around a rain puddle at the end of the street. "I beg you to forgive me, but that hotel does have a certain reputation."

"I've only recently discovered that."

"I had no desire to upset you, Mrs. Toby. I take it you are married?"

"My husband died earlier this month," she said indignantly.

"And you're not in mourning clothes?"

"I have been in mourning for him ever since he was seriously wounded last December. I don't need to wear black after I've been grieving for him so long."

"I fully understand, Mrs. Toby." He gazed at the entrance to the Monody Hotel and turned to her. "Again, my apologies. I hope we have the pleasure of meeting in the future."

Sara took a parting glance at him as he walked away. *I wish he were white. I could use the money.*

Chapter 46

Matt trudged past a sawmill, an iron works, and a warehouse and elbowed his way past the crowd at the shipyard as he attempted to return to the waiting gunboat. Just this afternoon, everyone in town was in happy spirits, rejoicing over the expectation of the arrival of the steamboat *Sultana*, making its way up the Mississippi. Over 2,000 men, mostly Union soldiers, were returning home, elated over the war's end. Many of them were Yankee prisoners of war who had served in compounds such as Andersonville and boarded the *Sultana* further down south in Vicksburg.

A woman in a light blue work dress, her reddish hair crowning her wrinkled forehead, grabbed Matt's sleeve. "What will I do?" she wailed, her gray eyes searching his for an answer. "My husband had departed on the *Sultana* and was to join me here."

"I will pray for him and the others. That is all I can do. Now if you will excuse me."

Matt, his feet muddied earlier when he had slogged along the riverbank, almost tripped on the plank leading to the boat. Waiting hands of men with the 42nd Wisconsin helped him board the vessel.

The boat left at once and Matt had to grab the railing to keep his balance. As the crowd along the shore slowly disappeared from view, the waters of the Mississippi spread out before him, far and wide.

A Union sailor standing next to him shook his head. "Dear Lord in heaven! After spending all that time in rebel prisons, our boys had to suffer and die in this needless tragedy."

Matt, his stomach soured by the news, nodded in silent agreement and slumped into a chair. He closed his eyes in prayer but soon his thoughts drifted to Mary. *I am indeed fortunate to have had the foresight of mind to send that telegram*

to her in St. Louis. Surely, Tinker and Nellie will understand.
I'm needed in Memphis to help the wounded and dying.

The waters of the Mississippi rocked and slapped the boat as it continued its steady course southward. Matt exhaled deeply, reflecting on the misery he would likely confront in Memphis. How many sleeping soldiers—freed from their bondage in Confederate prisons—were blown apart by the boiler explosion and how many had to endure the horror of drowning?

*****

Chicago
The next day

After unpacking her things at the Jackson Hotel, Jessica went to see Nellie and Tinker first before visiting with her publisher. According to his last letter, Matt would be arriving today, so this would give her an opportunity to talk with him.

I wish I didn't have to deceive Otto like this, convincing him he had to stay with the children in Washington. I know you wondered why I would want to see Lincoln's funeral again, but it wasn't the funeral I wanted to see again. It wasn't even Nellie.

Jessica wished she could have taken the past back to re-live those earlier days with Matt Lightfoot. Why could he not understand that what she really needed was more time. Pressuring like that about marriage when she had so many other concerns simply was not fair. Why could he not understand that?

Mama's words haunted her…*"Bein' understood don't matter as much as understanding, child. More important that you understand."*

But she was beginning to understand, wasn't she? Matt was a good, decent man, who would make a great husband. It didn't matter any more what his attitudes were about slavery or his strong devotion to his ministry. As far as she was concerned, love was the most important ingredient in a marriage, and she realized she truly did love him. He had always told

335

her how deeply he cared for her, and she had never known a man that expressed his love and devotion as he did. She was a writer, after all, and she told herself she ought to know that love really did conquer all and that it was not just a platitude.

It was ten in the morning when she rapped on the door of the Longfellow house. To her delight, Nellie herself answered. They squealed at the same time and hugged each other. "I feel a bit damp from all this rain we've been having," Jessica said, "but other than that, I'm fine."

"I am too," Nellie said, with a touch of sadness Jessica attributed to Lincoln's murder. "Please come in," Nellie added. "I have another visitor with me right now."

Jessica's heart leaped when she thought the visitor might be Matt Lightfoot, but it was a woman she did not recognize. She was an attractive lady about forty with brown hair and blue eyes, and with a face that smelled of rose water.

"This is Mrs. Sara Toby," Nellie said. "She came by this morning to see how I was doing. Her husband bought me from that evil man and I used t' live with them in Tennessee."

Jessica shook Sara's hand. "Yes, of course. I've written to you, Mrs. Toby. Thank you for taking care of Nellie all that time. Both you and Roger deserve our gratitude."

"Roger's wounds did not survive the battle at Franklin," Sara said, "and he died about two weeks ago."

"How dreadful."

"I was telling Nellie how delusional he had become in his last days. He talked incessantly about beautiful angels he claims to have seen on the battlefield."

Nellie's eyes sparkled. "I think they be pretty angels, dressed in white, 'n smilin' 'n happy."

"No, the entire incident was tragic," Sara said. "A doctor told me his retinas were probably shocked into blindness by an exploding shell." She took a deep breath and glared at Nellie. "Now let's not have any more silly talk about angels. They simply do not exist."

Nellie, eyes downcast, played with the edge of her apron.

336

"I am rather hoping," Sara added, turning her attention to Jessica, "that I will find work on the Chicago stage as an actress."

Jessica nodded. "You should. Chicago does have some fine theaters."

"They may at that, but I don't know what hostilities might await former supporters of the Confederacy."

"I am sure they will be dealt fairly and with compassion just as Lincoln would have wanted."

"I'm goin' to Lincoln's funeral," Nellie interjected, looking at Sara. A long pause ensued before Nellie added, "Are yah goin' too?"

"No. Don't see any point to it. I can't see why everyone is making such a fuss over this."

"What do you mean by that?" Jessica said, fuming. "If anyone deserves special recognition, it would be Mr. Lincoln."

"I didn't mean anything by it. You forget that as a Southern woman I look at this whole event a bit differently than you."

Jessica folded her arms and turned to face the window. "He was president of all the people and he deserves your respect."

Nellie looked at Sara and Jessica, her face hopeful the sudden frost would soon melt. "How 'bout we all have some coffee and pie? I made a nice apple pie, I'm shore you'll like. I been waitin' for Tinker to join us, but I suppose he's out somewhere lookin' for work."

"I'm looking for work myself," Sara said, taking her handbag from the chair, "and I will need to spend much of my time in the search. Perhaps we can get together at some future date, Miss Radford. I would enjoy conversing with you."

"And I as well. I apologize for my temper. This assassination has unsettled me. But I did hear that Mr. Booth and another conspirator had been captured. I just hope there isn't a wider conspiracy undertaken by the Confederate government."

"Yeah," Nellie added. "Tinker tells me he thinks they plannin' now t' kill Johnson 'n his whole Cabinet."

337

A vein in Sara's head throbbed. "The only conspiracy I see is that the victorious Yankees are now going to want to crush the South."

*****

Washington, DC

Otto straightened the framed photo of the children on the dining room wall. *In a way, leaving me alone with the children was the best thing for me, Jessica. Whenever I am tempted to take a drink to ease the pain of Lincoln's death and your absence, all I have to do is to look at the imploring faces of Mitzi and Emma.*

"What does Miss Radford do to entertain you when you have returned from school?" he asked when he spotted the two girls seated on the davenport.

"She reads us stories," Mitzi said, "and sometimes she asks us to make up our own endings."

"Yeah," Emma added, "and sometimes she writes the stories herself."

Otto scratched his head. "Well, can you find one of hers that I could read to you?"

"I think so," Mitzi said and ran to Jessica's bedroom. She returned in a minute and handed her father a sheaf of handwritten pages. "This was the one she was going to read to us before she went on her trip to Chicago."

Otto scanned the pages. "Interesting title: 'The Man Who Saved the Slaves.' Hmmm. Maybe this is a story about Lincoln. Do you want me to read it to you?"

"Maybe you can read it to Emma," Mitzi said. "I'm going to practice my piano."

"Very well, then. I will read it to Emma." He cleared his throat. 'Once upon a time, there was a man who was born in Germany but came to the United States at a very early age. His father told him to always treat the next person the same way you would want to be treated. So he did, and when he discovered that people with a different color of skin were forced

338

to be slaves, he rescued them and brought them back to a place of safety. In fact, he brought thirty of them to freedom."

Mitzi's playing of "Aura Lea" spread its sadness throughout the room. Otto dropped the sheath of papers to the floor as he dried his eyes with his sleeve. "Let me read this another time, Emma." He went to his room and looked out the window at the darkened afternoon sky. More storms coming. One tragedy after another. Penelope was gone. Now Lincoln.

Strange how this rain continues. Will the heavens ever stop crying for Lincoln?

He thought of that story she had written for the children. *Damn you, Jessica. You didn't have to write about me. I never meant to be a hero. I just did what I thought was right.*

Chapter 47

April 28
Chicago, Illinois

"I will consider it." These parting words that she said to her editor this morning at the publishing offices on Jefferson Street resonated in her mind after she closed the door behind her. The firm was not interested in any more novels dealing with the slavery issue. "Readers are weary of the topic," the editor had told her before returning her manuscript. "They've suffered through four long years of contention over it, and the states are now debating the merits of an amendment to our Constitution. Surely there must be another topic or another cause you can address other than slavery."

Her muscles tensed and she worked her tongue around the corner of her mouth as she thought about telling him he could find another writer. But instead, she grabbed her manuscript and left in a huff after promising she'd consider it.

But what was there to consider? Emancipation from slavery wasn't the end of the slavery problem, but just the beginning. *Another topic or cause I can address other than slavery? How absurd!*

Well, she'd just have to put this conversation out of her thoughts for now. She would go to Nellie's again this afternoon to see if Matt had finally arrived.

Her skirts rustling, she hastened to the Jackson Hotel, where she would toss her rejected manuscript on her bed and take a walk. But the hotel clerk called her by name as she skittered by. "Telegram for you, Ms. Radford."

"Telegram?" Thinking it might be Matt, she hastened to open it. Her face fell when she discovered it was not him…

Jessica Radford—
    I learned you would be in Chicago this week, and I was hoping you would join me and several ladies with the Women's Suffrage Association. You are a marvelous writer, and we could use your talents

*for our group. We are meeting on Friday, April 28 at
5 PM at the Jackson Hotel. I sincerely hope you will
join us.*

Elizabeth Cady Stanton

Elizabeth Cady Stanton? Oh yes, she was the founder of
an abolitionist group—the Women's National Loyal League.
Jessica recalled how Elizabeth had supported Jessica's anti-
slavery speech and garnered signatures to petition Congress
for the abolishment of slavery. Jessica stuffed the telegram in
her dress pocket. *Elizabeth was a good woman, but I am too
occupied with other matters and have no time to be involved
with another organization.*

After primping herself in her mirror, she strolled through
the city, hoping the cool, damp April air would calm her frail
nerves. Pausing before crossing the bridge over the Chicago
River, she watched a ferry make ripples as it headed northward. That boat had a purpose and a direction. So did she.
Marriage with Matt was a distinct possibility. But she had to
see him and ask how he felt about her, that she realized she
was wrong in not agreeing to his marriage proposal. *I just
needed more time, darling. That's what I will tell him.*

In her last letter, she told him how much she cared for
him and how she wished she could turn the tide in their relationship. But he didn't write back, probably realizing at that
time he had nothing more to add. Perhaps he imagined himself being in love with Mary—"Apple Mary," her childhood
friend. Ever since Jessica learned he had been intimate with
Mary when he served with the Eighth Kansas, she suspected
that Mary was a special person in his heart. But "love"? No,
Matt had always loved her. Now all she had to do was convince him she felt the same way about him.

She noticed the signs over some of the shops that mourned
the President: "A GREAT MAN HAS BEEN TAKEN"..."NOW IN
THE ARMS OF HIS MAKER"..."GOODBYE, MR. PRESIDENT!"

People passed by her with heads downcast and she rarely
saw anyone in conversation. She dropped down on a bench

near the lake and watched angry waves pound the rocks at the shoreline. A threatening gray cloud formed a fist as if it were Booth himself raising it at the audience. *Sic semper tryannis.* She shuddered at the suddenness of it all.

There was a Whitman line about death that had always intrigued her, and she asked him about it as he scribbled his autograph on her copy of *Leaves of* Grass....

> *"Mr. Whitman, you once wrote that 'Great is Death—sure as Life holds all parts together, Death holds all parts together.' I've never understood what that meant."*
>
> *The poet folded his hands and his eyes explored the room as if he were looking for the answer. "See all this suffering? This is what we experience as the War of the Rebellion moves on. It becomes a grinding stone, crushing out lives like a mill crushing grain into flour, which eventually becomes bread, the staff of life. If Life holds all parts together—marvelous joys commingled with tremendous suffering—then surely Death, the flour from the war mill, must also hold all parts together."*

Jessica stared at a lone iron-hulled steamer on Lake Michigan and at a formation of birds disappearing through a cloud. A slight breeze tussled her hair, and she flicked a strand away from her forehead. A gray sky above, a horizon formed by an endless lake, and trees with branches bending graciously with the wind. Everything fit into a pattern. According to Matt, that was the way God made everything.

Was it? Jessica took in a deep breath and exhaled her frustration. *Mr. Whitman, if what you had penned were true, then how could you say the death of our beloved President holds all parts together? What about his determination to finally put an end to the slavery issue? Regarding husbands now resting in graves while their widows struggle to survive—what about those parts? And what about the hope of reconciliation with the*

342

South? All these parts, Mr. Whitman…so many parts…how will Lincoln's death hold them together?

As the breeze picked up, two children shrieked as their kite grabbed up more of the overcast sky. An elderly gentleman seated on another bench nearby fed pigeons crowded all about him. Their feathers flew and their coos increased as he tossed more crumbs their way.

On a calmer day, she could envision herself sitting here, truly relaxing with the sight of a glassy smooth lake before her. She'd read something from Charlotte Brontë, such as "light airs stir a sleeping lake, the glassy calm that soothes my woes." Jessica despised the grayness of the morning and the lingering sorrow over Lincoln's unexpected death. If only she could be as free and unconcerned as those children or that colored man and woman holding hands as they sat under an elm watching the lake.

Jessica took another look at the black couple. The woman who had turned her head and let that gentleman kiss her looked very much like Nellie. Jessica turned away, not wishing to be noticed. That man who had kissed her did not appear to be Tinker. This man was slimmer and younger. But Jessica, from where she stood, could not identify him.

Rising from the bench, she moved slowly toward the lake, not wishing to take a second look until she reached the camouflage of a thick oak. That woman had to be Nellie. Or was she someone who only looked like her? And who was that young man she was with? Now safely hidden behind the tree, Jessica took a second glance at them. They were kissing again. She waited for the man to turn his head so she could identify him.

Should she run up to them and catch them in that awkward situation? She did not wish to interfere with Nellie's life, but she was her adopted sister and Jessica had every right to demand to know what was happening.

She gazed once more at the iron-hulled steamer in the distance, and then turned her head, but the couple was gone. Jessica moved briskly toward the spot where they had been. She looked about. There was no sign of them anywhere.

Had she been mistaken? Could the woman have been someone who only resembled Nellie?

*****

Yesterday Jessica found Nellie's house neat and orderly, proud that her adopted black sister did not shun housework. But this afternoon, Nellie had not bothered to sweep the kitchen or rinse the plates, and laundry had piled up in her bedroom.

"Something is wrong," Jessica said. "What is it?"

"Nuttin's wrong." She grabbed a teapot and, her hand shaking, filled it with water. "Maybe yuh want some tea."

"I don't want any tea. I want you to tell me what's wrong."

Nellie stood by the stove, her back toward Jessica, her body quivering. "I don't wanna lose him."

"Lose who?"

She spun around, the water sloshing out of her teapot. "Tinker. I don't wanna lose him." She crumpled to a chair and dropped her head in her hands, sobbing.

Jessica found a rag and wiped up the spill on the floor. "What makes you think you're going to lose him, Nellie?"

"Mr. Alcott tol' me 'bout what happened yesterday."

"Mr. Alcott?"

"Y'know—that musician? Devin Alcott. He 'n Tinker were in the Eighth Kansas t'gether."

Jessica tossed the rag into a pail as she recalled the young black musician who had shown an interest in coaching Mitzi with her music. She had no idea he was in Chicago.

"Mr. Alcott done tol' me," Nellie said, her voice now raspy and angry, "that he saw Tinker with a black lady. They was walkin' arm-in-arm down Michigan Avenue, lookin' at things in the store window. Mr. Alcott say that lady be his cousin Charlotte. Tinker tol' Mr. Alcott he met her long time ago."

"Perhaps she's just a friend."

"I think she more than a friend. Mr. Alcott say he be with Mrs. Toby yesterday at the Monody Hotel. He hear lotsa laughin' goin' on, so when he open his door, he done see

344

Tinker 'n Charlotte t'gether in the hallway. They look like they havin' lotsa fun."

Jessica was puzzled. *Why was Sara with Devin in a hotel room? And why was Tinker at that same hotel with some lady named Charlotte? And was that Nellie in the park kissing a stranger? If so, who was the stranger?*

"Nellie, who were you with at the lake today?" Jessica asked, trying to remain calm.

Nellie's eyes widened. "The lake?"

Jessica steadied her eyes at her, but Nellie averted her stare "I not be at the lake today," she said, her voice straining.

"But I saw you with some gentleman."

Nellie's lips were parted as if she were about to answer when there was a knock on the door. Nellie took in a deep breath as if she was relieved by the interruption.

Jessica's pulse quickened. *Could that be Matt?* She got up and insisted on answering the door.

But it wasn't Matt Lightfoot. It was Mary, and she carried a rolled-up bedcover under her arm.

"Why Mary," Jessica said, struggling for words, "what a surprise!"

"This is for you," Mary told her, handing her the bundle she had been carrying. "It's a quilt I had been working on and finally finished. I thought you'd enjoy having it."

"Why thank you," she said, taking the quilt. "But I am rather surprised to see you here."

"Mr. Lightfoot could not make it," Mary said. "He had planned to be here, but at the last moment, he needed to be in Memphis to console the friends and relatives of the men who have died on the *Sultana*."

"I've read about it. It was an awful tragedy."

"Yes, it certainly was. I understand about 1,700 men perished in that horrible disaster. Many were prisoners of war who were so close to obtaining the freedom they longed for. So very close. And then to die like that, so senselessly." She exhaled slowly. "I simply cannot comprehend it."

Jessica nodded. *It seems I cannot comprehend anything anymore.* She unrolled the quilt, wishing Matt would have

345

come to Chicago as he said he would. *Couldn't someone else have gone down to Memphis instead?*

Mary smiled weakly. "Anyway, I am glad to be here to pay my last respects to President Lincoln. He was a great man."

"Yes, he was," Jessica said, studying the quilt design.

"The original theme for that," Mary explained, "was the reconciliation of North and South. But, I guess, it's subject to other interpretations, such as our friendship."

Jessica glanced at her. *That was a long time ago. Friendships change. Besides, was a person who betrayed you a friend?*

She draped the quilt over the chair. "Thank you for this, Mary."

"You are quite welcome."

"Hello, Miz Delaney," Nellie said, smiling, although her cheeks were still wet from crying.

Mary greeted her with a kiss. "Where is Tinker?"

Nellie's face soured. "He tol' me he was out lookin' fer a job. He be out a long time."

"Has he found one yet?"

Nellie shrugged. "Don't know if yah can call it a job. Mr. Alcott helped him get a small role in a minstrel show playin' at the Academy of Music. Not much money, but he don't like it 'cause it put down negroes. Makes dem look stupid."

"It is wonderful that Devin is helping him find work," Mary said.

Jessica took a deep breath to relax her frayed nerves. *Was that Devin in the park with Nellie?*

"Do you know Devin Alcott?" Jessica asked, placing the quilt on a chair.

"Of course. I met him in Tennessee when I was with the Eighth Kansas. I understand he resigned his position with the School of Practice at Governor's Island and decided to search for work here in Chicago."

Jessica shrugged. "I suppose Devin did not have the time or courtesy to tell me about his plans as well."

"I don't know," Mary started, "I suppose that he—"

346

"Mr. Alcott be a good man," Nellie interjected, her face beaming. "He play nice music 'n he talk to me real nice. Made me feel like real lady today."

Jessica's muscles tensed. *Oh, was that you kissing him?*

"Today?" she asked, eyeing her carefully. "You talked to him today?"

Nellie nodded slowly, as if she had just been scolded.

"Is that all you did?" Jessica asked, her voice rising. "Talk?"

Nellie's mouth dropped open. "I dunno what you mean, Miz Jessica."

"Never mind." *Why do I even bother with her problems?* She turned her attention to Mary. "How are things back in St. Louis? Do you enjoy living there?"

"I have a wonderful position as a nurse, and Matt is pastor of a small congregation."

Jessica tapped her foot impatiently and folded her arms. "And?"

Mary frowned. "And what?"

"And are you and Matt seeing much of each other these days?"

Mary's lips parted in surprise at the question. "Why do you ask?"

Jessica fixed a steady gaze at her friend before answering. *You know why I am asking, Mary. Have you become intimate with Matt Lightfoot, a man I had known for the past five years?*

"I just assumed, Mary, that since you both live in St. Louis you would have a far better opportunity to see him than I would, being some eight hundred miles away."

"Why, yes," Mary said, "we do see each other quite frequently. He is doing excellent work in his ministry, and I daresay, in woodcarving. He has sold several of his creations to raise funds for the needy."

Jessica felt her headache return. *Why was Mary being so evasive?*

347

Chapter 48

Back in her hotel room, Jessica ripped the pages from her latest manuscript and flung them against the wall. Papers flew about the room like huge, disoriented butterflies. "Damn you, Tinker, damn you Nellie, and damn you, Devin! Why did I bother with any of you?"

She tossed the rest of her manuscript to the floor and dropped face down on the bed, sobbing. *Write my passion, Mr. Whitman? How can I write my passion when it's disappeared? I have nothing left in me to write about. Nothing. I really don't give a damn about the negro situation anymore. I really don't.*

She choked as her tears seemed to drain into her throat. Maybe her editor was right. There was no point in writing about an issue that the public was tired of hearing about. When Lincoln died, the cause died, and she died with it.

If at least she could have seen Matt again. It was unfair that he failed to appear when he said he would. And wasn't love supposed to be eternal? If he truly loved her, he would have answered her letter, he would have come to see her. They would talk about their future together.

The quilt Mary gave her was spread over a chair in her room. "Hands clasped in friendship," Mary had said about that quilt. Friendship? You mean when a friend steals your man from you, you're to remain friends? How was that possible? Look at that quilt. Two hands clasped. North and South. Mary and Jessica. No, probably more like Tinker and Charlotte, and Nellie and Devin. Maybe that was the theme.

Feeling herself drifting to sleep, she turned over on the bed so that her back pressed against the mattress Soon she found herself running through a field, escaping from white slavers who intended to kill her. Lightning streaked across the black sky as a light rain continued to fall. She ran alone, wondering what had happened to all those negroes who had been racing along with her earlier. Were they all dead? Was she like Melville's Ishmael who reflected on those soul-piercing words—"and I only am escaped alone to tell thee?"

But maybe I won't escape. The sound of gunshots behind her intensified, as did the death-rattling screams of the men chasing her. Jessica heaved with each breath. *How will I ever get free?* The persistent yelp of the dogs taunted her, reminding her of Whitman's lines....

> *I am the hounded slave....I wince at the bite of the dogs,*
> *Hell and despair are upon me ....*

She vowed these men would pay for her torment. Maybe, after all, she was a negro slave, but they had no reason to chase her like this. *I am not an animal to be hunted down.*

Her foot caught an object in her path and she fell face forward into the wet grass. She raised her aching body up just as a bolt of lightning crashed in front of her. It had the brightness of cannon fire and everything about her turned into a brilliant white. The boom that followed was deafening, and Jessica rolled over on her back, her arms outstretched in surrender.

"I don't give a damn," she said. "Go ahead and kill me. I want to die anyway. I have nothing to live for."

"But God is not through with you yet," a gentle, childlike voice said.

Jessica opened her eyes and blinked in disbelief. *An angel? A young black angel? Sissy?*

"You have a lot more to give to others," the angel said, her young face radiant with joy. "People need you."

"No, that is not true. I have nothing to give. Nothing."

She heard a rapping sound and turned about. The angel had disappeared. So did the rain. So did the field. So did everything. She was encased in total darkness.

The rapping continued. Jessica opened her eyes and found herself lying on the bed.

Realizing that someone was knocking on her door, she groaned her way out of bed and opened it. Before her stood a round-faced woman with short brown-and-gray hair curling across her forehead. "Please forgive the intrusion, Miss Radford, but the hotel clerk indicated you had not checked out yet and that I might still find you here."

"Elizabeth Cady Stanton, what brings you here?"

"Did you not get my telegram?"

Telegram? Oh yes, the telegram. Jessica reached in her dress pocket and took out the wrinkled message. "I apologize for not replying, Mrs. Stanton."

"That is quite all right. I would be pleased to have you join us. Some Chicago ladies were interested in becoming involved with our women's suffrage group, and I thought you'd like to meet with them this afternoon."

"Well, I—" She turned toward her room. Papers from her manuscript were scattered about.

Jessica cleared her throat and put her hand to her warm forehead. "I'll be there. But first I need to clean up this awful mess that I've made."

Epilogue

While relaxing with Mary in the rear of the riverboat, Matt watched the giant paddlewheel churn the Mississippi into streams of foam. The darkening sky of twilight formed silhouettes of trees on both sides of the river. In the distance, the gas lamps of Hannibal flickered as if to bid adieu to the boat journeyers.

"Mary," he said, turning to her, "did you know that the first railroad to cross the entire state of Missouri was built four years ago, extendin' all the way to Hannibal?"

"No, I didn't," she said, without looking up from her book.

"Darlin', mind if I ask what are you readin' now?"

She showed him the cover. "It's Jessica's novel, *A Slave Only Once*. I find it reads almost like a biography of Nellie, but with Jessica's traits."

Matt nodded. "I know. She's captured the slave experience quite well."

"Unfortunately," Mary added, "the protagonist in her novel has to deal with some rather painful experiences resulting from the War of the Rebellion." She closed the book and thought a minute. "It conjured up some sad memories for me."

"It did for me as well." Matt rose from his seat and walked to the railing. The churn of the paddlewheel was relentless and the wake it formed in the water reminded him, in a way, about the war. Good people on both sides fought and died for what they truly believed. Still, the nation moved on, like this boat, and it left in its wake many painful memories. One of them was Jessica. He reached for the metal chain about his neck. He never told Mary that this ornate hand-carved wooden cross he wore every day was originally intended for the woman he had almost married.

The last time he saw Jessica was when she left on a train bound for Washington. She didn't look out her window as the train pulled from the St. Louis station. But surely that departure must have been as painful for her at the time as it was for him.

At least he wanted to believe it was. But in a way, Jessica did him a favor. He took a new look at Mary and found a kindly, loving soul within. A person he wanted to live with the rest of his life.

Some things would always be difficult for him to believe. But there were many things he still could not fathom—particularly how people living in this same country could slaughter each other for four long years.

The churning of the river by the enormous paddle wheel of the boat brought him back to the present. He felt Mary's hand on his shoulder. "What are you thinking about, Matt?"

The stillness of the early evening was as quiet as death, and yet there was still enough light for him to see how the Mississippi stretched into eternity.

"Was it worth it?" he asked, aware of the embarrassing warmth of his tears. "In the end, when all the results are tallied by the Lord God Himself, was it worth it?"

 *—— the end ——*

Highlights of Battles Described in *All Parts Together*

Chattanooga, TN
First Battle: August 21, 1863
Second Battle: November 23-25, 1863

(Note: There was also an earlier battle that occurred in Chattanooga—on June 7-8, 1862—but this was not alluded to in this novel, so it is not discussed below.)

As part of his campaign to capture Chattanooga, Maj. Gen. William S. Rosecrans, commanding the Union's Army of the Cumberland, directed Col. John T. Wilder's brigade of the Union 4th Division, XIV Army Corps to march to a site northeast of Chattanooga where the Confederates could see them and thus reinforce Gen. Braxton Bragg's belief of a Union attack on the town from that direction. After reaching the Tennessee River near Chattanooga on August 21, Wilder had the 18th Indiana Light Artillery shell the town while Chattanooga's citizens were observing a day of prayer. Two rebel steamers docked at the landing were sunk, causing fear among the townspeople. While this Union shelling of Chattanooga continued over the next two weeks, Bragg's attention was focused on the northeast, where the bombardment was occurring, while most of Rosecran's army crossed the Tennessee River and proceeded southwest. On September 8, Bragg learned that Union soldiers were now strongly entrenched in an area just southwest of town, Bragg abandoned Chattanooga. But he responded by cutting off Union supply routes to the town, hoping to starve out the enemy. However, Major General Ulysses Grant took command of the Western armies in October and helped establish a new supply line. Bt mid-November, Major General Sherman brought in four divisions and prepared for an onslaught against the rebels, who had been occupying key defensive positions on Lookout Mountain and Missionary Ridge. The Union, on November 23 & 24, captured Orchard Knob and

355

Lookout Mountain. Then on November 25, the Union army managed to rout the Confederates from their entrenched position on Missionary Ridge. The Union victory allowed Chattanooga to become a major supply and logistics operational base for General Sherman's eventual siege of Atlanta.

Chickamauga, GA
September 18-20, 1863

On the heels of his success at Tullahoma in Tennessee, the Union's Major General William Rosecrans, went on the offensive to drive the Confederates from Chattanooga. He split his army into three corps and each headed for Chattanooga by separate routes. Later, by consolidating his forces that were scattered in Georgia and Tennessee, Rosecrans forced Confederate General Bragg out of Chattanooga. But Bragg, heading south, planned to meet Rosecran's XXI Army Corps, defeat them, and then reoccupy the town. On the 18th, Bragg encountered Union forces, including many armed with Spencer repeating rifles. Although hard fighting followed on the 19th, Bragg was unable to break the Union line. However, a fortunate turn of events for the rebels occurred on the 20th, when Rosecrans believed he had a gap in his line; but by moving units to close the nonexistent gap, he created one. Confederate General Longstreet took advantage of that error and drove a third of the Union army (including Rosecrans himself) from the field. Rosecrans was forced to relinquish his command to Union General George Thomas, who consolidated his forces on Horseshoe Ridge and Snodgrass Hill. Despite a heroic assault by the rebels, Thomas held back the Confederates until evening, when he retreated under cover of darkness. While the rebels held the field, the Union forces returned to Chattanooga.

Baxter Springs, KS
October 6, 1863

Having decided to attack Union troops near Baxter Springs, Kansas, rebel leader William Quantrill split his men into two columns—one under his command and the other under David Poole. When Poole's men later encountered black Yankee soldiers with the Second Kansas Colored Infantry, they chased and killed a few in their retreat toward Fort Blair in Baxter Springs. Once at the fort, the surviving blacks, along with the rest of the garrison, prepared for battle. The rebels attacked at once, but Lieutenant James Pond used a howitzer to help fight them off. The men under Quantrill, a short distance away, had a chance encounter with a Union detachment that was escorting Maj. Gen. James Blunt and his wagon train en route to Fort Smith. Since Quantrill's men wore Yankee uniforms, Blunt assumed they were part of the garrison who had come to greet him. Quantrill's men soon overpowered them. While the Union men, including unarmed musicians, tried to surrender, the rebels killed them. Blunt and a few mounted men managed to escape. Today, the Baxter Springs episode is commonly referred to as a "massacre" rather than a military battle.

Franklin, TN
November 30, 1864

Confederate General John Hood, had lost an opportunity to capture Union troops at Spring Hill, Tennessee. As a result, he pursued Maj. Gen. John M. Schofield's retreating Union army. Schofield managed to reach Franklin in the early morning of November 30 and immediately worked on forming a defensive line on the southern edge of town. Schofield considered Franklin only a temporary location where he could repair bridges for his supply trains since his real objective was to join other Union forces in Nashville for an anticipated major confrontation. Hood, however, went on the offensive in Franklin, marshaling a frontal attack against Schofield. Although two Union brigades who had held a forward position retreated from the rebels, Schofield's forces still held, despite heavy losses on both sides. After an extremely brutal battle of hand-to-hand combat, six Confederate generals, including the highly respected Patrick Cleburne, were killed.

Meet the Author

Tom Mach has two grown children, Michelle and Mark, and lives with his wife Virginia in Lawrence, Kansas. Part of his inspiration for *All Parts Together* came from Michelle, who has some of Jessica's best traits and from his brother-in-law Terry Blum, who faced his own death with hope and determination. While Tom won several awards for his various writing projects, he actually prefers to talk about two things that matter most to him— compassion and forgiveness. "That's why I love writing my trilogy about Jessica Radford," he says. "It allows me to probe into the very essence of souls who are given an opportunity to show kindness in the midst of hatred and brutality. While Whitman believed that death holds *all parts* together, I contend that it is love that holds *all of us* together."

Book Discussion Questions

1. What does the title of this book mean to you?

2. What surprised you about Lincoln or Whitman?

3. How did Jessica's character change from who she was at the beginning of this book to the end?

4. How would you compare Mary Delaney's personality with Jessica's?

5. How would you compare Devin's personality with Tinker's?

6. Were there any interesting outcomes in this novel—outcomes you would not have predicted?

7. What feelings did Matt initially have for Mary Delaney? What were her feelings for him initially?

8. What do you think might have convinced George Radford to put Nellie in his will?

9. Are you surprised at what happened to change Sara's concept of morality?

10. What was the climactic event for Jessica in this book?

11. What new challenges now await her?

Save on your next purchase of *Sissy!* or *All Parts Together*

$2 off list price for either copy

Clip coupon below and mail with payment.

Enclosed is my check or money order for

___ copies of *Sissy!* at **$13.95** [reg: $15.95]
___copies of *All Parts Together* at **$14.95** [reg: $16.95]

Total of above: $_____
    Add: $2.05 for shipping per copy
    Add: 7.3% sales tax if Kansas resident

TOTAL ENCLOSED: _____

Hill Song Press P O Box 486 Lawrence, KS 66044

NAME_____
ADDRESS_____
CITY_____STATE_____ZIP_____

www.HillSongPress.com